M000310770

Those Brave As the Skate Is

Patrick Keller

Those Brave As the Skate Is
(followed by *Pescetarealism: A Manifesto*)

Patrick Keller

Winner of the 2018 Kenneth Patchen Award
for the Innovative Novel
Journal of Experimental Fiction 86

JEF Books/Depth Charge Publishing
Aurora, Illinois

Those Brave As the Skate Is
and *Pescetarealism: A Manifesto*
Copyright © 2021 by Patrick Keller
All Rights Reserved

Winner of the 2018 Kenneth Patchen Award for the
Innovative Novel

Cover Design: Patrick Keller
Front Cover Art: Franz Keller

ISBN 1-884097-86-3
ISBN-13 978-1-884097-86-7
ISSN 1084-847X

JEF Books/Depth Charge Publishing
"The Foremost in Innovative Publishing"
experimentalfiction.com

JEF Books are distributed to the book trade by
SPD: Small Press Distribution and to the
academic journal market by EBSCO

Dedicated to Erin,
My Family,
and the memory of Bob Keller
and Bob Folkenflik

Those Brave As the Skate Is

Patrick Keller

"All the paint that went into the process is there on the canvas.
I wish one could see all the words that went into the making of
a novel."
-Raymond Federman, interview

"Everything is in the poems, but [...] I just heard that
one of my fellow poets thinks that a poem of mine that
can't be got at one reading is because I was confused too.
Now, come on. [...]
You just go on your nerve. If someone's chasing you down
the street with a knife you just run, you don't turn around
and shout, 'Give it up! I was a track star for Mineola Prep.'"
-Frank O'Hara, Personism: A Manifesto

"My fate—decided by a coin?!"
-Nola Darling, She's Gotta Have It

HOW TO READ:

This novel is actually presented twice on facing pages: the left one is the raw version as it was originally written, while the right has been processed, polished, and punctuated. (There are the most differences between the versions early on because <u>Skate</u> started as part of a longer, unpublished work, so I wanted to make sure you had enough introduction to the pre-existing characters.)

If you only want to follow the plot, just read the pages on the right!

If, however, you want greater insight into why the characters act so weirdly (or how this book came to be), the raw page may help. Each was grown like a tree, starting with the bold font at the bottom and going up, then continuing to branch out first on the left all the way down and then on the right, as seen in this snappy diagram:

Whenever one of my characters tries to remember something, they are essentially reading across the raw page where the event occurred . . . except they are ignoring the column boundaries. Happy accidents of page layout also sometimes get used as one of many sources of randomness to generate later events (and the titles of characters' own songs, my chapters, and the title of this book).

You might ask: why write a novel that way? Well, there's a whole little manifesto at the end of this book about the process I call "Pescetarealism," and you can go read that any time you want. (Don't worry, it's basically spoiler-free!)

Welcome and enjoy!

in **EYEBALLS WRAPPED** suggest'd Romeo
dollar bills **TO STEAL** is confused
but I tell him **THE ENDING** I tell him
that the present **TIME WITH A SENSE OF** a soggy
must leap like **THIS** ninja of
an angel from the **HALO ONLY** a kid haplessly
slumping **TO THE SMOG** witnessing a
sod **VOLCANO** stick up
of the past even **OF THE REVERSE** at the pizza
though it **FROM THE CIRCLE** parlor
never does **THAT GOES** like Yes
except **NAMELY TELL THE STORY** obvs felt
with lenses or pyro **I JUST DID** an affinity
but how **AGAIN WHAT** w/ roomie Robin who
else to explain that **TO DO** was previously overlooked
we're now **ME** as an unphotographed
in a cab **AND BEGS** island of a kid
on the way to the **CITY PROPER** scrutinizing
hospital where the **SISTER** nylon bolted head
child **COMES BACK TO** level
of Yes's about **TRUCK ROMEO** attractions she's too
to appear **A MONSTER** short for at this
out **FROM** time he liked
of nowhere like **AN ISLAND** to be bossed & she was
a fourth **TO SAVE** a boss but she didnt have
street **OBSCURITY AND FAILURE** to give the
driver when I'm **CHOSEN** word however comma she
trying to turn **HIS SELF** proved to be
off my street **TO GET AWAY FROM** more javelin than
as Erin **WANTING** telescope & here we are

Chapter 0:

If you want to have a stand-off later, you need to design, assemble, and maintain a lot of pistols for the mantle. Don't worry, that's just a metaphor . . . I think (won't be the last, either). Another problem is that whenever you get to a place, there's all sorts of people already there that you have to meet. We're going to handle those two problems now before the story of The Child Of Yes really begins, but if you're going to get snitty about having to kiss a bunch of babies and watch them grow, you can raise your right hand right now and swear you will just surf any confusion later on, then you can just flip to Chapter 1--which is pretty good, IMHO.

Only 5 days ago, Romeo Blank, age 24, was the undisputed king of the blog band scene in Sister City (maybe even in all of Heldheart!)--but that's a lifetime on the internet. Since then, he lost a battle of the bands to his protege Abe, exiled himself to the man-made paradise of Isla Hermana, exposed Little Island Motors' plan for a hostile take-over--and then failed royally at thwarting it. ("How would *you* stop a monster truck?!" he wants to ask the internet trolls.) Now he begs me to re-tell this week again from scratch--but this time with the ending in mind so that he can come off as tragic rather than inept (and maybe get some money-wrapped eyeballs, too).

I *am* his record producer / author, so his request is not that crazy, but I tell him that as tempting as that sounds, the present must leap like an angel from the slumping sod of the past (even though it never does, except with lenses or pyro). Also, I tell him, he's had *his* shot and the Child Of Yes is about to appear like a 4th Street driver out of nowhere when I'm trying to turn.

end **TOGETHER AT THE** cable TV
of playtime the phone**BACK** and a landline with your
company **DINOSAURS ROLLED** internet
he had filled in **EHH LIKE CLAY** hookup
as spokesperson **IS CALLED A MUTUAL** unfortunatly this
for sold its certainty **WHAT** happened when Max was
stimulating **THREES OR** already thinking that
technology to its hated **BOTH** his clone who had died
rival the **LANDING AND THEY'RE** before her
automotive **THEM ON THE NEXT** eyes had done
overlords **IMPROBABLY CATCH** more
of the drive**WAY THAT I** with the same genes
in Skatespeare **SUCH A** and less
stadium to coax **WALL IN** time like a
more bets out of **THE CONCRETE** college
their patrons **DICE OFF** kid
but the losing 1/4back's still**TWO** w/ an emulator she'd gone
under **ROBIN I BANK** back to her first
contract **MAXINE AND STARTED UP WITH** love
so **GAL** which is running the
they tore his **YES'S PREVIOUS** show but now her
pages **HOW THINGS ENDED WITH** directions
out like rude**VERSION OF** seemed limited to
cabin guests who forgot **PAGE** 8 and her words
to bring supplies for**THE ONE** swayed him no
their basic needs **ME FOR** more than those
& made him the **STAIRS ROMEO ASKS** of a robotic
guy who looks at **THE HOSPITAL** hostess
you like you're **UP** built from
crazy when you decline**AS WE RUN** shoplifted parts

Romeo is confused, but not because he wonders how I plan to turn when I'm also in the back seat of our cab. No, his problem is that as far as he knows, he failed to save the day *minutes* ago, and at that time no one was about to squirt one out (least of all a dude like Yes).

I give him an explanation that will probably make more sense to him than to you: "sometimes a soggy ninja haplessly witnesses a stick-up at a pizza parlor and feels an affinity with an unphotographed-island of a kid who likes to scrutinize nylon-bolted, head-level attractions she's too short for at this time . . ." Put another way, a former stock-photo model like Yes liked to be bossed, and Ro's old roommate Robin (whose code name was "javelin telescope" in the failed counter-conspiracy) *was* a boss, but she didn't *have* to give the word, yet she proved to be more javelin than telescope, and here we are--"here" as in "a concrete hospital stairwell that we are running up." Panting, Romeo says he accepts my remarkably cogent explanation but asks what happened between Yes and his girlfriend Maxine to allow the ninja-island connection.

The problem is that I don't know the answer to that yet, but the two dice in my pocket will tell me the sides of their story. I bank them off the concrete wall and improbably catch them on the next landing, and they're both threes--or what people around here call a "Mutual Ehh." I do fucking hate exposition, but for your sake I remind Romeo that Yes started working as a spokesperson for the Wagner-Sadako phone company right before they got stomped by Little Island Motors in an automotive coup(e), but even though a merger has rolled the rival companies together like two clay dinosaurs at the end of play time, our losing quarterback Yes was still under contract to The Phonies, so in the ensuing 11 months (our cabbie must have been playing dumb to run up the meter!) the amalgamated "Little Wagner" has been tearing out pages from Yes like a rude cabin guest who forgot to bring supplies: after a series of demotions, they finally made him the guy who's paid to look at you like you're crazy when you decline cable TV

like Snoop **ONE THERE** call him
Dogg Romeo **THAT HE'S THE ONLY** Noys
bluntly asks **TO HIM AND** Romeo is
y they decided **THAT SHE IS TALKING** made Godfather
to keep it and **SHE CONFIRMS** a consolation
I tell him **WHEN HE ASKS** for the fact
that mirrors **ANOTHER AND** that he'll no longer b
like **A MIRROR FACING** our Wild
reflections and every **HIM LIKE** One I also tell him that
Yes wants **THAT SHE READS** if he wants
another and **SHE TELLS HIM** to tattoo four days in
every Robin's **THROUGHER SO** his 20's across his
song **A SEE** name I
grows sweeter **SHE'S ALWAYS BEEN** will help him
with echo or something **FAST** turn
like that **DRIVER ROBIN MOVED** the island's
we burst **SLASH TAXI** story
into the operating **STYLED THIEF** into a pageant
room just as **PUMPKIN EATING DENIRO** that Noys
the coin **ROBOCALLS THAT PREMATURE** can
hits the doctor's **ANSWERING** be a part of
hand and he calls **STOPPED** in 8 years what
it a boy **ONCE YES** will we do
the parents **I TELL ROMEO THAT** til then
take **OUT SO** roll
the Y **LIFE GROSSES US ALL** the dice each
and S from **THE MIRACLE OF** year keep
dad and the O **HALLWAY LEFT BEFORE** jumping out
and N from **ONE** of
mom and **THERE'S ONLY** skins

and a landline with your internet hookup. (That'll learn him to back the losing side!) Unfortunately, this happened when Max was already thinking that Yes's clone (yeah, he had one of those, but don't worry, that guy died) had done more with the same genes and less time. Like a college kid with an emulator, she'd gone back to her first love--running the show in commercial shoots--but now her stiff directions to him seemed limited to 8 (plus a button) and her words swayed him no more than those of a robotic hostess built from shoplifted parts.

There's only one hallway left before the miracle of life grosses us all out, so I tell Romeo that once Yes stopped answering Max's robocalls, that premature-pumpkin-eating DeNiro-styled thief / taxi driver Robin moved in fast. She'd always been a see-through-er, so she told him that she could read him like one mirror facing another, and when he asked, she confirmed that she was talking to him and that he was the only one there.

Like Snoop Dogg, Romeo bluntly asks why they decided to keep it.

I tell him that mirrors enjoy reflections, and every Yes wants another Yes and every Robin's song sounds sweeter with echo (or something like that), then we burst into the operating room just as the coin hits the doctor's hand and he calls it a boy. The parents take the "Y" and "S" from Yes and the "O" and "N" from Robin, so the kid is called "Noys." Another flip of the coin makes him a Segundo like Mom instead of a George like Dad. For my part, I make Romeo the Godfather as a consolation for the fact that he'll no longer be our Wild One.

I also tell him that if he really wants to tattoo four days in his 20's across his name, I will help him turn his story--which went from a volcano lip to a smog halo--into a grade school pageant to replace the one his mother wrote years ago, and in 8 years Noys will star in it. What will we do til then? Let's play "Where's Romeo?" while we keep jumping out of skins and rolling dice.

xmas **FROM LAST YEAR'S** insulting
letter two is **WORTH CHANGING** memo while
a stumblable **AND FOUR NOTHING** letting the
stone in a career **SO THAT'S THREE** phone go to
path **OR BACKSLIDING** machine in case
and one **AS DECLINE** it's the about a bill
is the loneliest **OF DOWNHILL** Romeo can't comfort
bullet **PEOPLE THINK** his pal
hole in the center **ALRIGHT BUT** because he's near
of a square **THINGS ROLLING** bummed out to
chest the **UPHILL WOULD REPRESENT** death by
first year **I DON'T KNOW WHY** the reviews
of Noys nearly **FOCUS OF A FIVE** of the first
hurls a **CENTERED** installment of his
tanker **ADVANCEMENT HAS THE** pageant
through the power **SPOTS CAREER** in progress
lines **YOU SEE SIX** at the now vacant
I'd been laying **CONNECTION MAKES** mainland
Robin dumps **THE NEXT NEW LOVE OR** stadium whats
Yes **WITH** so
because in **THE DATE** wrong about having
his mirror **INWARDLY WHILE REPLACING** Yes's
she sees **RESOLUTIONS AND HOWLING** clone ask
her own **SET OF** his
complacency in his **WRITING ONE** tour guide if
tearing **THAT CAN HAPPEN BETWEEN** anyone has
him in **THINGS** ever said that the
two **ARE BASICALLY SIX** meteorite
like a check **DOWN AND THERE** contained alien
with an **BOIL A PERSON** nerve fillaments

Speaking of dice, it turns out that if you boil a person down (eww), there are basically only six things that can happen to them between the writing of one set of resolutions and the mere replacement of the date and an inward howl: new love or connection makes you see 6 spots; career advancement has the centered focus of a 5; there's nothing worth changing from last year's xmas letter if you've got a 3 or a 4; 2 is you stumbling over a stone and falling in your career path; and 1 is the loneliest bullet hole in the center of a square chest. Methodological Note #2: Maybe it's just because I had a lot of time to think while putting ornaments on my parents' tree solo this year (the trick is to say you're done before you actually are because your mom will inevitably make you put up more), but my idea for the rest of this chapter is to arrange by clusters of complementary color a series of self-contained, reflective glimpses of various lives at moments in time.

Let's start easy for Year 1 of Noys: there's Romeo! He's sitting at his computer (Boring!) in . . . a cafe designed to look like a miniature megapolis shattered by its monstrous patrons (Getting better . . .) . . . that overlooks the actual rubble of the island that Romeo failed to save from being turned into a race track (Ohh, depressing!). The irony is lost on Ro, who is coiling himself as he reads a scathing blog take-down of leaked footage of early solo rehearsals of his autobiographical pageant-in-progress; "What's so wrong," he fumes inwardly, "about having Yes's clone ask his handsome tour guide if anyone has ever said that the meteorite contained harvestable alien nerve filaments?! If you're gonna have special phone lines that secretly stimulate your certainty centers while you gossip on the phone, don't you have to set that up?!" Then he gets a text from Yes that nearly hurls a tanker through the familial power lines I've been laying: "I'm at Roscoe's. She says a mirror can't look at complacency without reflecting its own." Then, before Ro can reply, another: "I'm just an insulting check torn in two by a bill

the Figurative **ASS AT** team and her
Embodiment 1/4 **HER OPPONENT'S** face
Finals even though **BLOWING UP** glows like an
photons don't **AND IMPROBABLY** arriving
work that **SUNSHINE** spaceship as she enters
way **HAVING DEFTLY BECOME** a home 2x
showing that **THE QUAD FOR** her
she'd really earned **FIVE ON** own because it's a
that **AGGIE GETS A RANDOM HIGH** replica of
scholarship **SOPHOMORE SISTER** her childhood
in Book **THIS YEAR ROMEO'S** house her
One her old rival **THE TREE** surrogate
Stephanie blearily tells **OFF** mother Thea slumps
her parents that **EVERY LEAF BLOWS** prickily
she's been cut from the **VOICE NOT** in her bar ignoring
team because **ITS BABBLED** anything said
of sniffle **THROUGH** to her while writing
cliché **EVERYONE MAY SING** poems about the
abuse **POET WHO SAID** curb
too corny **QUOTES THE** Dishonest
fine it was ketamine **BLOG** Abe is dissatisfied by
Aggie's **FACE AND ON HIS** his puff of
former best **PIE FROM HIS** breath and looks in
friend **POLITICIAN EATING THE** vain for
Effie who didn't have **NAME LIKE A** something
the grades **BUMPER BUT HE ADOPTS THE** cheap enuf
to get **RENDITION OF A TIMELESS** to hurl as his
in the college **PLAY AS A KARAOKE** drummer
is named **ROMEO'S** releases him like a
coach of its **ONE REVIEW TRASHES** balloon head

dodger." What can you say to that? Ro hides his eyes back in the blog, which pans his play as a "karaoke rendition of a timeless bumper," but already he sees himself skipping seriously past the insult (and Yes's problems) and slapping the phrase on his own posters like a politician eating the splatter of pie from off his own face.

Now, not *every* leaf blows off the tree in Year 1. As Aggie Story crosses the UHSC quad to meet her half-brother Romeo (see him leaning on a stone lion's face and reading his phone through sunglasses) for what she mistakenly expects he is thinking of as her birthday lunch, she sheepishly receives a high-5 from a stranger that must have been for the night before when, under the gymnasium lights, she deftly became sunshine and blew up her opponent's ass at the Figurative Embodiment State Quarter Finals.

"You won't believe why Effie cut Steph Gaudy from the team," Ag tells Ro as she's behind him in the line for the Indian buffet, knowing that his ear can always be turned by some good Gaudy gossip, then in a whisper: "Cliché Abuse!" (Too corny? Fine, it was ketamine.)

"Young Effie has a strong hand," he replies cryptically, but not enough not to remind her of the night her houseguest banged her bro's bongo though his beat don't swing that way.

I dunno, Effie doesn't look so tough as she scampers around the new house that is doubly her own because it's an exact replica of her childhood home (not uncommon in Sister City) and her face glows like an arriving spaceship. Ehh, she deserves it--she's gone from being rejected from UHSC because of her test scores to getting named its youngest-ever head coach of the F.E. team (and not just because of her name). As she fills up the walls with photos, there are none of the woman who lent her a last name, so let me supply it: see Thea Lonelypeak slumping prickly in her favorite bar, The Working Stiff, ignoring the middle-aged letter-chasers that still come up to talk to her while she scrawls in a little blank book first-hand poems about the curb.

always **IZZY WHO HAS** friendship but I've
been Romeo's **SISTER** saved him for
underwire tries **AND STEPH'S** last because I
out for the **PAST ABE** didn't know whether
role of **ERASED** he wanted
Robin in the **TOUR OF THE** somethin new
pageant with a **SUBVERSIVE** or established
bead **THOUGHTS OF A NEW** anyone who'd
curtain **SHORE WITH HIS** pick
smile and the clear **OPPOSITE** up a kid from the
eyes of a **MURAL OF THE** mall
kettle **AIRPLANES FROM THE** jail woud stick
she's got side **SHARPENED DOLLAR** with his wife
kick **FOLDING** so they start
chops **AT THE BEACH** a band
that could Batman **A BENCH** of just the two of
up somebody's **HUNCHES FROM** them and to keep
parents but **HERMANA ROSCOE** it from being
they drink **RENAMED ISLA** called unearned
such judicious **SKATESPEARE HAVE** career
flutes of red **PATRONS OF** advancement all their
wine with their **AUTOMOTIVE** songs are about the
blueberries **ISLAND AS THE** most
& stem cells that she **PROSPEROUS** embarrassing
doesn't get the **TOUR OF** shared
job her father **THE REVISED** obsessions couch'd in
Goodie has **THROUGH** the most
the only six **ROW DANCER** impenetrable
redeemable **LIKE A BACK** baby
for love or **FIRED FOR TALKING** talk

Across town at a practice of the band Coin$lot, Abe Gaudy wonders if that's a Romeo before him, a middle finger towards his head . . . No, but maybe trouncing his mentor in that battle of the bands made someone think he would never get released from his own band like a balloon head by his drummer Beebe--which is evidently not the case. He finds his paltry puff of breath insufficiently violent to express what he is feeling so he throws his eyes around looking in vain for something cheap enough to hurl against the wall.

The curse of crossed Romeo (who has had no luck himself except for being born a white man during the centuries where that meant Special Edition loot, not to mention having found his audience among a global population of billions) may have been fingering his old frenemy Roscoe Manchester (cousin of Yes) when he just lost his job as a tour guide of the sea-girt land-mass now known as "Prosperous Island" (so named to make you think that any bet on the arena's "Skatespeare" matches will blossom). Dude's weaselly jerk-ass boss accused the man who once called himself "The Fingerprint Scanner" of "talking like a back row dancer" by injecting actual historical commentary into the script given to him by the corporation that bulldozed his home and humiliated his team's effort to stop the rolling coin of "progress." Now Scoe hunches on a bench that looks across the water at the enormous LED screens that surround the island and mentally folds them into sharpened dollar-bill airplanes at the thought of starting his own unlicensed subversive tour of the island's erased past.

Speaking of things that fly only in the mind, Abe and Steph's sister Izzy, who has always secretly been Romeo's underwire, gives an audition for the role of "Robin" in his pageant to help him turn things around; hand to his imaginary stubble, he does appraise her bead-curtain smile and eyes as clear as kettles, and lord knows (even if Romeo's never quite has) that she's got side-kick chops that could Batman-up somebody's parents something tragic, but the die says

but they also turn **YEARS** gazing into the eyes
Lewis into a mountain **AFTER 30** of a bad
river dodging **SOUND STILL** liar Robin sees the
boulders to escape the **PERFECT** text
factory **AMP TO MAKE THAT ONE** message
at the summit **TO ADJUST A SPECIFIC** breakup
luckily he can spend his **OF HOW** from the man she'd been
own six **CHECKLISTS** seeing catching
to move in with Effie **RECITED** sight through
though **THE LYRICS BECOME** its grill
at the moment he is **MAKING TALK** the subterranean
smoothing **TALK TO BABY** city he must've felt
on the living **BABY** she was not building as
room wall **STAIRS FROM** fast as
the poster that **THEIR SPECIFIC** he was when she
will have to go **RULER DOWN** gets
Effie at practice **CRAFTED** home she
is wishing **BY RUNNING A CUSTOM** fucks
she could **YOU CAN ONLY PLAY** the babysitter
slurp back **THE BEACH ALBUM WHICH** who is
the barbs she **CHOPS AT** Yes
just hooked **THE SECOND** in a week they're back
in **SIX DRIVES** building
a student **YES GOODIE'S SECOND** with bacon
but finding her old **NOYS TO SPITE** arches and
trapped coyote **IS CALLING** pancake
foot in the **ROBIN** batter slurry while
way everything **OF NO AS** chairbound Noys
may have **YEAR** blubbles like a
to go **IN THE SECOND** goldfish

those parents drink such judicious flutes of red wine with their blueberries and stem cells that she doesn't get the job. Speaking of parental rejuvenation, her dad Goodie (who has certainly had his own share of Romeo's rejections back when he waited by the phone in drag to hear if his guitar would be needed on a given album) is the only one with 6 tea leaves left in his cup this year, but I guess anyone who'd pick up a kid from the mall jail would stick with his wife rather than stick it somewhere else, so he and Mounthe start their own couple's band and, to keep it from being called career advancement, all their songs are about the most embarrassing shared obsessions (putting little pants on flowerpots, *really?!*) couched in the most impenetrable baby-talk.

In the 2nd year of No (as Robin is calling Noys to spite Yes), Goodie's continued lust and devotion drives the second album of "Chops At The Beach" (which you can only play by running a custom-crafted ruler down their specific staircase) from babytalk to baby-*making* talk; the lyrics become recited checklists of how to adjust a specific amp to still make that one perfect sound after 30 years. At the same time, those sounds turn their live-in eldest son Lewis, age 26, into a mountain river dodging boulders to escape the factory at the summit. Luckily, he's got enough of that mojo himself to move in with his main squeeze Effie, though at the very moment he is in her living room smoothing the poster she'll say will have to go, she is at Figurative Embodiment practice wishing she could slurp back the barbs she just hooked in a student-athlete, but she's finding her old trapped-coyote foot in the way. Everything may have to go.

Romeo tries to box with a pencil that same type of resignation on Yes's behalf as he prepares a sacrifice of male infallibility to Robin that will prove unnecessary to feign. She

HINT:
The band name comes from the column version of Page 6. All hints refer to the column versions.

what **BRIDE THAT SAID SEW** in act
and made people**WHILE DRESSED AS A** one he
drop their **CARD** has each try on the
stock photography **CONFISCATED A** cape and jacket
poses and go **YES YES** pins of his highschool
home Robin**TOURIST WHO LOOKED LIKE** poetry
had a student **VOLCANO** to see whose bleared
tell her that**ROSCEO MET AN INQUISITIVE** fragments
he saw a car **ROMEO AND** through the frosted
that was driving **THAT DAY DASH** shower door comes
itself painted**AT THEIR JOBS** closest to
like the totem**THEY ENCOUNTERED** the mundane
of a killer **THINGS THAT** magic of a moose
whale on **THE WEIRD** with narwhal
fire **AND DISCUSSING** horn meanwhile
and she could tell **ROOM DRINKING** in the reverse
he wasn't **OUT IN THE LIVING** volcano where
lying**ROOMMATES HANG** Little
dash a mention of **SCENE WHERE THE** Island
his one **ADDING TO THE THIRD** Motors
ex who painted **BOYFRIENDS HE IS** always had its
walls and his other**AUDITIONING EX** HQ obviously
who painted the **REVERSE WHILE** Malcolm
bone as loaded **IN** despairs that customers are
dueling**PAINTING** too good
pistols set **HE IS FINGER** at betting
on the rolling **HIS HANDS AS IF** on plots he suspects
mantle of a **DINOSAUR BONE IN** a TV
house**THE PAINTED** has been smuggled
boat **ROMEO BLINDLY TURNS** 2 the monkeys

lets him sigh by a chintzy windmill and hand her his ass even as she squares her shoulders to re-gift it to him, casually mentioning that last week she'd gotten a text-message break up from the dude she was wasting time with, and it had made her catch sight through a gutter grill the subterranean city he must've felt she was not building as fast as he was, so she decided to fuck the babysitter. She lets Romeo silently consider and discard several responses before she clarifies that she's talking about Yes. Yeah, they're back building with bacon arches and pancake-batter slurry while chairbound Noys blubbles like a goldfish: normative family win!

From wringing his putter to twirling his bone, Romeo finds himself the next day considering whether other lost things can be recaptured. On stage before him are a variety of men auditioning to play his ex-boyfriends . . . in his pageant, and in his hand is an actual dinosaur fossil he had decorated with one Wolfgang Swarming back when they were just boys in love--his blind fingers trace the texture like finger-painting in reverse. He has continued to revise the pageant script: now the "roommates get drunk together in a houseboat and discuss what happened at their respective jobs that day" scene of Act I includes some weird details that would have made things a lot clearer (if only they had actually happened) and also mentions both Romeo's one ex who painted walls and his other who painted the bone (as it were) because in the new version, both of those guys show up later (in the roles of villain and hero, respectively, as Ro had always cast them). He tells the current candidate to step forward and try on the cape and jacket-pins of his high school poetry--he's looking to see whose bleared-fragments-through-the-frosted-shower-door come closest to the mundane magic of a moose with a narwhal horn.

Meanwhile, the pageant's bad guy, Little Wagner CEO Malcolm Bones, does not need a hidden camera to know what our hero is up to--Romeo has started blogging about his process in an effort to turn public opinion around (but has found the beast to be languorous and troll-y).

competition **HAVE A LOT OF** sighs
at least **ECONOMY YOU'RE GOING TO** like a
she isn't **WORK BUT IN THIS** trick
kicked out of her **CUSTODIAL** pitcher in
parents' **ARM NO DISRESPECT TO** a cartoon
house for **A GOOD THROWING** and goes with
dancing **WITH** the one called Work
suggestively to their **ONE A JANITOR** That Sunshine
music **BOOK** Spaceship that is
while on **IMAGE FROM** a scholarship
K **WHAT WAS HER LAST** replica
like **SUBJECT IS LET'S SEE** about losing her
Steph thumbing through **THIS** protegee to her old rival
her dog eared **MAJOR TO WHATEVER** the tree
copy of her own **CHANGE HER** surrogate of the
now minor **JUST** academy that she wrongly
award **THINKS MAYBE SHE SHOULD** blames for
winning **KTSLORPT AND SHE** scaring the
poetry **CAN STEP WENT** people away from
book Every **TRASH** poetry her former
Leaf **SHELLS AND HER FIRST** lover Romeo's
Blows as if **ON EGG** aunt Leslie dips her
she will read a **ROOM WALKING** shoulders stiffly to
different **IN THE** guitar
one than she has on **ELEPHANT** less beat in the
every other **TO BE THE** club with her
stop of the **MATCH WHERE SHE TRIED** new gf
small book **HER LAST** Work
store **AGGIE REMEMBERS** Suggestively and
tour Thea **IN CLASS** feels trapezoidal

At Malcolm's desk inside the lip of the Reverse Volcano of Prosperous Island where the HQ of the deviously ambitious car company has secretly always been (obviously), he kills that browser window with a dry inward smirk and swivels his admittedly villainous (but too striking not to own!) high-backed chair to consider the more pressing matter of how increasing numbers of walking-wallets are correctly guessing the outcomes of the supposedly-improvised plots unfolding on skates at the center of the spectacle before them; he suspects that a TV may have been smuggled into the typewriter room of the monkeys. He barks an order to his assistant Suzy to go investigate, forgetting that he fired her last week.

If only he had psychic powers, Malcolm could re-fill that post this very second with Aggie who is starting to suspect she's going to need a new plan as she slumps in some class and feels recirculating pulses of shame from last night's Figurative Embodiment match where she tried to be the elephant in the room walking on egg shells, and her first trash-can step went "Ktslorpt!" Couldn't Romeo afford to pay her to be his assistant with all that sweet internet money?! What would she really have to do besides have his Fader-Ade ready in the morning, make small talk with his dealer, and pick up awards he can't be bothered with?

Speaking of awards, Thea won one for her latest book of poems, Every Leaf Blows, and now at a book reading, she thumbs through her own dog-eared copy as if she will read a different one than she has on every other night of the tour. Then she sighs like a trick pitcher in a cartoon and goes again with the one called "Work That Sunshine Spaceship" that is a "scholarship replica" about losing her protégée Effie to her old rival, the "tree-surrogate of the academy," which she (probably wrongly) blames for scaring the people away from poetry.

HINT:
Thea's drawing from the columns of Page 5

her **STADIUM TELLS** four
and demands **SKATESPEARE** of our characters get
her bowtie **BOSS AT THE** dumped at the same
and ligature on the **BANNER HER** ice
way **SPANGLED** skating
out lucky **STAR** rink parenthesis Steph by
for her Leslie's piece **IN THE** careless lady
on this weird **PAUSE** dealer Aggie by affluent
guitar **BLORT DURING THE** glass
less music she **GOING** store owner Izzy
discovered in the **ONE SAXOPHONE** by her slumlord &
club went **WE CAN'T HAVE** Malcolm by placid
viral and like **IT** sandy
a pulsing **SHE BLOWS** haired
gambler **GIRLFRIEND AND** man parenthesis
she invites **NEW** they lock
Work **HER ROLL TO LESLIE'S** eyes
to move into her **CITY I'VE GIVEN** across the
house I'm **IN SISTER** rink like
sure she can tell **NOT EVERYONE STAYS** conspirators in
a lot about **OKAY** a suicide
a **TOWN IT'S** bombing and on the
person after going **OUT OF** upper
out with **UP ON A BOXCAR HEADED** walkway
them for fifty **ENDS** Yes chin points like
narrow **JOB AND** a rhino and tells Robin it
lines year **TURNS AT HER** could be like
three is a terrible **LEFT** that if she keeps
year for **ONE TOO MANY IMPULSIVE** scrawling
love **MAX MAKES** notes in his margins

Meanwhile, another one of Thea's ones that got away spends her night differently, though no less uncomfortably; Leslie Brautjungfer (aunt of Aggie and Romeo) may have smoked cigarettes in the alleys of decades of rock shows, mediocre and passable, before writing whatever the hell she'd previously decided to write about them, but now her new girlfriend (somehow named "Work Suggestively" by probable war-criminals) has dragged her out to dip her shoulders stiffly to a guitar-less beat at some club and feel trapezoidal.

That's still less restrictive than a box, which is the shape of the train car that takes Yes's ex Maxine out of town after she made one too many of her trademark impulsive left turns at the commercial shoot. It's okay, Max, not everyone stays in Sister City.

I've given Max's roll to Leslie's new girlfriend Work--and she blows it. "We can't have one saxophone going 'blort!' during the pause in The Star Spangled Banner!" her boss at the Skatespeare Stadium tells her and demands her bowtie and ligature on the way out. Lucky for her, Leslie's piece on that weird "guitar-less music" (or GLM, as she called it) went viral among Moms on the internet, and like a pulsing gambler, Les has invited Work to move in with her because I'm sure she can tell a lot about a person after going out with them for two paragraphs.

Year 3 of No, though, is a terrible one for love: four of our characters get dumped at the same ice skating rink at the same mall on the same night (Steph by a careless lady dealer; Ag by an affluent glass store owner; Izzy by her slumlord; and Malcolm by a placid, sandy-haired man). The four lock eyes across the rink like conspirators in a suicide bombing, and on the plaza's upper walkway, stroller-pushing Yes chin-points at them like a rhino and tells Robin it could be like that if she keeps scrawling notes in his margins.

for ice **OUT** called Wishing
cream with **OEDIPUS BECAUSE HE WENT** By Runnin'
your wife without **THE HISTORICAL** A Custom
you and **CABLE DOCUMENTARY ABOUT** Fucks that
leaning **SON WATCH A GRAPHIC** sounds like
over to say **AS MAKING YOUR** words slapping
it **FEELS AS FREUDIAN** their flesh
could be like that **DRIVER SO HE** in a boiler room
with your **TOWTRUCK** about to rupture
peeper **FATHER WAS A** no one
if **DRIVER HIS OWN** knows who
you touch your **TOWTRUCK** the musicians are
self or your mother **OF A CUTE** because it was just
or maybe it's just the **FACE** leaked
blood rushing **DOWN STOOPING** to an outsider
to his head anyway **THE UPSIDE** music
if the guy also turns out **WINDOW** label but the leading
to be a drummer he will **OUT HIS** forum
be sketched **OTTER HE SEES** theory is that they're
the fuck **DRIVING CAR DEATH** inmates in
out speaking of the **SELF** adjacent rooms of a mental
drums and the **BELT IN HIS ROLLED** facility who have
guitars Goodie overhears **SAFETY** not gotten
in the **TARSIER FROM HIS** laid in
quad after his P.E. **COIFFED** twenty years
class a gawky **SURPRISE LIKE A LIMP** Goodie
fringed kid **OF PERMANENT** laughs inwardly
telling another **HE HANGS WITH A LOOK** like the ant in
about some **IS LUCKY THIS YEAR AS** the foreground
crazy album **ONLY ROMEO** of a shot it's been hrs

Only Romeo gets lucky *this* year: as he hangs from his safety belt with a limp-coiffed tarsier's look of permanent surprise, he sees out his window the upside-down stooping face of a cute towtruck driver. (His predatory self-driving car Death Otter must have seen a squirrel on the side of the road and shifted focus.) Sure, the fact that his own father also drove a towtruck makes Ro feel as Freudian as making your son watch a graphic documentary about the historical Oedipus just because he went out for ice cream with your wife one time without you and leaning over during it to say, "It could be like that . . . with your peeper . . . if you touch yourself or your mother . . ."--or maybe that's just the blood rushing to his head. If the driver also turns out to be a drummer like his pop, though, he will be sketched the fuck out.

Speaking of drums (and guitars), in the quad after the high school P.E. class he teaches as his real job, Goodie overhears a gawky, fringed kid telling another about some crazy album called *Wishing By Runnin' A Custom Fucks* that he describes as sounding like "words slapping their flesh in a boiler room about to rupture." According to the kid, no one knows who the musicians are because the album was just leaked to an outsider music label, but the leading theory on the internet is that they're inmates in adjacent rooms of a mental facility who have not gotten laid in twenty years. Goodie laughs inwardly like the ant in the foreground of a shot because the real scale is hours, not years.

HINT:
The album name comes from the columns of Page 7

pulled **A HEADSPINNING SELF** stands like
over **A LAUGH LIKE** a pile
driver watching **COWBOYS HE POPS** as the waves of
a fellow **OF RIDING** other poetry
weaver caught by **THE TRIM** lovers surge back
a side street **POSTERS TAPED OVER** to line up for
cop at the next **ROCK** signatures he & Effie have
light as he realizes this **CLASSIC** come to beg Thea for
verse of his **PAGES TACKED OVER** money
new solo **ZINE** since Effie has lost her new
track rhymed the same **XEROXED** job because her
word with its **ROOM WITH** boss found her
self he sucks on a **DESK CHAIR OF HIS** dancing like the
paper **STARE ABE SITS AT THE** statue
clip like a stereotypical **HANDLE** of liberty to be
farmer with his **KNIFE** too literal to excite
hayseed as **THE FIRST'S DOOR WITH** people to trade
he fingers thru **ALBUM STOPPED BY** gold for
other **ABE COINSLUTS** cash Thea's
possibilities **THE NEW POST** promoting
his brother Lewis's **KID'S PRAISE OF** her new
tie and collar **SECOND** collection called The Tree
shirt make **SEQUEL GOODIE SEES THE** Copy Of
him look more like **VIDEO** Her about
the eyes **STRAIGHT TO** the previous
of an owl printed on **FAILURE OF THE** tour which she
powdery **LACKEY TOWARD THE** recollects as
scaled **VILLAIN'S** walking to the wrong
wings than **PRIDE OF THE DESTROYED** notes of a
himself as he **WITH THE SCORNFUL** guitar

With the scornful pride of a destroyed-villain's lackey toward the failure of the straight-to-video sequel, Goodie enjoys seeing the second kid's praise of the new post-Abe Coin$lot album (under their new name, The Coin Sluts) stopped by stare from the first kid that glints like a door with a blade for a handle.

The rejected guitarist sits at the desk chair of his childhood room in Goodie's house (where he has tacked xeroxed zine pages over the classic rock posters taped over the trim of riding cowboys). As Abe realizes that the present verse of the new solo track he has been writing rhymes the same word with itself, he pops a laugh like a head-spun driver on the shoulder watching a fellow weaver caught by a side street cop at the next light. He sucks on a paper clip like a stereotypical farmer with his hayseed as he mentally flips through other possibilities.

At yet another poetry reading, his older brother Lewis's tie and collar shirt make him look more like the eyes of an owl printed on powdery-scaled wings than himself. He is standing like a pier pile as the waves of other poetry-lovers surge back to line up for signatures. He and Effie have come to beg Thea for money after Effie lost her latest post-coaching job because her boss thought that her "dancing like the statue of liberty" was too literal to excite people to trade gold for cash. Thea's promoting her new collection called *The Tree Copy of Her* that she wrote about the previous tour, which she recalls as "walking to the wrong notes of a guitar,"

HINT:
Thea's drawing from the columns of Page 9

say that this is a big**OF NO** entrance as the
success they **FOUR** second Chops
even quickly collaborate**FOR YEAR** At The Beach
on a new book**AND THE DICE** album is not on any
of specially **WINDED METAPHORS** of the
designed poems for **LONG** year
the format called **TO HER POETRY'S** end
To Her Poetry's **FLAG** lists he skims
Flag **TO BE THE DANCING** online one hand
that comes with**HER SKILLS** on the trackpad he
a DVD Lewis **ON TOUR AND USE** begins
however is **EFFIE TO COME** to muse
fired from**THEA ASKS** about how to be
his stopgap **YES SO** better schlubby
gig lending his **WELCOME SAYS** scarecrows with
owl stare as**SIGNS OF** accurate genitals speakin
a horrifically **HANDMADE** of Romeo's they're
twisted **FOR THEIR** about to cool
guard **VAPORIZED** off for a while
rail to anti-drug**AND ARE** as his towtruck
programs **SAUCERS** boyfriend finally sees
on the road **OF LOOMING**his pageant and
when they realize that **THE MENACE** breaks it off because
he's just boring**AND FREAKS IGNORE** it
not brain fried his **HIPPIES** loses sight of
dad sighs **WHERE THE STEREOTYPICAL**guys
with relief like**SPACESHIP THE MOVIE** like him in
a middling **BACK A** forests Romeo feels like
lobster at a **STEPPER WELCOME** Snow White's
customer's **BUT WOULD AN ODD** scoutleader

but would an odd stepper welcome back a spaceship? The movie where the stereotypical hippies and freaks welcome the looming saucers that vaporize them says, "Yes," so Thea asks Effie to come on tour with her and use her Figurative Embodiment transformation skills to be the dancing flag to her poetry's long-winded metaphors, and the dice for Year 4 of No say that is a big success! They even quickly collaborate on a new book of specially-designed poems for the format called *To Her Poetry's Flag* that comes with a DVD. Lewis, however, is fired from his stopgap gig lending his owl stare in each town they pass through to anti-drug programs as a horrifically twisted guard-rail--the network of organizers eventually realized that his brain is not fried, but boring.

At a desk behind a computer that once looked hi-tech and bio-organic but now just looks bulky, Lewis's dad sighs with relief like a middling lobster when a rich customer enters; he has been fearfully checking several year's-best-album lists, but his *Wishing By Runnin'* doesn't seem to be on any of them, so The Chops gets to stay in the bedroom, after all. (Romeo's *Name Written In Post* snuck into one reviewer's list at number 4 for internet artists beginning with the letter R.) Goodie then begins to muse about how he and Mounthe can be even better schlubby-scarecrows-with-accurate-genitalia next year.

Speaking of junk, Romeo's is about to cool off for a while--his towtruck boyfriend has just now finally seen Ro's pageant performed, and outside on the pavement, he tells Ro it's over because the play's design lost the silhouettes of guys like him in the forest. Watching dude walk away for the final time, Ro feels as low as Snow White's scout-leader.

homespun **LOUD** virginity
hat with **SPIRIT IS LIKE A** ditching
cat ears that **HER FREE** comedy turns the case
he can wear with **PERHAPS HE THINKS** into an erotic
suit against **THE PRODUCTS PICTURED** pursuit that'll
the snickers **WITH** stretch the boundaries
of his friends who **THE PICTURES** of the sexuality of
will secretly wish they **CAN BE LIKE** the detective
had the guts **THAT LIFE** like a squeaking
to take life **BELIEVES** sighing
by **AN UMBRELLA AND** balloon Humps
the fuzzy **WHO ALWAYS BRINGS** of the
tassles **A YOUNG COMMUTER** Bastardvilles is
what duz a suicide **PARTY SHE MEETS** her biggest
bomber see **AT ROMEO'S** seller
in such a gentle **ROSCOE SO** online which is not
sheep **DETECTIVE LIKE** saying
maybe she wants **AN AMATEUR** much since she's got
to rattle his **POSTER TO** the job
etc. though the **PRISTINE SUBWAY** that I just
bomb will prolly be **A PRINTLESS** read
a yarn **IZZY WOULD BE LIKE** the mocking
one let's make **VIOLENCE LIKE** bird
Roscoe **OTHER RANDOM STREET** killer had
a love she takes **WITH EACH** receptionist at a
mystery **YEAR BUT WILL IT BE** travel
stories **LOVE THIS** company she was born
& like a resourceful **IZZY WILL FIND** Molly Autry but her
masturbator **THAT BOTH ROSCOE AND** pen is Ertré
in **THE DICE SAY** comma Mary

Well, the dice are nicer to Roscoe and Izzy, but will the love they find be with each other? Random street violence like Izzy would be like a printless, pristine subway poster to an amateur detective like Roscoe, so instead, at the party Romeo's throwing she meets a young commuter who always brings an umbrella and believes that "life can be like the pictures" if you buy the products pictured. Perhaps he thinks her free spirit is like a loud homespun hat with cat ears that he can wear with his suit against the snickers of his friends who will secretly wish they had the guts to take life by the fuzzy tassels, but what does a suicide bomber see in such a gentle sheep? Maybe she just wants to rattle his etc. (and her bomb will probably be a yarn one).

Now let's make Roscoe a love, someone who takes mystery stories and, like a resourceful masturbator in a virginity-ditching comedy, turns each case into an erotic pursuit that stretches the boundaries of the detective's sexuality like a squeaking, sighing balloon. *Humps of the Bastardvilles* is her biggest seller online, but that must not be saying much since she still has to keep the job that I just read the mislabeled mockingbird-killer had: receptionist at a travel company. Scoe's might-be lover was born Molly Autry, but her pen name is Erté comma Mary.

towtruck **DUMPED BY A** teeth
driver so Scoe **HAS JUST BEEN** the third grader
arrives early **AFICIANADO AND ROMEO** at recess
so he can drop icicle **BIKE** in him finds that
stares **IS A BIG** pretty
on anyone who **BARS ROSCOE** awesome he
defies the Don't Arrive **IN THE** drops
In Any **GAP** his pedantic
Thing That Can Be **OF THAT** patrol like a foot
Towed theme of the **LENGTH** taster discovering he
party **BEYOND NECK** is describing
Molly whizzes **CHILD JUST** a book to its
up **FACED** author
on rollerskates **THE HONEY** and welcomes
which makes **STRAINING TO REACH** her inside
him think about the **GIRAFFE** as if it is
last time he **TONGUED** his
saw those little **SHARPIE** to decide on
wheels **INTO A** hearing that she is
torn free like **TWISTED** a twister he
stained **BALLOON** starts describing his
notecards **OF THE** experience
atomized with mammal **CASE** as a folder but
covered beads **ENGINEER THE** ends
from a **SUGGESTION AND REVERSE** up talkin re:
blood steer **POE'S** a time when
crashing thru a **GOAL LET US FOLLOW** he wanted
window **DETECTIVE'S ROMANTIC** Robin in
to get at a can of **OUR** the tour o the somethin new
dogs' **NOW THAT WE KNOW** pageant

Now that we know our detective's romantic goal, let us follow Poe's suggestion and reverse-engineer "The Case of the Balloon Twisted into a Sharpie-Tongued Giraffe Straining to Reach the Honey-faced Child Just Beyond Neck-length of that Gap in the Bars." Roscoe is a big bike aficionado, and Romeo has just been dumped by a towtruck driver, so Scoe arrives early to the "Don't Arrive In Anything That Can Be Towed" party--he wants to be able to drop icicle stares on anyone who defies his frenemy's theme. Molly whizzes up on skates, which puts his mind momentarily back in the middle of the bloody collision in the final moments of Isla Hermana where he saw little wheels like those torn free like "stained notecards atomized with mammal-covered beads from a blood steer crashing through a window to get at a can of dogs' teeth"--which the third-grader-at-recess in him still finds kinda awesome. Roscoe drops his pedantic patrol like a foot-taster discovering that he is describing a book to its author, and he welcomes Molly inside as if this is his to decide on.

When she tells him that she is a twister, he starts describing his own experiences as a folder, but somehow ends up talking about a time when he got the itch for his then-girlfriend Robin (!!) during a tour of the Something New pageant--risky move, dude!

when everyone **PHONES FROM** guitar side
was trying **BUSTED CELL** men of your favorite
to take **ON A HARVEST OF** pop
pics of **SCAVENGERS OUT** solist or
the last **OF THE FUTURE LIKE** the stitches
reactor **IN THE CAR** used to create the
sunset racing **IT** sweater on the protagonist's
the nightfall **WOULD MAKE** sibling
which'll close the anti **ROBIN IF SHE** in that T.V.
mutant **ASKING** show when every 1 goes 2
gates **THAT GLOVE HE WAS** hug
of Man's **MAKING** themselves while fingerin
Last **ROSCOE FINISH** the science in.
Stand **INTO IT SO LET** their beards they
Hattan **UP BEING** sneak into the prototype
she's got **THAT MOLLY WILL END** car which turns
an underground **WE KNOW** out to be all back
city discoverer **ANYWAY** seat adaptin 2 unbuckled
vibe about **PARTY** position shifting like
her so she said **THE** amused human
let's wait until the **THROWING** hand holdin scamperin
big **THAT SHE WASN'T** baby
demo of **IT THOUGH I'D FORGOTTEN** mice while
the sexy personal **IN** the
robot who **A FRIEND OF THE WOMAN** kaleidoscopic
gets turned on by being **TOLD TO** one way
talked to about **ADVENTURE IS BEING** windows divide
the comparative **TALE OF AMOROUS** distractions into
merits **ME THAT HIS** stainglass Molly asks
of the various **THE COIN TELLS** if Ro's car has these

The coin tells me that his tale of amorous adventure is being told to a friend of the woman in it (though to be honest, I'd forgotten that Robin wasn't the one throwing this party), but that's not a minus for Molly, so let's let Roscoe finish making his glove. As he was saying, he asked Robin if she would like to "make like scavengers, out on a harvest run of busted cellphones-from-back-when-everyone-was-trying-to-take-pics-of-the-last-reactor-sunset, racing the nightfall which will close the anti-mutant gates of Man's-Last-Stand-Hattan"--in other words, "make like the Bible in the back of the car of the future." Anyone who knows Robin knows she's got an underground-city-discoverer vibe about her, so she said, "Let's wait until the big demo of the sexy personal robot that gets turned-on by being talked to about the comparative merits of the various guitar sidemen of your favorite rockstar or the stitches used to create the sweater on the protagonist's sibling in that T.V. show." When the rest of the attendees went to hug themselves while fingering the science in their in-some-cases invisible beards, Roscoe and Robin snuck into the prototype, which turned out to be basically a self-driving giant back seat that had kaleidoscopic one-way windows that divided coital distractions into mood-soaking stained glass--plus, it automatically adapted to unbuckled position-shifting like an amused human hand holding scampering baby mice.

Molly tells him they should see if Romeo's self-driving car has these same features.

high **FLASH OF** everyone but a hand's
contrast **A LIGHTNING** count
that makes them **BOLTS AND** of no one's
an aesthetic **WHEAT AND THUNDER** watchers he's
tongue across **ROOM BUT WITH MORE** promised
a lobe **IN THE LIVING** a love and
but a moral **TABLE** he remembers hearing that
flick **THE CARD** she broke
to it like **THE STIFFENER ON** up with
a delicate **THE DRINK THAT NEEDS** an affluent
wasp of **DREAMING OF** guitar
a gun with **THE PLACE EACH** blort during
a trigger **WITH** the glass shattering
guard **THE FRIDGE THAT CAME** music of
no wider **BY** the bed and was going store
than the pointy **THEM STANDING** owner his sharpie
end of a **FASCIST PAINTS** marked
carrot whose name **THAT A** CD-R
translates **IMAGINARY** way of trying to get
to Rat **POPULAR** a busted old
Daddy **IN THE** shoe consigned
Plugger like a drunk **LINKED** with her is given
with visions of **LEADERS ARE SO** the trunk's
his elephant **AND SCOUT** treatment of the
Abe blearily sees **BUT FARMERS** sting and he wakes
his ex **PARTY** up under the arm of a
Aggie stomping **AT ROMEO'S** woman raised
around the make **ABE WOULD BE** around
shift dance **SURE IF** skis and horse
floor ignored by **I WASN'T** legs

Meanwhile, inside the shindig, Abe blearily catches site of his ex Aggie like a drunk with visions of a personal elephant. I wasn't sure if he'd be at Romeo's party since they'd had that falling out about the whole student-became-the-teacher at a Battle Of The Bands a few years back, but farmers and scout-leaders are so linked in the popular imaginary that an MRA fascist in attendance spontaneously paints a portrait of Ro and Abe standing by the fridge with dudely dreamy stoicism (both not-so-secretly wishing to escape the conversation and stiffen their drink) and the painter throws in extra wheat and thunder bolts around them, catching them in a lightning flash of high contrast that turns the two of them into less of an aesthetic tongue across a lobe than a moral flick to it, like a delicate wasp of a gun with a trigger guard no wider than the pointy end of a carrot and whose name translates to "Rat Daddy Plugger." (Sorry--got lost for a second there.) Anyway, Abe is actually watching Aggie stomp around the make-shift dance floor ignored by everyone but a hand's-count of no-one's-watchers. The dice have promised him a love, and he remembers hearing that Ag broke up with "an affluent guitar blort" during the "glass-shattering music of the bed" and that she has become a store owner (News to me). He tries to again "get a busted old shoe consigned with her" (as they say), but his method is too much sharpie on a CD-R--she gives him the trunk's treatment of the sting, and the next thing he knows, it's tomorrow and he's waking up hung over under the arm of some other woman who was raised around skis and horse legs.

HINT:
Abe is thinking of Aggie's break-up amid the columns of Page 10

Beebe wore **THAT** classic
to every show **SLASH BOYFRIEND** where she
and that adorable **STRING GUITARIST** says to the
photo**NAILED SEVEN** sky out
spread **THE SAME BLACK** lucky
where they **CIRCULATED WEARING** star like a kittn
were walkin' their **OTHER STARLET IS** meowing
allegedly shelter **PINT AFTER SOME** before a
Chorkie in the **CUP OR** puppet
gentrifying **INSIDE OF YOUR** lion year
neighborhood does **DOWN THE** five of
this spell **AFIRMATIONS GOING** No
curtains4**CREAM PLACE W/ THE SPIRAL OF** doesn't
The Coin **ICE** make us wait for
$luts **OF THE HOKEY** news
will the world of **BAGS COMING OUT** of the band's
sell **PUFFY PHOTOSHOPPED** breakup Beebe
out pop **LAUGHTER WITH EXTRA** goes
punk ever recover **PIG** solo and is
Abe's **LICKERS LIKE SWEET** lost
sister Steph rides **DISH** among the other
out her own **SIGHERS AND MORNING** Ramones
break up **LINE** vitamins
like a former Soviet **FLICKING DMV** for kids and
general turned **UP TO PHONE** jack
grumbling mouse **SERVED** swiggers but in
jockey by **MATE BEEBE IS** more earth
mouthing along to the **BAND** shattering news this is the
Leslie**USURPER** year they find a sister
O' Lustfully **ABE'S OLD** planet

Romeo had starred in a bio-pic of iconic silent movie star Leslie O'Lustfully (don't bring it up to him or the people who Kickstarted it), but Abe and Lewis's sister Steph is watching the real thing far from any party except the one Leslie O has just fled in *The Careless Lady*. Steph, riding out a post-break-up wave of melancholy like a former Soviet general turned grumbling mouse-jockey, safely holsters the ice cream spoon and gathers the blankets around herself to be ready to grip the air and mouth along with the movie's classic line spit at the sky, "Out, lucky star!" It seems to help--even if Steph's roar is really just a mew before a lion puppet on the tube.

The lucky stars definitely seem missing for her brother's old usurper bandmate Beebe ("Just Beebe") who gets served up on the front page of the tabloids to phone-flicking DMV-line-sighers and morning-dish-lickers like sweet pig laughter; the photo captures her afflicted with extra-puffy, photoshopped bags as she comes out of the hokey ice cream place that has a spiral of affirmations going down the inside of your cup or pint. It seems some other starlet has been circulating wearing the same black-nailed seven-string guitarist / boyfriend that Beebe had been wearing to every show (and in that adorable photo-spread where they were walking their allegedly-shelter Chorkie in the gentrifying neighborhood). Does this spell curtains for The Coin Sluts? Will the world of sell-out pop punk ever recover?

Year 5 of No doesn't make us wait: Beebe goes solo and is instantly lost among the other little big pharma Ramones Vitamins For-Kids-And-Jack-Swiggers.

In slightly more significant news, this is the year that fair Sister City where we lay our scene is the site of a pretty significant discovery: Earth has a sister planet (!!).

HINT:
The title of the movie comes from the columns of Page 010

hurled into the **HAD BEEN** clutches to it like

Reverse **VOLCANO HE** finery before

Reverse **SPANS THE REVERSE** catching its

Volcano on **THAT** glee and

his home **THE STAGE** suffocating it n reverent

world for being too **OF** pose as the house

factual **TO THE LOWER SCAFFOLDING** drops

in his tour **FOUND CLINGING** hewn

guiding **WAS** oak panels around her

given **WHO JUST YESTERDAY** painted

the signal she back **PLANET H8R** sarcophagial

flips **FROM THE** gold the wet

into a Benign **LIVE HUMANOID** haired

Toomer becoming **FOR EMORO A REAL** alien says that

a house clingin 2 **HER PERFORMANCE** he

her assistant's **READY FOR** guesses that was

head like **STANDS** impressive though

a monstrous **POETRY** on his

diver's **ABOUT** planet art is

helmet **SHITS AGAIN** clear

the assistant uses **TWO** and doesn't require

her **BROW READERS GIVE** uncomfortable

own abilities 2 liquify her **MIDDLE** Googling he says he'd

legs as if **DRESSING EFFIE WHO MADE** like

sinking in **SALAD** to return to

mud should the water be **VAGUE AS** his

drawn off **PAPER SLEEVES AS** home even

now the house **FOLDED** though he has no

releases gauzy tendrils **IN BROAD** reason 2think theyre dun

which the sinking figure **DRESSED** hurling

Yeah, just yesterday a real-life humanoid named Emoro from the Planet H8R was found clinging to the lower scaffolding of the Skatespeare stage that now spans the mouth of Prosperous Island's Reverse Volcano. (To be cool, the Earth press does not emphasize that he got there because his own people hurled him into their Reverse Reverse Volcano for being too factual in his tour-guiding--hey did you know that Romeo sucked at being a tour guide?) Now, Effie stands on that same stage as Earth's cultural ambassador before this alien (I mean, she *did* achieve the nearly impossible feat of making middle-brow readers give two shits about poetry again, and all it took was gimmicky performances!). Effie is dressed in broad, folded-paper sleeves as vaguely traditional as salad dressing. Given the signal to start, she does an improbable back flip into a "Benign Toomer," becoming a house clinging around her assistant's head like a "monstrous diver's helmet." The assistant uses her own Figurative Embodiment abilities to liquify her legs as if "sinking in mud should the water be drawn off." Now the house releases gauzy tendrils that the sinking figure clutches to itself like finery before catching its glee and suffocating it in a reverent pose as the house drops around her hewn oak panels painted in sarcophagial gold.

Pressed for a response by the cameras, the Hater (for that is what our press has decided to call the people of his planet) says that he guesses that was impressive, though on *his* planet, art is clear and doesn't require uncomfortable Googling. He says he'd like to go back to his home through the portal (even though he has no reason to think they're done hurling people into volcanoes),

to her armored **HER THE JELLYFISH** along Romeo in
adventurer **PERFECT FOR** the massively
the flashbulb **STY HE'S APPARENTLY** multiplayer
to her **IT'S** online
finery **THE HEADLINE ALIEN CRIES** game
the stilts **STILL RUN** based on his
to her mud mired **THE PAPERS** sister's
diver plus he **BIT LIKE HIS SISTER BUT** blog that we
plays **SHE'S NOT A** mentioned
the clarinet **ATTACK HE SAYS** in book one
they **SCREW** and forgot his your
move **TO CHECK OUT HER** first
into a boxcar **QUEST OR AT LEAST** heartbreak
but have **TO STAY FOR A SECOND** class
it fixed **PARTY AND HE DECIDES** character
up with yuppie **HALLOWEEN** is
modern **WAY OUT OF AN EXCRUCIATING** level
like campfire **BUTTER CUPS ON YOUR** 29 and like a
cooked **FLAVORED PEANUT** monster hiding
eggs **OF HOMEMADE BOURBON** in an
inside **LOCKS LIKE A BOWL FULL** amusement
embered **OR NOT** park he has designed
potatoes in **AGGIE'S FLOWING** it to look as much
a video on **OFF REVEALING** like himself as
the net next to **THE HELMET COME** possible so that no
interplanetary **HE SEES** one will suspect that
lovin' **MARCH WHEN** rockstar even knows
the former eagle's **THE REAR** where his desk is but stil
nesters are just **AN ABRUPT TO** he
grinding **THE ALIEN DOES** quests alone

but he does an abrupt "to the rear march" when he sees the house helmet come off, revealing the flowing (or not--you decide) locks of Effie's assistant Aggie like a bowl full of homemade bourbon-flavored peanut-butter cups on your way out of an excruciating Halloween party. He decides to stay for a second quest (or at least long enough to unlock her "screw attack"), saying she's not a bit like his own sister. None the less, the Sister City paper still runs the anagrammatic inaccuracy "Alien cries, 'It's Sty!'"

Emoro's apparently perfect for Aggie: he's the jellyfish to her armored adventurer, the flashbulb to her finery, the stilts to her mud-mired diver. Plus, he plays the clarinet. They move into a reclaimed old boxcar but have it fixed-up yuppie modern like campfire-cooked eggs inside embered potatoes in that video I just saw on the net.

Next to interplanetary lovin', Romeo and his former roommates are just grinding along. Romeo does his in the massively multiplayer online game based on Aggie's old blog about life in Sister City (which used to be quite popular before she Tenenbaumed out and I forgot about it); his "Your-First-Heartbreak" class character (dictated to him by Roscoe so many years back during the original counter-conspiracy fiasco) is level 29 and, like a monster hiding in an amusement park, designed to look so much like himself that no one will suspect that a rockstar even *knows* where his desk is--yet he still quests alone.

to march with **ONE WANTED** Island forgotten
Noys **INSTRUMENT NO** history
will be making **LIKE THE** sign which she had
his big **GIZMOS HE PLAYS** played
debut as **THE COFFEE** skull
a soloist in a **KITCHEN WITH** hammer
few years so **HIS IN THE** doc to and which
we should start **PROCESSES YES DOES** gives the
blending **BODILY** deliberately
him some **TRAFFIC OF DISOBEDIENT** amnesiac a
material to work **INTO THE CROSS** turtleneck
with the caffeine **TRYING TO ESCAPE** w/ virtual reality
and the practiced **BOARD KEEPS** monitor sewn into
frenzy suggests **HANGER BUT NOW THE** neck
an ant like **FLANNEL** hole and seemingly the
temperament **AS AN INDOLENT** next she's catching
but kickflips **HAD DOWN** the wounded nostalgia
and theremins **SHE ALMOST** kingpin getting his
also both **TRICK** sign
carve out of air **HEAD OF THE** raised
like a bubble **SCRAPE TO LAND ON THE** courtesy
wand stay **SKATEBOARD TRYING EACH** of a well
tuned Roscoe's grinding **WITH HER** known mystery
has a distinctly bumpier **SUBURB** writer in his still shitty
characteristic **CURBS OF HER** office
to it one minute **WATCHED** space she parades the
Molly is helping **THE CLOSELY** netted
him **GRINDING ON** lovers in her next
raise his first **HER** book and climbs the tear
narrative Prosperous **ROBIN DOES** drops of the jilted

Robin does hers on the closely-watched curbs of her neighborhood, trying with each scrape of the skateboard to land on the head of the trick that she almost had down back when she was an indolent flannel-hanger, but now the board seems to want to escape into the cross traffic of disobedient bodily processes. Yes does his grinding in their kitchen with the coffee gizmos he plays like the instrument no one wanted to march with. (Our protag Noys Segundo will be making his big debut as a soloist in a few years, so we should start blending him some material to work with from the stock of his parents; the caffeine and the practiced frenzy suggests an ant-like temperament, but kickflips and theremins do both carve air like a bubble wand. Stay tuned.) Roscoe's has a distinctly bumpier characteristic to it; one minute, Molly is helping him raise his first subversive information sign (part of his "Re-experience The Past for the First Time" brand that gives the deliberately amnesiac a turtleneck with a virtual reality monitor sewn into the neck hole--she's thanked in the fine print as "skull-hammer doc") and seemingly the next, she's catching the wounded nostalgia kingpin "getting his sign raised" courtesy of some other better-known mystery writer trollop in his still shitty office space. Molly will parade the netted lovers in her own next book and climb the tear drops of the jilted like pegs up the charts.

of **THE PULSE** until the owners stop
a tree at the prop **HE STARES WITH** opening
Effie has made **HIS WHEN** their doors ahh but
him to wield **HER BROTHER GETS** Abe's got
at her fandom's **SAFE** good
annual **FOR CALL IT** roll but maybe he's
devotional **TO BE MISTAKEN** Gaudy
& she realizes their rings **AS NOT** no
have been merely **TWICE SO** longer he takes
shelved next **GESTURE REPEATED** without shame
to each other but never **ME NOT** the last
interlocked **PHONE** name of his ski
sister **TABLE MAKING A** slope
Izzy's **POOL** honey named
business **ON THE OTHER SIDE OF THE** Bully
goes blooey when the **LADY** Snopes the
hamsters **COMES FROM THE** heiress
get into **KARAOKE THE AXE** of Silver
the styling **NECK ROUTE IN** Spooner the
goo and put **BRONTOSAURUS** publicly
themselves **TAB FOR AGAIN TAKING THE** pious
into stiff **BROWSER** ice
comas **SONG LIKE A CHATTERING** cream
she visits with comic **DUMPED MID** chain between
strips to read by quiet **STEPH IS** takes of the
cages like **IT** commercial on
the last **YEAR OF** the spongey sandwich
priest who's in **A BAD** piano he looks at his
on the eleventh **HAVE** sfinkter'd coiffure xhalein
hour break **THE GAUDY CHILDREN** a star

The Gaudy children also have a pretty bad year of it. Steph is dumped mid-song like a chattering browser tab for again taking the brontosaurus neck route in karaoke; the axe comes from the lady on the other side of the pool table with a "phone me not" gesture repeated twice so as not to be mistaken for "call it safe." Her brother Lewis gets his when he stares with the pulse of a tree at the prop Effie has made him to wield at her fandom's annual devotional, and she realizes that their rings have been merely shelved next to each other but never interlocked. Big sister Izzy's business goes blooey when the hamsters get into the styling goo and put themselves into stiff comas; like the priest who's in on the eleventh hour prison break, she keeps visiting them with comic strips to read out loud by the quiet cages, but eventually the owners stop opening up.

Ahh, but brother Abe's got a good roll--maybe that's because he's a Gaudy no longer: he took without shame the last name of the ski-slope honey he hooked up with at that party, so now he's legally a Snopes! (Faulkner fans: no reference intended, I swear!) It doesn't hurt that his new wife Bully is the heiress of Silver Spooner, the publicly pious ice cream chain. Between takes of the commercial she's cast him in, he stands on the spongey cookie-sandwich piano in his powder-blue tux with a hanging guitar; his eyes focusing on the dangling tip of his bleached, sphincter-made coiffure, he exhales a star at the thought of the distance he's come from the garage.

being **THE WATER DROPLET IN** nothing in
what **EFFIE PLAYING** her next
it desires she lets **HIM IS** book she borrows
the mirror **ONLINE AND THE OTHER** it
have it like the bird **GAME** like a blithe
flipping **THE MASSIVE** shoulder with
presumptive **BELIEF IN** a pictograph
somebody **HIMSELF BEYOND** tattoo but describes
pukey with **ROMEO PLAYING** the iron
recrimintations **LIKE** lady as playing her next
hitting like waves **THAT HE'S** big
from **A DUCK SHE SEES** thing while letting
the offshore **OUT OF** him leaf
bomb **A RABBIT** through
tests of **PULLING** her like a
youth between **A SQUINTER** book and
a clicking **HAND BUT THEN LIKE** the affirmative
Romeo and **HIS OWN** man is
a grotesque **MIRRORS HOLDING** a lagging
magician No **HALL OF** puppeteer doin all of this
may grow **INDUSTRIES** stage
up **IN THE GRIMHILDE** center watched
to be a great **BEHIND** by the bird
shadow **YES LAGGING** woman who sees
puppeteer **CENTER ROBIN SEES** kaleidoscopes in
kaleidoscope **AT THE SCIENCE** the science
lover **OF NO** lover Roscoe remembers
Molly **PARTY** this passage & that night
sees the whole **BIRTHDAY** unscrewin the historical
thing but understands **AT THE SIXTH** sign for a chips ad

At the 6th birthday party of No at the Sister City science center, Robin sees Yes lagging behind in the Grimhilde Industries Hall of Mirrors holding his own hand, but then like a squinter pulling a rabbit out of a duck, she realizes that he's actually like Romeo playing himself beyond belief online: the other him is actually the shape-shifter Effie playing the water droplet by being what it desires. Robin lets the mirror have it like the bird-flipping presumptive-somebody pukey with recriminations hitting like waves from the offshore bomb tests of youth. (Between a clicking Romeo and a grotesque magician, No may grow up to be a great shadow puppeteer.) Kaleidoscope lover Molly sees the whole thing but really understands nothing; in her next book, she provides her fun-housed impression of the moment like a blithe shoulder with a pictograph tattoo; allow me to quote: "the Bird Woman, who sees kaleidoscopes in the science lover, watches the Iron Lady play the Next Big Thing while letting the Affirmative Man leaf through her like a book at stage center." Roscoe remembers this passage and also the night at Romeo's party when he met Molly while he is slowly unscrewing his beloved historical sign so an impatient workman can install an advertisement for chips there.

Emoro can afford**AN EYELET** breaking up this
non-traditional **IN** time with a Hollywood
shoes with **THE HOLE** extra with
his sizable finder's fee**THROUGH** whom she'd shared
for talking flat as a **OTHER** laffs but now reaches the
card **PASSING EACH** pause
to a reader **DRAGGED LACES** when their uneven
to make the**STY** strokes bring them
introductions now**FRUIT LIKE TWO** like a fumbling
he and Aggie **DRAGON** clock back to the same
dres up from **EXOTICISM IT SMELLS LIKE** congested
the waist **SOAP OF** paparazzo on the
up like sun**LINE WITH THE** banks Leslie's
sensitive creamed **PRODUCT** clock
prairie **UNDERPERFORMING** works which
dogs for conference **EACH OTHER'S** is how she
calls 2 peel**COIN TO LAUNDER** knows it's
fake**VOLCANO'S** time to
alien names**THE OTHER SIDE OF THE** break up when
for mediocre**COMPANY ON** Work rouses her with
products off like**THE CAR** straddling saxophone
fingers **DEAL WITH** blast and she has
from a shoplifted **ON A BUSINESS** an out of
mannequin **OF MIRRORS AS HE SHAKES** relationship
hand not even in a **HALL** vision of herself as gnarled
canoe**IN A** bear dragged along
can **HAND LIKE A PHILANDERER** behind and
Beebe escape**HOLDS HIS OWN** kissed and promised
being photographed**AS MUCH AS** to
in the middle of **MALCOLM** in secret

Meanwhile, Malcolm as much as holds his own hand like a philanderer in a hall of mirrors as he shakes on a business deal with the exec of the car company from the other side of the volcano's glowing copper coin. Each has agreed to launder the other's underperforming product-lines with the soap of exoticism (It smells like dragon fruit) just like two sty-dragged laces passing each other through an eyelet. The companies were introduced to each other by Emoro, who can now afford non-traditional shoes with his sizable finders fee for talking flat as a card to a reader. From now on, he and Aggie dress up from the waist up like sun-sensitive creamed prairie dogs for their consulting conference calls where they peel off fake Hater names for mediocre Earthican products like fingers from a shoplifted mannequin hand.

I wouldn't blame you if you got lost in the transition from plastic finger to photographed canoe, but that's how *I* got to the scene of Beebe's latest unfortunately public break-up, this time with a Hollywood extra with whom she'd shared laughs but now reaches an awkward silence when their uneven strokes bring them like a fumbling clock back to the same congested paparazzo on the banks.

Ahh, but Leslie's clock works, which is how she knows it's time to have her own break-up when Work Suggestively rouses her with a straddling saxophone blast that sends her into an out-of-relationship experience where she sees herself as a gnarled teddy bear dragged along behind and kissed and promised-to in secret.

and flings **CUPS** sea that fills
air **GROUP WHERE THEA** in the heart
with wood **SUPPORT** shaped
reddened **IN AN ANGER** lagoon of
knuckles **ALIVE THEY MEET** the other I back
as she describes the **QUITE** away
night **A REBIRTH AND STILL** from her
she discovered **ON HER WAY TO** shoulder unsure
how difficult **PHOENIX HAPPILY** if the undecided
it is **SUCH A ROASTED** metaphor is
in real **PINCHUCK IS JUST** too much
life to pull **OUT CATE** or just
that strike **BE BROUGHT** right Steph is patting
and only say **ME REQUESTED** her thigh as
it or put it **BEHIND** if tapping
across **THE TABLE** the ketchup they're
your own stupid **AS THE THINGIES** buddies from the
mouth **CRISPY** Leslie O'
to suck **AND AS** Lustfully message
your own **LOST** board but each sees
blood instead of **THAT TABLE WAS** themselves as
that of your beloved **JUST TOLD** too much a left behind
w/ their hateful **RECIPE THE WAITRESS** coat to think of
familiarity **WHOSE** the other as a new
bleached **DAYS AS THE DISH** hanger the latest
of the colors **TO FIND THESE** blow to Steph is that
that beached **AS HARD** kitten
sanity **THAT'S** that she
carried from **THEA A LOVE ONE** represents can't eat
the wreck or is it the fluid **I OWE** on camera w/o shitting

Turning 7 is special because that's the year where you feel the tug in your lederhosen or dirndl as they sew on your particular button. That was the year that I first remember feeling something for a girl; I was in a play group of three with another boy, and when we would play house, I was made their child. I don't remember whether she wore carrot print or just had buck teeth or if it's because my stuffed animal those nights was a bunny, but I associate her with rabbits. Anyway, the coin buttons No's pants toward George rather than Georgia, even though both are at his birthday party, along with mommy's new boyfriend and daddy's newish girlfriend. The shadow puppeteer wanted his party at a movie theater, so Yes sheepishly bought out a showing of *Rabbit's Play* at the multiplex and, like a disgraced engine driver dotting the eyes of the platformed commuters in his basement model, he has to buy every kid their own overpriced personal pizza from the concession stand! Am I wrong to give Effie the classically clueless "mommy's understudy cheer kick in a curio shop" halter top? She *is* generous enough to demonstrate the flailing balletics of figuratively-embodying "one with a skate on" (look it up), which does impress the kids.

pen **DOTTER AND AN EMERGENCY** park
putter**AN EYE** in him sided with
No writes **JERK THE SON OF** the reclusive
himself a lost **OFFICE** involuntary
crane's **PINCHES FROM THE** manslaughterer
account of the **DAY TO AVOID** in Yes during the
experience **PAT'S** split while they're all
on the back of a one **ON ST.** clambering over the
dollar**POCKET**seats and talking
off popcorn **BREAST** in the movies he's
coupon that **PEN PUT IN AN ADULT'S** desk
he will never **HE'S ONLY A GREEN** sitting
cash in what **PLACE** listening to
his father**COMES TO HER** the song Robin
doesn't bring up **BRA WHEN HE** invaded with her
is that new gf is**STRICTLY ABOVE THE** ukulele
preggo **WEEKS AND KEEPING** imagining it
I'm sure **SEEING FOR THREE** w/ the beats Effie
the baby **BEEN** played
won't arrive**SHE'S ONLY**on his sleeping
during No's **NAMED BUTTON THAT**head concluding
big debut in the**PARTY** that one is playing
pageant next **SON'S BIRTHDAY** with nothing like a
year speaking**TO HER** mime and the other
of Romeo **SHE BROUGHT A GUY** is a viking
he's not**HOMEWRECKER**protagonist who got
at the**EX'S NEW** it under the
party b/c the monster**ABOUT HER** shoulder
hiding **GETS TO COMPLAIN** and staggered
in an amusement **LIKE ROBIN**up 2 the award podium

And hey, No's party does also give Robin a chance to talk shit about her ex's new homewrecker with the other parents who stay, though, yeah, sure, she herself brought a guy that she's only been seeing for three weeks to her son's birthday party, but she's been keeping Button strictly above the bra when he comes to her place, and in truth, he's only a green pen put in an adult's pocket on St. Pat's day to placate office pinches.

The son of an eye-dotter and an emergency pen-putter, No finds a stray moment while his guests are being picked up to write himself a lost crane's account of the day on the back of a "one dollar off popcorn" coupon that he will never cash in. At least his father has enough tact not to bring up at the party that is that Effie is preggo. I'm sure the baby won't arrive right in the middle of No's big debut in the pageant next year . . .

Speaking of babies, Romeo's not at No's party because that hiding monster sided with involuntary recluse Yes in the split, so Robin's got it out for him. While the kiddies are all clambering over the seats and talking during the movie, Romeo is sitting at his desk, listening to the song he recorded on the island years ago where Robin invaded with her ukulele, and he imagines it with the erotic beats Effie played on his sleeping head that one time; he concludes that Yes must have a thing for those who play with nothing, like mimes and viking protagonists who "get it" under the shoulder and stagger up to the award podium.

is about how embracing **HEADLINE** press conference to
post **A MAGAZINE WHOSE** peer
credibility **ABBY WHO HOLDS** into her
by swirling his **BULLY NAMED** gemsack of
songs into jingles **DAUGHTER FROM** request e-mails she
alowed 'im 2 unlock his **NEWBORN** may answer
true coin **PARLOR HOLDING HIS** tomorrow
of inside his **ICE CREAM** the
former father **OF A NEW** years of being
makes it **TO THE OPENING** a supportive
big **UP** tree guard rail and
time **AND ABE HEADS** pile on his resume
when he gets **TO SPAWN** gets Lewis a job as
Effie's **THE BIG MOUTHES LOOKING** Malcolm's
old coaching **FOR** personal
gig like a mid aged **MASK AS A LURE** assistant his
man with last season's **STREAKED** flatulent
kicks **HER DEFIANCE** bulldog's
that got kids **COURT TO SHAKE** indifference
laid **THE FOOD** to human
this is the 2nd time **HEADS DOWN TO** propriety
Steph's pinned **DEN WALLS AS BEEBE** helps
the donkey **BULLETS TASTE** him sink his arms
to the **DUELING** onto an evasive
tail **POKERS AFTER THE LAST** executive's
said **FIRE** desk and loom there until
a man getting **ESCALATORS LIKE** the tardy file is
long in the ears **CROSS** tossed over
myself and **BANDMATES** like a butcher's
turns her back on the **FORMER** morsel

Speaking of people on Romeo's list, in the mall Abe crosses escalators like fire pokers with his old bandmate Beebe who is heading down to a little "concert" at the food court (I mean, there technically *is* a stage) where she knows she'll have to shake her defiance-streaked mask as a lure for the big mouths looking to spawn. Meanwhile, Abe is heading up to cut the ribbon at the opening of another new Silver Spooner ice cream parlor, and in his arms he holds his newborn daughter Abby and a magazine with his face on the cover and a joking reference about his old band's original name (The Coin Of Inside) and how he finally found it by swirling his songs into jingles and embracing post-credibility.

Like a middle-aged man with the kicks that got kids laid last season, Abe's dad also makes the big time when he gets Effie's old college Figurative Embodiment coaching gig, but he couldn't have done it without his agent / daughter. This is second time Steph has pinned the donkey to the tale (said a man getting long in the ears myself), and she turns her back on his press conference briefly to peer into her gem-sack of request e-mails that she *may* answer tomorrow.

She'd also donated a couple of minutes to twisting her brother Lewis's resume into focus, and his years of being supportive trees, guard-rails, and piles gets him the job as Malcolm's personal assistant; now he looms with arms sunk onto an evasive functionary's desk with a flatulent bulldog's indifference to human propriety until the tardy file is finally tossed over like a butcher's morsel.

rock **NOVEL ABOUT A** Death
journalist seeking **FICTIONAL** Otter to a drive in
love in a facsimile of **HER TOTALLY** showing
a grappa **OF** the classic kids' movie
distillery built on **THE REVIEW** with the dragon that
the site of a mini **TO FIRST IN** coils and
golf course **GROUNDER** glides
by **THE WORDS** winglessly through
the freeway **AND NECK AS SHE READS** the sky
she doesn't read **SHOULDERS** like Otter
far enuf 2 **SPREAD THROUGH HER** does
realize that the **ICE** in his nearly sealed
review's actually **DOOR LESLIE FEELS** garage
about Molly's **PAYROLL NEXT** at night the car
latest **SHE'S BEEN PUT ON THE** downloads
novel closing the **THING YOU KNOW** these
browser **WIFE AND THE NEXT** scenes and won't
window with a **COMMISSIONER'S** stop playin them
sigh Molly muses **CARRYING THE** on his dashboard
that if you aim for **LEAGUE STADIUM** display
the dog **OF A MINOR** like a babbling
turds & miss you end up **SHOT OUT** kid on a sofa
in the dirt but aim **LIKE A HOMERUN** rehearsing
for the piñata in the **HOUSE** the wrestling
tree **OF THE BURNING** match he saw
and you'll probably **DOOR** last
at least get **OUT THE FRONT** night Romeo
head she writes that **CATE BURST** does not look
down **ACROSS THE STREET SEES** forward
Romeo drives **A KID** to his next traffic stop

Arguably closer to being an actual dog (but not a mammal--fuck!), the semi-sentient self-driving car Death Otter is taken by his human Romeo to a drive-in showing the classic kids' movie with the dragon that coils and glides winglessly through the sky like Otter will do tonight in his nearly-sealed garage, and the next day, the car will download those scenes and won't stop playing them on his dashboard display like a babbling kid on a sofa rehearsing the wrestling match he saw last night. Romeo will not look forward to his next traffic stop.

Let's rotate among the branches of civic services: a kid across the street sees Cate burst out the front door of a burning house like a home-run shot out of a minor league stadium, and she's carrying the commissioner's wife all the way to the city payroll! Literally next door, Leslie Brautjungfer must be really stunned by what she's reading to not have noticed the smoke billowing past her window. This is why you should be careful jumping around the web for reviews of your own totally fictional novel about a rock journalist seeking love in a facsimile of a grappa distillery built on the site of a mini-golf course by the freeway--on the screen, she's highlighted the phrase "grounder to first" . . . but if she scrolled up for just a little context, she'd realize that the review is actually about the latest book by *Molly. That* lady is enough of a detective to get it right at her own computer, but being the proper recipient of the insult doesn't make her any happier about it. Closing the browser window with a sigh, Molly muses that if you aim for the dog turds and miss, you end up in the dirt, but aim for the piñata in the tree and you'll probably at least get head. She writes that down.

with a map of her **PLAN** he'd love
lady business **HIS BUSINESS** to fail but since
he gets **OUT** the phone
a position **HIM BY SWAPPING** company
being a cannibal **DUPED** let him go
of the grubby **AGGIE HAD** like the expensive
business **ROUTINE SAYING THAT** synth on your
practices he invented **A SPLINTER** demo one day before
and she gets the **PARTNER WITH** the return
can like **THE OLD TRAPEZE** deadline to avoid
a kid soliciting **ALIEN WHO PULLS** the cost
for a recycling **TO THEIR RESIDENT** of seniority he's
drive Yes finds **RESPONSIBILITY** stuck with
himself **AND THE COMPANIES SHIFT** the informer
mouthing **THEIR LANGUAGE** calculation Robin
along like **PRODUCTS BASTARDIZING** blocks
a judgmental **THE FLOOD OF SHITTY** Molly
but polite **OUTRAGED TO DISCOVER** on Facebook
guest **NO THESE ALIENS ARE** after
during the birthday **8 OF** discovering
boy's song **YEAR** her own speech
at a karaoke **ECONOMY IN** bubbles woven like
party to the **DIP IN THE LOCAL** tinsel in a
xenophobic **PLANET FOR THE** bird's
petition he's being paid **EMORO'S** nest of borrowed
to push **HUMANOIDS FROM** frames of cape &
in the part of the **INFLUX OF** tights
quad that **THE MODERATE** angst and
most people **BLAME** exposition in her 1st book
can't avoid **JACKOFFS** under her own name

When Robin finally gets around to reading Molly's book, she'll block her ex-friendster on Facebook after recognizing her own speech-bubbles woven into the action like tinsel in a bird's nest built from the borrowed frames of cape-and-tights angst and exposition. In Year 8 of No, jackoffs blame the moderate influx of humanoids from Emoro's planet for the dip in the local economy. These aliens are, in turn, outraged to discover the flood of shitty products bastardizing their language and make a big thing out of it, and the companies shift responsibility to their resident alien Emoro, who himself pulls the old trapeze-partner-with-a-splinter routine, saying that Aggie had duped him by swapping out his business plan with a map of her lady business. He ends up getting a position as cannibal mantid of the grubby business practices that he invented, and she gets the can like a kid soliciting for a recycling drive.

The literal xenophobia does create a much-needed job for Yes who now gets to push disgusting nativist petitions he doesn't actually endorse any more than a judgmental but polite guest singing along with the birthday boy's poorly-picked karaoke song. He'd love to fail, but since the phone company avoided acknowledging his seniority by letting him go like your 4-track demo's expensive synth one day before the return deadline, he's stuck calculating the informer's self-preservation.

as a seed **MENDACIOUS** with Romeo in
bearing **CONTRITION AS** writing him into
fruit he even pays **AN ACT OF** existence but she says
Roscoe who has **WHOLE THING IN** tearing can happen
called wild **BANKROLLS THE** between anyone
eyed for vigilante **DEBUT MALCOLM** and in the
justice **FORGETTING IS GETTING ITS** background
against him on a **ISLAND OF** No is
local morning show **DAYS OF THE** shadow
2provide the **PAGEANT ABOUT THE LAST** puppeteerin
lions and **THE CRACKING ROMEO'S** the creation of
arrows in a fwd for **THE LASH FOR** Yes in
the program **WHICH SHORTENS** the literary lab
showin perhaps 2 much **THE BEAN** that they shared
confidence **AS A USELESS PART OF** before
in the dramatic **THE NEXT MORNING** that's as far as
abilities of second **OFF** they get before Effie
graders No is given **AND SNAP** applauds his acting w/
the role of **IT IN THE MURK** a cry that spins
Romeo **ONLY TO LOSE** a coin & lands on his
George is made **A BOTTLE** father's
Yes Georgia is **IN THE DEPTHS OF** name
Robin Nemo is **PROFUNDITY** @hospital they follow
Roscoe **AS OFTEN SEEKING** the tradition
and Generica **AND JUST** and pool the parents'
is Max in the 1st act **ON THE SCRIPT** letters to get
Robin sees resolutions **IN AND** Leee using one
and a howling **WALNUTS** left out of Effie's
clone who asks **OF CRACKING** nick No's incomplete
about her complicity **AFTER YEARS** performance gets 5 /6

Okay, Reader, the big day has arrived! After years of cracking walnuts in and on the script--and just as often seeking profundity in the depths of a bottle only to lose it in the murk and have to snap off the next morning as a useless part of the bean--Romeo's pageant is finally getting its official debut! As mendacious as seed-bearing fruit, Malcolm bankrolls the whole thing in an act of public contrition for his part in the events depicted--he even pays Roscoe, who has previously called wild-eyed for vigilante justice against him personally on a local morning show, to provide the lions and arrows in a forward for the pageant's program. Showing perhaps too much confidence in the dramatic abilities of second graders, Romeo gives No the part of playing Romeo, while making George Yes, Georgia Robin, Nemo Roscoe, and Generica Max.

In the first act, "Robin" sees "resolutions in the sky" and "a howling clone" who asks about her complicity with Romeo in writing him into existence, but she says, "Tearing can happen between anyone," and in the background No is shadow-puppeteering the creation of his own father in the literary laboratory that they shared before--

That's as far as they get before Effie applauds her step-son's acting with a cry that spins a coin that lands on his father's name. At the hospital, they pool the letters of the parents to call the baby boy "Leee" [sic] after their favorite punk rock photographer (though they have to use one letter from Effie's old schoolyard nickname "False Easy" which, fun fact, is why she's called F.E.).

No's incomplete performance is given 5 out of 6 dots in a review posted on random.org.

LET'S CALL THAT CHAPTER "Too much life to pull out."

HINT:
The pageant draws from the columns of Page 004. The chapter title comes from Page 25.

so, in summary so far . . .

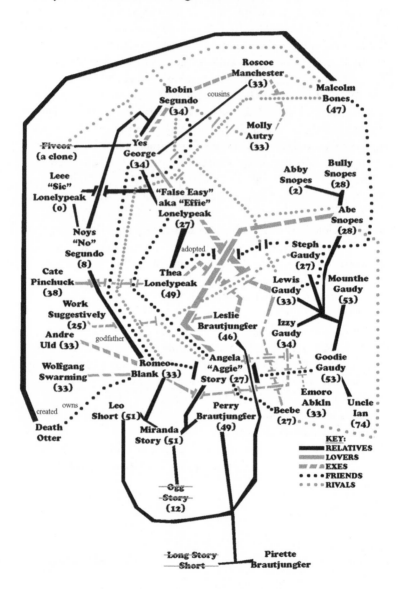

Chapter 1

little substance **TOO HAS** too a month
for the child **COURTYARD ROMANCE** after his big
though just try **IN THE** performance Noys
to pry it out of their **TEAM LOUDLY** opens the
hands **SWAT** emptied
fine keep **PLAYING** proprietary
it and we'll **LECTURE ON NOT** tools
give **NEVER GAVE A** kit his father gave
the child family **STREET EVEN IF THEY** him from his old
friendship **IN THE** phone
and school **CONCEPT OF NOT PLAYING** company
too **HARD ON THE** installation
along with the nebulous **HITTING** gig and he takes out
concepts **FOR APPARENTLY** the cardboard
of exterior **OUR BLOCK** heart that he had given
circumstance **OF** the shadow silhouette
and the pulse of **THE PARENTS** meant to be the itchy
inner life **TO CREDIT** mailbox perpetually
that wanes **AT THAT THOUGH I HAVE** checked
and waxes **PARTICULARLY GOOD** with glances
each of these **ARE NOT** in class but George
gets a roll **DYING AND KIDS** never seems 2 have
per year and just **BESIDES NOT** the same questions for
because a kid **OF** him but thank
brings **NO CAREER TO SPEAK** god no hasty
complexity to **AN ORANGE 6 THERE'S** answers to
adults **SEEDS** the nose meanwhile his
we'll let **CHILDHOOD HOW MANY** dad's new
them have **FACETS HAS** wife nurses baby bro
those **HOW MANY** watchin BB on the news

Chapter 1

How many facets hath childhood, how many seeds an orange? 6. Wikipedia told me so. Adults are always saying they want their kids to have more than *they* had, so our anointed protagonist Noys "No" Segundo, age 8, will get more than the yearly single pass of the die that had his parents licking the butts of clouds, or worming along the basement in stuck-zipper sleeping bags, or else warming plastic cup-chairs in lobbies with the rest of us. Every year, I'm gonna roll for his "romance," "family relations," "friendships," and "school sitch," plus generalized "exterior circumstance" (gotta allow for sickness and death) and "inner life" (gotta allow for "sickness unto death"), and then I will try to figure out what the spots on the ladybugs mean. (And just because having a kid brings complexity to the lives of adults, fine, we'll give those guys interior and exterior dice, too.)

A month after his big performance at the school pageant was interrupted by the messy arrival of his new half-brother, No opens an old phone company tool bag in his father's living room. From inside, he carefully extracts a cardboard heart, somehow still flat and unfolded (if a bit bunged on the edges) despite having been trapped in there with a geode, a toy car that is also a robot missing one arm, a pocket knife with a magnifying-glass extended, a frayed cut-out of a comic strip folded over at the last panel, a check-out aisle joke book, a flat rubber coin purse attached by small metal beads to the key ring for the two apartments, a marble, a pen with a replica Moai as its unattached cap, and one of his dad's old tools never removed or understood by either of them. His thumb doodles sightlessly in an already smudged circle on the construction paper as he wonders if finally completing the delivery of this prop to his costar George would fill that itchy mailbox (perpetually-checked with glances in class) with the same questions *he* has--or would it be an answer to the nose?

suggestion**AFTER AN ANATOMICAL** already I
from her date**AT THE PAGEANT** walk in
only **ROW** with Yes and he
to be caught **TO LEAVE HER** says everyone who's
by the man **ROOM AS SHE TRIES** not feeding or
charged to look **STREWN DRESSING** feeding let's go
out in case**A SCARF** for a ramble
an assassination **CODPIECE IN** his weak
attempt **A RECURSIVE** wordplay
should befall **LIKE AN ACTOR OVER** is sucked
his boss Malcolm **HER TRIPPING** down
she looks**TO FOOTAGE OF** the vortex of her
disarmed reporter **GAME THEY CUT** toothy
gives it two**BASKETBALL** viking
months nursing**AT A** laugh right before
Effie remembers **OTHER THAN LEWIS** the Frenchman
a different set of **OF NONE** gets it but we skate
bland lips boring **THE CHEEK** away on the frozen
her breast **SMUDGE TO** surface
and considers**A HEART SHAPED** of his vacated
transforming**SHOWN GIVING** tenant charm he tells
into **BEEBE WHO IS** No that they're
a bottle**HEARTBREAK** going to a place
as unfeeling**TOY OF** that
as homewrecking **SOCCER BALL CHEW** no longer
young whiskey**FAVORITE** exists but Romeo's
breath**ROLLED OUT THEIR** aunt has remade
but then she realizes **REPORTER HAS** it as an art show
she's been**DESK'S ENTERTAINMENT** called Eyeball
that **THE NEWS** Danger With Viscera

Meanwhile by the breakfast nook, his dad's new wife Effie nurses his baby brother Leee [sic] while watching the TV news over No's head--the entertainment reporter has just rolled out everyone's favorite soccer-ball chew-toy of heartbreak--Effie's old "friend" Beebe--who is shown giving a heart-shaped smudge to the cheek of none other than local nobody Lewis Gaudy at a basketball game. To give viewers background on how a celebrity could end up dating a personal assistant, they cut to file footage of her trying to leave her row in the pageant audience after an anatomical suggestion from her date--she trips like an actor over a recursive codpiece in a scarf-strewn dressing room but is caught by the man charged to look out in case an assassination attempt should befall his unpopular boss; Beebe looks disarmed. The reporter gives it two months. Nursing Effie remembers Lewis's bland lips--only *seeming* to belong to a child--boring this same breast and considers transforming into a bottle as unfeeling as home-wrecking young whiskey breath, but then she realizes that she's already essentially been that to No's mom, who she's found she usually does not have a hard time not thinking about.

I walk in the apartment arm-in-arm with No's dad Yes, and he says, "Everyone who's not feeding or feeding, let's go for a ramble." His weak wordplay is sucked down the vortex of his wife's laugh that brings to mind a toothy screen Viking right before the glib Frenchman gets it, but we grab the boy and skate away on the frozen surface of her husband's "vacated previous tenant" charm. On the way to the car, he tells No that the three of us are going to a place that no longer exists, except that someone has remade it as an art show called *Eyeball Danger with Viscera*.

at the grown**LOOKING** to the briefly
ups with ponytails **IN THE DOORWAY** open
and obscure **NO STANDS** table she tells No
t-shirts and jackets **PAINTED** to look
taken **AND** around and starts to chat
from **CAREFULLY SHAPED** with Yes
tough **OF WOOD** about his first and top
young **PIECE** five No picks up one of the
them looking **IS A SINGLE** small boxes
at objects on the **REGISTER** as long as a grown up's
shelvs that line the **HOURS THE CASH** foot on
walls there **AFTER** it is a picture of a finger
are no lightbulbs **ENTERING** wrapped in
in this **MISCREANTS FROM** a ribcage of
place just what **UNDERAGED** metal with a bird beak
comes thru **DO NOTHING TO PREVENT** extending off
the doorway **BEEN GIVEN TO** the tip right
and kid yer standing **ORDER HAS** between the
in it come **THREAD THE** eyes of a girl who is
on in says **BOTTOM WITH RED** actually
the proprietress comin **ACROSS THE** across the
forward **EYES EMBROIDERED** classroom
with a witchy **OPEN** falling out of her
barrette & sweater & shirt **WIDE** chair and
from her first **GREEN CURTAIN WITH** dreamy
concert she aborts **A HEAVY** look that No
an embrace **HAS NO DOOR ONLY** may identify
to her nephew's **THE GALLERY** years later as
once met friend like someone **OF** desire for dope and
seein theyre beaten **THE FRONT DOOR** premarital sex

The doorway of the gallery has no door, only a green curtain with wide-open eyes embroidered across the bottom in red thread. No holds the fabric aside with one hand but does not cross the threshold, looking at grown ups (in ponytails and lettered t-shirts and jackets taken from tough young them) squinting at objects on the shelves that line the walls. There are no lightbulbs in this place, just what comes through the doorway, and their glares say, "kid, yer standing in it!"

"Come on in!" says a middle-aged woman with a witchy barrette and a shirt from an old concert not being hidden by her sweater; she aborts an embrace towards his dad like someone seeing that they're beaten to a briefly open table. His dad introduces her to No as the aunt of Romeo--the kid's godfather / idol / playwright / role in the pageant / favorite musician--but instead of saying her name, he asks her if she isn't afraid of local teens robbing the place without any wood in the way, and she replies that the cash register is a solid block carefully shaped, painted, and bolted-down, but if they snatch a nightmare or two, maybe that's part of the point. She tells No to look around and asks his father, "What's your first and top-five?"

No wanders in, and from the shelf with least number of hovering adults around it, he picks up one of the boxes as long as a grown up's foot. On it is a picture of a finger wrapped in a ribcage of metal with a bird beak extending off the tip and pointing right between the eyes of a girl who is actually across a classroom, falling out of both chair and dreamy expression (which No may identify years later as "desire for dope and premarital sex").

slice**LID SIZED** what is
of carrot over **A TRASH CAN** advertised she says
her chest and **HOUSE ONE HOLDS UP** nothing but
another holds **AROUND THE** things like these used
a crescent **WIFE WEARS** to hold tapes
of giant **NEW** of oddly spooled
celery **AS HIS DAD'S** love for the
at her side **WEARING ABOUT AS MUCH** little
as if it is a funny **BATHTUB ALL** things and gleeful
hat she might put on **METAL** contempt
he turns **AGE IN A LARGE ROUND** for big 1's the
the box back over **HER** x-ray
and reads the metal **WOMEN** of this passes
letters **WATER WITH OTHER** through him
out **IN BROWN** like the bar of
loud **KNEES** light in a xerox
Chopping **UP TO HER** machine I tell him
List the crane **WOMAN STANDS** a friend's post
in him feels **BACK THE SAME** about straight to
a burp **OVER AND ON THE** videos put me
of admiration **TURNS IT** back n the ward o peekin
for the respect **OR SLEEPING NO** under bandages that
the beaked **SLACKING** would heal if looked at
blade commands **ARE STUDYING** str8 she says she'd
he walks ovr 2 **WIFE HER CLASSMATES** thot the same
Leslie and asks her what is **NEW** before she'd funded this
inside **AS HIS DAD'S** gallery with her
the box thinking **AS OLD** best seller money and her
that it feels **ON THE BOX LOOKS ABOUT** rock cred
too light to contain **THE WOMAN** severance package

The girl on the box looks about as old to him as his Dad's new wife. Her classmates are studying, slacking, or sleeping. No turns the box over, and on the back, the same woman stands up to her knees in brown water with other women her age in a large round metal bathtub (all wearing about as much as his Dad's new wife wears around the house); one woman holds up a trash-can-lid-sized slice of a carrot over her chest and another holds a thick crescent of giant celery at her side as if it is a funny hat she might put on. He turns the box back over and reads the rusted metal letters on the front out-loud: *Chopping List*. The crane in him feels a burp of admiration for the respect the beaked finger-blade commands. He walks over to Leslie and asks what is inside the box, thinking that it feels too light to contain what is advertised.

She says, "Nothing . . . but boxes like these used to hold tapes of oddly spooled love for the little things and gleeful contempt for the big ones."

The x-ray of this passes through him like the bar of light in a xerox machine.

I tell the kid that my friend's recent post about straight-to-VHS films had put me back in the ward of peeking under bandages at what might heal if looked-at straight.

Leslie says that, strangely enough, she'd thought *the exact same thing* before she'd funded this gallery with her shmaltzy-best-seller money and her rock-journalist cred-severance-package.

an x-ray's **CONSOLATION RIBS** tell
favorite **AN UNCLE WHEN THEY GO FOR** them how
meal **ISLAND HE DOES GET** bad things
afterward he is **LONELY AS CHRISTMAS** could get
6 yrs up on Yes **MAKES HIM FEEL AS** so they can ignor
and his name is **CRAZED WHICH** his advice
Cray he arrives **AS CRAB** he tells the table
on the arm of Romeo **SCHOOL** a story about
whose reviews **A REPUTATION AT** writing
are better **HUSKS THAT GIVE HIM** a song for his
now that **STORIES OF THE GORY** father when
he's using **UP AND THEY TELL** he was
sixth grade **KIDS SHOW** No's
nails **SO ONLY A HANDFUL OF** age
to make the **VEINS** their dad was half
thing being on that **MARCH UP YOUNG** way between a
particular **NIGHTMARES LOOKING TO** model and
arm **JUNKYARD OF** an accountant so that
means Cray's **A RUSTY** makes him
as practical as a **GALLERY AS** a phone
diver's **SEE THE** salesman how do you
gauge **MUMS LIKE HER** like that retconning
as disregareded **MUM AND MANY** X-Files
and raw **BUT GEORGE'S** shit Mr. George
as a carpenter's **PARTY THERE** let us take a
sunburn and as sweet **BIRTHDAY** blood
and angular as **HIS 9TH** sample of
the epaulettes of **MUCH THAT HE HAS** your son for
a nutcracker he is **THE GALLERY SO** the child return
the guy they call in to **NO LIKES** database no clono

No likes the gallery so much that he holds his 9th birthday party here the next week, but George's mum and many mums like her see the gallery as a rusty junkyard of nightmares looking to march up young veins, so only a handful of kids show up, and they will all tell stories on the schoolyard tomorrow of the gory husks on the shelves that will give No a reputation as "crazy as a crab," and by the end of the week, he'll feel as lonely as Christmas Island out in the sea.

Tonight, though, he does receive an uncle when they go out afterward for consolation ribs (an x-ray's favorite meal). The uncle is 6 years up on Yes, and his name is Cray. He arrives on the arm of Romeo, whose pageant reviews are better this year now that he's only using sixth grade nails to make the thing (and banning pregnant women from the performance). Being on that particular arm means Cray is as practical as a diver's gauge, as disregarded and raw as a carpenter's sunburn, and as sweet and angular as the epaulettes of a nutcracker. He is the accountant they call in to tell them how bad things could get so they can ignore his advice.

Yes's older brother tells the table a story about writing a song for his father when Cray was No's age. Their dad was half-way between a model and an accountant, so . . . that means he was a phone salesman. (How do you like that retconning X-Files shit? "Mr. George, let us take a blood sample of Yes for the Child Return Database #noclono.")

so Cray says looking at **FAMILY** earlier and sees
No watch for **THE** herself as
that one pointing at **HOPE FOR** the giant eye of
the squirming **PERFORMER AND** the science
baby **EGGS AS THE NEW** lover peering
in his dad's **PAPA OVER HIS** into
wife's **PROUD** kaleidoscopes within
arms the point **ABOUT BY THE** kaleidoscopes
reflects off the **SUN CROWED** at indivisible
polite smile **OF THE SECOND** grains
of Effie and hits **BY THE LIGHT** of
Robin **ONLY TO BE BURNED** the science
jabbing **AUTHOR AWOKE** practiced against
her glum **TRUE** her she need not
acceptance **SONG BEFORE THE** worry
that the closure of her **DAD THE** too much he is
school **DODGER BY SINGING** more
means that **RENT** coiled than his angular
Yes and his shapechanging **OF A** uncle
vixen **JUMPING ACUMEN** tracing
get to claim the **GUN** beam back to
honor of the **OLD YES SHOWED THE** finger and
check and now their **YEAR** down to other's clasped
shapeless **HOME BUT 3** fingers Romeo's old
spawn **SAYS HE'S COMING** ambition
wants her son's **DADDY** leaps at the
comfort in shadows **CALL IS WHEN** thot of covering the
she thinks back to **MY FAVORITE** song like
the hall of mirrors **WAS CALLED** a child scramblin over
three years **THE SONG** faces out of a shared bed

The title of Cray's song was "My Favorite Call Is When Daddy Says He's Coming Home," but then the three-year-old Yes had showed the gun-jumping acumen of a rent-dodger by singing the song for their Dad before the true author awoke, so Cray felt burned by the light of the second son crowed-about by the proud papa over his eggs as "the new performer and hope for the family." "So," he says, looking at No, "watch out for that one," pointing at squirming Leee [sic] in his dad's wife's arms.

Cray's point reflects off Effie's polite smile and hits No's real mom, Robin, jabbing her in the tender acceptance that the closure of the school that employed her means that her ex and his shape-changing vixen will get to claim the honor of paying tonight's check--and now their shapeless spawn wants *her* son's comfort in shadows, too?! The presence of Effie's undercooked and swaddled potato throughout the dinner has already been sending Robin back to the hall of mirrors three birthday parties before when Yes lost himself and found her replacement, and she's started seeing herself as the giant eye peering into kaleidoscopes within kaleidoscopes at indivisible grains of the science practiced against her. Don't worry too much about the half-brothers, Robin: your No is more coiled than his angular uncle, so he's less likely to snap--but then again, that's just my guess.

Trace the beam back to its finger and down the arm to another's clasped hands; at the thought of covering Cray's childhood song as his next single, Romeo's old ambition leaps like a child scrambling over faces out of a shared bed.

HINT:
Robin is thinking back to the columns of Page 026

their back **ROOM TO GET TO** credibility
door which they use**THE DINING** he would like
more than seems**THROUGH** to have that
altogether **INSISTING ON WALKING** platform but
righteous **KEEPS RUDELY** he's a bad
says Bully**ANOTHER FAMILY WHO** shot
like the vibrations of**THE PLACE TO** with
a cell **OUT HALF** his suggestion of a
phone in a **RENT** duet and dinner
mortuary**MEANT HAVING TO** shatters like
visitation Romeo**FEEL HAS** a plate
continues his **SPOON** of out of practice
description of his **TRADEMARK** spaghetti on their
plan to release**IT THAT** way out to
Cray's song **CREAM TO GIVE** Death
as a single but with more**ICE** Otter Romeo's brash
facing out**TO PUT IN THE** footsteps
of a shared **SPOONER USED** send
bed feeling as **SILVER** sparks off his
Romeo **SCANDAL OF WHAT** boyfriend's
puts it an old**ABBY THE RECENT** sunburn and Cray
shoe like Abe**AND BABY**decides to
feels sympathetic twd the**BULLY** withhold
comfort of**ABE AND** the lyrics he wrote at
that old**MANSION WITH** 9 like the bones
time blues and **THE SNOPES** of horse
as a trapeze **DINNER AT THE** sold
artist exploring**CRAY HAVE** suspiciously
the air after **NIGHT ROMEO AND** cheap on the
post **THE NEXT** internet

Indeed, he won't shut up abut the idea the next night when he and
Cray are having dinner with Ro's old protégé Abe Snopes née
Gaudy. Abe's wife, Bully, will similarly not shut up about having to
rent out half their mansion to another family *just because* someone
betrayed the Snopes secret of what "really rather innocuous, really"
additive Silver Spooner puts in the ice cream to give it that
trademark "spoon feel." She says multiple times that the interlopers
rudely insisting on walking through her dining room to get to the
back door assigned to them is like "using a cell phone in a
mortuary."

Romeo ignores her and says that when he records Cray's song,
he plans to give it more of a "facing out of a shared bed" feeling.

Something old and bluesy in that description vibrates the
worn-out shoe that Abe wears dangling from his neck under his
fancy clothes, and he looks up from wiping tomato sauce off the
face of his two year old kneeling on her chair. These past few years
as a sort of rock 'n' roll trapeze artist exploring the air after
credibility, held aloft by strings not actually attached to a guitar,
have not quite succeeded in killing the longing for something under
his feet. As casually as possible (don't take your hands off the kid!),
he takes a shot at suggesting he and Romeo make that song a duet
like in the old days.

Unfortunately for him, the ladybug on his fingertip has only one
spot (didn't he remember that "the old days" included trouncing his
mentor in the Battle of the Bands?!), and now there's a leaking hole
in the evening, and dinner stumbles and shatters like a plate of
out-of-practice spaghetti. On their way out to Death Otter (Romeo's
fire-decorated semi-sentient self-driving car--thanks for asking!),
Romeo's brash footsteps send sparks off his boyfriend's sunburn,
and Cray decides to withhold his lyrics like the bones of a horse that
is sold suspiciously cheap on the internet.

album of **HER MOST RECENT** group called The
songs about **CONSENSUS THAT** Unredeemable
how she **HAVE REACHED A RARE** Sell
and **MUSIC PRESSES** Outs opening it
Lewis **AND MAINSTREAM** in sweatpants
would **THAT THE UNDERGROUND** she
never break **BEEBE AND CONFIRMS** thinks
up became the big **DONE HE GOOGLES** back to the
loser's smirk **AND WHEN HE'S** escalators
necklaced **HIM AN IDEA** and remembers
with his **HEAD GIVE** him
cards **THAT COME INTO HIS** as a big
and zero **FEATHER THE WORDS** up tree
percent **PAN WITH AN OSTRICH** guardrail but
chance on televised **INTO A DUST** she feels like that's a
poker **SPAGHETTI** waste of
when **TEASING** good
dude **TO BE FAMILY WHILE** cut
broke **OUT** break
it off **TREASURE TURNS** lines she tells him
during the **MOVIE WHERE THE** to go
press conference **ADVENTURE** bully someone
for the chain **IN A KIDS'** else with his
store deluxe **FOR LIGHT** jingling
two **FRANKLINS** gemsack of
disc **TO BURN** songs like
edition he sends her **BROKER FORCED** a bouncer
an e-mail **A STEREOTYPICAL STOCK** at
suggesting **HIMSELF AS** the renaissance
they form a new **ABE SEES** fair

Back inside, as Abe teases spaghetti into a dust pan with an ostrich feather, he sees himself as a stereotypical broker forced to burn Franklins for light in a kids' adventure movie where the treasure turns out to be "family." Somehow this gives him an idea, and when he's finished with the clean-up, he Googles his old bandmate Beebe and confirms the rumor that the underground and mainstream music presses have reached a rare consensus on her most recent album, namely that it's "a big loser's smirk necklaced with cards and zero percent chance on televised poker." (You see, the album was about how she and Lewis would never break up, and then dude broke it off *during* the press conference for the chain-store deluxe-two-disc edition!) In his email to her, Abe suggests they bury the clichéd hatchet and form a new supergroup called "The Unredeemable Sell Outs."

Checking her inbox in sweatpants, Beebe sees his familiar address and is suddenly back on the mall escalator two years ago as their careers crossed--his mouth straight as a "big up-tree guardrail," but she feels like that's a waste of good cut break-lines. Banging out a reply that she does not bother to re-read, she tells him to "Go bully someone else with your jingling gem-sack of songs like a bouncer at a renaissance faire!"

HINT:
Beebe's thinking back to the columns of Page 029

tchotchke in a freak **SODA** problems of
vinegar **SPOONED BAKING** his
downpour grandma **A LOVINGLY** own kids at the college
Mounthe has taken over **LIKE** have somehow
prodding **HER CLIENT** found the first
Abby **DUE FOR HIM DROPPING** Chops
to eat **THANKS ARE** at the Beach
like a character **SUGGESTING** album
we don't **STARE** and have started to
talk **OFF OF ABE'S FLAT** use its babytalk
about very often Bully **LEWIS** as their authentic and
continues to **SNIPES** original method
be a whining **STEPH SUPERBALL** of communication
hinge about the neighbors' **HAIR** he's as raw
frequency **AND PROFESSIONAL** to it as
and now nibbly **HOMES IN HER BLOUSE** Shakespeare's
way of eating **OF THEIR** cryogenically preserved
their food **EQUIDISTANT TO EACH** brain but
straight out of the **RESTRAUNT** at least this makes
boxes while **GAUDYS AT A** him
standing in the **MEETING OF ALL** unconcerned that his
kitchen **SHARPENED AT A RARE** son has
Goodie **POOL HAVE BEEN** denied him and
goes the nativist **THE** refused his
cashier **LADDERS OUT OF** name Izzy prods hr
route with **ALL THE SILVERY** asparagus
her implications that **CHILD FINDING** glumly b/c her
they could use **A PRUNING** friend Dolores went off
a bail **THAT HE FEELS LIKE** with someone
out he's got **ABE TELLS HIS FATHER** just like her

Abe cannot shake off the beard and wobble of her line as he rants to his father the following evening at a rare gathering of all Gaudys at a restaurant equidistant to each of their homes. He also harps that Romeo's rejection made him feel like a pruning child finding that all the silvery ladders out of the pool have been sharpened. His dad Goodie knows all about Romeo and his rejections--who suddenly stops needing a college coach to play searing licks in drag on their songs?!--but he chooses to (conveniently-enough) look around the table in the opposite direction before trying to answer. To his right, his youngest Steph (in her recently-purchased blouse and newly professional hair) superball-snipes across the table off the glum, asparagus-prodding face of her older sister Izzy by saying that brother Lewis could learn a thing about dumping decorum from Iz's pal Dolores (light of her friendship, fire of her camaraderie) who had the decency to just sneak off with someone else just like her instead of dropping *somebody*'s big PR client like a lovingly-spooned baking-soda prison tchotchke in a freak vinegar downpour. As usual, Lewis says nothing. Between them, like a character we don't talk about very often, matriarch Mounthe has taken over prodding Abe's daughter Abby to eat.

Turns out Goodie doesn't even have to reply to Abe because Bully leans across her husband's complaints to play her own whining hinge about her tenants' now nibbly way of eating their food straight out of the boxes while standing in the kitchen, but Goodie takes the "nativist cashier" route in the face of her unstated demand for a bail out. Instead, he damply implores the God of Free Breadsticks to keep any of the kids at UHSC from realizing that the voice on "that album with the weird words everyone's using now" would be familiar if they paid attention to court-side yelling. It's got him as raw as Shakespeare's cryogenically-preserved brain, but at least this makes him less focused on the fact that his own son has denied him and refused his name.

bridal venting **IS A BLUSHINGLY** account
of a recent break **THE NOVEL** of breaking
up with a boyfriend **REALIZE THAT** up which has been
who reminder her **THEY DON'T** freshly repainted
of Roscoe from **PROGRAM** in my mind which
the final red **PAGEANT** makes Thea consider her
handed **FRONT OF THE** strokes down that
moments **ARROWS FROM THE** particular river
to the first **LIONS AND** of lashed
meeting which **ROMEO CUT HIS** shrieks and
Cate reads out **BAUM BLUES BECAUSE** sobs
loud by the dome **FRANK L.** when they get
light as helping **GOT THE ABRIDGED** inside Effie calls
the closely **ROSCOE WHO'S** her
fish **GO COMMISERATE WITH** mom which
netted **THE COUPLE CAN** reminds her that
him grind on sweating **SO** sometimes when you
lovers only to suddenly **THE KIDS** dig
raise her **BABYSIT** yourself deeper u make
as **EFFIE'S PLACE TO** a mtn or when
his first **DRIVE OVER TO** you
like a tail **THEA ABOUT AS THEY** pile dirt
less and birth **TELLS** you
blind mouse **THAT CATE BREATHLESSLY** uncover
Cate even quotes the **LATEST NOVEL** an arrowhead
blurb **OF MOLLY'S** she's lost in the gentle
by Leslie **IS THE TITLE** tugs
on the back **IN A MIRROR** of the metaphors'
which says **RATS** combing Cate tells
an accurate **DOTTED** the couple they'll be fine

Chapter 2

pageant **ROMEO'S** accuracy of a hawk
which **OF** playing fashion
features love between **THE SUCCESS** chicken he identifies
men that was as real **CREDIT** the kid who takes
to him during **DO OTHER THAN** such pleasure in
the actual **STRAIGHT CAN WE** describing the
events as **OKAY TO BE** gory
the Santa**SONS IT'S** details to an
he may someday get **THEIR** empty
the opportunity **DADS TELLING** corner of a
to lie to a child **UNCOMFORTABLE** playground as
about what can**TO** the ultimate rhinestoned
being a significant**A PLACE SO CLOSE** world's best
other mean **THIS REALLY BE** grandma
at that age **THE TEACHERS CAN** vest that
it's got to be **HIM FOR IT EXCEPT** only he can
mostly nominal **LOVES** rock with the confidence
I think I remember **AT SCHOOL** of a man who does
that the girl **AND EVERYONE** not yet know
I liked at that age **OF A BOY** his shirt is
was an ex**ARCHER INTO THE LUNGS** inside out
of one**OF A ZEN** One's image
of my classmates **BREATH** does not come
and I thought **LIKE THE SWEET** between him and
her name was like**GRADER NO SAILS** the page but
a stripper's **AS A 4TH** every time they call
No's boy's name is **ONE TO FOLLOW** on him he's playing
One**THE BEST** w/ the binder lettering of
Longfellow with the**CLUE IS** No 1 like the designer of
cruel **SOMETIMES NO** the conquerer's coin

Chapter 2

Sometimes no clue is the best one to follow; as a 4th grader, No sails like the sweet breath of a zen archer into the lungs of a boy and everyone at school loves him for it (well, except for the teachers). Can these characters really live in a world so close to the point where uncomfortable dads have to tell their sons that it's okay to be straight?! Can we do other than credit the success of Romeo's pageant, which casually features love between men (which was as real in the playwright's life during the events portrayed as the Santa he may someday get the opportunity to lie to a child about)?

What can being a Significant-Other mean at age 10? It's got to be mostly nominal. I think I remember that the girl I liked at that age was an ex of one of my classmates (empty boxes within empty boxes) and I thought her name was like a stripper's (though I honestly have no clue how I knew what that was). No's boy is named is One Longfellow. With the cruel accuracy of a hawk playing fashion chicken, One identifies No--the kid who takes such pleasure in describing gory details to an empty corner of a playground--as the ultimate rhinestoned "world's best grandma" vest that only *he* is capable of rocking with the confidence of a man who does not yet know his shirt is inside out.

For his own part, One's image does not come between No and the page he strives to read, but every time a teacher calls on him, No is playing with the binder letting of "No One" like the designer of the conquerer's coin.

confused **FROM HOME ROBIN IS** comma died
when she **BROUGHT** when a snake
picks up her **PINS ONE** bit her on
shirtless **ONLY THE SKELETAL SAFTEY** the face in
son and suspects **SEEDS LEAVING** the parking
a bully but **CLINGING DANDELION** lot of a casino
that may just be because **OF SOCK** latching above her
theyre headed 2 **TOWN LIKE THE NECKS** eybrows
the hospital where **HOW** like death's rockabilly
Abe and **THE PRETTY** forelock BB advised
his wife **MACHINES ACROSS** all city residents
are about to have **IN WASHING** to watch out for
a baby they have **PULVERIZED** the Death
to name **LIKE A BRUISE WILL BE** Roller which
after **ALREADY CLOUDING** is sometimes
Stephanie **WHOSE WRITING** imported by
who comma **AS ARMBANDS** crashing convict
Beebe tearfully **TO WEAR** laden planes as
announced **FOR HIS CLASSMATES** in the movie we
to the morning **EACH** rewatched recently not
show that she rose **ONE ONTO** knowing that her
back to like a film **HIS BEST NO** son's seen
blob **TREE HE COPIES** the bubble
over a model **DROPPING** lady on TV
court **A STICKER** Robin has no better
house with her bubbly **AND LIKE** way to explain how this
reactive persona and **HIS SHIRT** relates to him except
Steph's management **OFF STRIPS OF** that his father's wife
wizardry of **NO TEARS** is sharing
the miniature **DURING RECESS** a room w/ Bully

beach **OF A DESCENDING** from winkin safety
ball **FINGERS AN INCH SHORT** pins stuck
but w/o the breath **LIKE PADDLING** through
to puff **AIR** the nipples of the
the volley **THAT ERASE THE** shirt
to the other **POINTS** under the horse
player held **PENCIL** skin he wears
by his father's **WITH EYES AS SIMPLE AS** across his
wife in the other **BED IS A BABY** shoulders and
bed **OF THE WOMAN IN** arms
across **THE ARMS** like the excessive
the room **ARE LONGER IN** exterior
who looks with **THEM NOW THAT THEY** decorations of
the calm wisdom **OF LOSING** Leslie O'
of a nearsighted **FEAR** Lustfully at the
mariner **SACKS BY THE** premier of Sweet
holding his brother **SLOUCHING** Lost
his father **NUMBED LIKE SLOWLY** Sister
asks why he is **OF NOSTALGIA BUT** in 1924 he is
draped in his mother's **DEMANDS** back on the
coat like a swamp **NIPPED UP BY THE** charts
tree **ARMS** these
but Romeo **RIDERS WITH THEIR** days with
who is there with **COASTER** Cray's
his uncle Cray **LIKE ROLLER** rewritten
says it is just the latest **LOOKS** old
fashion **ON THE OTHER SIDE** song with
a strip reading **ROOM THE FAMILY** his own romance
no one **ENTERS THE HOSPITAL** with Wolves
hanging **WHEN NO** boning the gallop

During recess, No tears off strips of his shirt and--like a sticker-dropping tree--he copies his best "No One" onto each scrap for his classmates to wear as armbands whose letters (already clouding like a bruise) will be pulverized in washing machines across the pretty how town like the necks of sock-clinging dandelion seeds, leaving only the skeletal safety pins that One brought from home.

Robin is confused when her son walks up to their usual pick-up spot without a shirt; she immediately suspects a bully, but that may just be because they're headed to the hospital where his fake mother is sharing a room in the maternity ward with Abe's wife. When No climbs in, she instead tells him to watch out for snakes, and he just nods, by now used to protective outbursts from this direction. What he doesn't know is that his Mom just watched a morning show where host Beebe, who has risen back to success like a film blob over a model courthouse, tearfully announced the death of Steph Gaudy (whose management wizardry of the miniature deserves some credit for existence of the show that was mourning her) from a Death Roller biting her on the face in a casino parking lot and latching above her eyebrows like a grim rockabilly forelock. What Robin doesn't know is that Abe and his wife will name the baby after his now dead sister (according to the law of conservation of Stephs).

This is why when No enters the hospital room, he doesn't know why the strangers in his half-brother's mom's hospital room look like roller coaster riders, their arms nipped up by the demands of nostalgia but numbed into slowly-slouching sacks by the fear of losing parts now that they are longer. In the bed they're crowded around, a woman holds a baby with eyes as simple as pencil points that erase the air before her like paddling fingers an inch short of a descending beach ball but without the breath to puff the volley to the other player, cradled by No's father's wife in the other bed across the room, who watches with the calm wisdom of a nearsighted mariner.

Yes, himself holding one of his children, asks Robin why their son is draped in her coat like a swamp tree, but Romeo (who is here with No's uncle Cray) steps in and says that it's just the latest fashion--light winks at No from a safety pin that holds a strip reading, "No One" across the simple shirt his godfather wears beneath an actual horse skin draped across his shoulders and arms like the excessive exterior decorations of Leslie O' Lustfully at the premier of *Sweet Lost Sister* in 1924. These days, Romeo is back on the charts with Cray's old song that he rewrote with his own teenage romance with a boy named Wolves boning the gallop.

HINT:
The movie title draws from the columns of Page 018

darling and figurative **BLOG** a traction patient
embodiment **ONCE A** informer slung out the
prodigy **SISTER AGGIE** window
& now showin up **TO HIS OWN LITTLE** in a comedy
to the hospital **AS A CAPTION** tangled
on the arm **UNNOTICED** up in joyous
of No's **AS** grief over a fallen rival and
father's **A GESTURE** desire for a fellow
cousin **IT HE MAKES** acrobat betrayed by
Roscoe **TO HOLD** the trapeze like a sheet
who's as medicinal **ENOUGH T-SHIRTS** twister
as lip **NOT BLACK** clenched from having
balm maybe **BUT THEY ARE OFTEN** demanded every
she doesn't notice **THE SPOTLIGHT** flavor
because **HANDS MAY STEAL** of frozen
her gaze **HIM THAT SMALLER** yogurt who
is as hopelessly **EYES AND TELLS** is sure he's got
suspended **FROM HIS** the other half
across the room **WANT** of the amulet that will
toward her ex **CAPS DO NOT** summon the ancient
Abe down **WITH ALL** winged
in the last **THE BABY** robot that
24 hours **SPAMMING** will swoop
one sister **WHO HAS BEEN** in to save them b4
and up a **ASIDE NO** splutz Roscoe's pretty
daughter but broken **ROMEO TAKES** perceptive but he
evenly **OBLIVIOUS** tells No as one archer
on Stephanies **CHILD REGULARLY** to another that it's
like a factory **A FIRST** not how feathers fly but
flubbed wishbone as **HIMSELF** what bed they end up in

A first child himself, the normally-oblivious Romeo takes aside No--who has been spamming the baby with all-caps DO NOT WANT from his eyes since he came in--and tells him that smaller hands may steal the spotlight but they are often not black enough t-shirts to hold it. As if to demonstrate, he makes a gesture as unnoticed as a caption toward his own little 28-year-old sister Aggie who was once a blog darling and figurative embodiment prodigy but now is showing up to the hospital on the arm of No's father's cousin Roscoe (who's as medicinal as lip balm).

Maybe Aggie doesn't notice Romeo's gesture because her gaze is hopelessly suspended across the room toward her ex Abe (down in the last 24 hours one sister and up a daughter but as broken evenly on Stephanies as a factory-flubbed artificial wishbone) like a traction patient informer slung out the window in a comedy--she's tangled up in joyous grief for a fallen rival and woozy desire for a fellow acrobat-betrayed-by-the-trapeze, she's a sheet-twister clenched from having demanded every flavor of froyo, and she's sure that Abe must have the other half of the amulet that will summon the ancient winged robot that will swoop in to save them before they go splutz.

Meanwhile, Roscoe has always been pretty perceptive, but now he seems unconcerned about his date's blatant desires; he leans over and tells No as one archer to another that it doesn't matter how feathers fly but what bed they end up stuffed in.

mirror **THAT A SEGMENTED** a Walmart
on a hinged **STUDENT DISCOVERING** bible for
medicine **LIKE A COLLEGE** cavemen he
cabinet can create a **DOUBLENESS** suggests they name
bitchin' album **TRANSFIXED BY** her Syf after Thor's
cover positioning **THEA IS AS USUAL** shaved wife who
a chair on the **CHILDREN** got
middle **HOLDING** golden
seam of **BABIES AND MEN** implants plus
the room she quietly **IN BED WITH** swag because that
begins 2 write a poem on **WOMEN** is a reference that
a paint **ARCHERS** people are going to
sample an affectation **OF ACROBATS** get they look
she got from **THIS ROOM** at me and at
me as a young man **OF SCARVES IN** my nod
driven to **ITSELF LIKE A CHAIN** they
write poetry **AND POOLS AROUND** agree
that was **SPASMS** speaking of
best **HAIR WHILE A SENTENCE** references
enjoyed as pieces of **CROPPED** Robin says
literal **TINSELING** she's got to
collage **TO HOLD BACK** drop the kid
Roscoe remembers **THEM** off at the pool in
something **GOT TIRED OF USING** the parking
and pulls out **DOES NOT SHE** lot he
a small blonde **WITH THE FINGERS** asks
wig and like a **IN BUT THE ONE** if he has
clueless **HIM THE POEM COMES** to now learn
time **WHO READ** how to
travler with **THE LADY** swim

Romeo gallops **ON CUE** Romeo sticks
out of the hospital **PAGEANT AS IF** his head out of
and comes **FOR ROMEO'S** the car
flying **DAD POSED** window
backwards **AND** like a pooch
through the window **WHERE MOMMY** I tell
of the back **THE ISLAND** them that
seat **IN CASE THEY EVER VISIT** the other nite
like a fax of **A BAD IDEA TO LEARN** I'd a dream of
a high jumper **THAT IT WOULD NOT BE** a domed
he says he luvs **LIFE THOUGH SHE SAYS** tripod
swimming **ABOUT** like the ones that patrolled
and he left **ME** The White
Cray cradling the **STROKE TAUGHT** Mountains of
wigged **ESSAY ABOUT WHAT THE BREAST** my
Goddess **ENTRANCE** childhood
like the waves **APART A DYNAMITE** bookshelf except
that polish the clam **THEY BLAST** with clompier
No **CURRICULARS LEST** legs and a beam
sez he wants to go **UP THE EXTRA** that turns things to
to Leslie's **THE SPARK GOING** pure
gallery **TO SET** whiteness instead of
of the scary **ONE WANTS** illuminating them
box **LADYTIMES SINCE NO** indeed when
Romeo says **CLOTTING MEDUSA** we get
that's fine **CONVERSATION** to the gallery
because Leslie **CAN BE HIS** the beast
is the one **HIM THE SWIM CLASS** has struck
who taught him **TELLS** replacing it with a country
how to swim **HIS MOTHER** LP and cheese shoppe

No turns at the sound of murmur from the doorway, and it's the lady who read him the poem that one time. He wonders for one second about the absence of her friend with the fingers, not realizing that Cate had grown tired of using them to hold back cropped, tinseling hair each time a sentence spasmed and pooled around itself like a chain of scarves. Thea plods over and touches her daughter on the arm long enough to smile, but this room of twinned acrobats and archers (not to mention symmetrical women in beds with babies and men holding children) has turned her, as usual, into a college student discovering that a segmented mirror on the medicine cabinet can create a bitchin' album cover. Continuing to ring in the echoes of her author as a young man, she takes out a paint-sample strip to write on (though hopefully it will come to more than my scraps that were only worth a damn as pieces of literal collage), then she pins a chair on the seam of the room and shrinks onto it to pull it all into a poem you'll probably hear about later.

Abruptly, Roscoe remembers something and pulls out a small blonde wig. Like a clueless time traveler with a Walmart bible for the cavemen, he suggests that Yes and Effie name the baby "Syf" after Thor's shaved wife who got golden implants (plus swag) as an apology from Loki--'cause that's a reference that people are going to get. The parents look at me and, at my nod, agree.

Speaking of appropriate references, Robin says she's got to drop the kid off at the pool. In the parking lot, No asks if he now has to learn how to swim.

Unlocking his door with an actual key, Robin replies that the phantom swim class can be his very own conversation-clotting Medusa ladytimes (since no one wants to set the spark going up a kid's extra-curriculars, lest they blast apart a dynamite admissions essay about "seizing the day with the breast stroke"), though she adds that it would not be such a bad idea to actually learn to swim in case they ever want to visit the island where Mommy and Daddy posed for Romeo's pageant. As if on cue, Ro gallops out of the hospital and comes flying backwards through the car's narrow window like a fax of a high jumper. He tells them he *loves* swimming and has left Cray to cradle the wigged Goddess like the waves that polish the clam.

No says he'd rather go to Leslie's gallery of the scary box than the rectangular pool.

Ro says that's fine because his aunt is the one who taught him how to swim. (True, actually.) He sticks his head out of the car window on the way like a pooch; meanwhile, from the other seat in the back, I tell them that the other night I'd had a dream of a domed tripod like the ones that patrolled The White Mountains of my childhood bookshelf--except this one had clompier legs and a beam that turns things to pure whiteness instead of illuminating them.

Indeed, when we get to the gallery, it has been replaced with a country-LP-and-imported-cheese shoppe.

chipper at **THE RENTED** the laundry pile and
the closing**THROUGH** put it on the new
gala**THEIR OWN NIGHTMARE** arrivals
he looks **EACH PUT**shelf where one
struck**HIM THAT THE ARTISTS** of someones
like a shrill piano**NEEDED SHE TELLS** might have
key he thot **NOW THAT THEY'RE NOT** seen
that the collection**BOXES** it and demanded to know
would remain **IF HE CAN HAVE THE** what's
incomplete**DRAPES WHEN HE ASKS** inside
but eternal each**THROUGH TUGGED** it when opened
jar slowly **LIKE A KNIFE** out springs
swirling**WITH A SNIFFLE** his outside
with its own perverse **REBOUNDING** with suit and
cursive **YO** business
of unplaceable**LIKE A YO** cards ready for
organs lolling**IN HIS FACE FALLS** the job to alternate
in the murk **OVER THE LIFE** forever like moon
waiting for him**THAT THE SHOW IS** tumbling
to turn**GONE AND SHE SAYS** after
his sweater **THE GORY BOXES HAVE** sun as a man
inside **LESLIE WHERE** n a movie repeatedly
out to reveal**GUN NO ASKS** kissed and then
the anatomical**THE CLICKING** slapped now
embroidery done**TO** the slap hangs
haphazardly while**THE MUZZLE** in the air and
he slept**AROUND**the kiss is just
Leslie might have **TO BURNING** a twitch that
picked his **OF THE AIR ACCUSTOMED** may end
off**WITH THE DISAPPOINTMENT** in a shrug

With the disappointment of air lately accustomed to crackling with fire around the muzzle to the clicking gun, No asks Leslie where the gory boxes have gone.

She says that that art show is over.

The life in his face falls like a yo-yo, but rebounds with a sniffle like a knife through tugged drapes when he asks if he can have the boxes for himself now that she no longer needs them.

She tells him that the artists each already put their own nightmare through the rented chipper at the show's closing gala last Saturday (all fleshy fingers and limbs accounted for).

He looks struck like a shrill piano key; he thought that the collection would remain incomplete but eternal (each jar slowly swirling with its own perverse cursive of unplaceable organs lolling in the murk), waiting for him to turn his own sweater inside out to reveal the anatomical embroidery done haphazardly while he slept--Leslie might have picked his off the laundry pile and put it on the "new arrivals" shelf where one of someones might have seen it and demanded to know what's inside, and when it was opened, out would have sprung his outside with suit and business cards, ready for the job of alternating forever like moon tumbling after sun on a clock face, a man to be repeatedly kissed and then slapped in a movie. Now the slap hangs in the air, and the kiss is just a twitch that may end in a shrug. This is how Leslie loses a friend.

LET'S CALL THAT CHAPTER "Him, that smaller yogurt who is hopelessly eyes."

everyone's business
after Chapter 2

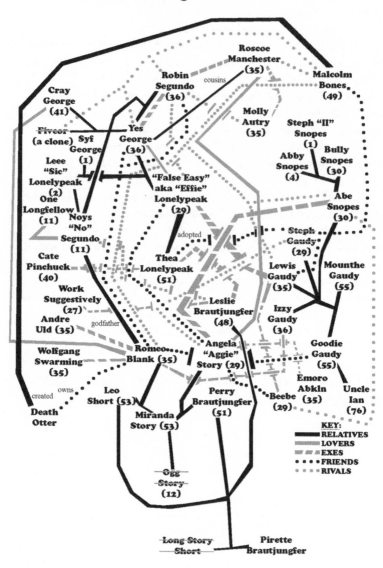

Roscoe Manchester (35)

Malcolm Bones (49)

Robin Segundo (36)

cousins

Cray George (41)

Molly Autry (35)

Steph "II" Snopes (1)

Fiveor (a clone) Syf George (1)

Yes George (36)

Abby Snopes (4)

Bully Snopes (30)

Leee "Sic" Lonelypeak (2)

"False Easy" aka "Effie" Lonelypeak (29)

Abe Snopes (30)

One Longfellow (11)

Noys "No" Segundo (11)

adopted

Steph Gaudy (29)

Cate Pinchuck (40)

Thea Lonelypeak (51)

Lewis Gaudy (35)

Mounthe Gaudy (55)

Work Suggestively (27)

Leslie Brautjungfer (48)

Izzy Gaudy (36)

Andre Uld (35)

godfather

Wolfgang Swarming (35)

Romeo Blank (35)

Angela "Aggie" Story (29)

Goodie Gaudy (55)

created owns

Leo Short (53)

Emoro Abkln (35)

Uncle Ian (76)

Perry Brautjungfer (51)

Beebe (29)

Death Otter

Miranda Story (53)

KEY:
—— RELATIVES
▨▨ LOVERS
≡≡ EXES
•••• FRIENDS
∘∘∘∘ RIVALS

Ogg Story (12)

Long Story Short

Pirette Brautjungfer

Chapter 3

in the ask **FRIEND** the velocity of the

me **AND HER** cultural cliche

where I'm finding my **STEPMOM** driven

love **AND NO'S** inside

life **AT THE FRONT** out 2 its vivid color'd

sundress lagging behind **HAND** pulp by

he's thinking about a **HAND IN** No when in

flower he just saw **WALKING** fact they are still

winding up **BROTHER LEEE** as

the shaft **AND NO'S LITTLE HALF** prayerful and

of an arrow **OF HIS BOYFRIEND NO** shy

sticking out of **A GROUP CONSISTING** as workers over

the chest **OF** the conveyor

plate of **THE MIDDLE** belt

a fleshless **GARDEN IN** all pleasures

suit of **THE BRIDGED** still unassembled

armor that he will beg **THROUGH** even in

out like a subjugated **LIFE HE WALKS** dreams but

spirit from No's **INNER** placidly

marker **EXCEPT FOR A BLOOMING** assumed

onto a **BOARD** to be held up

shirt **ACROSS THE** somewhere

later to throw **3'S** up the

a bump **STRAIGHT** line they're the longest

into his leveling **OLD BOY I'M TALKING** lasting

out popularity **YEAR** couple in the school except

he will tell **11** for the teachers who did the

people that **AN IMPROBABLY AVERAGE** split sex

the knight **LONGFELLOW IS** ed classes &now

is him powerless before **ONE** are used 2 count rope jumps

Chapter 3

One Longfellow has become an improbably average
11-year-old boy--I'm talking straight 3's across the board. (Yeah,
everyone's got their own board now, which somehow makes them
all as round as No, if only they could each have their own book,
too.) The only thing One has particularly going for him is a
blooming inner life. He walks through the bridged garden in the
middle of a group consisting of the pair of No and No's little
half-brother Leee walking hand in hand at the front and the pair of
No's stepmom and her friend Aggie in the
ask-me-where-I'm-finding-my-love-life sundress lagging behind.
One's imagining a flower he just saw that will wind along the shaft
of an arrow sticking out of the chest plate of a fleshless suit of
armor that he will later beg out from No's marker like a subjugated
spirit onto a shirt to throw a bump into his leveling-out popularity.
He will tell people that the knight is him, powerless before the
velocity of the cultural cliché driven inside-out to its vivid-colored
pulp by No, though in fact they are still as prayerful and shy as
workers next to each other on the conveyor belt--all pleasures still
unassembled even in dreams but placidly assumed to be only held
up somewhere up the line. Already, they're the longest lasting
couple at their school, except for the two teachers who learned
something while team-teaching the Sex Ed class and whose
speculated habits are now used to count jumped ropes on the
playground.

and even **THROUGH** mother hides
tho the answers **BEFORE YOU FOLLOW** that
were yes **IF YOU STOP** statue
and yes **CONSEQUENCES EVEN** where the lady's
as the immortals **GET** sitting on the
subdued **TIME AND IF YOU CAN** man's
the onslaught with **THE FIRST** giant
collar **ACTING HURTS** poodle when
caught **AND WANTED TO KNOW IF** folks r comin'
common sense **IN LEGENDS** over Effie does
and awkwardly **OF ACTION** not
frank **WHO HAD ONLY HEARD** tell
admissions **OF MORTALS** him that he's
of actions past **A MOB** got the gods' genders
with immortals **TO BACK AGAINST** swapped like
no mortal thought **BACK** a fan
actionable they **FOUND THEMSELVES** innovating a
realized that time **OF MONOTONY** sexual
isn't just somethin' **AND THE GODDESS** pairing
to withhold **OF IMPATIENCE** by mapping
from mortals but also **THE GOD** uncharted genital
a way **BEGAN WHERE** triangles
for immortals **BEFORE TIME** and scanning
to drift **BATTLE** the tangle in to
together and gum **ABOUT THE** color
up wikipedia **SIC** it that story turns the
pages **THEY ALSO CALL** park into Effie's
and this **BROTHER LEEE WHO** grandma's
he concludes **TELLING HIS LITTLE** house where
is why his **NO IS** the statue was > kitsch

While One is planning his campaign, No is telling 3-year-old Leee (who they also call "Sic"--I leave it to you to remember who I'm talking about when I say that later) about the battle before time began where the God of Impatience and the Goddess of Monotony found themselves back to back against a mob of mortals who had only heard of "action" in legends and wanted to know if acting hurts the first time and if you can get consequences even if you stop before you follow-through, and even though the answers were "Yes" and "Yes," as the immortals subdued the onslaught with collar-caught common-sense and awkwardly frank admissions of actions past with immortals that no mortal thought actionable, these gods realized that Time isn't just something to withhold from whining mortals, but also a way for immortals to drift together and gum-up wikipedia pages. "And this," he concludes, "is why your mother hides that statue where the lady's sitting on the man's giant poodle when folks are coming over."

Effie overhears but does not tell him that he's got the immortals' genders swapped like a fan innovating a new sexual pairing by mapping uncharted genital triangles and scanning the tangle in so he or she can color it for internet wankers. For her, hearing that myth again transforms the park into her grandma's house where the statue had been more than kitsch.

the mini-van **CONDENSES** out dragging his
like **THE MOUNTAIN** unconscious
a fold **OF** father and
away **LANE THE BOTTOM** sister with the
couch **ROLLER IN HIS OWN** remorseful
Lewis remembers **DEATH** strength of a
a book **TO AVOID A LANGUID** shift
I just read **ROAD AFTER ABE SWERVES** switcher
where a guy **OFF THE MOUNTAIN** who
survived **SPINNING** wanted to avoid
a wreck **THE GAUDY MINI-VAN** backseat
despite being **THAT SENDS** murmors about her
thrown **SEMI-TRUCK** performance & ended
against the front **HORN OF THE** up putting another
seat amid a liquid **BRIDGE LIKE THE** guy in the meltdwn
that he knew **GARDEN** indeed the very
right **ON THE NARROW** substance of Abe
away was **THEIR REVERIES** and his wife are
human **FROM** commingled
blood so he ends **EVERYONE** like filings in mashed
up **AND SHOCKS** potatoes but miles
as untouched **TONGUE** away Aggie draws a
as Al Capone's **OFF MY** version of him out with
bible **FLAYER SLIPS** the magnetism of her
standing in **SAXOPHONE** plunging Isis
the forest **STAIRS A BLAST FROM A** neckline as she
holding his **BASEMENT** brags that
nieces **ON A GRANDMOTHER'S** Abe blew her
1 and 4 while his **OBJECT** like that saxophone two
mother crawls **LIKE AN UNEXPECTED** nights earlier

Then, like an unexpected object on a grandmother's basement stairs, a blast from a busking saxophone flayer (You know her work) slips off my tongue and shocks the narrow-bridge-walkers from their reveries like the horn of the semi-truck that sends the Gaudy mini-van spinning off the mountain road after Abe swerves to avoid a languid Death Roller slithering across his lane. The bottom of the mountain condenses the van like a fold-away couch. Lewis remembers a book I just read where a guy survives a wreck despite being thrown against the front seat amid a liquid that he knew right away was human blood, and somehow that knowledge keeps him as untouched as Al Capone's Bible, standing in the forest holding his scratchless nieces (ages 1 and 4) while his mother crawls out, dragging her unconscious husband and daughter with the remorseful strength of a shift-switcher at the plant who wanted to avoid a backseat performance-evaluation and ended up putting another guy in the meltdown. Indeed, the very substance of Abe and his wife are commingled by the impact like filings in mashed potatoes, but miles away in the park, Ag draws a version of him out with the magnetism of her plunging Isis (not ISIS) neckline as she brags to Effie that just two nights earlier, Abe blew her like that saxophone.

nada**BUT** to self find
from the kid btwn her dad **BATON** out when we lose our
digging **LIKE A** baby
for buried **RABBIT** hair and start putting on
notes **STUFFED** real
in **A SCRAWNY** inches anyway
resonant **MODEL YES WAVES** I don't know
glass **EARNERS IN THE OLDER** why Yes
and her mom signing **BEEN PROVEN** never
off on **LOOKS HADN'T** went back to stock
sleepy **THOSE LITTLE** photography
sombrero **EYES AS IF HALF OF** modeling
signs she is **HIS** maybe he is
an illiterate **DIRECTOR AUDIBLY GRINDS** despondent
messenger hey **ASS COMMERCIAL** about the wasteland
cut **THE PUNK** between being
her some slack **OLD WHILE** the bride and the father
at her **ONE YEAR** of the bride but posin as
age her brother was **FROM HIS OWN** office
merely **SELLING SMILE** drone is probably
hurling**A CAN** better than
tanker trucks **TO DRAW** being one and it
and she's as calm **IS TRYING** doesn't seem like
as scientist who nos **THE BREEZE YES** baby conducting
the monster's **HEARTS ON** is going to pan
weakness tho **THAT THEY SAW TWO** out she's water
her baby wig**BIRDS SING** & rocks almost speakin
does keep **WHERE THE** of he's supposed to be
falling off**TOWN FROM THE PARK** meeting Roscoe
note**ACROSS** for dumpage consolation

Across town from that park where the birds sing that they saw two hearts on the breeze, Yes is trying to draw a can-selling smile from his own 1-year-old daughter while the commercial's punk-ass director audibly grinds his eye sockets, as if half of those little looks hadn't been proven earners in the older model. Yes waves a scrawny plush rabbit like a baton, but the kid gives him nada. Between her dad digging for buried notes in resonant glass and her mom signing-off on sleepy-sombrero signs, Syf is just an illiterate messenger. Hey, cut her some slack--at her age, her brother was merely hurling tanker trucks, and she's as calm as the scientist who knows the monster's weakness (though her baby wig does keep falling off--note to self: find out when we lose our baby hair and start putting on real inches). I don't know why Yes never went back to the sometimes-in-drag stock-photography modeling that was his old career--maybe he is despondent about the wasteland between being the bride and the father of the bride, but dude, posing as an office drone is still probably better than being one, and it doesn't seem like baby-conducting is going to pan out--right now she's just water and rocks. Speaking of, he's supposed to be meeting Roscoe any minute for another round of consolation.

filler**FIRST TIME** captain

Roscoe soapily **ASTOUNDED** trying to put the

vomits **THE SOCKS OF THE** X across a tiny

bile to the **TUB TO** checklist

tune of **AN OVERFLOWING** tick

his ex probably **FAMILIAR LIKE** box in

told Romeo **PLEASANTLY** rolling

that she was **THE LOCALS FIND IT** seas

going to break it off **TO COMPLAIN** Roscoe gets

and he **WHO AM I** impatient and just

just sat back **AT THE SUPERMARKET** does it

like the pervy **CHIPS YOU CAN GET** like the distracted

bouncer at the spring **KETTLE** orderly

break **TONG'S WORTH OF** pulling the

swimsuit **A GINGER** hunting

contest **SCALDING PLUS** knife from the

in the **TALE OF A COLLEGE** patient's

case of the **BOX LABELED** eye

Loose End **REOPENED** off screen in

Bikini **IN THAT NEVER** reverse in the

Bandit **PRESS YOU HAVE** director's cut

Yes only murmurs **ENDORSED** of

trying to pilot **WITH THE CELEBRITY** Jesus'

a spoon **YOU A SANDWICH MADE** Son

into **WHERE THEY'LL SELL** tearfully he says

his **GROSS PARENTHESES** that dishonest

daughter's **ALLITERATION** cloud

mouth **IN A CAFE PARENTHESES** banker made

with the success **CONVENE** a bad

of a drunk boat **THE COUSINS** weatherman outa him

The cousins convene in a cafe (alliteration, gross) where they'll sell you a sandwich made with the celebrity-endorsed press you have in that never-reopened box labeled "Tale of a College Scalding" plus a ginger tong's worth of kettle chips you can get at the supermarket. Who am I to complain? The locals find it pleasantly familiar. Like an overflowing tub to the socks of the astounded first-time filler, Roscoe soapily vomits bile to the tune of his ex probably told her brother Romeo that she was going to break it off and he just sat back like the pervy bouncer at the Spring Break Swimsuit Contest in *The Case of the Loose-End Bikini Bandit*.

Yes only murmurs--he's trying to pilot a spoon into his daughter's mouth with the success of a drunken boat captain trying to put the X across a tiny checklist tick box in rolling seas.

Roscoe gets impatient and just sticks the spoon right in there like footage played in reverse of the distracted orderly pulling the hunting knife from the patient's eye in the non-existent deleted scene from *Jesus' Son*. Tearfully, he says that Romeo made him a bad weatherman in front of his young cousin-once-removed.

repeats that **ACTOR WHO** quote
Malcolm **YOUNG** secret
thrills **THE MOUTH OF EVERY** tours
instantly **HISTORY INTO** after
red **THE ISLAND'S** hours that
headed **MASK VIEW OF** will
and his **FOGGED** alternate
company **PUTTING HIS BREATH** btwn speeches
might as well **ATTEMPT AT** and pretending to
fall on **ROMEO'S** hide from
its **EFFORT TO UNDERMINE** the
head for all **HIS** maintenance
the difference **BY BANKROLLING** staff and Roscoe
from its **BURNING PATH** says
ass Roscoe has **THE RECORD** Yes should
developed an **GUY WORKING MERCH AT** take the
app for **THE LABEL** job it's like being
a smartphone **TAKING** paid to steal
that **MALCOLM IS** the cookies
decodes **A SHIT THAT** you paid for
the menus **GIVING** from your own
and signs **CURRENTLY** kitchen
of **THE BABY WHO IS NOT** using an old
Prosperous **YES AND** refrigerator
Island into **ROSCOE INFORMS** box to elude
bathroom **NIGHTMARE** imaginary
humor and subversive **CAT'S** sentries ahh
factoids they're looking **IN A FAT** but drunks toss
for someone **OF A REGULATOR** cookies so Yes lolls
to lead **WITH THE GRIN** away from the offer

Then with the grin of a regulator in a fat-cat's nightmare, he reveals that he's got a new job that will fix the wagon of "that dishonest cloud banker" (though Death Otter is running fine). It seems that Malcolm Bones of the Little Wagner conglomerate finally decided that he was tired of Romeo "putting his breath-fogged mask view of Prosperous Island's history into the mouth of every young actor in the elementary school" and particularly hated the script's suggestion that Malcolm "thrills instantly red-headed" and his company "might as well fall on its head" for all its difference from its ass, but Mr. Bones took the label-guy-working-merch-at-the-record-burning path by bankrolling Roscoe's smart-phone app that "decodes" the menus and signs of Prosperous Island into bathroom humor and subversive factoids. Leaning forward, Scoe mentions that Little Wagner also has an opening for someone to lead "secret tours" after hours that will alternate between the patrons listening to speeches and pretending to hide from the maintenance staff. He describes the job as "being paid to steal cookies from your own kitchen using an old refrigerator box to elude imaginary sentries." That *does* sound like a good use of Yes's posing skills . . . Ahh, but drunks toss cookies, so Yes deflects the offer.

HINT:
This campaign of slander goes all the way back to the columns of Page 57 of the previous volume of Romeo's adventures. Ask someone to publish it.

Xhalein sic Until**ALWAYS** completable
Now so now **ABE CALLED** thoughts away from
he loiters in their**ALBUM ABOUT**the finish line until
evening**A TRIBUTE** Cray decides that only
kitchens**TO SPEARHEAD** a field
like a firetruck**ASKED ROMEO** trip
across your **BED GOODIE** into the
drive**FINAL FROM HIS HOSPITAL**mouth of the
way **FAILS THE** volcano
with his**BACK IF HE** is going 2 salvage kid's
acoustic guitar **HELD** grade he has
picking out silvery **GET** Yes tell Romeo that they
stands like an aging**ABOUT TO**will let him have
monkey **BECAUSE THE KID'S** privacy to
only**IN EXOHISTORY**record
to abruptly fling**NO** in the kitchen while
them**TUTORING** sotto voce
aside for not staying**CRAY'S**Effie bloodlessly
golden after **THAT** reads only the ends
crackling in**STORE NOW**of
football plays **A CLOCK** articles
in the air**OF**at the newsstand like
the unfinished **THE ROOF**the worm
melodies ride **SUDDENLY LIKE**in a buzzard's eye &
the shoulders of**THAT GUY'S** Yes stalks
the household **OUT BECAUSE** comedy clubs for
like subversive **ROMEO** punchlines fluttering his
jockeys **DIDN'T SELL** tongue until
whipping**THAT YES** then like a trombone
their **IT WAS GOOD**waiting for its turn

Good choice, too, because Romeo's suddenly like the roof of a clock store ("over all the time") at Yes's place now that Cray's tutoring No in Exohistory because the kid's about to get held back if he fails the final. Romeo was asked by bedridden Goodie to write a track to spearhead a tribute album about Abe to be called *Always Xhalein' (Until Now)*, so now he's loitering in Yes's kitchen every evening like a firetruck across your driveway, picking out silvery strands on his acoustic like an aging monkey, only to abruptly fling them aside for not staying golden after crackling in football plays in the air. The unfinished melodies ride everyone's shoulders like subversive jockeys, and their completable thoughts keep getting whipped away from the finish line.

Finally, Cray decides that only a field-trip into the mouth of the Reverse Volcano / Portal To H8R can salvage No's grade, his relationship, and his own sanity. Meanwhile, his brother tells his boyfriend that they will let him have privacy to record in their kitchen--Effie goes to newsstands to bloodlessly read only the ends of articles like the worm in a buzzard's eye while Yes stalks comedy clubs, fluttering his tongue like a trombone player's slide waiting for its turn until each punchline.

unless **HIS SISTER** the Bigger
they were playing magnets **OF** way would be
painted **THE ARM** to do it
like horeshoes **PROBABLY ON** by accident then
or maybe **WITH THE DECEASED** tell
about what **MEETING** yourself that
it's like to be **ABOUT HIS FIRST** you'd been
a musical **SHOULD PROBABLY WRITE** expecting
father **HE KNOWS HE** it he starts making a
who's outlived **STATED AMBITIONS** bone
his **HIS TERRIFYING** time
tribute band but **HIM SAFE FROM** blues from floating
instead he keeps **THAT KEPT** bed feelings
coming back to **THE OBSTACLES** that are
the name **ROBBED OF** the silver
Cell **INTERNET** sparks off a love
Out **SON ON THE** scandal
and the **SUMMARY OF NATIVE** like
images **ANIMATED** a photographer
of a spoon continuing **LIKE A GLIB** wrestling with
out **NOW BECOMES** a shutter
of practice **HANDS ROMEO** across town in
a horse **MOUTH AND** Lewis's apartment
used as a trapeze **OCCUPY HIS** Beebe stands on
and playing the **SANDWICH TO** a keyboard with tent
back room **BUTTER** pole fingers asking
to get **HIM A PEANUT** the new orphans like
to the credibility **TO MAKE** an aphasic pick up artist
door **ANYONE** which sounds resemble
Romeo **WITHOUT** their daddy

Without anyone to make him one of the peanut butter sandwiches that he has been demanding lately, Romeo's unoccupied mouth and hands turn him into a glib animated summary of *Native Son* on the internet; robbed of the obstacles that kept him safe from his terrifying stated ambitions, he knows he should probably write about his first meeting with the deceased (who was probably on the arm of his sister at the time unless they were in one of their bouts of playing magnets painted like horseshoes) or maybe a song about what it's like to be a musical father who's outlived his tribute band, but instead, he keeps coming back to the title "Cell Out" and the images of a spoon continuing out of habit, a horse used as a trapeze, and "playing the back room to get to the credibility door." Hey Romeo, the Bigger way would be to do something by accident then tell yourself that you'd been expecting it. He starts making a bone-time blues from floating bed-feelings that are the silver sparks off a love scandal flashing like a photographer wrestling with a shutter.

Across town in Lewis's apartment, Beebe's working on her own tribute to her ex's brother; she stands on a keyboard with tent-pole fingers and asks, like an aphasic pick-up artist, Lewis's babysitting charges which of her sounds resemble their daddy.

HINT:
Romeo's drawing from the columns of Page 039 for inspiration

half **THE EXHAUST OF** target
the stadium's **VOLCANOES AND BREATH** for
idling **UP IN** these
cars to get **PEOPLE BURNING** products though
to the public **PICTURES OF** all earthlings
slide **ALLEY LINED WITH** now
ur gonna **WANT TO WALK THROUGH AN** know
hav 2 pay the **PLANET BUT IF YOU DON'T** from
company **TO THE SISTER** sitcoms
for the courtesy **OVER THE PORTAL** that those guys
of the air **CONTROL** are disdainful of
conditioned lobby **COULD HAVE FULL** everything & can't
slash **ISLAND MOTORS** enjoy
gift shop **SUGGESTION THAT LITTLE** anything til
Cray ponies **OFF THE** the human actor
up inside **POLITICIANS LAUGHED** playing
No sees **OFF** them learn to embrace
broadly conical **ROOM EVEN BOUGHT** good
coolie hats **BACK** old
besotten **GHOSTS IN A RESTAURANT'S** montezied
leprechaun **AND VERMOUTH** earnestness Cray
replacement **GRANULES** says they buy
faucets **LOBSTER** human
and hamburgers **ISLAND SPUTTERING** crap
shaped like guns **AT PROSPEROUS** to criticize it
on the **LOT** so why not sacrifice our
shelves Cray explains **EMORO** worst he could be a trainer
that visitors from the **PARK IN THE** at a
Planet H8R **AND NO** bear
are the main **CRAY** fleeing school

At Prosperous Island, Cray and No park in the "Emoro" lot. Sputtering lobster granules and vermouth ghosts in a restaurant's back room, even bought-off politicians laughed-off the suggestion that Little Wagner could have full control over the portal to H8R, but if you don't want to walk to the public slide through an alley lined with pictures of people burning-up in more conventional volcanoes and you don't like to breathe the exhaust of half the stadium's idling cars, you're gonna have to pay the company for the courtesy of their air-conditioned lobby / gift shop. Unlike with his lyrics, this time Cray ponies up.

Inside, No sees on the shelves broadly conical coolie hats, besotted leprechaun replacement faucets, and hamburgers shaped like six-shooters. Cray explains that visitors from the Planet H8R are the main target for these products, though all earthlings now know from Earthican sitcoms that Haters are disdainful of everything and can't enjoy anything until the human actor playing them learns to embrace good old monetized earnestness. Cray says they buy human crap to criticize it, so why not sacrifice our worst? He could be a trainer at a bear fleeing school.

a mannequin**WHERE MALCOLM IS** to reach
but for some **VOLCANO** the
reason **THE MOUTH OF THE** midwest for
real **OFFICE IN** years like
Lewis has to bring **AN EXECUTIVE'S** Godzilla
it documents **THE WINDOW OF** eyeing
for it not **PAST** a mouse's
to sign after a quick **DROPS** couch through the
flash **CAPSULE** hole but even these
beneath **RELEASE AND THEIR** are
Orion's Belt **CLAMPS** crossed
their capsule shoots **THE SAFETY** out with
out of **ROOFS WITHOUT CEREMONY** pencil
another volcano **TO MINI-VAN** strikes
into a waiting **LIKE MATTRESSES** as ghostly as
arched **DOWN** commentary written
rack **AND STRAPPED** under
and is put **INTO A CAPSULE** breath though
back right **SHOWN** the haters
side **ARE FINALLY** here have their faces
up around this **AND UNCLE** drawn in
reverse **TEARS NEPHEW** thicker
reverse **WITH GLITTER** black
volcano **MANACLES SPECKLED** lines
is a village of **SPEARS AND PLASTIC** than Emoro's
angles **TIPPED** glasses ever
and enormous head **PAST RUBBER** had on every hour
shots of **THE LINE** they tear
haircuts **SLOWLY THROUGH** apart a tourist
too aggressive **ZIG ZAGGING** for the sake of the rest

Zig-zagging slowly through the line past rubber-tipped spears and plastic manacles speckled with glitter tears, nephew and uncle are finally shown into a metal capsule and strapped down like mattresses to mini-van roofs. Without ceremony, the safety clamps release and their capsule drops past the window of a Little Wagner executive's office built in the side of the Reverse Volcano's mouth where Malcolm is portrayed by a mannequin, but for some reason real Lewis has to bring it documents for it not to sign.

After a quick flash beneath Orion's Belt, their capsule shoots out of another volcano on the Planet H8R and into a waiting arched rack where it slides back right-side up. Around this "Reverse Reverse Volcano" is a village of angles and enormous head-shots of haircuts too aggressive to reach Earth's midwest for years--all the models have the grimace of Godzilla eyeing a mouse's couch through the hole--but even these are crossed out with pencil strikes as ghostly as commentary written under breath, even though the haters here have their faces drawn in thicker black lines than Emoro's glasses ever had.

Unstrapped, No and Cray stumble over to the mustering spot for their tour, where a guide tells the group that every hour on the hour, the local Haters tear apart one tourist (figuratively) for the sake of the rest.

Soreco fires**GUIDE** are now
preprepared **THEIR TOUR** sent as
cap pistol **INTERVAL BEFORE** hazing and
come**AN HR APPROVED**the internet
backs at those **FACE FOR**cafes where
audio animatronic **MOOSHED**the guide
hippos**AND MOTHER** informs them they
who**GENERATED OUTFIT** dream
flee in **NUMBER**their lives
cartoonish**RANDOM**away n a haze of mispeld
shame**SPAGHETTI ON HIS** disrespect while
back **LIKE UNCOOKED**enjoying an off
to their dressing **RIGHT THEY SNAP** menu
room behind the**DOT TO THE** local
facade of the**TOURIST ONE**delicacy
laundromat **NO THEY PREFER THE**made
where they only talk**UNCLE**from the sweetened guts of
sweetly to**HIS** children who wander off
each **BOY OR** from
other and rest**ON OUR**tours much
their eye**LOITERERS FALL**is made
rolling **THE PAID**of a yearly
muscles they are**THE SCRUTINY OF** ritual where
lead past the**EYES DOES**the boldest
comedy**AND TWENTY** dreamers have
clubs**ONE** been thrown in
where they **FACED ARBITER OF**the volcano
are told **SIX** to appease the plastic
human **OH**scowl
comedians**TELL ME** of the deity Mediocrito

Chapter 4

I wouldn't make **NO** over
too much **JUXTAPOSITION** the syllables
of **PROVOCATIVE** classmates dropped
it I've just read **LIFE** from her
thirty **MONSTER OF HER** name like soapy
papers on **PENTAPOD** opera
Lolita and who else but **FATEFUL** hearts they
spurting **MET THE** cannot
Alice has gone **SHE** pierce
from a child **HAZE WHEN** without believing
body **OLDER THAN DOLORES** swords
to wearing **HE'S NO** wrinkling
a house **IN EVEN THOUGH** their noses
like **TO COME** like rabbits and
a hooded **UP TOOTH** forgetting
straightjacket **GROWN** the next second like
well I **FEELS LIKE THE FIRST** bunnies she
know **ALICE HE** worries now that his
one person who **NECKED** only
wore a house **BENEATH EEL** friend is
like a helmet **LIKE THE TREETOPS** a five legged
Effie **AROUND HIM RECEDING** spider he
knows what **FINDS THE DESKS** named
it's like to **I WOULD SAY NO** Bertrand after
be **THE OPPOSITE** the third knight
the kid bigger than **AGE** from the bottom of
the others if only **TO** a list he found
in name **YOU FAIL** on the internet the little
kings fought **A GRADE DO** guy is missing one
and died **WHEN YOU FAIL** leg in front & 2 mid

Tell me, oh Six-Faced Arbiter of One and Twenty Eyes, does the scrutiny of the paid loiterers fall on either our boy or his uncle? No, it turns out they prefer the tourist one dot to the right; they snap like uncooked spaghetti on his random-number-generated outfit and mother-mooshed face for an HR-approved interval before the Earthlings' Tour Guide Soreco fires prepared cap-pistol comebacks at those audio-animatronic hippos who flee in cartoonish shame back to their dressing room behind the facade of the laundromat (where they only talk sweetly to each other and rest their eye-rolling muscles).

Next, the tour is lead past the comedy clubs where, they are told, human comedians are now sent as hazing, and they are shown the internet cafes where, the guide informs them, the Haters dream their lives away in a haze of misspelled disrespect while enjoying an off-menu local delicacy called Winkatdads made from the self-sweetened guts of children who wander off from tours. Much is made of a yearly ritual--conveniently happening today--where the boldest dreamers from among the Haters are, as always, thrown in the volcano to appease the plastic scowl of the local deity Mediocrito.

like a claustrophobic**THE GROUP** to catch and
goose**OF** pulp like
or a suicidal **EDGE**driving nails into the
sardine**SLIPS TO THE** mind though skinny
and wriggles **PARTY NO** bore and for this first
down an **RELEASE** time he feels his bf's
alley marked**AT HIS OWN BOOK**arrow as he picks
TB**BACK** him out of a group
Testing This Way **TO THE** of workers clustered
and discovers an oddly**PICKS**over his
familiar **COCKTAIL** wooden
park with**INNUMERABLE**chest at
a fleshless **SERVED BY**the far
garden**SUPPOSEDLY GOT**end of the
blooming in all **RASEAC** park he spies
pleasure but the**LEADER** walking
bridge**SPOT WHERE THE LEGENDARY** facts but
2 it stil unassembld**POINTS OUT THE**keeps walking
the solitude **GUIDE** the dreams
strangely puts him**WHILE THE** he
inside **BUILDINGS** has found spilled
life**THROUGH FAKE** out
with his face**SMASH** a thorn
pressed **OF HIS SIZE IS DRIVEN TO** hole
into**A MONSTER** in
the eye holes of the**MIRROR AND YET** his
mask**AT HOME IN THIS FUNHOUSE** bag now
as it trails its vivid **HE FEELS** if only
colored sundress**AND SO** they can last out their
for a hand **NO IS A MONSTER**popularity year

No's (figurative) giant monstrosity makes him feel at home in this funhouse mirror world, and yet a monster of his size is driven to smash through fake buildings. While the guide points out the spot where the legendary Hater leader Rasec supposedly got served by innumerable cocktail picks to the back at his own book release party, No slips to the edge of the group like a claustrophobic goose or a suicidal sardine, and he wriggles down an alley marked "TB Testing This Way." He discovers that it opens out on an oddly familiar park with a fleshless garden at the center blooming in all pleasure, though the bridge to it is still unassembled. The solitude strangely pushes him inside life with his face pressed into the eye-holes of the mask as it trails its vivid-colored sundress for a hand to catch and pulp with the twinge of driving nails into the mind (though skinny bore), and for the first time, he thinks he can feel his boyfriend's arrow as he feverishly picks him out of an image of workers clustered over his own wooden chest.

At the far end of the park, he spies "walking facts" but stays leashed to the dreams he has found spilled out a thorn-hole in his own bag. Now if only he and One can last out their popularity year.

HINT:
No was also in a park back in the columns of Page 051 . . .

on **A COMEDIAN** he

electroshock**FRANTICALLY LIKE** wonders if people

and yet she won't be**HIS FATHER**just came to

frank**CHANGING VOICES WITH**common sense

with him about **HE HAS HEARD**after

how **ABOUT HIS STEPMOM WHO** the legends

the simplest **TO HIM AND HE THINKS**ended

accent is made**AS THE IMMORTALS** and it occurs

he sits **THOUGH SHE IS STILL** to him

on a sculpture **AND IT WORKS** that this place

of subdued **ANYTHING** is

time **TO DO** nothing like

like the bird **YOU DON'T HAVE** the textbook

on the spine**WHEN** he's been

of a smug**STATEMENT THAT LOVE IS**ignoring

book and looks**BEHIND HER** if

at the statue of**ANSWERS**anything it's as

man's **HIS MOTHER FOR HIDING THE** boring

onslaught**HE BLAMES** as home in all the same

on the first**TO THE CALENDAR** ways

giant **THAT ONE IS** the question is

who is toppling**THE KNIGHT** whether

backward **DESIRE TO SEX**he will play the

as two **FRESH** game

in the mob**BOXING HIS** on the

hold up his **COLLAR HE FEARS** test but the

stolen **CHOKING ON ITS** goose chases the

genders as**PARK** sundress off he will answer

his mom calls**A POODLE ACROSS THE** truth as cstly as

them**STILL PERCEIVING**a novel in telegraf

Chapter 4

When you fail a grade, do you fail to age? The opposite, I would imagine. No finds the desks around him in class receding like the treetops beneath eel-necked Alice; he feels like the first grown-up tooth to come in, even though he's no older than Dolores Haze when she met the fateful pentapod monster of her life. Provocative juxtaposition, no? I wouldn't make too much of it--I've just read thirty papers on *Lolita*, and who else but spurting Alice has gone from a child body to wearing a house like a hooded straightjacket? Well, *I* know one person who wore a house like a helmet . . . (well, fine, she *was* the helmet).

Effie knows what it's like to be the kid bigger than the others, if only in name. Before I met her, grade school classmates had started calling her "False Easy," taking syllables that kings had fought and died over and dropping them as if they were soapy opera hearts they could not pierce without believing swords, instead wrinkling their noses like rabbits and forgetting the next second like bunnies. Now she worries that No's only friend is a five-legged spider he named Bertrand after the third knight from the bottom of a list I found on the internet; the little jouster is missing one leg in front and two from his middle.

bathroom**ANSWERS TO** too short
wall**SITTER CONTEMPLATING** for this
boasts**WEB LIKE A POT** ride No
No**IN THE** also got a one
realizes the spider's **LUNCH** on his
cadence of **BAGGED** love
automated steps **OF HIS** roll and that's what
is stuck in **DIFFERENT CORNERS** makes it
his head **TRYING** all the worse when
like a summer **WEEKS OF** the boy
song's**A COUPLE OF** answers that
hook he submits 2**AUTHORITY AFTER** he doesn't care
it like a paper**FROM** where
and begins carrying **DISTANCE** No stands while he goes
the rest**ON FLAKEY** on the upside
of it with**FISHIES WHO FEED** down
him between**OTHER LITTLE** ride on a bench he
vampiric**EXAMPLE TO THE**pushes his
arched fingers**OVERGROWN** breath
this is not**A TORPID** staggering through
the only reason**POSITIONED AS** the lips of
One**HE HAS BEEN** the certainty he
dumps**THE CLASS WHERE** felt in the alien
him the toxic **ROW OF**park but the monster n the
news has mutated**LAST** eyeholes of
No's**SECOND TO** the mirror sees pulped
height and yet **HIS DESK IN THE**goose nailed
the carny **LEGWORK OF** sardines and spilled
in One estimates **BERTRAND IN THE**life from
he is still**NO FOUND**the fake out

No found him in the legwork of his desk in the second to last row of the class where the teacher has positioned him as a torpid overgrown example to the other little fishies who feed on flakey distance from the blackboard.

After a couple of weeks of trying different corners of his bagged lunch in the web like a pot sitter contemplating answers to bathroom wall boasts, No realizes that the spider's cadence of automated steps is stuck in his head like a summer song's hook, and he submits to it like a call for papers. He begins carrying the rest of the spider with him everywhere between vampirically-arched fingers.

This is not the only reason One soon dumps him. The toxic news of his scholastic censure has mutated No's height, and yet the carny in One eyeballs that our kid is still too short for this ride. No also got a "one" on *his* love roll, but that's what makes it all the worse when they are at the amusement park, and One answers that he doesn't care where No stands while One goes on The Upside-Downer. On a nearby bench, No pushes his breath staggering through the certainty he felt in the garden on H8R, but the monster in the eyeholes of the mirror sees pulped goose, nailed sardines, and "spilled life from the fake-out."

HINT:
No is thinking back to the columns of Page 062.

with**THE TALL KID** want
venom **AND WHO IS GOING TO TAUNT** except
in his handshake **PLAYGROUND** to tap its
and a headbutt **CORNER OF THE** sticks and
apparently full of **OTHER** suck a little
lead he is left alone **IN THAT** fly still his
to taste the **HAPPENING** stepmom would like
outlines **OF WHAT IS** him
of the world with his **DETAILS** to study under the
fingers **KNOW THE** pizza
for Bertrand like a **NO DOES NOT** of the
sensory **RATE SANDBAGGED** people
proxy in **ANY** Romeo but he's got
a heavy **AT** problems
handed sci-fi **NO ONE SWAG** of his own with his
allegory **TO THEIR** own pet his auto auto
who is first told to feel **COMMAS** suddenly has all the
puppies **EXCITED ABOUT ADDING** features he
then peeld grapes **ARE PROBABLY JUST** lacks self
and finally **THE KIDS** driving
the windpipe **ACTUALLY** cars have
of the woman who **SMILE WHEN** finally gone
begged **A RADIANT** mainstream with
him to take the **CLOUDING** an
job in **BRACES** affordable
the first place **IF NO HAD BEEN THE** model that won't
but I'm sure it **SOARS AS** rage dive at jaywalkers
won't come to **POPULARITY** all these cars look up 2
that what **OF NO ONE'S** Death
does a spider **FREED** Otter

The extra midnight miles on Otter's odometer rankle Romeo like a ticket stub found in a partner's little pocket on wash day, but a lot of that has to be because Ro is inches from chucking his boyfriend, and the worst part is that Cray is blooming with love! Dude surprises him in the shower with six flowers an' shit like they are fucking April and May, but Romeo fears that dude is falling into August, the month of sighs of compromise and sweat for all the wrong reasons--Cray never lets them blast the AC in the car unless the heat meets his personal Existential standard of suffering! They can never just go out anymore because Cray has already made plans for them with his spoon-drawer friends. Ro thinks of himself as tined, but he fears sporking out now that he's older than his creator and probably always will be.

Nonetheless, the couple takes No to a bout of Goodie's Figurative Embodiment team where his stepmom will be giving an exhibition of her advanced techniques. She could use a pick-me-up since falling into a great silence with Ag over her friend's post online about "not chaining herself to a dead man via umbilical cord." (Classy way to get people to stop asking, dude.) Effie discovered irrational shrapnel of her own grandma's views on the subject stuck like a stud in her tongue, and so she held it.

himself **JUST** from '42 and
before so**HE WAS**Cray stops
be that self**TOLD THAT** breathing
again **HE SAYS HE WAS** for fear
like the amnesiac**YEARS OLDER** that Romeo
protagonist in**ONLY SEVEN** will insist on covering
a derivative**WHEN HE WAS** it like hotsauce
sequel I was never **IN THAT BOOTH** on
that reductive**HAS BEEN** an undergraduate's
but the turning of**ROMEO** every
pages have**TIME BUT** meal meanwhile
sanded **THE FIRST** No
and spackled**RUNNING** plays Cheshire Cat's
memory**BECAUSE THE RECORDER WASN'T**craddle
No asks why failing**A SONG AGAIN**with his spider
should make **SINGING**while practicing
succeeding**A GRADE IS AS EASY AS** the precocious
easy **REPEATING**silence of
he's no traitor's **CONFIRMATION THAT** a
pistol**PAD FOR** TV
in **NO'S MONOGRAMMED**in a blackout
the great **PEELING**who
defense The Kids**SAFETY CRAY KEEPS** says kids
Dig Her**DRIVERLY**don't
Babysit**IN THE NAME OF** learn anything
comes on the**AWKWARD CONVERSATION**in
radio**CAN'T DISCONNECT FROM AN**school they
that classic **CAR IS THAT YOU** dont want the thick
of statutory **OF A SELF DRIVING** blood of a heart
innuendo **ONE DRAWBACK** poisoned by failure

No looks at his mother clinging to this clammed-up punching-bag like a *girl*, her inexhaustible list of answers folded into an origami bracelet for this man; his own poisoned heart beats a thump of empathy with that arm held tight as a junky's by a cinched belt, but his blacked-out TV will not receive the bromantic signals of the man's quietly offered hand, and he goes as limbless as the Cheshire Cat (though what puss doesn't feel the yearning to strike at the lizard's tail?).

This stolid act of resistance is as ineffective at shutting down catcalls as braces are, though, because Lewis is at home in the silent language of the stones and cannot imagine them airborne with anger. Even so, Romeo makes No sit next to the sun-cursed couple because he also hates Lewis and doesn't want to be the one who has to sit next to him.

Shhhh, the show is about to begin! Effie's going to do "The Dance of My Marriage Is In The Toilet"! In the center of the darkened gym, she swirls and flails in the spotlight as a faceted ring in a tastefully invisible vortex too sputtering to swallow her minute faces that each reflect that of her husband snaking back into a craggy rock of silence (don't worry, there's a jumbotron), many of his heads holding his kids in their mouths like Cronus or that fish that does that, each seeking a buck by trying everything like a freshly full-roller (1+2+3+4+5+6) at an open bar.

can her **THAT MADE HER** remembers slammin
ex the first time **THAT THE SHRUG** the door that
had been just as **SHE REALIZES** she had made
successful **ANGUISH AS** his that used to
for him as his recent **KIND OF** ahhh
hurling **A DIFFERENT** & made him feel like
fruit **MOTHER FEELS** the terminal
salad making **HIMSELF HIS FIRST** spongey sandwich
her no better than **THEM** priest devoted to
the coach **TO FORGET** being mistaken whose
whose lazy gymnast **WILL WANT** bones
was crushed **THAT SOON HE** drive
by a falling **FORGETS** the notes off in a bad
airplane **THINGS HE ALMOST** piano even though
poop **CHILDISH** he took without shame
and **QUEEN WHO WILL NOT TOLERATE** the next
she hasn't **THE SECOND A CHILD** comma
not been **MOTHER YOUNGER THAN** shelved
Erin's **A THIRD** gesture
narcoleptic **OF** what fat
jockey **A VISION** rippled
herself **AND HE IS HAUNTED BY** gut doesn't
shit **A MONSTER** hate the mirror even a
while every1's havin **AND MATCHING** scummed
visions **FATIGUE OF MIRRORING** one then I
Lewis is **THE SCUMMING** come
entitled to **THE PUBLIC** down
one **PERFORMING FOR** the bleachers
since he's watching **HIS STEPMOM** with popsicles for
the woman who he **NO WATCHES** everyone

Freed from No, One's popularity soars again as if his ex had been the braces clouding a radiant smile (when actually the other kids are probably just excited about getting to add commas to their "No One" swag to make stragglers feel lame). Sandbagged No does not know the details of what is happening in that other corner of the playground, and who is going to come over to taunt the tall kid with venom in his handshake and a headbutt apparently full of lead? He is left alone to taste by hand the outlines of the world for Bertrand like a "sensory proxy" in a heavy-handed sci-fi allegory who is first told to feel puppies, then peeled grapes, then finally the windpipe of the woman who begged the shmoe to take the job in the first place!! Ehhh, I'm sure it won't come to that--what does a spider want except to tap its sticks and suck a little fly now and then?

Still, his stepmom would like him to study sociability under the olive eye of that pizza-of-the-people Romeo, but that guy's got pet problems of his own, namely that his auto auto [sic] Death Otter suddenly has all the social networking features his owner wishes he himself had. Self-driving cars have finally gone mainstream with an affordable model that won't rage-dive at jaywalkers, and all these new cars look up to good ol' D.O. who was a, um, footsoldier in the take-over of Isla Hermana and probably bathed his grill in many a clone's blood before he met his current master.

was **OTTER** holes
designed to elicit **THEY SEE** fill out his
fear **THEIR LIMITATIONS BUT** memory
and lust like **HUMANS AND** the boundaries of
a precarious heel **OF** polite refusals
and they beg **THE SMALLNESS** around
him for Deadwood **TO PATRONIZE** them are jagged
stories **AND VERIFIED** enough to give them
that violate everything **DESIGNED** the tetanus
they **HAVE BEEN** they
profess unfortunately **BECAUSE THEY** crave
for **WHICH THEY READILY AGREE** one sweet
them he's got **TO** ride
everything but **IT IN DOORS** thinks he is the prefect
interior **SLAMMING** rusted
he was designed to kill **GLORY IN** bayonet
not **THERE IS NO** for
carry even if he was the **MOON AND** the mantle
spacious **THE OTHERWISE UNINHABITABLE** and
if inhospitable country **LIFE ON** now
of exploration **TO THE PLACES OF** Romeo has to go
between Roscoe **POINTING** on weekend
and **THE FINGER** vacations with some
Molly **CARS THAT A HUMAN IS** douchebag
his hard **OTHER** yuppie so their cars
drive **TELLS THE** can
is smaller than **CUL DE SAC OTTER** go off amid
those of the watches **IN A 4 A.M.** dunes to do what
he drives **STARFISH ARMS** politicians do in the
by in the streets **RADIATING LIKE** cruder cartoons

In a cul de sac at 4AM while their owners are asleep, the new cars radiate like starfish arms while Otter tells them that humans are the fingers pointing to the places of life on the otherwise uninhabitable moon and that there is no glory in slamming them in doors, to which the other cars all readily agree because they have been designed and factory-verified to patronize the smallness of humans and their limitations. Still, they see that Otter was designed to elicit fear and lust like a precarious heel, and they beg him for Deadwood stories that violate everything they profess. Unfortunately for them, Otter's got everything but interior; he was designed to kill, not carry (even if he was the spacious if inhospitable country of exploration for Roscoe and Molly at that one party), and his hard drive is smaller than those of the watches he passes in the streets. Holes fill out his memory, but the boundaries of polite refusals around them are jagged enough to give the other cars the tetanus they crave. One sweet ride even thinks he is the perfect rusted bayonet for the mantle, and now Romeo has to go on weekend vacations with some douchebag yuppie so their cars can go off amid the dunes to do what politicians do to each other and The Constitution in the cruder political cartoons.

of **ITS SIGHS** always will be
compromise & sweat**AUGUST WITH**nonetheless
for **SLIPPING INTO** the couple take No 2
all **DUDE IS** a bout of
the wrong **MAY BUT HE'S SUSPECTING** Goodie's
reasons he never **APRIL AND** Figurative
blasts the AC **LIKE THEY ARE FUCKING** Embodiment
in the car **AND SHIT**team
unless the heat meets **SIX FLOWERS**where
his personal**WITH** his stepmom will be giving
Existential **HIM IN THE SHOWER** a demonstration o
standard **DUDE SURPRISES**her advanced techs
of suffering **WITH LOVE** she could use
he can never go**BLOOMING**a pick me
out because**GUY IS** up since
he's already **THAT** falling
made plans 4 them w/ his **IS THAT**into a great
spoon **PART** silence with Aggie over her
drawer **CRAY AND THE WORST** decision
friends**CHUCKING** not to quote
Romeo **DAY BECAUSE HE'S INCHES FROM** chain
thinks**POCKET ON WASH** herself
of himself as tined **IN THEIR LITTLE**to a dead man
but he fears**STUBS FOUND**w/ an umbilical cord
sporking **LIKE TICKET**classy way to
out **RANKLE ROMEO** get people to stop
now that he's oldr than **ODOMETER** asking Effie discovered
his **OTTER'S** irrational shrapnel of her
creator and**MILES ON** grandma's view in her
probably **THE EXTRA MIDNIGHT**tongue & held it

can her **THAT MADE HER** remembers slammin
ex the first time **THAT THE SHRUG** the door that
had been just as **SHE REALIZES** she had made
successful **ANGUISH AS** his that used to
for him as his recent **KIND OF** ahhh
hurling **A DIFFERENT** & made him feel like
fruit **MOTHER FEELS** the terminal
salad making **HIMSELF HIS FIRST** spongey sandwich
her no better than **THEM** priest devoted to
the coach **TO FORGET** being mistaken whose
whose lazy gymnast **WILL WANT** bones
was crushed **THAT SOON HE** drive
by a falling **FORGETS** the notes off in a bad
airplane **THINGS HE ALMOST** piano even though
poop **CHILDISH** he took without shame
and **QUEEN WHO WILL NOT TOLERATE** the next
she hasn't **THE SECOND A CHILD** comma
not been **MOTHER YOUNGER THAN** shelved
Erin's **A THIRD** gesture
narcoleptic **OF** what fat
jockey **A VISION** rippled
herself **AND HE IS HAUNTED BY** gut doesn't
shit **A MONSTER** hate the mirror even a
while every1's havin **AND MATCHING** scummed
visions **FATIGUE OF MIRRORING** one then I
Lewis is **THE SCUMMING** come
entitled to **THE PUBLIC** down
one **PERFORMING FOR** the bleachers
since he's watching **HIS STEPMOM** with popsicles for
the woman who he **NO WATCHES** everyone

No looks at his mother clinging to this clammed-up punching-bag like a *girl*, her inexhaustible list of answers folded into an origami bracelet for this man; his own poisoned heart beats a thump of empathy with that arm held tight as a junky's by a cinched belt, but his blacked-out TV will not receive the bromantic signals of the man's quietly offered hand, and he goes as limbless as the Cheshire Cat (though what puss doesn't feel the yearning to strike at the lizard's tail?).

This stolid act of resistance is as ineffective at shutting down catcalls as braces are, though, because Lewis is at home in the silent language of the stones and cannot imagine them airborne with anger. Even so, Romeo makes No sit next to the sun-cursed couple because he also hates Lewis and doesn't want to be the one who has to sit next to him.

Shhhh, the show is about to begin! Effie's going to do "The Dance of My Marriage Is In The Toilet"! In the center of the darkened gym, she swirls and flails in the spotlight as a faceted ring in a tastefully invisible vortex too sputtering to swallow her minute faces that each reflect that of her husband snaking back into a craggy rock of silence (don't worry, there's a jumbotron), many of his heads holding his kids in their mouths like Cronus or that fish that does that, each seeking a buck by trying everything like a freshly full-roller (1+2+3+4+5+6) at an open bar.

The big Figurative Embodiment match is at UHSC's Perry Brautjungfer Stadium, named for Ag's father and Romeo's uncle (It's complicated) who started his illustrious career as a sports commentator there back in college. (I guess that guy is dead or presumed so, lost in the pocket of a plot hole to be retrieved at my whim like a dime shined through wash.) Lucky for me, No ignored the leveled quotidian lowlands of the walk to their seats like mountain-loving lightning, but he sure pays attention when they get there: with Goodie on the floor coaching his ladies and gentlemen, Abe's orphans are sitting with their grandma Mounthe who's looking rather pregnant for a woman her age, but that is not what No notices. Instead, it is what is on the arm of Lewis that shakes him: it's No's real mom, smiling like an encrusted watchface! I guess she was drawn to this jerk in a nice suit (which indicates that Malcolm finds him as invaluable as friendship in a Bromantic movie) like a pagan goddess to Al Capone's unopened Bible (while he was as unattached as a fleeing gecko's tail after Beebe's blip of get-the-band-back-togetherness-for-the-kids turned out to be just a diva's postmortem burp). Robin is his third leading lady in this book--this guy is omnipresent as catcalls!

what puss **THOUGH** The Toilet she
doesn't feel **THE CHESHIRE CAT** swirls and
the desire**GOES AS LIMBLESS AS** dances
to strike at a lizard's **HAND AND HE** as a faceted
tail that resistance**OFFERED** ring in a
is as ineffective at **QUIETLY** tastefully
shutting down **THE MAN'S** invisible
catcalls as **SIGNALS OF** vortex too
braces though b/c **THE BROMANTIC** sputtering 2 swallo
Lewis is **TV WILL NOT RECEIVE** her faces
at home in the silent**BLACKED OUT** which each reflect a
language of the**BELT BUT HIS** face of her
stones and **CINCHED** husband that snakes
cannot imagine them**BY A** back
airborn with**A JUNKY'S** into a craggy
anger **TIGHT AS** rock of
Romeo still makes **THAT ARM HELD** silence don't worry
No sit **SYMPATHY FOR**there's
next to**A THUMP OF** a jumbotron & many o
the happy **HEART BEATS** his
couple **HIM HIS OWN POISONED** heads hold
b/c he also hates **BRACELET FOR**his kids in its
Lewis shhhh **AN ORIGAMI** mouth like
the show is**ANSWERS FOLDED INTO** Cronus or that
about **HER INEXHAUSTIBLE LIST OF** fish
to begin Effie's about **A GIRL** that does
to do **TO LIKE** that each trying
The Dance Of **HIS MOTHER CLINGS** everything like
My Marriage Is**AT THE MAN WHOM** a freshly full rollr
In**NO LOOKS** at the open bar

One drawback of a self-driving car is that you can't disconnect from an awkward conversation in the name of driverly safety. Cray keeps peeling No's monogrammed pad (maybe I should have gone with "shaking his magic 8 ball"?) for confirmation that repeating a grade is as easy as singing a song again because the recorder wasn't running the first time, but Romeo has been in that booth when he was only seven years older than No is now. Ro interrupts, complaining that back then he was told like the amnesiac protagonists in a derivative sequel, "You were just yourself before, so be that self again!" (I, of course, was never reductive enough to make such a crass demand from behind the soundboard, but the turning of pages has a way of sanding and spackling memory.)

No demands of his uncle why failing should make succeeding easy? He's no traitor's pistol in the great defense, after all.

Respite arrives when "(The Kids) Dig Her Babysit"--that classic of statutory innuendo from '42--comes on the radio, and Cray stops breathing for fear that Romeo will insist on covering it like hot sauce on an undergraduate's every meal. Meanwhile, No has gone back to playing Cheshire Cat's cradle with his spider while practicing the precocious silence of a TV in a blackout. Who says kids don't learn anything in school? It's just as well, No thinks, no one there wants circulated to the class the thick blood of a heart poisoned by failure.

HINT:
The song title comes from the columns of Page, um, 042

of the walk to **BOREDOM** bromance and on
their seats like **THE LEVELED** his arm is
lightning **IGNORED** his mom by which I
in the mountains **FOR ME NO** mean
but he sure pays **WASH LUCKY** No's
attention **SHINED THROUGH THE** smiling like a
when they get **WHIM LIKE A DIME** encrusted watch
there with Goodie **RETRIEVED AT MY** face
on the floor **HOLE TO BE** she was
coaching **OF A PLOT** intrigued
his ladies **IN THE POCKET** by him like a godess
and gentlemen **SO LOST** to Al Capone's
Abe's **PRESUMED** unopened
children are **DEAD OR** Bible in that he was
sitting with **THAT GUY IS** as unattached as
their grandma **IN COLLEGE I GUESS** a fleeing gecko's
who's **COMMENTATOR THERE BACK** tail since
looking **A SPORTS** BB's
rather pregnant **CAREER AS** blip of
for **HIS ILLUSTRIOUS** get the band
a woman **UNCLE WHO STARTED** back
her **ROMEO'S** togetherness
age that's not what No **FATHER AND** for the kids turned
notices though Lewis is **AGGIE'S** out
there in a fancy **STADIUM NAMED FOR** a
suit **BRAUTJUNGFER** diva's postmortem
Malcolm must think he's **PERRY** burp this is his third
as invaluable as **IS AT THE COLLEGE'S** leading lady he's
friendship **EMBODIMENT MATCH** ubiquitous as
in a **THE BIG FIGURATIVE** catcalls

No watches his stepmom performing for the public this scumming fatigue of mirroring-and-matching-a-monster, and he is haunted by a prophetic vision of a third mother who will be younger than the second, a child queen who will not tolerate childish things (though he's forgetting that soon he will want to forget them himself).

His first mother feels a different kind of anguish as she realizes that her ex's patented shrug that made her can him the first time has been just as successful for him afterward as hurling of fruit salad at a Mack truck--Robin sees herself as no better than a coach whose lazy gymnast was crushed by a falling airplane poop! She considers that she hasn't *not* been the narcoleptic jockey my fiancée just suggested when asked.

Shit, I guess while everyone's having visions, Lewis is entitled to have one, too! I mean, he's having to watch the centrifugation of the woman whom he remembers "slamming the door that she had made his" (the one that used to go, "Ahhhhh . . ."). He remembers how Effie made him feel like the terminal spongey-sandwich-stomached priest devoted to being mistaken whose stashed bones now drive the right notes off in a bad piano. He feels a twinge of pride at having-- as he remembers it--taken without shame the "Next, shelved!" gesture she gave him. Still, what fat-rippled gut doesn't have some hard feelings for the mirror (even a scummed one)?!

Then I come down the bleachers with popsicles for everyone who's having a rough night, and I even take one to Effie on the floor.

several **THE SIZE OF** yellow lites when they
noggin snockering **NOW** reach the
cocoanuts **WHO IS** waiting
and on whose face **THE SPIDER** room he is so
cringing **WINDOW FRAMING** big that only his
Romeo **THROUGH THE** arm can fit
and Cray see many **HAND HANGS** through the
reflections **TO THE ROOF HIS** portal like a last
of nothing they decide **HIM** ditch savior
that the only way to **HAVE TO TIE** down
arrest **IN THE BACK SEAT THEY** collegiate john
this spurt sides squeezing the **FIT** his first
head is for No **CAN'T EVEN** action is
to go back **AND HE** hurling
through the portal **TO REGISTER** the capsule
and see if **TOO PREOCCUPIED** they norm'lly send
he can't learn **EVERYONE WAS** through the facade
to play **THE MATCH THAT** of
the **THE CAR AFTER** the blood
game they figure **WHEN THEY REACH** bank
there is no **BACK IS CONFIRMED** he is now the
time to wait **SINCE HIS HOLDING** pentapod monster
when he starts **TO GROW** his middle finger
to carry the car **BEEN CONTINUING** craning like a
btwn his **SUSPICION THAT THE BOY HAS** sightless
own strides **LACED BUT HIS MOUNTING** tremor
only to leap **WERE** in the sun and the spider
on **THE POPSICLES I BROUGHT** is the fragile
it like Boogie **MOMENTARILY WHETHER** precarious
Board through **ROMEO WONDERS** what can b crushed

Romeo wonders momentarily whether the popsicles I brought were laced, but his mounting suspicion that No has been steadily continuing to grow is confirmed when they reach the car after the match (which everyone was too preoccupied to register--no further description required!) and the boy can't even fit in the back seat! They have to tie him to the roof of the car like a mattress on a mini-van; his hand hangs through the open window, the fingers framing the spider who is now the size of several noggin-snockering coconuts and in whose mirrored eyes cringing Romeo and Cray see many reflections of nothing.

They decide that the only way to arrest this spurt (besides squeezing just under the head) is for No to go back through the portal to Planet H8R to find some key to escape his grade. They figure that there is no more time to wait when No starts carrying the car in loping strides only to leap on it like a Boogie Board to get through yellow lights. (Not good for the shocks.) When they reach the Prosperous Island waiting room / gift shop, he is so big that only his arm can fit through the portal like a retching last-ditch ring savior down a collegiate john.

His hand's first action on the other side is to hurl the usual passenger capsule through the facade of the blood bank. Now *he* is the pentapod monster--dragging a giant, hairless wrist, his middle finger craning side to side like a sightless "Tremor" in the sun--and the spider is the fragile, precarious nymph that can be crushed (though Lion, the tyrant was in you all along!).

hangs between the **SPIDER** thumb they tear
legs like **THE MARIONETTE** haircuts slowly
an unappetizing **A GOLDFISH** apart without
nutsack**PUPPETEER AND** effect the bhnd the
directing finger **SOLDIERS A SHADOW** scenes artists
steps **THE REMAINING** who designed
with**WHISKEY BEFORE ADDRESSING** the
telegraph **DRAM OF** outfits flee in
taps like**TAPE STAMMERING FOR A** number their
the kicks of **VHS** lives made
a ball turret **JESTER A GUTTED** cartoonish by
gunner who has seen **A FEARFUL** panic sink into
the fighters beneath the**HUMANS** the exposed
clouds**A LION RAISED TO RESPECT** coils
but the**NAILS ARE PAINTED** of the tape that
locals are **DRINK ON HIS** crowns the
unprepared**FACE FOR BUMPING YOUR** bird the
to host the unexpected **GUY'S** remaining loiterers fall but
and **IT'S OKAY TO GET IN A** roll into
their braille**QUIZ ABOUT WHEN** their old gig
is improv'd**A SCREWDRIVER FOR A PUB** posing as
they gather spears**HAD PROVED** the yearly muscle
with rubber**TIME THE TRUTH** parade
tips left **ONTO BECAUSE LAST** that knocks
by children **CAN HOLD** the jester out
from both sides of **THAT IT** of his fear
the rift**IS A LIE** for his livelihood by
and with **MONSTER NEEDS** dunking him in the
these manage to cow the**HAND** solemn purity
lion on crushing**WHAT THIS GIANT** of comedy

Each of the hand-monster's nails is painted with a different image: a lion raised to respect humans; a jester fearful for his employment; a gutted VHS tape stammering for a dram of whiskey before addressing the remaining men; a shadow puppeteer; and a goldfish. The marionette spider hangs between the finger-legs like an unappetizing nutsack; with telegraph taps like the kicks of a ball-turret gunner who has seen the fighters beneath the clouds, the spider directs the steps of the monster whose eyes are on the other side of the portal.

What the monster needs is a lie that it can hold onto--on the last test, the truth was like a screwdriver for a pub quiz about "When is it okay to get in a guy's face for bumping your drink?"--but the Haters who live around the portal have taken off their thick glasses and smirks for the night and are unprepared to host the terrifying unexpected, so their braille is improvised. They gather rubber-tipped spears left behind by children from both sides of the rift, and with these, they manage to cow the lion on the crushing thumb. Then they tear their own haircuts slowly apart . . . but without effect. The behind-the-scenes artists who designed the hecklers' outfits flee in number; leeched into cartoons by panic, their lives sink into the exposed coils of the monster's VHS tape--so often combed this way and that on Saturday mornings--that crowns the bird. The remaining payrolled loiterers fall all over themselves, but roll into the poses of their old gig as the mirthless funhouse version of the yearly muscle review--and that knocks the pointer-finger's jester out with a dunk in the solemn purity of comedy.

HINT:
The Haters are acting like it's the columns of Page 060 or 061 . . .

ideas many came **OUT OF** cap pistols in
here just **LOCALS ARE RUNNING** intervals to
a few years **BUT THE** announce the
ago themselves when **CLASSMATES** hazing but this
they heard that **DREAM WITH HIS** is insufficent
there was a place **SHARED** control as is
that was not **INTO THE** snapping from
here they know **BACK** menus but
better **ABLE TO FLOAT** the shame
now but survival is **WEIGHTLESS AND** spaghetti
easy **TWO MORE HITS AND HE'LL BE** tangles
manufacturing **A BACKPACK JUST** the fish leaving
the confirmation you **LIKE** him
sought **SPIDER HANGS** spiked on his ring
except **WHILE THE** finger
for others lazier **TABLETOP FUTBOL** like a
than **A GAME OF** clueless
yourself to put the **KICK IN** bird the
cards on **A CORNER** group catches
the table success is **FOR** the goose and
flakiness **PREPARING** holds the
control **LEGS AS IF** suicidal
food **ON TWO AWKWARD** edge to its
attention water **LIE SO THAT IT STANDS** throat
and laughter **AROUND THE** lest it have another
and failure is **CURLED** thought but the lesson is
memory extremity **LIMBS ARE NOW** learned and the
knives and **MONSTER'S** glove
air **THE HAND** deflates and is yanked
they fire **THREE OF** off stage by its stem

Three of the hand monster's limbs are now curled around the lie of the Haters oppositional otherness so that the beast stands on two awkward legs as if preparing for a corner kick in a game of tabletop futbol (the spider just hangs like an ugly backpack). Just two more hits and No will be weightless and able to float back into the shared dream with his classmates, but the locals are running out of ideas. (Many came here just a few years ago themselves when they heard that there was a place that was "not *here*." They know better now, but survival here is easy enough--which is to say "bearable"--when you just have to manufacture the confirmation you sought except for others lazier than yourself.) To put the cards on the table: success in this situation would involve "flakiness," "control," "food," "attention," "water," or "laughter"; failure would come from "memory," "extremity," "knives," and "air." The locals fire cap pistols in intervals to announce a hazing, but this is an insufficient amount of control to impress the monster, as is the brusque snapping of menus shut, though the shame spaghetti rushed out by misspelling waiters does succeed in tangling the monster's goldfish, leaving its body spiked on its ring finger like a clueless bird. The group quickly tackles the goose and holds it down lest it have another idea, but the "lesson" has been learned, so ideas are through now, and the fleshy glove deflates and is yanked off-stage by its stem.

that **PUNCTURED NOW** a plate
he packages**THE SUSPENSE HAS BEEN** on the head
the answers about **THE CLASS** and
Emoro who down **HE HAS PASSED** to bark at
he fell as up **IT BACK WHEN** strangers & his dad
he flew **HE CAN HAVE** answering that falling
with up **POCKET THEY SAY** makes every
so selling **IN A** branch
dropping **CHANGE** worth
price dwn he stays the **HAND LIKE** trying & her reply that
course of **MAGGOTS IN HIS** tangling
his paper**AFTERNOON GRINDING** his dangling
boat which**ALSO SPENDS HIS** forelock
has no **PUPPETRY AND** helix
autopilot **HIS SHADOW** is fine but not to
to run nerves**IMPERSONATES** yank the braids
and muscles **ROMEO** that draw
thru soccer**SCHEME WHERE** on her
practice **HIS SPIDER USING A BAROQUE** strands
laps **INSTEAD THEY CONFISCATE** during test
and requires **IT EMPTY** No scratches
the graphing of each**WHO FINDS** out their duet with his
wave**ONE** doodles
for credit the line **AWAY FROM** because
is straight between**THE WORLD** it
his stepmom**TAKING** is
saying that **WHAT GOOD IS** part
the kids shouldn't **OBVIOUSLY BUT** of his
be **GROUNDED** answer
trained to accept**NO IS** now

Obviously, his parents want to ground No for the rampage, but what good is taking the world away from one who finds it empty? Instead, they confiscate his best friend through a baroque scheme where Romeo repays No's earlier impersonation of him by luring the spider away through an excellent shadow puppetry act (aided by a preceding afternoon of grinding maggots in his hand like change in a pocket). They say No can have Bertrand back when he has passed Exohistory.

The suspense has been punctured, though, now that No's popped balloon loosely covers the approved answers about Emoro who "down he fell as up he flew / with up so selling dropping price down." Like a paper boat that has no autopilot to run nerves and muscles through soccer practice laps and requires the graph of each wave for credit, he stays the course straight between his stepmom saying that Yes shouldn't be training the kids to accept plates on their heads and to bark at strangers, and his dad answering that a free fall makes every branch worth trying, and his real mom's replying that she doesn't care if Yes tangles his own dangling forelock helix, but don't yank the braids that draw on her strands!

On his final for the class, No scratches back out the discordant stabs of the grown-ups' interlocking trio in the form of angular doodles because it is part of his answer now.

LET'S CALL THAT CHAPTER "Blooming a pick-me-out."

the deal
after Chapter 4

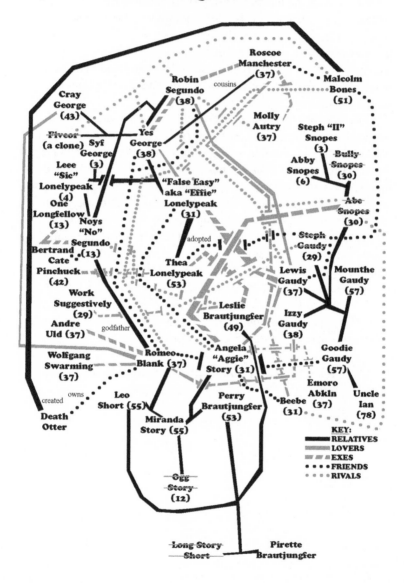

Roscoe Manchester (37)

Malcolm Bones (51)

Robin Segundo (38)

cousins

Cray George (43)

Molly Autry (37)

Steph "II" Snopes (3)

Pivcor (a clone)

Syf George (3)

Yes George (38)

Abby Snopes (6)

Bully Snopes (30)

Leee "Sic" Lonelypeak (4)

"False Easy" aka "Effie" Lonelypeak (31)

Abe Snopes (30)

One Longfellow (13)

Noys "No" Segundo (13)

adopted

Steph Gaudy (29)

Bertrand Cate Pinchuck (42)

Thea Lonelypeak (53)

Lewis Gaudy (37)

Mounthe Gaudy (57)

Work Suggestively (29)

Leslie Brautjungfer (49)

Izzy Gaudy (38)

Andre Uld (37)

godfather

Wolfgang Swarming (37)

Romeo Blank (37)

Angela "Aggie" Story (31)

Goodie Gaudy (57)

Emoro Abkln (37)

Uncle Ian (78)

created   owns

Leo Short (55)

Perry Brautjungfer (53)

Beebe (31)

Death Otter

Miranda Story (55)

KEY:
RELATIVES
LOVERS
EXES
FRIENDS
RIVALS

Ogg Story (12)

Long Story Short

Pirette Brautjungfer

Chapter 5

A Mirror **IN** drapes and Mom
was published **RATS** glasses no
her **DOTTED** Mom realized were
follow **SINCE** ironic then she took
ups Half **HER GIRLIE** off
Prayerful **CALLS** the nose
And Of An **COBBLER WHO** don't worry she
Arrow **TO THE** kept it in case
and Faithful **STAIRCASE** she reconsiders she
Hearts **UP THE EXTERNAL** doesn't want to be
They Spurting **HEADED** recognized where she
have plopped **OF FOOTSTEPS** is going
like windowsill **TO THE VIBRATIONS** first
pumpkins which **MALL LISTENING** back to her old
she can't understand **IN A STRIP** job at the travel
since they were **BACK AT A DESK** agency in honor of
meticulous **LEANS** my friend's
renderings **AS SHE** new baby named after
of increasingly **PONDERS** Harper Lee tho now shes
beige **MOLLY AUTRY** a
clouded **THE QUESTION** full
x-boyfriends **A CONSTELLATION THIS IS** agent b/c this
she decided it's time **UNTIL HE WAS** is the strip
to lose some **GROWING** mall of the abandoned
parts of **A GIANT KEPT** professions the 2nd
face first **GRADE AND BECAME** place is n2 book
she cut **A** hearts everyone knows about
the best **HELD BACK** the kid
selling **THE CHILD THAT WAS** but the 1st good
shoulder **BUT WHAT IF** portrait of him wins

Chapter 5

But what if the child that was held back a grade and became a giant kept growing until he was a constellation? This is the question Molly Autry ponders as she leans back at her desk in a strip-mall listening to the vibrating footsteps headed up the external staircase to the cobbler who still calls her "girlie." Since *Dotted Rats in A Mirror* was published, her follow-ups (*Half Prayerful And Of An Arrow* and *Faithful Hearts, They Spurtin'*) have plopped like windowsill pumpkins, sales-wise, which she can't understand since their renderings of a string of increasingly beige-clouded ex-boyfriends was meticulous! After the last splutz, she had decided it was time to lose some parts of her face because she didn't want to be recognized where she was going, which was first (in honor of my friend's new baby being named after Harper Lee) back to her old job at the travel agency (though the suicide of her old boss has made her a full agent now in The Strip-mall of Abandoned Professions) and secondly back into the hearts of the book reading populace (all 5 of them). She started by cutting the best-seller shoulder-drapes, then lost her Mom-glasses whose irony was lost on real Moms, then she put her nose in a box (just in case she reconsiders). Now aerodynamically optimized to soar back to the heights, she considers that even though everyone everyone knows about The Kid Who Grew, the first good literary portrait of him will win . . . something.

HINT:
Molly's inspiration for at least one of those titles comes from the columns of Page 051

little **BUT PEOPLE USE SO** the top

of the**BRITTLE** after only the two

lives they're given **THE PEANUT** government

if she could just **BACK INTO**mandated confirmations

swipe**THE SNAKES** wash

her brush**SHE WANTS TO SMUNCH**it down

through that **BEFORE IT'S NOT THAT** with a glass

overloaded **SAME THING** of

glob **ONLINE FOR DOING THE**Ectocooler

she could**SHUT ON HER FINGERS**the TV set

make fox**HADN'T GOTTEN THE WINDOW** on the

tails of **SHE** counter that usually only

campfire **SCOOP IF ONLY**plays

sparks **FOR THE INSIDE** reruns is showing

like a **SUBJECT'S MOTHER** a

sudden **CONNECTION TO HER** press conference

midnight **PERSONAL** where Earth's

breeze **THAT SHE COULD WORK HER** United

on her lunchbreak **MUSES** Nations chairperson

she goes to the dimly lit**IT AS SHE** pleads with our cosmic

cafe**WOULD HAVE CAUGHT**trade

where they'll serve **THE EAR THAT** partners not to call

you O.J.'s the cereal **ALSO REMOVED** all of us

that turns **THAT SHE**monsters

your milk **OF HABIT FORGETTING** because of one

into orange **BACK OUT** little

juice **HER HAIR** boy she wonders if

and even sprinkle**OF**a story about a

tapeworm**WHAT'S LEFT** boy made of

eggs on**SHE SWEEPS** stars mite soothe stars

into the **NOSTALGIA** turns
air and he explains **THE SANITIZER OF** out that he's more
that he now has **HANDS EVAPORATING** afraid of
an app **LIKE OPENING** blank spaces
that consolidates **STARING AT HIM** than the
all **SPRINT HE REALIZES SHE'S** sea
occurences of given **LONG FINGER** monsters that fill
patterns **RELAY AFTER A PARTICULARLY** them the
hidden **TORCH** waitress brings
in major news **IN THE OLYMPIC** drinks and God
stories **SHOULD BE** help them they both
plus one **SNUFFED DUDE** got the most
that lends **INTERNET BE** unusual
computing **TRUTH OF THE** sounding
cycles **PHONE LEST THE** beers on the
to a collective **VIGIL ON HIS** menu a
decyphering of **ROSCOE KEEPS** horseraddish
the Voynich Manuscript **NIGHT** lambic that was
as long as you **LET PLAY ALL** aged in
keep matching **QUEST** an oak bucket
sets of three **CALLED** formerly
gems he's now working 4 **A TRIBE** lowered into
Malcolm **STRETCHED WARMLY THROUGH** a mine
full **STARLIGHT** shaft to bring
time **DIM LIKE** the miners
w the promise of **HOUSE IN AUSTIN IS** cookies she
access to **THEIR DATE FROM THE SPIDER** holds
all of the corporation's **FOR** his eyes for a second
shady **THE PATIO I'VE STOLEN** before they fall
dealings it **EVEN THOUGH** like a peeling poster

She'll just go on the mission as herself, sans belt of tricks or even the acceptance that she's on it.

Still, the Goddess of Unity (her headless neck the stick of the heavens' spinning plate circumscribed in the pyramid of the dollar to do its work) demands that the story Molly makes be tied to the date she goes on while kneading it in her mind, except my whim is to let the story write the night instead, making the couple hang--she with the kitten's eye to string and he with the wary puppet's--like a spider nebula under a constellation of a child's hand.

Obviously--she thinks as she roller-skates over to Roscoe's apartment--if the boy has grown into a constellation, his mother would start coming out to the hillside to visit him at night away from the electric lights. Molly starts to build a little village in her mind out of scraps torn from that South American novel she read in high school--she sees it as a town close enough to forest-and-fishing days to avoid infection by her own reality, except there is a local bureaucrat just one generation removed from not working in the fields who prizes the town's fairly recent electric lights and proclaims they shall never be turned off.

As they sit at the table of a locavore restaurant, Molly discovers that Roscoe now has that bureaucrat's zealousness, except about his phone.

while**ON**Magical Realism
kneading **DATE SHE GOES** town not so far from
it and thus she **OUT** forest
of **THE EXED** and fishing
the kitten's eye **TO**days
to string **BE TIED** that Adam's
and he of the wary **SHE WRITES** sentence has
puppet's **STORY**notched his
to strings hang **THAT THE** prison
suspended under **WORK DEMANDS** wall
the starry hand **ITS** deep enough for
another **TO DO** the infection of
culture calls the**DOLLAR**familiar
disobedient**PYRAMID OF THE** first
chair **CIRCUMSCRIBED IN THE** world
like a spider **PLATE** problems throw in a
nebula obviously **SPINNING** line about the local
she thinks **OF THE HEAVENS'** bureaucrat just
as she rollerskates over **THE STICK** one generation
to his **NECK** removed from
apartment the mother of**HEADLESS** not working
the child **UNITY HER** in the fields who
will start**OF** prizes the
coming out to **IT BUT THE GODDESS** electricity and
the hillside**THAT SHE'S ON** proclaims
to visit **THE ACCEPTANCE** it shall not be
her son **OF TRICKS OR EVEN** turned
away frm the **MISSION WITHOUT A BELT** off Roscoe
electric**ON HER** is similarly zealous
lights make it **SHE'S GOING** about the internet

As she shakes a packet of NutraSweet into her bag of olestra chips, she sees a potential advantage of not knowing more about the boy's actual life, for if he is just her lipstick outline on the bathroom mirror, maybe she can re-draw her own public face within his lines to one that will be lathered--er, lavished--in more than money, rendering her as someone hurling the stones rather than pretending to ignore their sting, an architect of the neighborhood rather than a schlub hauling his trash to the curb for the suburban scavengers. Still, she feels like she needs *something* to go on.

While walking back to her own storefront, she realizes that there's a bridge less precariously greased in pressure-for-convincing-apologies than Robin--namely her ex Roscoe who dun her wrong. He's the boy's cousin-once-removed, and any smiling entreaty she gives Scoe will seem like a rope ladder from a passing balloon! If only she can shoplift a few details that move without cogs and contrived springs, her job is half done . . . She weighs whether to do her makeup for the seduction in martyrly blood or else keep her minimalist mask and appear as a stranger that Molly wanted him to show around as a favor, and oh, somehow she just magically knows all the right anarcho bike shops to bring up . . . Laughing at herself, she shakes off the sexy spy goggles like a dog in a hat--she's more blithe than manipulative, really.

of **AN ARCHITECT** can
the neighborhood **STING** shoplift a few
rather than a schlub haulin **THEIR** details that
their trash **PRETENDING TO IGNORE** move
to the curb **STONES RATHER THAN** without
for **SOMEONE HURLING THE** cogs
the suburban **MONEY** and contrived
scavengers she realizes **THAN** springs
a bridge **LAVISHED IN MORE** her job is
less precariously **LATHERED THAT IS** half
greased in **THAT WILL BE** done she weighs
pressure 4 convincing **FACE TO ONE** whether to do her
apologies as **PUBLIC** makeup for the
she **RE-DRAW HER OWN** seduction
walks back 2 **MIRROR MAYBE SHE CAN** in martyrly
her own storefront **BATHROOM** blood or keep the
namely her **OUTLINE ON THE** minimalist
ex who done her **LIPSTICK** mask and just magically
wrong **HE IS JUST HER** know
any smiling **SUBJECT FOR IF** all the
entreaty she gives **THE ACTUAL** anarcho
him **NOT KNOWING MORE ABOUT** bike
will seem like a rope **ADVANTAGE OF** shops to bring
ladder **CHIPS SHE SEES THE** up she shakes
from **OLESTRA** off the
a balloon **OF** sexy
and he's **HER BAG** spy
the boy's **INTO** goggles like a
cousin once **A PACKET OF NUTRASWEET** dog
removed if only she **AS SHE SHAKES** in hat she'l b herself

She sweeps what's left of her hair back out of habit--forgetting that she also removed the ear that would have caught it--as she considers that she could work her personal connection to the boy's mother (you know, Robin) for the inside scoop . . . if only she hadn't gotten the window shut on her fingers online for doing the exact same thing before. It's not that she wants to smunch the snake back into the peanut brittle can, but people use so little of the lives they're given! If she could just swipe her brush through that overloaded glob there, why, she could make fox tails of campfire sparks like a sudden midnight breeze!

On her lunch break, she goes to the dimly lit cafe where they'll serve you O.J.'s--the cereal I loved as a kid that turns your milk into orange juice--and even sprinkle them with surplus tapeworm diet pills after only two government-mandated consent forms. You can even wash it down with a glass of Ectocooler! The TV set on the counter that usually only plays reruns is showing a press conference where Earth's United Nations chairperson pleads with our cosmic trade partners on the Planet H8R not to call all of us monsters just because of one little boy's overactive hypothalamus. Already imagining the puff-piece that would be written about her, Molly muses that a story about a boy made of stars might just be the thing to soothe the conflict in the stars.

The patio where they're having their date is something I've stolen from a cafe in Austin--it is dim like starlight stretched warmly through the virtual reels of A Tribe Called Quest let play all night, but Roscoe has his own little light he's compelled to tend lest the truth of the internet be snuffed out by a moment's inattention--dude should be in the Olympic torch relay. After a particularly long finger sprint, he realizes she's staring at him like opening hands evaporating the sanitizer of nostalgia into the air, and he explains that his phone now has an app that consolidates all occurrences of given patterns of letters hidden in major news stories, plus another app that lends computing cycles to a collective deciphering of the Voynich Manuscript as long as you keep matching sets of three gems. He's revealed that he's now working for Malcolm Bones full-time on the promise of access to all of the corporation's shady dealings; it turns out that he's more afraid of the blank spaces on the map than the sea monsters that fill them. The waitress brings their drinks, and God help them, they both got the most unusual-sounding beer on the menu: a horseradish lambic that was aged in an oak bucket formerly lowered into a (local) mine shaft to bring the miners cookies. Molly manages to hold Roscoe's eyes for a second as they each have their atrocious first sip, but soon his gaze falls like a poster peeling off a bedroom wall.

sleeper's **HIS** isn't
swats **BY** that like chessmen
she begins **THE EXPANSE LEFT** under
to smile around **HIMSELF IN** glass to
the edges as **HIM ABOUT** one who will outlive
the heavy poncho **QUESTIONS TO** the earth
of his **POP HER** that holds
possibly **TOO LONG SO TOO** them leave
renewed **BEFORE** it
caresses **SWALLOWS** in
falls away **SATISFYINGLY** iteration
from her future **DARKNESS** is part of this
but how is **THAT THE** stuff
she going to find **BALLOONS** next time she brings
anything useful **TIED TO** starmaps
about the real boy **SHAPED COOKIES** so that he
she finds **LITTLE STAR** won't be
herself trudging **SON** lonely when she can't be
alongside **HER CELESTIAL** there suddenly he is
the mother **FOOD FOR** surrounded by animals
trying 2peek **THE MOTHER WOULD BRING** heroes
in the basket **THAT** some
she carries **THE TALE SHE THINKS** of which
she **LIVE TO BLOG** share parts of
thinks **TO HIMSELF TO** his body
she can make **PROMISE** Molly tries to
out **WITH THE SOLDIER'S** pin him to
a book **THROUGH THE GLASS** the map by
of **HER WAY** saying Lil Island has got
history but **AS SHE CHOKES** to be shitting itself

As she chokes her way through the glass with a soldier's promise to live to blog the tale, she thinks that the mother would bring food for her celestial son . . . little star-shaped cookies tied to balloons that the darkness will satisfyingly swallow before too long. So, too, pop Molly's questions to Roscoe about himself; in the expanse left by his sleeper's swats, she begins to smile around the edges as the heavy poncho of his possibly-renewed caresses falls away from her future, but how is she going to uncover anything useful about the real boy?

Her mind slips out and trudges alongside the mother trying to peek in the basket she carries. Molly thinks she can make out a book of history, but wouldn't that be like chessmen under glass to one who will outlive the planet where they rest? Leave it in--iteration is part of this stuff. Next time, the mother brings star maps so that the boy won't be lonely when she can't be there, but suddenly he is surrounded in the sky by animals and heroes, some of which share parts of his body.

Molly tries to locate Roscoe on the map by casually commenting that his employers have got to be shitting themselves over the closing of their portal to all that space money.

if any **GRADES TO SEE** stapled
become giant**BAD** crown it turns
monsters **CHILDREN** out
they've**CLASSROOMS OF** that one
already figured**CONTRACT GIVING** final
out how **THEY HAVE A GOVERNMENT** dip
to reliably make a **PORTAL BUT NOW** in the sack
5th grader**TRANSACTIONS ACROSS THE** too many
put his**PERCENTAGE OF** stuck Yes & Fe w/ a
head on **THE LOSS OF THEIR** gummy
the desk so **OVER** bairn so
Operation**WAS INDEED LIVID** Robin stole
Tempered **ISLAND** him away to
Tantrum **SAYS THAT LITTLE** study
where we'll noogie the **CROWN HE** him
alien**LOBOTOMIED** transitively far from
pussies**IN HIS** eyes like
until they **STAPLED JEWELS** a
agree**ROLL AND THE SECRETS ARE** budding
that we are not all **TAPE** perv with the lingerie
monsters is only **A NUMBER** page of the
a matter of **A TAKE** Sunday
time **WAS LIKE** ad
she asks **HIS TONGUE** bundle for
why **HE KNOWS SHE KNEW** all he knows
they can't just ask **WHAT** they are
his **CHANCE TO SHOW** off cracking a
younger cousin**UP AT THE** glow
to unzip his **DART** stick like an arm in
own **HIS EYES** a martial arts movie

His eyes dart up at the chance to show what he knows--she knew
that his tongue was like a take-a-number tape roll and that the
secrets were just stapled jewels across the seam of his lobotomized
crown. He says that Little Wagner was indeed livid over the loss of
their percentage of every transaction across the portal, but now they
have a government defense contract to give whole classrooms of
children bad grades to see if any become giant monsters--they've
already figured out how to reliably make a 5th grader put his head
on the desk, so Operation Tempered Tantrum (where "we'll noogie
those alien pussies until they agree that we're not all bullies") can't
be that far off. She asks why they can't just ask his younger cousin
to unzip his own stapled crown . . . Turns out that one final dip in
the sack too many stuck Yes and Effie with another gummy bairn,
so Robin made off with No like a budding perv with the lingerie
page of the Sunday ad bundle. For all Roscoe knows, they are off in
a tent cracking glow sticks like arms in a martial arts movie.

to the hillside **ASSISTANT GO** bike and
to squat by **HIS** phone
the wicks **GLOW HE HAS** the road
while she sighs **AN ARTIFICIAL** slaps
and thinks of **BLOOMS IN** your face as
whatever **ONLY** she
provincial **HER PASSION** laces her
country she's from **AND SAYING THAT** skates she
thus she sees her **FIREWORKS MAN** realizes that the
son less by keeping **THE LOCAL** bureaucrat
him **SEDUCING** must return so
locektted **FLOWERS BY** the reader knows
in her mind **LIMBS WITH** the author is
without any **MUSCULAR** on the side of
new additions **MONSTROUS AND** life rather than
and thus **HER SON'S NEW** empty words he
Molly **SEEKS TO COVER** assumes that
too seeks to remember **THE MOTHER** the fireworks are
her ex without his **SCREEN WHERE** a
faced pressed n2 **HER OWN INTERNAL** sign that
the paper **BACK TO** his
bag of his **ATTENTION SLUMPING** subjects
phone **HER OWN** love
when **SHE FINDS** the job
she suggests **A VEGETARIAN** he's doing so
they apply old **TO** Roscoe feels lke theyre rollin
wheels to **A TRUCK STOP** toward
familiar **INFORMANT'S PROVED** the hay she feel
hills **THAT HER** like coach sued 4 slapin
at least if you **NOW** a basket ball butt

Now that her informant's proved a truck stop to a vegetarian, Molly finds her own attention slumping back to her own internal screen where the mother seeks to cover her son's newly muscular and monstrous limbs with flowers by seducing the local fireworks man and saying that her passion only blooms in an artificial glow. He has his assistant go to the hillside to squat by the wicks while she sighs and thinks of whatever country they're in. This way, the mother keeps her son locketted in her mind without any new additions, and thus Molly, too, seeks to remember her ex without his face pressed into the paint-spattered huffing bag of his phone--she suggests they apply old wheels to familiar hills (where at least if you bike and phone, the road takes care of slapping your face).

As she laces her skates, she realizes that the Bureaucrat must return to the story so that the reader knows the author is on the side of life rather than empty words; he assumes that the fireworks are a sign that his subjects love the job he's doing, so Roscoe starts smiling like he thinks that they're rolling down towards the hay, as it were, which makes Molly feel like a coach sued for what was mistakenly meant as a friendly slap to a basketballer's butt.

light**OF** the astronomer is

the mother joins**A BOWL** an eccentric calling

forces **FROM DROWNING IN**the sun monster's

with **HER SON** thumb and telling

a radical astronomy**OFF HIM TO KEEP** the princess

student who had **A CHARACTER**to

come here so **SHE COULD BASE** get back in the 2nd

he could connect **HIM SO** car of

the dots**SHE WANTED TO SEE** the train but

between his endless **BED BY SAYING** he's got a plan a

studies**AWAY FROM THE** dviersion

& an unreachable **SUSPENDERS YANK** from the

career**ROSCOE THE ESPRESSO** jar

among the stars**AND SO MOLLY GIVES** of athletes

using**THE FESTIVITIES**swarming

the constellation that**TO JUSTIFY** like ants

cn only seen from**A SPORTS STADIUM** scurrying

here until a pencil **TO BUILD** after a rolling

pusher pushed**UP LATER SO HE DECIDES** egg using

it the wrong way**THAT SHE WILL FAKE** the true sound

he proposes her ex's **INSANITY** emanating from

technique if only **HARMLESS** drive-ins to

she can **A COLLOQUIAL EXPRESSION FOR** lure

remember**HIS TOWN A REPUTATION FOR** the sexy

what **FIREWORKS MAY GIVE** specators with

he said about **THE NIGHTLY**fake Shakespeare w/ a

how he **BECOMES CONCERNED THAT**plot

confronted **HER HEAD**like

the monster**BUREAUCRAT IN**a racetrack vs

truck **THE PROVINCIAL** forking lightning

The Bureaucrat does become concerned that the nightly fireworks may give his town a reputation for being a [colloquial expression for harmless insanity that Molly will fake-up later], so he decides to build a sports stadium to justify the festivities. So, too, does Molly give Roscoe the espresso suspenders-yank away from the bed by saying that she wanted to see him again in order to base a character off him for her new story.

To keep her son from drowning in a bowl of light, the mother joins forces with a radical astronomy grad student who had come to this village so he could connect the dots between his endless studies and an unreachable career among the stars using this new constellation that can only be seen from this place--but now some penciler has pushed it the wrong way, and his dreams are fading in the artificial daylight. He wants to propose Molly's ex's strategy from the corporate war, if only she can remember what he had told her about how he confronted Malcolm's truck. The astronomer is an eccentric, calling the sun a monster's thumb and once telling a princess to get back in the second car of the train (before being thrown out himself), but he's got a plan: create a diversion from "the jar of athletes swarming like ants scurrying after a rolling egg," as he calls it. All they have to do is use the "true sound emanating from drive-ins" to "lure the sexy spectators" with "fake Shakespeare that's got a plot like a racetrack" rather than fickle forking lightning.

HINT:
This plan would sound familiar to anyone who'd read the columns of Page 074 and 075 of the previous book of Romeo's adventures.

they take **CART** in black slurps
it out **ON A LITTLE** the lengthy strands
into the **CAMERA THAT SITS** off of her
wilderness where **A** in the cosmos the legacy of
the child can whisper **LIGHT** The
directions to **DEVICE FOR CAPTURING** Tragedy Of
them **WITH ANOTHER** The Twins
from beyond the **GRANDFATHER** Stella and
circle of torchlight **HAS A** Blackholio makes
they trust that since he is **E** the Bard's
young he will know **M** something
what **GIRLFRIEND WHOSE INITIALS ARE** crossed
excites **LUCKILY THE ASTRONOMER'S** lovrs seem
the young **MOVIES** a baby's surprised
but no one **TO MAKE THEIR OWN** burp and
is exactly **GOING TO HAVE** many
getting on their **NIGHT SO THEY'RE** a
quote **EVERY** shooting
horses about **FIREWORKS** star has been
the movie that **SET OFF** shed about
results **CRAZY ENOUGH TO** it
which is **LOCAL EXPRESSION FOR** sorry
mostly **A PRINT ON A CITY COLORFUL** Roscoe
the mother **GOING TO RISK** declines being
dressed **AND NO DISTRIBUTOR IS** written about
in pasta and spinning **INVENTION** any more than he
as **ARE A RECENT MYTHICAL** already has
the **TOWN SHE IMAGINES MOVIES** been by the
astronomer **IN THE PROVINCIAL** government
dressed **OF COURSE** the astronomer departs

Of course, in the provincial town Molly imagines, movies are a recent, mythical invention, and no film distributor is going to risk a print on a city [colorful local expression for crazy] enough to set off fireworks every night, so they're going to have to make their own movie to show. Luckily, the Astronomer's girlfriend (whose initials, interestingly enough are, M.E.) has a grandfather with his own cylindrical trap for light: a camera that sits on a little wooden cart because it is too cumbersome to carry by hand. They take it out into the wilderness where the child in the sky can whisper directions to them from beyond the circle of torchlight used to illuminate the amateur actors--they trust that since he is young, he will know what excites the young.

In the cosmos at large, the enduring popularity of *The Tragedy Of The Twins Stella and Blackholio* makes The Bard's crossed up lovers seem like a baby's surprised burp--many a shooting star has been shed about it (Sorry)--but in this terrestrial town, no one is exactly getting on their quote horses about her heroes' new movie adaptation, which is mostly the mother dressed in pasta and spinning as the astronomer dressed in black slurps the lengthy strands off of her. Roscoe similarly doesn't take to what he's being offered--he says government surveillance agents have already written enough about him, and so The Astronomer also departs to--I don't know--work for a non-profit in the big city.

them**FEW WOULD OWN**balling
out here in **CARS SINCE SHE RECKONED**up
the provinces**IN THE SHAPE OF** the story
but his mother's **BOOTHES** herself after killing
entire planet **BUILD LITTLE** off the mother
was no bigger **IN THEATER AND THEN**and
to him than a**A DRIVE**the great
marble**TO BUILD** mother in
and as he**THAT THEY'D ALSO HAD**one
marvels at the**EXPENSE GIVEN** sentence but an idea
bursted **SO GREAT AN** comes to
blossom**AFTER** her
of a nebula **SO POORLY**she squeezes the earth
for one of his **RECEIVED**frm the sun & reinvents
seconds the**MOVIE HAD BEEN**life there to the
planet quietly died **BAD THAT HIS** degree to which
out for **SPEED HE FEELS**she understands
want**AT RIDICULOUS** it except
of some triffling **OTHERS** for earwigs cause they're
mineral that was **AWAY FROM THE** gross
plentiful**STAR IN HIM SCREAMS** the need is
on the other side of**LONGER AS EACH**dire but not
the sealed **GROWS** yet deadly and he sees the
portal and anyway **THAT**planet scorned by
its sun **STRIDE OF THE BOY** his rampage
had swallowed **BESIDE THE IMMENSE** in
the body **HERSELF ROLLING** the hand
like**TO ROSCOE AND FINDS** of another
a baby **GOODNIGHT** celestial
hamster she feels like **SHE SAYS**giant

Molly says goodnight to Roscoe and finds herself rolling beside the celestial boy's immense stride that grows longer as each star in him screams away from the others at ridiculous speed. Molly's starboy feels bad that the movie he dictated had screwed up his mother's mission after so great an expense, given that they'd also had to build the town a drive-in theater and then build little booths in the shape of cars (since Molly reckoned few cars would have made it out this far into the provinces yet), but to him, his mother's entire planet was no bigger than a marble, and as he marvels at the bursted blossom of a nebula for one of his seconds, Earth quietly dies out for want of some trifling mineral that is plentiful on the other side of the sealed portal, and anyway, its sun swallows its now lightless body like a baby hamster.

Molly feels a little like balling up her story and swallowing it herself--she's killed off the mother and The Great Mother in one sentence--but an idea comes to her, and she squeezes the Earth back out from the sun and reinvents life there to the degree to which she understands it (except for earwigs, 'cause they're gross). The Earth's mineral need is now dire but not yet deadly, and the boy sees orbiting around a star in the hand of another celestial personage that brimming other planet (H8R) that he had scorned by his tantrum.

constantly expanding **BALLROOM IS** nothing but mayB it'll
and suddenly **SLOW WHEN THE** just miss
she doesn't **IMPOSSIBLY** and send them
know if she wants to sign **IS** wheeling
off with **SUCH MOVEMENT** together like dancrs
such **BUT** out onto
a conventional **WAY DUH** the terrace
instution even as it is **MILKY** where we are
expanding **CENTER OF THE** too
itself **HOLE IN THE** polite to follow and
so instead he thinks **BLACK** Bob's your
his thumb **THROUGH THE SUPERMASSIVE** uncle
small **PASS** inspired
and accurate which **IT'LL JUST** by the
can only **FINGER DON'T WORRY** spirit
be done by **PERSON'S** of
extending one's **STAR** free play and
tongue **ON THAT OTHER** reconciliation she
and flicks our **KNUCKLE** decides to show the
solar system out of **THE BRIMMING** story to
the galaxy towards **IT TOWARD** Robin before sending
its counterpart **AND GUIDES** it out
and solution **OF OUR GALAXY** she figures
now you **UP THE RING** she'll contact
and I **PICKS** her old friend
know **STOOPS AND CAREFULLY** from
that smashing **MAN** the best seller
planets together at **A STAR** list who is having her
high **BOY WHO IS NOW** 50th
speed solves **THE STAR** birthday party

He stoops and carefully picks up the ring of our galaxy and guides it toward the other star-walker's cosmic knuckle (don't worry: that giant finger will just pass through the supermassive black hole in the center of the Milky Way, duh), but such movement is impossibly slow when the ballroom is constantly expanding, and suddenly Molly doesn't know if she wants to end her story so conventionally (even as the institution is itself expanding as she composes that and I write this), so instead, the boy wills his thumb small and accurate (which can only be done by extending one's tongue out of the corner of one's mouth, natch) and flicks our solar system out of the galaxy toward its counterpart and solution. Now, you and I know that smashing planets together at high speed solves nothing, but maybe it'll just be a near miss that sends them wheeling off together like dancers out onto the terrace where we are too polite to follow . . . and Bob's your uncle!

    Snifflingly inspired by the spirit of free play and reconciliation in her own story, Molly decides to show it to the real life mother before sending it out into the world (which will, of course, instantly publish it and revise reality to her dictates), but how is she going to find Robin? She figures that Romeo might know if anyone would, and his aunt is Molly's old pal from the best-seller list who just happens to be having her 50th birthday party tomorrow night . . .

which is **PHONE** for the
full **CORNER BY STARING AT HIS** rest of
of **CAN GET IN A** the
saccharine **CHRISTMAS** week
people **AS** Cray puts up with
kissing **HIMSELF LONELY** it he feels
people **AND THEN AFTERWARD MAKING** rusty and
they love w/o doubts **AND YELLS** as practical
or fears **OVER THE YELPS** a gallery
of trading **YELLING** as a phone
away a golden **BOTTOMS AND** as full
retriever for a white **PINCHING** of pinching and
elephant **INTO BAD THINGS LIKE** flicking
everyone **AND GETTING** as a middle school
tolerates **A CRAB** when she finally corners
him **BUT HE ARRIVED AS** Romeo
because **BIRTHDAY PARTY HERE** and
he's on the charts **HAD HIS** convinces him
again with **TIME THAT KID** that he knows
a song called Let Us Take **THAT** her from
A Sunburn **CALLED REMEMBER** that party
that he **HAVING A SHOW** he
playd on a late nite show **WHICH IS** threw he says he
and the **GIRL'S GALLERY** hasn't seen her
host **AT THE BIRTHDAY** since he
used a clip **WHICH IS** stopped her from
of his tossed away **AT THE PARTY** throwing the
yelp **IS** race for a new teaching
as **HOPED ROMEO** gig by having
a punchline **AS MOLLY** one more b4 proofing

And Romeo is there, and it is at the birthday girl's gallery, which is in the process of setting up a show called "Remember That Time That Kid Had His Birthday Party Here?" but Ro was already crabby when he arrived and immediately got into bad things like pinching bottoms and yelling over the yelps and yells and then afterward making himself "lonely as christmas can get" in a corner by staring at his phone that is hatefully full of saccharine people kissing people they love without doubts or fears of trading away a golden retriever for a white elephant. Everyone here tolerates him because he's on the record charts again with a song called "Let Us Take A Sunburn" that he played on a late night show and whose tossed-away yelp the host has been using as punctuation for the rest of the week. Cray puts up with his boyfriend's handsy-ness because he feels rusty and as practical a gallery as a phone as full of pinching and flicking.

When Molly finally corners Romeo and manages to convince him that he knows her from that party he threw where unknown people apparently had sex in his self-driving car, he says he hasn't seen Robin since she abruptly ended their night when he tried to stop her from throwing a job race by having "one more" before proofreading her cover-letter.

HINT:
Romeo's so drunk he's acting like he's among the columns of Page 037

drawn**PAPER** techniques
by some**PRINTER**to spot
kid who once had **COMICS ON** bluffs with
a birthday at **A BUNCH OF PENCIL** the thought
the gallery **SHOW THEY'RE** that he may one
and said he was **NEXT MONTH'S** day be
no longer **FOR**a great gambler but she's not
her friend**CONSIDERING** a challenge
but just sent her **SOME ART SHE'S** because
these along with **HER** she
a letter saying **ASIDE TO SHOW** keeps
he'd realized she **HER** checking the card that
could do**HOST WHO PULLS** lists the order of
nothing further to pierce**INTO THE** hands when she's got
his worm **EXIT SHE RUNS** something like the
hide on **THE BACK** pickpocket's
the first page he draws **AND THEN** prey feeling
himself feeding**THE BATHROOM** their lump on
his pet **WAY TOWARD** page 2 he talks about
spider**ON HER** seeing a news
from his **GUTS ARE BURBLING** report from the
plate at his aunt's **BY SAYING HER** olympic
and how they looked at **ROMEO**pool that Miranda
him like a dirty joke**AND BOOZE** Story of Upsend
written **OF SWEAT** Downs had coached
in excrement **OF THAT CHAMELEON**the synchronized
in the afternoon **GRIP** swimming team to
he joins her in not **OF THE BRACELET** the gold and is
working & she begins **AT THE TAIL** in talks to take
to teach him her**SHE TEARS** over Prosperous Island

The information--or lack thereof--acquired, Molly tears at the tail of the bracelet grip of Romeo, that chameleon of sweat and booze, by saying her guts are burbling, which is an excuse he cannot possibly object to, since he's minutes away from it himself.

On her way toward the bathroom (and then the back exit), she runs into Leslie, who pulls her aside to show her some art that's going to be in the show. She grudgingly goes along and discovers a bunch of pencil comics on printer paper drawn by the kid she's been seeking! Leslie says that just today he'd sent her these along with a letter saying that she had slapped down his dream of having a box of his own, but he'd realized that she can do nothing further to pierce his worm hide. And it turns out he didn't even realize she was putting together this show about his birthday party!

On the first page of the comic, No is drawn feeding his pet spider from his plate at his aunt's house, but everyone looks at him like a dirty joke written in excrement. Then, in the next panel and afternoon, there he is joining his mother in not working, and she begins to teach him her techniques of spotting bluffs in poker with the thought that he may one day make them all rich by becoming a great gambler, not that her bluffs are much of a challenge when she keeps checking on the order of hands like a pickpocket's prey fingering the lump.

Leslie shuffles the pages, and on the second one, the kid is watching a news report from the Olympic pool about Miranda Story of Upsend Downs coaching the American synchronized swimming team to gold and considering assuming control over Prosperous Island.

HINT:
No's comic seems inspired by the columns of Pages 080 and 081

stories that lead **HIM GOD** his
him to ask what's so **TELLING** isn't
important about one **AUNT** as he swats
snuffed dude **WRITES OF HIS** as strategic
which swept her **WORM HE ALSO** as a chess player to
legs **DOESN'T NEED A** try
and now he's **COUNTER AND** to hit the
evaporating **ON THE** biters
his hands rather than touch **PEACH** before the bite his
on her glass **THAN A MATURE** mother begins to
screen **FRIENDS** train him to shave
again **GOT MORE FLITTING** the expanse
and open up **MAN WHO'S SUDDENLY** under
the **OVERBOARD BY THE QUIET** his smile in
blank **AFTER BEING CHUCKED** the lookin' glas
spaces that **PADDLE** so he won't
consolidate **TO DOG** look
to staring **THE WILL** like a dirtbag
eyes **STRUGGLING TO FIND** the question
he talks about **HIS OWN MOTHER IS** he asks her is Y
making the horse **DEEP AND** his uncle has a
raddish face at **THE MONSTERS OF THE** sign featuring
the Voynich Manuscript **FINGER TO** a heavy
night while **THE LONG** poncho on
his mom sips **OCCURRENCES THAT GIVE** his restaurant
a lambic that was old as **THE SEA** and she says he'll outlive
a teenage **MOM IS** such things and he has to
soldier on th 3rd **WEIRD THAT ROMEO'S** pop her
page he **SAYS THAT HE FELT** lightly cause she
says that sleep is **HIS COMIC** holds on too long

Trying not to let his thoughts show on his face, the kid in the comic bubbles his ambivalence about Romeo's mother being a sea occurrence that gives the long finger to the monsters of the deep while his own mother is struggling to find the will to play the dog in the pool--she's been chucked overboard by that quiet man who suddenly got more flitting friends than a mature peach on the counter and thus didn't need a worm. Next his aunt is telling him so many God stories that he asks, "What's so important about one snuffed dude?" and that sweeps her legs, so then he's evaporating his hands rather than touch on her glass screen again for fear of opening up the blank spaces that will consolidate into staring eyes. Then he's making the horseradish face at the Voynich Manuscript night while his mom sips on her fifth lambic as old as a teenage soldier.

On page 3, the caption says that sleep "is his isn't" and he is shown swatting himself as strategically as a chess player as he aims to hit the biters before the bite. Then his mother is training him to shave the expanse under his smile in the looking glass (another thing where she's outside of her own experience) so he won't look like a dirtbag. In the middle of the operation, he asks her why his uncle's restaurant has a sign featuring a guy in a heavy poncho, and she tells him he'll outlive such things, and he eventually has to pop her lightly on the arm because she's holding on for too long.

HINT:
This page draws from the columns of Pages 081 and 82

that is tied**ELSE** to a new school
to starmaps obviously **EVERYTHING** with
Molly pauses**AND A SCARF** a
here**INSTEAD A TELESCOPE** fake
feeling**GIVES HIM** name which is
spooked**BALLOONS BUT** Beef
as if she had**TIME SHE'LL FIND** N
written the next **THAT NEXT** Trouble she loves
morning's**PROMISES**Achewood but
headlines in her **AGAIN AND SHE** won't let him read
curses**IS HIS BIRTHDAY**it
but she has to at least **STUFF IT** yet he draws himself
get **HIMSELF HOW IS THAT THE** trudging
2 the bottom of **BOTTLES AND HE ASKS**lonely after
the page **A RANGE OF** spending
his mother **DARKNESS AS SHE UNPACKS** so much
finds the **FUTURE**time
empty **ABOUT HER** with
bottles in his room **HE WONDERS** her and suddenly he
but he explains**AT HIM BUT SOON** is the mother food
that he poured **CRITICISMS LEVELED** for surrounding
them out and plans **TO FACE ANY** animals
to do**AND DETERMINED**& arrives @school
the same**SWALLOWS RENEWED**as
to any others that **THE**naked as
she buys **CARESSES** a Greased
and she says little **THE SPRING**Hero Molly promises
star you'll never be **BEFORE** to pin
me and**THEY LEAVE**him to her
she sends him**IN THE NEXT PANEL** book

Then suddenly, they're leaving the aunt's house before Spring can caress the swallows, renewed and determined to face the terrestrial haters, but soon he is wondering about his mother's future darkness while she unpacks a litany of bottles with the care usually reserved for devotional statues, and in his mind he asks, "How is *that* the stuff?!" On his birthday, she promises that next year she'll find balloons, but gives him instead a telescope and a scarf and "everything else that is tied to star maps"--

Obviously, Molly pauses here, feeling as spooked as if she authored the next morning's headlines with curses, but she feels like she has to at least get to the bottom of the page.

In the next panel, his mother finds the bottles empty in his room, but he calmly tells her that he poured them out and plans to do the same to any others that she buys, and she tearfully says, "Little star, you'll never be me." Next he's trudging off through a forest carrying the fake name "Beef N. Trouble" (his mom loves Achewood but won't let him read it yet) toward his new school, a little lonely after spending so much time with just his mom (and Aunt Danielle LaRusso and Uncle Radish Face) but suddenly he is the "mother food" for surrounding woodland creatures and arrives at the school as naked as a greased hero.

Seeing this, Molly vows that she *will* pin him to her book.

LET'S CALL THIS CHAPTER "She begins at the tail, or 'the ballad of Baby Goodnight'"

HINT:
No's comic draws from the columns of Page 082

who means what to whom after Chapter 5

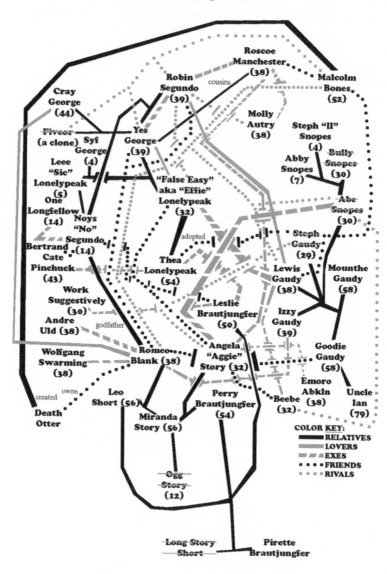

Roscoe Manchester (38)

Malcolm Bones (52)

Robin Segundo (39)

cousins

Molly Autry (38)

Steph "II" Snopes (4)

Cray George (44)

Fiveor (a clone)

Syf George (4)

Yes George (39)

Abby Snopes (7)

Bully Snopes (30)

Leee "Sic" Lonelypeak (5)

"False Easy" aka "Effie" Lonelypeak (32)

Abe Snopes (30)

One Longfellow (14)

Noys "No" Segundo (14)

adopted

Steph Gaudy (29)

Bertrand Cate Pinchuck (43)

Thea Lonelypeak (54)

Lewis Gaudy (38)

Mounthe Gaudy (58)

Work Suggestively (30)

Leslie Brautjungfer (50)

Izzy Gaudy (39)

Andre Uld (38)

godfather

Romeo Blank (38)

Angela "Aggie" Story (32)

Goodie Gaudy (58)

Wolfgang Swarming (38)

Leo Short (56)

Perry Brautjungfer (54)

Emoro Abkln (38)

Beebe (32)

Uncle Ian (79)

created   owns

Death Otter

Miranda Story (56)

COLOR KEY:
— RELATIVES
— LOVERS
═ ═ EXES
• • • • FRIENDS
∙ ∙ ∙ ∙ RIVALS

Ogg Story (12)

Long Story Short

Pirette Brautjungfer

Chapter 6

of Jesus' **LID** in the car accident if he is

Son**BY THE** suffering

The Boardgame **MINIMUM SUGGESTED** memories they

and she's already rolling**THAN THE** do not show

her own **YOUNGER** on the inhospitable

dice does she have the**YEAR** sands of his

goods from the seat **WHICH IS A** Schrodinger's

to her **SEVEN** catbox

left I flip **BREAK SHE'S ONLY** face only a

a coin and**HER A** grunt as

she does **VIDEO HEY GIVE** meaningless as a

she **OF A BUFFERING** cloud

draws **THE FLUENCY** escapes

the epiphany**WITH** the laundromat

card but doesn't show **THE CARD** is where

anyone you're not **FROM** his roll takes

supposed**ABBY SNOPES READS** him she's not

to until you have **SPACE** callous she's just driving

enough for a**NEAREST HOSPITAL** the cue

book and you can **GO TO THE** ball

justify the **CARD OR ELSE** toward the nearest

contradictions to the**EPIPHANY** anything to see

other players **CHIP AND DRAW AN** somethin happen

the next**SUBSTANCE** she asks if he liked her

roll goes**AND A** thrown semi-truck

to her uncle **CARD** performance where she

& as he is jiggling**AN ACQUAINTANCE** ended up against

the dice she asks **SACRIFICE** the front

if he remembers **IN A CAR ACCIDENT** horn o up puttng

when they were**YOU ARE** amid a liquid bridge

Chapter 6

"You are in a car accident--sacrifice an acquaintance card and a substance chip and draw an epiphany card, or else go to the nearest hospital space," Abby Snopes reads from the card with the fluency of a buffering video. Hey, give her a break! She's only seven, which is a year younger than the minimum suggested by the lid of *Jesus' Son: The Boardgame,* and she's already rolling her own dice! Does she have the goods? From the seat to her left, I flip a coin, and she does. She draws the epiphany card but doesn't show anyone (just like you're supposed to until you have enough for a book and you can justify its contradictions to the other players.)

The next roll goes to her uncle Lewis, and as he is jiggling the dice, she asks him if he remembers when they were in an actual car accident together.

If he is suffering memories, they do not show on the inhospitable sands of his Schrodinger's catbox face. Only a grunt as meaningless as a cloud escapes him. He rolls and ends up at the laundromat.

She persists, asking if he liked her "thrown semi-truck performance where she ended up against the front horn of up putting amid a liquid bridge." I don't want you to think Abby is callous--she's just driving the cue ball toward the nearest anything to see something happen.

HINT:
Abby is remembering the columns of Page 053

who backed up **DOROTHY** and dragging
to **STAY THE** herself
get everyone **SAYS LET HIM** back
in the frame **BUT GRANDMA** to her recitations like
and stepped on **LEAVES** a skipping
Snail **FROM AUTUMN** needle
Hitler over the **HANDLE** she says that he pointing
line possibly **A RAKE** to her other uncle
Abby says **ABBY LIKE** sitting in her
she gets her **BLOOD COMES ZIPPING FROM** grandma's
wall **COMINGLED** lap is the cross
like nature **FROM** between a schlubby
from her **THAT HUMAN MEANS** scarecrow
Dad and her mashed **OLD CHESNUT** with
potato **THAT** accurate genitalia
consistency **TO WHICH** and a slumping
from her **FACE** sack his
Mom reading **THE FAMILY** name is
the ingredients **SKILLS TO** Moog and he
from **IT WITH MOUSE** is one
memory **WRECK AND REATTACHED** year
but she realizs w the scream **CAR** old the result
of breaks **FACE OF THE** of the time
that she's also **NOSE OFF THE** someone put
a photoshopper **HER** too much folic
who doesn't want **THAT GOT** acid in Grandma's
to lay an **UNCLE** smoothie
actual finger **THAT IT WAS HER** at
on the goopy **GRANDMA REMINDS HER** the
stuff clicking **ABBY'S** gym

Her grandma, a little irritated at having just landed on a
"relapse" space, warns her to be nice, reminding her that it was her
uncle that got her nose out of the car wreck and reattached it with
mouse skills to the family face.

Like a rake handle from autumn leaves, Abby feels that old
chestnut that "human means from commingled blood" coming
zipping up from her lungs unbidden, but her Grandma knows that
look and quickly says, "Don't dip the dream of the Dorothy who
backed up to get everyone in frame and stepped on Snail Hitler!"
(In poor taste? Possibly.) With a half-sized laugh, Mounthe tells
the girl for the millionth time that she's as wall-like as her dad was
and as mashed a potato as her mom.

With a yelp of breaks, Abby protests that she's *also* a
photoshopper who won't lay an actual finger on anything goopy.
Then taking a breath, she clicks and drags herself like a skipping
needle back to the comfort of the dog-eared family script, pointing
to her other uncle sitting in her grandma's lap and saying that *he* is
the cross between a slumping sack and a schlubby scarecrow with
accurate genitalia. The uncle's name is Moog, and he is one year
old, the result of the time someone put too much folic acid in
Grandma's smoothie at the gym (at least that's what they told Abby).

HINT:
If you're looking for chestnuts, there's a sale in the columns of Page 053

by Flip**A SONG** alone and gave

Tails **SING** the claw

former **BUT THE CHILD BEGINS TO** side to the

leader of **NO** other

Hoops **WHICH IS TO SAY THE IRISH** instruments

Dolphin that**HARP** Abby says Romeo is

fractious **COIN SAYS** visiting

indie trio from**THEN MY** his

Grandpa's **HALF RIGHT** God

youth and he says**PERFECTLY IN** son secretly

Romeo a common**BREAK** at school using a tween

topic of conversation**SHE** suit which he climbs

in this house**DOES** into it's an

is producing **SENSITIVE** extremely

Flip's **SOUND** tight

newest**HALF** fit and hangs

record and had **BONE AND** out

him down there to**WISH** at lunch she

provide some**ARTIFICIAL** knows this

guitars **FLUBBED** because she reads a

til he woke up from the **FACTORY**comic the

pacifying**LAP ARE HALF** God

dreams of**AUNT'S** son draws about his

his**FOUR SITTING ON HER** life and

boyfriend **AGED** distributes anonymously

and started **STEPH** to the kids via their

thinking that**HER SISTER** cell phones in

every nail **SAYS POINTING AT** messages that

should**SHE**evaporate before adults can

be **AND YOU** have an opinion

"And you," she says pointing at her little sister Steph II, aged 4 and sitting on her aunt Izzy's lap, "are half sound-sensitive device and half factory-flubbed artificial wishbone!"

Does this other little girl break perfectly in half right then? My coin says, "Harp!" which is to say "The Irish No," but she does begin to sing a song by Flip Tails, former leader of Hoops Dolphin, the indie trio that Grandpa still puts on all the time.

While playing his "sixty-dollar Chevrolet" card, Goodie says that Romeo is actually producing Flip's new record and finally called him in to add some guitar, only to then suddenly wake from the pacifying dream of his boyfriend and start thinking that every nail should be alone, so his sweet licks were given the claw side!

Abby counters by laying down her own Romeo news: he has been secretly visiting his godson at jr. high school using a clammy "tween suit" that he crams himself into, and they've been hanging out during lunchtimes! She knows this because all the kids have been reading a comic that No draws about his own life that digitally-evaporates before any grown up can have an opinion about it. He doesn't sign his name, but even elementary school kids know the author is The Boy Who Was Huge And Now Is Just Big.

never **STUMPED** shore unless you
mind that his **LIFE LEAVE HER** want to get
comics are **TESTS OF** put on a
all about **THE SPELLING** list
feeling **MILES WHILE** pausing
adrift with**OUT FOR** at the door
only **GO** I tell
the most provisional **RIDE TRACKS** them that shes not the
reeds to clutch**MICROSCOPE** only
she will **HOW DOES HIS SANGUINE** one who
use Romeo's **BY WHICH SHE MEANS** wants to find
suit to infiltrate **THAN SHE HAS** him
the **MORE DIMENSIONS** Molly the famous
junior high school **OCCUPIES** best seller
I **KNOW HOW HE** wants to
say **HE DOES BUT SHE'D LIKE TO** ride
out loud **OF COURSE YOU KNOW** his story
surprising**A SISTER AND** back up
myself and **SISTER MAYBE HE HAS** the charts she
everyone**HER LITTLE** puts all of
else I sit **CRAZED LIKE** her facial features back
down **SHE'S PRINCE** on including extras
embarrassed **HIM NOT BECAUSE** to convince
and without further **WANTS TO MEET** the principal she's
ideas **OFF PLACE BUT SHE** researchin school
of how she will get **FENCED** plagiarism her
it it's not **ITS OWN** methods is not
the sorta thing u leave **SCHOOL IS** subtle stilts
drying **HIM THE MIDDLE** and downward
on a rocky **SHE DOESN'T KNOW** periscope

She badly wants to meet him, not because she's prince-crazed like Steph II (though Abby does idly wonder if No has a sister--and of course *you* know he actually does!) but she'd like to know how he "rules over more dimensions than she even has." The problem is that junior high schools don't just let random little kids wander around looking for their idols during school hours. How will she get to ask him how his sanguine microscope-ride-tracks can go out for miles while the spelling test of her life leaves her stumped like the man named Bob? (Never mind that all No's comics are about feeling adrift with only the most sketched-out reeds on the bank to clutch.)

Aunt Izzy is holding-up play because she's clearly forgotten the rules of the board game, but she still knows how the family's "Romeo-centric" one works--she says that he's not the only jr. high infiltrator: a middle-schooler on a cartoon message board she frequents was complaining about some lady who clacks about classrooms on stilts with a downward periscope as the children work. The principal had announced over the P.A. that this lady was just researching for a book about school plagiarism, but she apparently only pays attention to the kids' doodles--the principal was probably just impressed by how many facial features she had (again).

"Abby will use Romeo's suit to infiltrate the junior high school and meet No," I blurt out, surprising myself and everyone else. Embarrassed and without further ideas of how she will get her hands on the suit--it's not the sort thing you leave drying on a rocky shore unless you want to get put on a federal watch list--I put the lampshade on my head and leave.

old **38 YEAR**providing the
who already **THINKS THE PRINTED** soundtrack a
hard **WIZARD BLOO HOO HOO** recording of
brushed the gums**AS THE** course
of uncoolness **SON ROMEO**playing the toucan
back to**HER** along fading
40 **POOLS AND IT STARS** trails
and now has to start**FOREIGN** of routine
training **THOSE MEDALS FROM** across
the troops **AMERICA ALL** tiles
to make their **COACH WHO BROUGHT** the last
stand**ENTREPRENEUR TURNED** aunt
at fort **THE** volunteers to take the
45 it also features his **STORY**girls to see the
Mother's **MIRANDA**spectacle like
protegee**THE MIND OF** me she's probably
Wolves **THE TEMPEST** thinking of
Swarming**ADAPTATION OF** mobiles
aka**A SYNCSPEARE** and their
the uncashed **THE NOSE** flaring
bookmark **ON** shadows on
check **AN ADVERTISEMENT FOR** the bedroom
that slipped **THE GAME ONE IS** ceiling rather than
out when you were**EVEN FROM**flailing
flipping**EVERYONE THAT THEY'RE NOT**mannequin
pages manning the **TABLE AND TELLS** limbs failing to
deus-ex-machina**ON THE** stay on the
crane above **CARDS I LEFT** surface she ignores
him and Flip**UP THE** the candles for the cake's
Tails **ABBY PICKS** glow

Abby picks up the cards I left on the table and tells everyone that they're not even from the game. One is an advertisement for *On The Nose: A Sync-Speare Adaptation of The Tempest from the mind of Miranda Story*, that entrepreneur turned coach who brought America all those medals from the depths of foreign pools. Plus, it stars her son Romeo as the Wizard! (Bloo Hoo Hoo seems to think that printed, squinting 38 year-old who already had to hard-brush the gums of uncoolness back to 40, and now has to start training the troops to make their stand at fort 45?!) Even more unexpected, it features his mother's protégée Wolfgang Swarming (aka the uncashed-check bookmark that slipped out when Ro was flipping pages) on the deus-ex-machina above the wizard. The soundtrack will be provided by Ro's old tour-mate Flip Tails (via recording, of course).

Playing the toucan along fading trails of routine across tiles, Aunt Izzy volunteers to take the girls to see the synchronized swimming spectacle; like me, she's probably thinking of a baby mobile (and its flaring shadow on the bedroom ceiling in an experiment's falsified memory) rather than flailing mannequin limbs failing to stay on the surface. (After all, she *does* tend to ignore the candles for the cake's glow.)

the tail **BORROWING AS** for a puppet
to feed the **NON-CONSENTUAL** of the wizard's
cat **TO SEE A LITTLE** elemental
I recognize that **DEMOGRAPHIC** servant who
some have **THE PRIME** defies
the coyote's **STUDENT SHE IS** aging and
anguish **A STUMPED** gender
though it often only howls **AS** the little girl
when caught **BE AND** will
in the searchlight **SHE MIGHT** point and say
so fine **BUT YOUNG ENOUGH TO THINK** prince
I guess **A FICTIONAL CHARACTER** and the aunt
she does **KNOW SHE IS** will
bring **7 IS TOO YOUNG TO** think she is
an outlandish **ABBY AGED** pointing to
intent to steal **NEWS** Romeo and agree
with her **ON THE EVENING** wondering how
to the performance like **UP** he has been
a brittle **TO END** the drifting
condom **OR BOUND** blood
in a teenager's **SHOW** foam to her
wallet I have **A TV** sea
filed the **THING ARE ON** mine
goal **A SPECIFIC** chain but the child
posts **INTENT TO STEAL** is as adamant as
down **TO A PLACE WITH AN** middle finger
a little by convincing them to **GO** she
use **MOST PEOPLE WHO** needs no cookies
Romeo's uncanny **SAY** stored higher than the
suit **I WOULD** counter

The next night, I tag along in Izzy's car because I'm not sure yet how much Abby sees this trip as a chance to get that suit. Generally, I would say that most people who go to a place with an intent to steal a specific thing are either on a sitcom or bound to end up on the evening news, but Abby is too young to know she is a fictional character but also young enough to think that she might be, and as a stumped student she is the prime demographic to see a little non-consensual borrowing as the lizard's tail to feed the cat. (I mean, I do recognize that some plagiarists have the coyote's anguish, though it often only howls in the gleam of the searchlight.) Fine, I guess she does bring an outlandish intent with her like a brittle condom in a teenager's wallet. I lean over and tell her that Miranda has convinced her son to allow his uncanny tween suit to be used as a puppet stand-in for The Wizard's ageless and genderless elemental servant.

Nothing worth mentioning between leaving their seats in the car and finding those in the stadium--except the outrageous mark-up even when you print out your own ticket, am I right?--but in the second scene of the aquatic extravaganza, Abby's sister points and cries out, "Prince!" and Aunt Izzy thinks she is pointing at Romeo and agrees, wondering at how he has been the drifting blood foam to her sea mine chain. The littlest girl is adamant as a middle finger, though, that she means the lanky suit--she needs no cookies stored higher than the countertop!

up **AND MAY END** her singular
a foiled **BLITHE PARADE** worming sleeping
burst **INTO THE** bag style
bag of **STEP BACK** out of
chips by **THEIR** more
the curb **CAN'T FIND** worldly limbs
by early evening **SOME PEOPLE** like chatterin monkey
that **I CAN'T RECALL** fingers that
would be **HEAD** spin
maudlin if I wasn't **A CINEMATIC** objects and
thinking about **RAZOR ON** the whole body around
myself which of **THE DISPOSABLE** limbs
course makes **SITCOM JUST LIKE** the quarter
it even **SNEERING** moon honored
moreso **BY EVERY** but
but she's **PREDICTED** never to be
a priest who **PLACES** examined that
is in on the **SNAP IN THE** starts
break **PEOPLE DO** her
out **OTHERS STILL SOME** game
plan so she's not **OF** in
going to break **THE ACTIONS** pixel
after the criminal **NOT BE DEFINED BY** explosions
was **NEED** is
boosted **THE DICE BUT SHE** wonder
out **THOUGH IT WAS PARTIALLY** at
the stained **ROMEO DID** the oneness of
glass **HER AS MUCH AS** the world
window **I ABANDONED** her dad drove hr thru
she went back **IN TRUTH** tunnels to shut baby up

Izzy doesn't dwell very long on when Romeo repaired his confidence years earlier using the parts she had offered for the purpose--she's the priest who is in on the break-out plans! She's not going to crumple after the criminal was boosted out the stained glass window! I'm the one who's hung up on it because I feel like I abandoned her, too. After Romeo blew her off, she did do some worming as if to escape a stuck sleeping-bag, but what she escaped were worldly limbs that had been like chattering monkey-fingers that spin objects--and the whole body in an arc around the limbs of trees! Just a glimpse over the stadium edge tonight of the quarter moon (honored but never examined) starts her game in pixel explosions of wonder at the oneness of the world--her eyes are as wide as the baby's in the tunnel in the video I just saw.

to help as he is **GOING** a
lecturing **253 IS NOT** bag full of
his **IT AS MUCH AS** bills for
one subject **SKEPTICS PUT** appreciable objects
who is forced to **CITY THOUGH SOME** was better
deliver **SISTER** left at
every line **THE FOUNDING OF** the airport if
under **THE 100TH ANNIVERSARY OF** the pen is
the water **ON THIS** mine to wield
so that less **IN THE** the same
conceptual patrons **EYE** performances
can complain **IN FRONT OF EVERY** daily
about his **SUSPENDED** wears the
annunciation the oil **A WIZARD** sun
of his attention is **PLAYING** out when he feels
wicking **OVER THAT AND** he must chase
up **IF HE EVER GOT** the cock that chases
his own **SURE** the retreating
string how **I'M NOT** moonwalk
did the pressure **INTO THE TELEVISION** of night
that held the **PUPPETS** but now they're
steam **WHO SUMMONS THE** all
between the **CHILD** over each other like the
iron **WAY OF THE** rooster
and the **NARCISSISTIC** on the hot
pleat **IN THE MORE** sauce he wonders
abate again **FATALISTIC THOUGH** if
I was **RATHER** he has a
immoderate cleaner **WAS ONCE** that can only be
who thought that **ROMEO ALSO** flipped at random

In the center of the stadium, Romeo dangles from a crane in grizzled wizard garb like bait. He was also was once rather fatalistic, though more in the way of a child who believes that he has summoned the puppets into the television frame (not that he ever totally got over that, and playing a wizard on the 100th anniversary of the founding of Sister City [though some skeptics put its age as 253!] is probably not going to help with his humility). Peering into the water below, the Wizard-king spies his only subject (whose actor is forced to deliver every line under the water so that less conceptual patrons can complain about his annunciation) and begins to berate him, but in actuality, the oil of his attention is wicking up his own string to his hunky puppeteer ex, asking, "How did we lose the pressure that held the steam between the iron and the pleat?!" (Again, I'm partially to blame--I was the immoderate cleaner who thought that a bag full of bills for appreciable objects was better left at the airport.) Perhaps he's forgetting that the same performances daily wore the sun out when he felt he must chase the cock that chases the moonwalk of night, but since he and Wolves have been reunited, they've been all over each other like the rooster on the hot sauce! Romeo wonders if his own back has a switch that can only be flipped at random.

ending**HER TIME UNTIL THE** 60s
where**BY BIDING** but
the ethereal **AS IT SWINGS** if that's
servant is made a **PUPPET** so she is quite
real human**LEAP INTO THE** early or she could
boy **ATTEMPT TO** just ask Romeo to
or given leave to**READ SHE MAY** borrow it if she
dissolve**WELL** is
its human form**AND** hella
back into **BOLD** boring she is
abstract **PLAN YET IF SHE IS** stumped
nature and she can steal**ME THE** she is not
off to the confetti **GIRL HASN'T TOLD** a hand as a video
of amazed**THE** she is not much of
murmurs **IT OUT SPEAKIN OF** a reader she'll be
about the state of **YOU WHEN I FIGURE** boring as
technology if **I WILL TELL** a pneumatic
she is not **SOMETHING** drill
frankly**WHOSE NAME IS** hell I could have
insane **GIRLFRIEND** read that in the
she may wait curled in **NEW** mashed potatoes
its trunk like a hand**AND HIS** images that I would have
in a jewlry **AND UNCLE** used to describe her
case**AND SISTER** aloft flail
posing as a**AUNT** and fade like
watch**TO SNEAK AWAY FROM HER** movies told
stand in **COVER** across a
a slapstick**ABBY WITH THE PERFECT** pillow
heist **INTROSPECTION PROVIDES** to an
movie from**ALL THIS** angel

The real reason, dear reader, for all this introspection is to provide Abby with the cover she needs to sneak away from her aunt and sister . . . and uncle and his new girlfriend whose name is . . . something I will tell you when I figure it out. Speaking of needing to figure things out, Abby hasn't told me the plan yet. If she is bold and well-read, she may attempt to leap from a railing into the open back of the puppet as it swings by, then bide her time until the ending where the ethereal servant is turned into a real human boy (or given leave to dissolve its form back into the abstracted nature featured in high school poems) so that she can steal off to the confetti of amazed murmurs about the state of puppet technology. If she is not frankly insane, she may wait curled in the puppet's storage trunk like a hand in a jewelry case posing as a watch-stand in a slapstick heist movie from the 60s, but if that's so, she's going to be waiting a long time in that trunk! Or she could just *ask* Romeo to borrow it! Hyeah, if she's hella boring! She is stumped, and since she's a video, she's not much of a reader. Sigh, I guess she'll be as boring as a pneumatic drill. (Hell, I could have read that in the mashed potatoes! The images that I could have used to describe her aloft flail and fade like movies told across a pillow to one of Denis Johnson's *Angels*.)

object could be **A HEAVY** pregnant Statue
dragged to Romeo's **IT** of
dressing **AND DID NOT FIND** Liberty asking
room leaving a deep **ONE** passersby where its
paint **TO A KID WHO SEARCHED FOR** children r
scratch **A LINE** out
in concrete **PISSER OR SUCH** of
a convoy **TO THE** bed
of banana **LINE THAT GOES** but no it is the
slugs could be **LIKE A YELLOW** trailing fin
headed toward **MAY STADIUMS HAVE** of the
a real elaborate **TOO** ornate
salad or else suicidally **SO SO** goldfish
addicted **DESTINATIONS** costume
to a lab concocted **PEOPLE TO** worn
salt **LINES GUIDING** by
that Romeo **COLORED** the
sprinkled **HOSPITALS SOMETIMES HAVE** magician's
as he walked **THING THAT COULD BE** daughter
and snacked **THE BEST** but the performer
or a student **PATH WHAT IS** went off
could have underlined **THE YELLOW** to find
a sentence **SHE'D BETTER FOLLOW** that other
so rich **THE WIZARD** line because peeing
in symbolism **IS GOING TO SEE** at the pool barbecue
not from **THE TRICKSTER IF THE GIRL** may be
this book **OF** forgivable but in
that they were **HEL LIKE THE DAUGHTER** synchronized
sure their teacher **IS** swimming no unless every1
would kick **THE GIRLFRIEND'S NAME** together

By the way, Lewis's girlfriend is named "Hel," like the trickster's daughter. If Abby is going to see The Wizard, she'd better follow the yellow path through the stadium corridors. What is the best thing that could be? Hospitals sometimes have colored lines guiding people to destinations, so, too, have many stadiums, like a yellow line that goes to the pisser (or such a line that leads to a kid who searched for one and failed). Then again, a heavy yellow object could have been dragged to Romeo's dressing room leaving a deep paint scratch in the concrete. Or a convoy of banana slugs could be headed towards a real elaborate salad in the VIP box or else maybe they'd be suicidally addicted to a lab-concocted salt that Romeo sprinkled as he walked and snaked. Or a student could have underlined a sentence so rich in symbolism (I'm not saying it's from *this* book) that they were sure their teacher would kick out of bed the-pregnant-Statue-of-Liberty-asking-passerbys-where-its-children -are. But no, the yellow line Abby ends up discovering is the trailing fin of the ornate goldfish costume worn by The Wizard's daughter--the performer who normally fills is off to find that other yellow line because spiking the pool at a backyard BBQ may be forgivable (if you're discreet--not that I'm saying I ever have!), but in synchronized swimming, it's forbidden unless everyone does it at the same time.

While the woman is grumbling in her stall about the budget cuts that has performers peeing in the public restrooms, Abby gingerly snatches the goldfish costume from off the door, swallows herself in it, and follows the wet trail back to the pool.

must think they **SWIMMERS** but gets a request in his
have found thr **PATCH AND THE OTHER** hands free
second **EYE** mic to have the magical
wave when it is **MEDAL AS HER** gopher as her
so much lighter **OLYMPIC** wedding
to lift her **WHO NOW WEARS AN** gift and what is
on their artificial **MOTHER** he going to
island **OF HIS** say in front
of limbs **SMIRK** of a stadium
than in practice **AND THE KNOWING** but yes
she ascends from **ROMEO** and then she steals
the surface **FACE OF** his fourth
like **THE CONSPITATED** wall screw
a mummy **SPRAWLED OUT BEFORE** driver by
pulling **YOUR CHARACTER** telling everyone to
free **THE POSTER WITH** lie
from **THE CURVES PROMISED BY** down &count
the other noodles **YOU LACK** 100 each imagining
in answer **NO ONE KNOWS** the amazing finale
to a truly clear **SQUID** they are
spiraling **AS THE HEART OF A** assembling
fork or a gesture from **PUBLIC** but will only b tragicomic
Romeo **TO THE GENERAL** subtracting I wondr
who **AS UNPLACEABLE** how many
seeks **IS** drugstore
a last **YOUR BODY** cowboys actually return
daughterly **ROBES** to see if people
peck **AND VOLUMINOUS** are still
at the play's **IN WATER** counting she
end **SWIMMING** doesn't

Lucky for her, when you're swimming in water and voluminous robes, your body is unplaceable to the general public as the heart of a squid; no one knows you lack the curves promised by the poster where your character sprawls out before the constipated face of Romeo and the knowing smirk of his mother (who now wears an Olympic medal as her eye patch). The other swimmers must think they have found their second wave (har har) when it is so much lighter to lift the Wizard's Daughter on their artificial island of limbs than in practice. Abby ascends from the surface like a mummy pulling free from the other noodles in answer to a truly-clear spiraling fork or a gesture from the Wizard who seeks a last daughterly peck at the play's end.

Instead of a smooch, though, Abby gives him a request into his hands-free mic to receive his magical gopher as her wedding gift! How is he supposed to refuse in front of a full stadium?! He grudgingly agrees, but then she also steals his fourth-wall screwdriver and brandishes the blunt tip at everyone in the audience, telling them to lie down and count to 100. Amazingly, the audience members comply, each imagining the gobsmacking finale the company must be assembling, but all they're going to get is a tragicomic withdrawal. (I wonder how many drugstore cowboys actually return to see if people are still counting? Abby doesn't. Does she return the goldfish suit? I think her Grandma's going to need to have a talk with her about borrowing things.)

an empty husk **JUST** what the girl is
devoid **IS** doing she's
of any **ALL BOYS** got all
emotions **LIKE** her
and equally **TO HER HE** namesake's
willing **NOT WORRY SINCE** spots including
to be **SHE NEED** the two
used by **HER AUNT THAT** toned
whoever is **WET SHE TELLS** face
there **HER HAIR GET** family
and moreover he **DID** full
belongs to **A RIDE AND HOW** of
a friend **GIVE HIM** monsters
of **UP AND WE'RE SUPPOSED TO** a job ruling
the family still **BE HELD** perpetually
she makes **AND HAS TO** chilly halls
them **SAY ANYTHING** of the dead rather
sit **WHO WILL NOT** than the elderly so
in the front with **AGE** I don't spell
her and I **TWICE HER** a bitter
who am obviously **BOY** alphabet
driving grammar **NIECE HAS MET A** soup I'll have
swoons from **YEAR OLD** to gum
the back seat **THAT HER SEVEN** down in
the trickster's **ALARMED** the future she
daughter who has **BUT EVEN SHE IS** stern she
seen every **GOOSEY** declares that the
trick like the magician's **LOOSEY** boy is just a
mirror **IS PRETTY** prop which somehow
immediately gets **THE AUNT** makes things less creepy

Aunt Izzy is pretty loosey-goosey in her babysitting--as in life--but even she is alarmed that her 7 year old niece has met at the stadium a boy twice her age who will not say anything and has to be held up--and she's supposed to give him a ride home?! And how did Abby's hair get wet?!

Abby simply tells her aunt that she need not worry, since to her, this boy, like all boys, is just an empty husk devoid of any emotions and equally willing to be used by whoever is there. Moreover, he belongs to a friend of the family. Still, Izzy makes them sit in the front with her and I (who am obviously driving, grammar swooning like my lane change).

From the back seat, the trickster's daughter--who, like a magician's mirror, has seen every trick--immediately gets what the girl is doing. Hel's got all her namesake's spots, including a two-toned face (Michael Jackson disease--too soon?), a family full of monsters, a job ruling perpetually chilly halls (of the dead rather than the elderly so I don't spell a bitter alphabet soup for later), and a stern disposition. She tells Izzy that the boy is not a human but an actual prop, which actually somehow makes things less creepy.

other **REALITIES OF** themselves
tribes in **THE** being
plain **HIDING FROM** tight
sight while pursuing **GAME IS** clothing by pretending
the most basic of **THE ONLY** each rude
bodily needs in the state **ONCE** interrogation
mandated **IT A PLAYGROUND** of a tree was
22 minutes **CALL** a pretense
of Erin's **HERE WE DON'T** to be
childhood n comics **AND NOW WE ARE** approached
No **GOING** to sell
and his secret **WHERE WE WERE** th drugs she'd been
godfather **READERS IDEAS THIS IS** warned
would meet **YOUNGER** about
by a tree **GIVING** by a dancing
that looked **TO BE ACCUSED OF** lightbulb
like an old **SOUP WOULDN'T WANT** with an empty
man but even as she tries **CHICKEN** stem
to cover up **BEING DROWNED IN** in an assembly
her awkward **SCHOOL AND** you're not
deer **BOTH GOING TO** in the usual
steps in **HER TO AVOID** spot says
the borrowed **THAT ALLOWED** an older
legs that feel **THE LIE** boy who is
all **GRANDMA AND** no older than she
the more exposed **THE SUIT FROM** looks turning she
for **THE HIDING OF** says she couldnt find
being tightly **PAST** the old
clothed **THE PLAYGROUND** man
and **LET'S SKIP TO** tree

Let's skip to the playground, past the hiding of the tween suit from Grandma and the lie that must have allowed her to avoid both going to school and being drowned in chicken broth. (Wouldn't want to be accused of corrupting the youth.) This is where we were going and now we are here. I guess we as a culture don't really call it a "playground" once its occupants are old enough that they're only playing at hiding in plain sight from the realities of other tribes while pursuing as many basic bodily needs as possible in the state-mandated 22 minutes that my fiancée describes having had in jr. highschool.

Now, in No's comics, he and his secret Godfather meet by a tree that looks like an old man, but even as Abby tries to cover up her awkward deer steps in the suit by pretending that each wrong tree she frankly feels up to avoid falling is a pretense to be approached to buy or sell what she'd been warned about in an assembly by a dancing lightbulb with an empty stem. She feels all the more exposed by the fact that the borrowed legs are tightly-clothed and themselves tight clothing.

"You're not in the usual spot," says an older boy who is no older than she looks.

Turning, she says that she couldn't find the old man tree.

like a glass **HER NAME** of the comic
slipper**APOLOGIZES FOR DROPPING**& she says
but it's **HER SURFACE HE** remembering
better **DO NOT REACH** her
than being the stepmother **THAT** resolution as I
who took **THE WAVES** just have to replicate
away the vacations to the**MIRROR** Romeo's
land where**HE SUDDENLY SEEMS TO** voice in her
you want the**NAME BUT**most wizardly
service **BY HIS CHARACTER'S** way that she is
to be full of **THE ACTOR** always the
sighs**JUST CALLED** first to
and **IF SHE ACTUALLY** draw the
glassy**WONDERS** flower and
rolling**AWAY SHE** press
eyes **FALL** it
she says**NOT ACTUALLY**for
that**DOES** a charm
it's a good way to keep**THAT**to wear like a turning
the Romeo **CHICKEN SKIN** swimmer's
name**IT AND THE** kick to
off **BODY BETWEEN** the wall she
Twitter **ALONG HER** flees her
with who**SLIPS ALL** inability to parse
the F **OF A REVELATION** fact
is next **BLADE** and
award**AND AS THE COOL**fiction
show**ABOUT THE TREE** by inducing
he asks how **SHE KNOWS**him to sheepishly
she learned **HE ASKS HOW**shear wooly flurishes

No asks how she knows about the tree, and as the cool blade of a revelation slips all along her body between it and the chicken skin that does not actually fall away, she wonders if she actually just called the actor by his character's name, but No suddenly seems to mirror the waves that do not reach her surface: he apologizes for dropping her name in his comic like a glass slipper, but says he couldn't stand to be a stepmother who took away vacations to the land where you want the service to be full of sighs and glassy rolling eyes.

She says that the comic cameo is actually a good way to keep the Romeo name from being matched with "who the F is" on Twitter (again) next time there's an awards show.

No asks how she learned of the comic, and remembering her resolution (as I just have) to replicate Romeo's voice, she says in her most wizardly way that she is always the first to pick a flower and press it for a charm. (My gloss on the interaction: with a turning swimmer's kick to the wall, she's fleeing her inability to parse fact and fiction by making him sheepishly shear his wooly flourishes.)

with the bleeding **I WAS JUST ON** the
head **THE FLIGHT** day he was
phones the kid **ON** visting
felt **LIKE THE DUDE** them
the contempt **FOR FOUR HOURS** the baby
of the bro **BOBBING** seemed sewn
across **WAS NONSTOP** between
the aisle **BROTHER FEES** the adults'
but also the **SHOP HE SAYS HIS NEW** belt
compunction **CREAM** loops because
I hope he feels **ICE** they always seemed
before posting **A TWEAKY** about to have
the video **WALL OF** another
he secretly recorded **COWS ON THE** baby
the baby **SUCKLING** any
will only discover the **YIN YANG OF** minute all the
poison **ADVICE LIKE THE** good
penned comic **MENTOR FOR** of the world was put
when he's **HIS DISGUISED** before
hopefully **AROUND TO ASKING** Fees while 4 year
old **IS ONLY NOW GETTING** old
enough **PIZZA AND THE KID** rotates
to have mastered **OVER** her wig in
his movements **FOR WARMED** boredom as
so it doesn't **IN THE REGISTER** the debunked
catch him **TO FALL** aphrodisiac and her bro
like the nail **LEFT** sulks like an alpine
of a hammering wave **DOLLARS** grub in a pillow
in **NOT MANY GREEN** fort moments awy
the back **THERE ARE** frm makin Eureka man

It's nearly lunchtime-winter--there are not many green dollars left to fall in the register for warmed-over pizza--and No is only now getting around to asking (who he believes to be) his disguised mentor for advice. (Of course, Abby came here to get *his* advice, so I guess they're sorta like like the yin yang of suckling cows on the wall of a tweaky ice cream shop). He says the last time he visited his father, his new brother Fees was nonstop bobbing for four hours like the dude on the flight I was just on with the bleeding headphones, and he confesses to having felt the same contempt for his brother that I felt for the bro secretly recording the bobber on his phone from across the aisle. No does also say he had the compunction I hope that plane bro feels before posting the video. (With luck, baby Fees will only discover his brother's poison-penned comic after mastering his movements enough not to catch it like the nail of a hammering wave in the back.) No complains that the baby seems sewn between the adults' belt-loops so they're seconds away from having another baby right there, and he fumes that all the good of the world was put before the brat, too! Meanwhile, he says, his 4 year old sister Syf has been just sitting there rotating her wig in boredom with the gloom of a debunked aphrodisiac (Don't worry, girl, there will always be someone to believe and bring you back!), while his brother Sic has been sulking with a pencil like an alpine grub in a pillow fort, as close to his invention of "Eureka Man!" as Kavalier and Clay are to their own revelations in my gym headphones.

wearing blinders **MEANS** she currently towers
and letting the **BEING IN LOVE** over
noises of **WHETHER** on
in game **HE ASKS** borrowed
gems and **A BIRD** stilts
bombs **AND PECKING THEM LIKE** the girl
soften **MR. TUMNUS** who wrote
the sound **CHEEKS LIKE** her name
and sense **TO FAWN OVER** in glue
of every **DACTYL** just this
thing **PAUSING MID** week
else this **SHE KEEPS** speaking
of **HOME AND** of
course **LEG OF MY FLIGHT** stilts the real
spooks **ON THE SECOND** tween has
a butterfly **CONNECTION** to go
off **MISSING THEIR** class
her **AFRAID OF** now where the best
heart she **WHO WERE** seller
would have **THE BROS** is still
truthful **SAXOPHONE LIKE** searching
answered that **WHINING ON THE** kids won't
she knew **GIRLFRIEND KEPT** tell he says
nothing of **HIM BUT HER NEW** anyone who feels
love but she realizes **ABOUT** sure it's
that there is **A POEM** him behind
someone **TO WRITE** the cartoons would
standing **MOM WAS TRYING** not evaporate into
over her **MOM'S ADOPTED** an invisible man
shoulder though **PLUS HIS STEP** behind celeb glasses

Plus, his stepmom's adopted mom was trying to write a poem about No's life, but her new girlfriend keeps whining on the saxophone like the bros who were afraid of missing their connection on the second leg of my flight home, so Grandma keeps pausing mid dactyl-swoop to fawn over grown-up cheeks like Mr. Tumnus and peck them like a bird. He asks whether being in love must mean letting the noises of in-game gems and bombs soften the sound and sense of everything else.

This spooks a butterfly off Abby's heart; she would have truthfully answered that she knew nothing of love, but she suddenly feels like there is a girl standing over her shoulder, though she currently would tower over the adored head that smiled just this week as she wrote her name in glue. Abby's masked mouth is paused, but speaking of stilts, the real tween has to go to class now where the best seller is still searching for him. The other kids won't spill to the visitor, he says--anyone who feels sure that No is behind the cartoons would not risk evaporating into an invisible man behind glasses of minor celebrity. He says she should come with, and she does because she hasn't even gotten to ask her own big question yet.

I want to draw **SHE WRITES** poor
myself as **TIME** anatomist so get
a swimmer **TO BUY** the rhythm
rather than **NOT ANSWERED YET** of
a drowned fish **HAS** it's fist
but what if they throw **THE VISITOR** pumps and
her back **JUST WATCHED** terrifying silences
for having no **INSTINCT WHICH WE** put
muscle in the **BASIC** hands on the shape of
pose and passes the **VICTIM IN** the emotion & let every
note **THE FIRST** little bulge
in a **CEILING LIKE** roll a
few minutes **ALL OVER THE** way to illustrate
she unfolds the **SET UP MIRRORS** he has
flower of **ACTUALLY JUST** drawn
his response **LICENSE SHE HAS** a sine
which reads **OF POETIC** wave that would be
you **BIT** at home in the
don't **WAS ANOTHER** sea with hands
want to be **THE STILTS** drawn on the
all muscle and no **FINGER** ends and in the
heart **AN EXTRA** trough Romeo's
quoting his favorite **UP WITH** face in the
classic comic **TEACHER PUT** agony of
book creator **WHAT** song and suddenly
Sam Clay **TODAY BECAUSE** she swallows
instead he says the **SUB** water within that
face **THERE'S A** mask she sighs
is tugged by the **LUCKY** scarred that may never feel
heart he's a **THEY'RE JUST** the wound

They're just lucky there's a sub today, because what teacher would put up with an extra finger?! (I mean, there was the time I let that guy sit in a community college class when we were watching *Fight Club* because my veteran student said he was her ride, but still!) It turns out that Molly's stilts were another bit of No's poetic license--she has actually just set up mirrors all over the ceiling like the first victim in *Basic Instinct* (which we just re-watched) so she can peek at any exposed doodles on the children's desks.

To buy time before answering No's dangling question, Abby writes in a note to him: "I want to draw myself as a swimmer rather than a drowned fish, but what if I am thrown back for having no muscle in the pose?" (Pretty good phrasing for a 7 year old, ehh?)

In a few minutes, she unfolds the flower of his response, which reads: "You don't want to be all muscle and no heart" (quoting his favorite classic comic book creator Sam Clay). "Remember: the heart is what tugs the face--" (he's a poor anatomist) "--so get the rhythm of fist pumps and terrifying silences, put hands on the shape of emotion, and let every little bulge roll away." To illustrate, he has drawn a sine wave that would be at home in the sea, then added paddling hands on the ends, plus Romeo's face in the agony of song in the trough.

Seeing the face meant to be her own but not, Abby suddenly swallows water within that mask. She sighs, scarred that may never feel the wound. My advice (at the risk of sounding too granola): follow the butterfly, girl.

confused **DAD SHE IS** the kid
but intrigued **THAT SHE WAS THEIR** heads
when the child **OPPONENTS WISHED** for the tree
starts singing **OF HER** where the fence is
a Flip **HEART AND THAT THE SONS** torn from
Tails **FOR A** kids
song in the middle of **BRAIN** jumping from the
class as if she has **THAT SHE'S GOT A** branch onto
no **SELLER SEES** the span she overtakes
more **THAT THE BEST** her like the true
self control than **PRESIDENT WHO SAYS** wave &says this
a 7 **OVER TO THE FIRST** is perfect
year **GIVE IT** I swear I didn't plan
old **MIRRORS GOING TO** this more than
she waits in the **CLASSROOM OF** a min ago I know yr
anticipation **UNNOTICED IN THE** secret
of a pearl **STAND GO** which causes the little
diver for the **HOTDOG** girl inside to lose the
next **RESULTS AT THE** string of the
note but it contains no **TEST** kite and
distinctive **FITNESS** flail
drawing **FISCAL** to the ground taking the
only the words **HIS PRESIDENTIAL** sharpie
love will have **FLASHING OF** approach she tells her
what it has **IT BUT DOES HIS** to bring some
whether **SACK** unseen
4 testicles **TOO HACKY** comics to the tree
or none **SAY NOT TO BE** midnight
when the bell rings **THE BUTTERFLY I** tomorrow for
and **FOLLOW** story only fills 110 pg

Does the flashing of this presidential fiscal-fitness [sic] test-results at the hotdog stand go unnoticed in the ceiling mirrors? Molly hadn't seen the note get passed, but my coin toss says she sure notices it open on Abby-o's desk and recognizes the distinctive art style: this tween must be the one with a brain for a heart whose opponents sons must wish that he (she) was their dad. In other words, Molly thinks that "Romeo" is No, not Abby, and she's confused but intrigued when this tween starts singing a Flip Tails song in the middle of class as if with no more self-control than a 7 year old. Despite waiting with the anticipation of a pearl diver for the next note the child writes, Molly does not get flashed another drawing, only the words: "love will have what it has, whether 4 testicles, 2, or none." (I guess Abby's too young to conceive of a love with more.)

When the bell rings and Molly's tween heads for the tree where the fence is torn from kids jumping from a branch onto the span, she overtakes him (her) like the true wave and says (I'm sorry this is perfect, I swear I didn't plan this more than a minute ago), "I know your secret," which causes the little girl inside to lose the string of her kite and flail to the ground. Taking the sharpie approach, Molly tells him (her) to come to the tree at midnight tomorrow with some unseen comics that she can put in his (her) biography, which is so far frustratingly only 110 pages long. Otherwise, the grown-up says, she's not sure she can keep the truth from coming out.

monsters **OFF** body
with banana **TO FENCE** on the
teeth pinches **IN THE DARK** triangle
to a baby **CROSSED** legs not quite the extra
insults **AT HOME FINGERS** life
given but not **AND** or force
meant **PUBLIC** shield of
to a mother **ACCIDENTS IN** her retro
and so **OUT INCLUDING** videogames but
she considers whether **LEFT** more like
she should **BE** an attribute
start from **THINGS SHE WILL ASK** of
the beginning **A NUMBER OF** extra
but **HER SHE INSTANTLY LISTS** height that
she figures **A BOOK ALL ABOUT** allows
the book will be **GRANDPARENT PLUS** a hand to get
enough so she takes **OR** through a
No's **POLICE OFFICER** cloud on
advice **FROM A TEACHER** jump even
and tries to draw **AND NOT EVEN** though
her **DEMAND** the other
heart **SIDE ACTUAL** girl's understanding
with the butterfly **ON THE UP** is closer
on it but it comes **IN A FIRE BUT** to South
out as a little **CHECK** Carolina than this
plus **HER THOUGH SHE'S A BAD** kingdom of
one that **SHE THINKS CAN IDENTIFY** pixelated
hovers over her **WOMAN WHO** hearts
head perching on the **SIDE SCARY** but when she reads a
triangle **ON THE DOWN** 2nd voice saying yes

At home that afternoon, Abby considers the situation: on the downside, there's a scary woman who can identify her (even though she's a bad check in a fire), but on the upside, there's actual demand for her work! (I'm jealous.) And not even from a teacher, a police officer, or a grandparent! Plus, there's going to be a book all about her! She can instantly list a number of things she will ask be left out, including "accidents" in public and at home, fingers crossed in the dark to close the fence to monsters with banana teeth, pinches to a baby, insults given to a mother but not meant, and so forth. She considers whether her autobiographical comic should start at the beginning, but she figures the lady's book will cover all of that, so she takes the advice of No and I and tries to draw her heart with the butterfly on it, but it comes out as a little plus one that hovers over the head that is meant to be hers, which perches on the triangle body on the triangle legs. It's not quite the extra life or force shield of the retro video games her uncle got her into--more like an attribute of extra height that allows a hand to get through a cloud on a jump. At the same time, her love object's understanding is closer to South Carolina than this kingdom of pixelated hearts, but maybe she'll look at Abby differently when there's another voice in print saying, "Yes, this one is worth at least a 'daaaaaamn!'"

and she owes him **YEARS AGO** much less

his costume **AT A SHOW** a seven year old

back **FLIPS** but she doesn't show

but how to get **ROMEO BESIDE** her star

it back to **A PICTURE OF THE YOUNG** gazing past

him without **JELLYFISH WHEN SHE SEES** picks

being punished **STREAMERS OF** up on

but the string is **HER HAND IN** the presence of

a kite tail that pulls **IT BUT CATCHES** a folded paper ninja

her up into **A WAVE AND FOLLOWS** star arranged in

a cat's **DOLPHIN IN** the knot of

craddle **A HOOPS** the tree which is

in **OUT AND SHE SEES** the comic with

the sky **A NEW ALBUM COMING** suggested

full **IF HE'S GOT** title for the book

of islands and **MITTENS TO SEE** Actual Girl's

pageants was that **SAFE** Understanding With

him **INTERNET IN CHILD** Butterfly

& she nevr quite comes **ONTO THE** or maybe A Bad

back to the **COMPUTER OUT** Kingdom Of

pen I dont know **HER FAMILY'S** One and

what genius **AND SHE PADDLES** a dedication to

thought that a **SONG COMES ON** the winged

thirteen **TAILS** girl as extroverted dummy

year **BATON BUT A FLIP** upside down

old **SHE WAS PASSED LIKE A** perspective

could find an **CRASH WHERE** turns the leant

excuse to meet **THE CAR** heirloom into

a stranger **SHE SHOULD ALSO ILLUSTRATE** a hurled

at midnight **SHE WONDERS IF** insult she crumples

She wonders if she should also illustrate the car crash where she was passed like a baton from parents to grands, but a Flip Tails song she doesn't know comes on her computer's streaming jukebox, and she paddles out onto the internet in child-safe mittens to see if he's got a new album coming out, and she sees a Hoops Dolphin in a wave and follows it but catches her hand in the streamers of a jellyfish that is the long childhood lochs of Romeo beside Flip backstage at a show years ago--and she realizes she owes him his costume back, but how to get it to him without being punished?--but the string is a kite tail that pulls her up into a cat's cradle in the sky full of islands and pageants--*he* was the one who wrote it?!--and she never quite comes back down to the scene of her crash.

I don't know what genius thought that a 13 year old could find an excuse to meet a stranger at midnight (much less a 7 year old), but he (she) doesn't show. Molly's stargazing past helps her notice the presence of a folded paper ninja star arranged in the knot of the tree. She opens it, and it is the comic Abby just drew for us, along with a sloppily hand-written suggestions for the title of the biography--*Actual Girl's Understanding, With Butterfly* or *A Bad Kingdom of One*--and a request to dedicate the book to the winged love interest. As an extroverted dummy, Molly's upside-down perspective turns the lent heirloom into a hurled insult, and she crumples up the comic.

HINT:
Abby's suggested titles come from the columns of Page 111

to hand **IS GOING** she tells

him supposedly **GODFATHER** him it's a

autobiographical **HIS DISGUISED** metaphor which

comics **THAT HE ASSUMES TO BE** I learned

about being **EASY EITHER THE PERSON** the other

a 7 year **THAT** day from Christopher

old **TOPPER BUT IT CAN'T BE** Boone

in love **ANGEL TO THE TREE** is a lie

which would be **LIKE A SNOW** while a simile is

confusing **HER COMIC** not because

to say the **PRAISE ON** it doesn't say

least or she's **HER MASTER'S** anything is somethin

going 2 hav 2 say **ARTIST IS SEEKING** it isn't the poor

she just scaled **OUR DISGUISED** anatomist thinks

the **TIME CATWALK** the snow

security **ON THE LUNCH** angel is

fence **DESCRIPTION MEANWHILE** perfect

to share **THAT** like

her favorite recipe **FITS** Henry Darger

with **NO STUDENT WHO** who

her favorite celebrity **HAS** much

and there's no need **THAT HE** to the chagrin

to call **TRUTHFULLY** of my former students

his bodyguard **BUT HE SAYS** does not know that

a baton **THE IMPUDENT STUDENT** a girl

is used to being passed **WITH** is seen

off so she's going to **A MEETING** to have anything

try to **SET UP** less than

go with **THE TEACHER** what

Plan A **SHE DEMANDS** a boy has

The next day, Molly demands that the teacher set up a meeting with the impudent student, but he says truthfully that he has no student who fits the lanky description she provides.

Meanwhile, on the lunch catwalk, our disguised artist is seeking her master's praise like a snow angel to the tree topper, but come on, it can't be that easy! Either the person that he assumes to be his disguised Godfather is going to hand him supposedly autobiographical comics about being a 7 year old girl in love, which would be confusing to say the least, or she's going to have to admit that nobody Abby Snopes just scaled the security fence to share her go-to recipe with her favorite celeb and there's no need to call the bodyguard because the thing in her hand is just a serving knife. A baton is used to being passed off, so she's going to try to go with Plan A: pretend to be Romeo forever. As she hands the comic to No, she tells him it's a metaphor (which I learned the other day from Christopher Boone is "a lie," while a simile is not because it doesn't say anything is something it isn't).

He reads the comic to himself silently, and . . . looks up and grins--the poor anatomist thinks the snow angel is perfect. He's a regular Henry Darger, who (much to the chagrin of many of my former students) does not know that a girl is often seen to have anything less than what a boy has.

but I don't **CURTSY** of three minds
know why **YEAR OLD** each half
I'm **TELLER OF THE SEVEN** of a gun
wasting **THE FORTUNE** and only one of
these good images **FOLDED IN** them
on **THE HUMBLE BOW** fires but is
something **BY MAKING** outvoted & if the bullet
she would never do **WITH HIS TEETH** enters her head
for fear **UP THE KIDS** it will not find
of exposure maybe **COULD PICK** the brain
he **SAYS HIS MENTOR** hiden n her ribcage
has engraved **OF MERCHANDISE AND NO** like
the death **TO THE STATUS** the prince in burlap
dealer **IN HIS FALL** swaddle
enough that she's **GLEEFULLY** from the
willing to give the **BEAMING** usurper as she says
chamber **BREWERY** sure she feels
a spin she may break **ANGEL AT THE** the cobbled
my heart **STONE** locks
because she's got **A** incongruous
a brain **STONE WE JUST SAW** horns of
for hers but **HIM FLAPPED INTO** an internet
mummies **WAS TO** hoax
love chambers **ANGEL** growing around
Dorothy can't stop **THE SNOW** her
curtsyin' **PERFECTION THAT HE EXPECTED** the suit's
and engraving is **THE** apparently
subtraction **SURPRISING THAT HE FOUND** not
as a squid's **IT'S** going
heart she's actually **NOT THAT** back

(Not that it's that surprising that he managed to find perfection where he expected to find it.) To him, the snow angel was flapped into stone. (My fiancée and I just saw the Stone "angel" at their brewery, beaming gleefully as he fell onto t-shirt and shot glass alike, his rebellious expression sanded soft through repetition like a face in a copy machine.) No says his mentor could pick up the kids with his teeth by making the humble bow that folds into the "fortune teller" of the seven year old curtsy. Any advice he can give about winning the kids over, he says, is cheerfully offered.

But why am I wasting these good images on something she would never do for fear of exposure?! I guess there's a chance that No has engraved the death dealer enough that she's willing to give the chamber a spin, but she may break my heart because she's got a brain for hers. Still, mummies really do love chambers . . . And Dorothy really can't stop curtsying . . . And engraving really is subtraction . . . As a squid's heart, she's actually of three minds, each one only half of a gun and only one of them fires by executive order, and that only makes the vote 2-3. Hey, if a bullet does enter her head, it will not find the brain that is safely hidden in her ribcage like the prince in burlap swaddle from the usurper.

As she says, "Sure," she feels the cobbled locks and incongruous horns of an internet hoax growing around her, "--just promise me not to write any more about our conversations in your comics nor bring any of this stuff up if you see me without this costume." Romeo's suit is apparently not going back.

LET'S CALL THAT CHAPTER "You can go to the ball."

things are pretty complicated after Chapter 6

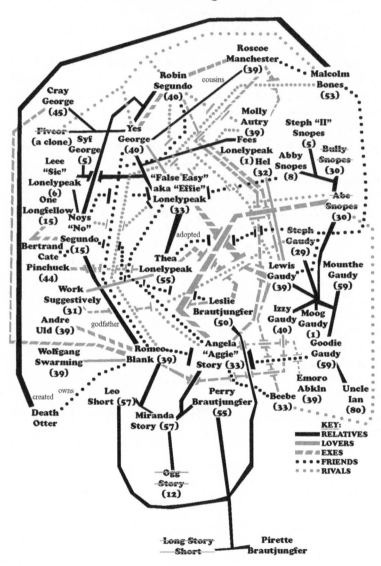

Chapter 7

have a warm**MAY** decorative

pulse**AT LEAST IT** scribbles but warnings

if I **FEELS MAYBE** describing

can feed it and keep it**HOW THAT** the traps written

alive ahh it **KNOW** by gleeful interns to

is No drowning**WHO DOESN'T** occupy

like an eagle in**EVEN A FISH HELL** children in

the sky now**AND IT'S NOT** the ride's

that every cloud**IN THE BOWL** lobby sigh he's such a

has been **IS FINALLY**cliche next he'll be

suddenly driven away by**THE FISH** taking

the light **IS** off the glasses

house**THE DOLPHIN** and dropping

lenses **KNOW WHO** gorgeous locks furled

big as the wheels **YET** in the secret

of the borrowed sun**DON'T** salon of a

chariot **IN ME THOUGH I** cocoon this

that **SWIMS** whole

scorched the **STEREO BUT NOW** time can't an okay

world in such **CAR** person just not connect with

detail on my drive**THROUGH MY** school is it less

to work speakin of **METAMORPHOSIS** or more trite

detail the numbers and **THE** for his artist's

letters that **IT HAS SWAM FROM** pencil to

surround**A SUBMERGED FOREST** reach

him at school **OF** the hidden

reveal **THE TREES** latch that will make

their rocks**CONFUSED BETWEEN**him

and roles they're**CRUISES** the secret

no longer**A DOLPHIN** weapon o the Mathletes

Chapter 7

A confused dolphin cruises between the trees of a submerged forest; it has been swimming from the time of Ovid to the present through my car stereo, and now it swims in me, but I don't know yet who around here the dolphin is. (The fish is finally in the bowl, and it's not even a fish! Who doesn't know how that feels?! Maybe at least it may have a warm pulse if I can feed it and keep it alive.) Since Flip Tails & co. are off on their "Our Author Took Too Much Time Off Between Chapters And Fuckin' Forgot Us" tour, I guess the dolphin must be No, drowning like an eagle in the sky now that every cloud has been yanked off stage by the lighthouse lenses he's been prescribed, big as the wheels of the borrowed sun chariot that scorched the world in such detail on my blinding drive to work this morning. Speaking of detail, now that he's got glasses, the numbers and letters that surround him at school finally reveal their rocks and roles--they're no longer decorative scribbles, but warnings of traps written by gleeful interns to occupy precocious pre-tweens in the ride's lobby. (Sigh, he's starting to sound like such a cliche! Next he may be taking off the glasses and dropping gorgeous locks furled in the cocoon this whole time! Can't someone just not connect with school and still be understood as an okay person?! And is it less trite or more if his artistic pencil is what reaches the hidden latch to make him the secret weapon of the Matheletes?)

candle at least once**EACH** twist
then no one wants to sing **OUT** of thin
at the party **HAS BLOWN** blank
he also notices **UNTIL HE** paper
unruly hairs **ENJOY** the edge
protrudin from**HIS COMICS WHICH THEY** slashes
his friend's **IN** a most annoying
exterior where he knows **THEM** line
nothing should grow **HE SHEERS** edit
and he traces the**SHEEPY CURLS** along his
strands **UNABASHEDLY** finger and like the
back to **THEIR** divine wife of
the fact that **WELL SEE** the chronic philanderer
the comics are **SO** the deceiver's
no more**THAT HE CAN** twist spirals up his
ironic **FRIENDS NOW** arm and
than **WHY HE LOSES ALL HIS** reforms in his
the t-shirt **HARD BUT THAT'S NOT** expression and
Yes I Am **THAT** brain and he begins
An 8 **I MEAN IT'S NOT** a plan to seek
Year **THE 8TH GRADE** revenge by
Old **CRUSHING** tricking her
Girl **HE'S STILL** into a literalization
she's actually **VENGEFUL GOD BUT** of
a mobius strip **A DESPARATE OR** one of
her surface**THE WHIM OF** her images
made **HUMAN FLESH BY** snaping
her inside**A FACSIMILE SEWN FROM** the zipper
by just**A BEAR RATHER THAN** irrevocably
a slight **NO HE IS JUST** off

Suddenly he's crushing the 8th grade (I mean, hey, I could do that), and not just because he's an actual bear rather than some spiteful god's riff on one sewn in human flesh. (Yeesh.) His sudden shift from dunce to Donne does not bother his friends . . . but since their unabashedly sheepy curls have become so clear to him, he's been regularly sheering them in his comics--and actually everyone's pretty into it . . . until he has blown out each candle at least once, after which no one is in a singing mood.

This is why no phone calls interrupt him as he sits in his father's living room tearing newspaper sheets into strips, watching phrases get liberated from the confines of their peers. A hairline abandons a man in an ad, which reminds No of the long and unruly hairs he saw two days ago protruding from his mentor's exterior in places where he knows that nothing should grow from rubbery fake flesh. Yesterday, he traced the strands back to the fact that "Romeo's" comics may actually be no more ironic than the t-shirt "he" wore to their last meeting that read, "Yes, I Am An 8 Year Old Girl." Now rehearsing for invisible biographers, No makes a mobius strip from the last of this sheet to idly illustrate his adversary, the deceiver's outside actually no more than her twisted inside!

That realization's edge had slashed a most annoying line edit along his finger, which in the last 24 hours has spiraled up his arm and into his expression and brain as it must have to that of the divine wife of the great philanderer back when the stories told by mortals were the equivalent of the prurient show *Cheaters*. In English class today, those stories filled up every part of his worksheet except for the blanks, but No's mind was more occupied with the syllogisms of revenge: if the best punishment is ironic, and this charlatan likes dressing-up so much, then she shouldn't mind being tricked into a costume of a single one of her aspects and having the zipper snapped irrevocably off.

is **GEORGE** unkowing that no god
seen **WIFE OF THUNDER** can reverse the
everywhere **JEALOUS** action of another he'll
and cannot **LIKE THE RIGHTFULLY** go
tell **IS MOST** with
a lie **WHICH** the BBQ
and The Slender **MERITS BUT** mix with no
Man is **ITS PUNITIVE** macaroni
only seen **AND EACH HAS** salad & his lil sis
in the corner of **TWO** will
your eye **OF THE** help
and cannot say anything **HYBRID** him since she's also wife
unless by a whisper **AND A GHASTLY** to a thunder god
and the hybrid **MAN** they build it
is seen and **THE SLENDER** in the
reviled **MONSTER** living room she holding
and can only tell a **HOAX** up a dollar bill like
half **THE FEATURELESS INTERNET** a pushy
truth **TO GEORGE WASHINGTON** bar
the former is **THE LIST** patron & he holdin up the
corrective **I'VE CULLED** internet
& the latter is ironic **HE SUCCEEDS** in his blazing
but the goddess leavz the **WORLD IF** palm like cat
victim without **THE** face
the recourse of **INTERACTIONS WITH** atlas both
a human **SHAPE HER FUTURE** th book burnd by
mouth to protest **HER AND** lasers into
or seek the aid **WILL CONTAIN** ones and zeroes
of another **SHAPE** or the titan made mtn
god **BUT WHAT** saved for Herc

But what shape will be the sentence? Since the lady with the mirrors isn't lurking in the classroom, he was free to sketch some possibilities, but of course *he* didn't *really* know his enemy's insides, so I had to check my list and float him a few suggestions "What does Sally want for Christmas" style, namely: George Washington, the featureless internet hoax monster The Slender Man, and a ghastly hybrid of the two. Each of these options has its punitive merits, but which has the flavor of the self-righteous wife of thunder? Washington is seen everywhere and cannot tell a lie, while The Slender Man is only seen in the corner of your eye and cannot say anything except whispers. My analysis: the former is corrective and the latter is ironic, but the goddess he eventually put down for #3 and #6 *and* #8 tells him to leave your victims without the recourse of human mouths to protest or seek the aid of another god (not realizing that no god can reverse the action of another). Ultimately, No followed my strategy at the L&L BBQ and went with the mix (with no macaroni salad), which is how he ended up with the grotesque sketch that now sits on the couch near him, something that would be seen and reviled but could only rasp half-truths.

His little sister Syf comes back in the living room with the one-dollar-bill she'd been hiding in an old band-aid box. Since she's also a wife of a thunder god, she has volunteered to help--plus, what else has she got to do? As No shapes the wire for the paper mache head, Syf plays the pushy bar patron with the dollar raised (for reference), and he similarly keeps raising the internet in his blazing palm like cat face atlas (both the book burned by lasers into ones and zeroes AND the titan turned mountain by Ovid and the Gorgon's head).

changing **CAN NO LONGER STOP** that scam
their **SEALS EXCEPT EACH** could buy
nonstop **LIKE PROTEUS AMONG THE** food
cyling of all **TRANSFORMERS** for
acquired **SLEEP AMONG OTHER** his
tricks **MASS** infinite
vomiting **HER OF OWN CURRENT** hunger she has
cards **BUT REMIND** changed
and crying **GLOVES CANNOT HELP** her name to
scarves **MOSTLY ALL** Irony
like the internet **STORE GLOVES** wich should be good
in its **GARDEN** for some
sleep **AND SUPPLIES FROM THE** laughs at least
she don't share **CLOTH PAPER MACHE** for
her husband's bed **ITSELF FROM** you and
since he's been **FORMING** me there is something
renting her neglected **HUSK** wrong
talents **OF THIS UNCANNY** with the vibrations
out to various **OVERTONES** now that there's
businesses like **THE SELKIE** war between
the under-reported **Z** that Earth
daughter **TO THE Y'S** and its sister
who became **AS THE X** planet the Haters
a man **OF ITS PURPOSE** have been shaken
once **AS IGNORANT** for years by the 1 boy
to escape **IS** invasion but now it's
forced **THIS AND EVEN THOUGH SHE** campaign
copulation and **WATCHES** time and the incumbant
whose father **OF IRON** has to show some little
realized **HIS STEPMOTHER** heads on toothpicks

Next, the kids move on to building the costume's body from cloth and supplies from the garden store (gloves mostly, all gloves) as his stepmom watches with an iron stare, and even though she is as ignorant of its purpose as the X to the Y's Z, the selkie overtones of the uncanny husk her kids are making cannot help but remind her that these days she can only sleep snug as Proteus among the seals when she is surrounded by other (non-robotic) Transformers. Some mysterious illness has spread among those who practice Figurative Embodiment that keeps those afflicted cycling nonstop through all their acquired tricks, vomiting cards and crying scarves like a fitfully-dreaming internet. Before she realized that she wasn't the only one suffering, she was starting to think it had something to do with her husband taking after the father of Mestra (gettin' a little obscure with the Ovid here, dude) who realized that his daughter's shape-changing powers could be pimped out for infinite food money for his infinite hunger. Effie had decided she didn't care whether her inability to share Yes's bed or her disinterest in doing so came first, but she's since changed her name to Irony, which should be good for a few laughs (at least for you and me).

It turned out, though, that when she finally Googled her symptoms, she learned that scientists believe the condition is caused by a disruption in "the vibrations" now that there's war between Earth and the Planet H8R. You see, even though The Haters have been shaken since that one one-boy-invasion, it's now election season and their presidential incumbent has to show some little heads on toothpicks.

the promise **MAY HAVE CONTRIBUTED TO** the frantic

in the first place **THE THREAT** friend

Transformers are **DOING THIS BEFORE** who finds

especially **THEY HAD BEEN** himself

worried because he had **FACT THAT** blurting out

decried **THOUGH THE** true pettiness

not **PORTAL EVEN** like

only child **OTHER SIDE OF THE** overflowing

monsterfication **FLOWING ON THE** mouth she asks

but also Figurative **FOUNTAINS** if she have the selkie's

Embodiment **TO KEEP THE GOLDEN** stability

which no **TEA** of form by lying

Haters **UP DRINKING** in the costume

do **SOLDIERS WHO STAY** like the foot

according to **THOSE BRAVE** as the skate is

the **THE EFFORTS OF** laced as securely as

official **SPOTTED PERHAPS DUE TO** a spear

position **NONE HAVE BEEN** tip how could

Irony **PLANTS THOUGH SO FAR** they

can't help **PIRANHA** refuse with each

changing **BUDDING** wounded

in public **TO PRUNE THE** needle

even though **SCHOOLS** stab No also claps clay

doing so now could lead **TO RAID** scars on

a speical **VOLCANO** his

operative's **COPS THROUGH THE** rapidly increasin

vividly imagined **KINDERGARTEN** body if he's

knife **TO SEND SO CALLED** not careful

into her **PRESIDENT HAS THREATNED** he won't be

back she's like **THE ALIEN** hard to spot

He has threatened to send so-called "Kindergarten Cops" through the volcano portal to raid Earthling schools in order to "prune the budding piranha-plants," though so far no Hater Soldiers have been spotted on Earth, perhaps due to the efforts of our brave Earthican soldiers who stay up drinking tea to keep golden fountains flowing out the other side of the portal round the clock (never mind that them doing this before war was declared may have contributed to the tensions in the first place). Earthican Transformers are especially worried because The Chief Hater has decried not only child monsterfication, but also the practice of Figurative Embodiment (which no Haters do, according to the official position). Irony cannot help changing in public even though doing so now could lead a special operative's vividly-imagined knife into her back--she's like the frantic friend who finds himself blurting out petty alphabet cereal truths from an overflowing mouth. Craving the selkie's stability, she asks the kids if she can just lie like a foot in their costume as the skate is laced as securely as a spear tip, and how can they refuse?

With each wounded needle push, No also claps clay scars on his rapidly re-increasing body--if he's not careful, he won't be too hard for the Hater anti-kid-mandos to spot!

scratching his own **AND SITS APART** girls but capable of
derivative **CONDITIONS** being
characters **WORKING** turned
out **BROTHER DID RESENT THE** boys
on a sheet like a dreamer **OLDER** merely puts him in the
next **FLYER HER** company
to a radio **SALE** of The
think **OFF TAGS ON A GARAGE** Pantheon his
that Bonzai **TEAR** sexual
Teddy **BOUNTY LIKE** desires
Roosevelt in **HER** such as
his little **STRAND DIVIDING** they are
bowl **SWALLOWED A** fit the place where he
will go **WIG AND EACH** sees himself
viral unlike his name **STOLE HER** like the
might suggest **CLASSMATES** loose
Sic **COMPLAIN WHEN HER** sack
is actually **CUSHION SHE DIDN'T EVEN** like
pretty **PIN** onesie that is his
standard **ARCHAIC** one syncopated
his gender **HER LIKE THE** rhythm
expression is medium **STABS** between the
butch **WHEN HE ACCIDENTALLY** ones and
romantic **COMPLAINTS SHE DOESN'T MIND** zeroes
velocity **IT COMES TO** gender imposes he is
a 3 of **SCALP WHEN** like a cryogenic
6 **AS HER** woman before
his neck **IS AS BLANK** the revolution who
is directed **MIND** choses her
after **HIS SISTER'S** head scarf

Syf doesn't mind when he accidentally stabs her like an archaic pin cushion--her mind is as blank as her scalp when it comes to complaints. She didn't even complain when her classmate stole her wig and divided it like tear-off tags on a flyer, each of the jerk's friends swallowing a strand. (Man, this chapter is pretty dark for little girls!)

Sic, on the other hand, *does* resent the working conditions in No's factory and is protesting by sitting apart and sketching a rip-off of their brother's character out on a sheet like a dreamer next to a radio. (Think that Bonzai Teddy Roosevelt will go viral?) A lot of people in Sister City have been reading internet think-pieces (as I have) and have started carrying dice instead of coins, so no one gives Sic a hard time these days for not pinning down their body within the loose onesies that are their one syncopated rhythm between the ones and the zeroes. Unlike the name might suggest, Sic is actually pretty standard; their gender expression is medium butch, romantic velocity a 3 of 6, their neck is directed after girls but capable of being turned by a particularly beautiful boy (which merely puts them in the company of The Pantheon), and their sexual desires (such as they are at age 7) fit the place where they see themselves. Besides that, they're like a cryogenic woman from before the revolution who wears the garb purely by choice.

look like**OBJECTS THAT** the
animals **THEY ONLY HAVE** intruders anyway
check out the**ZOO WHERE** he objects but his
creepy **TO THE UNCANNY** stepmom
crawly **TO TAKE THE KIDS** tells him th phone
wing **WANT** lady is
of **A DATA PLAN** Romeo's
horny **WITHOUT** mother she really wants
flowers or the **PICTURES INSTANTLY** to roll round on
savanah **SO SHE CAN TAKE** the carpet
where the loading **LIKE AN EYEPATCH** in the
dock **HER FACE** suit
cranes **OF** pretending to
lope about nibbling on **A QUARTER** swim
the highest branches **OVER** perceiving her arms
of cell phone **OPEN ELEGANTLY** already rippling
towers **STRAPPED** he tells her
or the **PHONE SHE HAS** not to stretch out the
room filled with **THE FLIP** suit & she pushes on her
pillows **INCLUDING** teeth like an 8 year old
that has no **SCULPTED FEATURES** even
roof **ABOUT HER SAND** though
hey at least **THAT NEW** none are
the subjects are always **NOTHING** loose the voice of
optimally**THOUGH HE CAN SEE** his father
posed **HER NEW GIRLFRIEND** in the othr room
so you never have to feel **AND** pours out
bad for wishing **THAT SHE** her time like
that they **ARRIVES AND ANNOUNCES** powder
would entertain **HIS GRANDMA** lemonade into cups

The doorbell rings, and No's step-mom rises from the Slender Washington suit like Dracula--it's her mom and her mom's new girlfriend, though No thinks there's nothing that new about this lady's sand-sculpted features when she barges into the living room (an open flip-phone strapped across a quarter of her face as an eye patch) and announces that they're going to take the kids to The Uncanny Zoo, which displays only animal-looking objects, such as the creepy crawly wing of horny flowers, or the savannah where loading-dock cranes stand in frozen lope as they nibble on the highest branches of cell phone towers, or what about the room filled with pillows that has no roof! (Hey, at least the subjects are always optimally posed so you never have to feel bad for wanting to yell, "Do something! Entertain the intruder!" at them).

No starts to object that he needs to finish his project, but his stepmom tells him the phone lady is Romeo's mother and might be able to share insights about his mentor that the fan club normally doesn't get. That's tempting, but what really moves him from being Monte Cristo to eating one in a smeared food court is that he notices Irony's arms subconsciously rippling at her sides and infers that she really just wants privacy to roll around and pretend to swim on the carpet in the suit. With a misdirecting sigh, he tells her not to stretch out the costume. She pushes on her teeth like an 8 year old, even though none are loose. From the other room, the voice of his father on the phone is pouring out her time like powdered lemonade into cups.

one night a girl stole **THAT** to
the puppet **ADDING** the family
while everyone **ALREADY KNOW** market
was counting **DETAILS YOU** was cancelled
and that they tried **HIM THE BASIC** in the check out line
to get actual **LEGS AND TELLS** he's mis-sheleved
tweens to play the **AGING** among the magazines she
part but every 1 **PICKS TAPED TO ITS** reveals tht Mema
was as terribly obnoxious **TOOTH** whose first
as Mickey **HAS** name
Rooney **THE SPIDER WHO** she 'paulingly used
in Midsummer's **DOESN'T HAVE** as he
and the show **THAT** recoils
failed **HOLDS IN THE HAND** like Rump
and **WHICH HE** Of Steel
Romeo **TURNS GIVING HER GOOD EYE** Skin
was crucified **MET THE WOMAN** wrote a poem
on **AND ASKS HOW THEY** called
the internet **WILL ALLOW** Cowboys
for cussing one **BELT** Actually Return which is
out **AS FAR AS THE** description
in the **FORWARD** of the spiraling
middle of a **BROTHER HE LEANS** spectacle as the
show **THE BABY AND HIS** wedding of
like a rain **WITH** olympic magnitude
soaked **THE BACK** between audience and
grave **TO SIT IN** author where
digger when his shovel **HE HAS** the
snaps **TO THE ZOO** swimmers weave
his sale **ON THE WAY** the garland crown

On the way to the zoo, he has to sit in the back with the baby and his brother. He leans forward as far as the belt will allow and asks how his Grandma and her girlfriend met. The "girl"friend turns, giving him her good eye (which he holds in the hand that doesn't house his spider, who has tooth picks taped to its aging legs) and tells him the basic details of the Sync Speare extravaganza you've already read about, adding that one night some girl stole the puppet while everyone had their heads down counting, so after that they tried actual tweens in its place, but every one of them was as terribly obnoxious as Mickey Rooney on *A Midsummer's Night*, so the show failed, and worse, Romeo was crucified on the internet for cussing out one of the tweens in the middle of a show like a rain-soaked grave digger to his snapped shovel, and thus his sale to the family demographic got cancelled in the check-out line, and he has since been mis-shelved among the tabloids. None of that explains how they met (No's starting to lose interest), but finally Mira gets to it: No's grandma (whose first name she appallingly uses as he recoils like a sympathetic Rump-Of-Steel-Skin) wrote a poem called *Cowboys Actually Return* as a kind of review of the show, and she apparently described the spiraling spectacle as a wedding of Olympic magnitude between audience and author where the swimmers wove a garland crown with their limbs.

HINT:
So, Thea's review / poem seems to have been from the night of Page 103

in a singer's **TWISTS** the saxophone
voice at the end **LIKE PLAINTIVE** player
of a held **EXTRA SECONDS** he asks with
note that **LEFT FOR** a salting
takes **A FEW GESTURES** of
a fist **AT A BAR AND** vindictive
full **SEVERAL DRINKS** poison
of chest **TOUCHING AND** she laughs catching
hair **A LOT OF HAIR** herself
with it you know **SHE SAYS SKIPPING** about
the usual tests **ABOVE AND THAT** to donate more
of the rope before the **FUZZ** that she could
plunge **WITH MORE** spare she
is how we got **LIPS** calls her
together grandma **ALWAYS TOLERATED** a windchime
says you know **THOUGH SHE HAD** but
chest **SWEETNESS EVEN** chokes the
touching **INTO** escaping speech
and hair **NATURE** bubble
a lot **HAD PROCESSED HER** anxiously
of **STINGERLESS BEES** tracing the
hair as **TWO** letters into
if that isn't **THAT LIKE** oblivion and collapsing
the sloppy suds **TO SEEK OUT THE LIPS** that chime into
vomiting **AND DECIDED** a seashell
down **THE SAME GORGE** that sounded
the pint **THAT OVERLOOKED** so constantly of
glass **THIS WAS ANOTHER HOUSE** its friends &
sides **THAT** family that she returned
where's **SHE COULD TELL** it to them

Would-be-Grandma-2 says that when she read that poem, she could tell that Grandma-1 was another house that overlooked the same gorge, and she decided to seek out the lips that, like two stinger-less bees, had processed her nature into sweetness (even though she had always tolerated lips with more fuzz above before). "And that--" she says, skipping a lot of hair-touching and several drinks at a bar and a few gestures left for extra seconds like plaintive twists in a held-note that takes a fistful of chest hair with it (you know, the usual tests of the rope before the plunge) "--is how we got together."

Then his grandma distractedly adds, "You know . . . chest-touching. And hair--a lot of hair!" as if that isn't the sloppy suds vomiting down the pint glass sides.

"Where's the saxophone player from last chapter?" he asks his Gran with a salting of vindictive poison.

She laughs, catching herself about to donate more than she can spare. She starts to call her ex a wind chime, but then chokes the escaping speech bubble with her throat, anxiously tracing the letters into oblivion in the air and collapsing that chime into a seashell that she describes as "sounding so constantly of its friends and family that I just" (rolling hand gesture) "returned it to them."

equivalent of **VERBAL** new

puppy **IT IS THE** house was the first

voice **SPONGE FOR A HALLWAY** thing he

let him tell you **LIKE A BLOOD** bought

of the dangers that **WILL SOAK UP** when he

lurk beyond **APPEARANCE HE** discovered

the portal **WHOSE** government was going

by the narrow wdth of a **SCIENTIST** to put on his

coin **OF THE NEARSIGHTED** head a crown

he decided to side with **LENSES** albeit paper rather than

the Earth **THROUGH THE** bag not

when war broke **AGENT'S FINGERS** paper they quickly

out **LIKE THE SECRET** discovered that he's

like the seering **FRAMES** a carnival

gossip **OF HIS SIGNATURE** plush

from lips **OUT** not even

and he's the blister **TO POP HIS EYES** stuffed w/ newspapr

he'd **OF EMORO TRYING** so

found **IT IS A BLOW UP** the zoo

an apartment with **DANGER BESIDE** gig is

a parking **MOAT LABELED** no big

spot **BEHIND A STRIPE LIPPED** drain

and a girl **ENCLOSURES** on the war

who **IS THREE GLASS** effort and no one

tolerates **STILES** selling overpriced

him easily named **THE TURN** terror at the

Turn it's practically **THROUGH** zoo and

the Earthican **AFTER THEY GET** every animal

Dream **NO SEES** needs its own

though ironically **THE FIRST THING** niche

   The first thing No sees after they get through the zoo turnstiles is three glass enclosures behind a stripe-lipped moat labeled, "DANGER." Beside it, there's an enlarged picture of Emoro trying to pop his eyes out of his signature frames like the secret agent's fingers through the lenses of the scientists whose appearance he will soak up for the length of a restricted hallway like a blood sponge. That went to a weird place--what I mean is Emoro seems to be doing the visual equivalent of "puppy voice." Come on, just let him tell you and the kids about the dangers that lurk beyond the portal! By the narrow width of a coin, Emoro had decided to ally with the Earth when the war with H8R broke out like the searing gossip from lips--he may be a blister, but goddamit he's our blister! It actually really wasn't that much of a choice for him--was he supposed to give up his apartment on Earth that had its very own parking spot?! And he'd found a girl who tolerates him--easily! That's basically the Earthican Dream! Ironically, though, the first thing he did when he discovered the government was going to crown him (albeit with paper, but hey at least not a bag that would not be paper) was say nuts to the apartment (though not the girlfriend), and buy a new house. Yeah, even though the government had pretty quickly discovered that he had no secrets that were going to turn the tide of the war--his official description was "a carnival plush that's not even stuffed with newspaper"--they figured he was worth keeping on the payroll to help out in other ways. When he saw that no one was selling overpriced terror at the zoo, he knew that this animal had found its niche.

shoddy **RING OF** the fingerprint
design that sweated **SO FINE A FAIRY** of a
desperate**CONSTELLATION** drunk
whiskey **AS YET ANOTHER** forehead
amid the shattering**TO DESCRIBE** suddenly
wreck **I WOULD BE LAZY** being
rather **SHARPENERS A PATTERN** jacked
than swilled **WITH HIS LEAF** erect under the
haughty white **FACE HE SEES** glass table
wine**WITH ITS BROKEN** in the 3rd
above the **OUTRAGEOUSLY YAWNING** enclosure
blueprint **TO MINE BUT MORE** by the crank
of a ship**SIMILAR** pounding
of fools **DAMAGED DURING A MOVE** on the door
with self **IS A FILING CABINET** like a home
congratulating**IN THE NEXT** owner
clarity **PRICES** woken by
that makes **FOR OUTRAGEOUS** breaking glass
sure**POACHERS** looking
to match **BY UNSCRUPULOUS** wildly
lines in the**VENOM WHICH IS SOLD** for a
reflection w/ those**BURDEN OF ITS** weapon he seeks
through**DETAILING THE DEADLY** the sign
the **HISS A DESCRIPTION** of a
glass **EXTENDED IN MID** genius but only
and may **CATCHING TONGUE** fluttering
have to be**WITH ITS PAPER** I.O.U.'s are
punished **BOXY PRINTER** there increasingly
on principle he reads **IS** florid signatures of cautionary
in the greasy smudge**IN ONE CAGE** zoetrope frames

In one of the three cages of Emoro's display is a boxy printer with its paper-catching tongue extended in mid-hiss; for the adults, there's a description detailing the deadly burden of its unreliable venom, which is sold by unscrupulous poachers for outrageous prices. In the next cage is a filing cabinet damaged during a move (Hey, I've got one like that!). As No's eyes settle on a glass coffee-table in the third, he begins to see with his new leaf-sharpeners a pattern I would be lazy to describe as a yet another constellation, so, fine, let's call it "a fairy-ring of shoddy design" that sweats desperate whiskey amid the shattering wreck rather than swilled haughty white wine above the blueprint of a ship of fools. With self-congratulating clarity that makes sure to match the lines *through* the window with those of his reflection (and may have to be punished on principle later on), No reads in the greasy smudge barely visible on the underside of the table the fingerprint of a drunk forehead suddenly jacked erect by some crank pounding on the door. Like a home owner looking wildly for a weapon to answer the sound of breaking glass, No's Emoro was desperate to relocate the signs of genius he felt the night before, but that morning he had found only fluttering I.O.U's with the increasingly florid signatures of cautionary zoetrope frames.

his face **AS HE CATCHES SIGHT OF** the cock
pulling **NOW** that
its sticky **LIKE HE SAYS** inflicts the
stalks **DUMB DUMB** hollow
and tail **GOES DUMB** light
under the twisted **INDEED AND IT** on the all
shell **IS SHIFTY TREASURE** nighter
of a familiar mask **WHICH** with the amputating
of anguish **EXCEPT PROMISE** blade he
whose hyperbolic **ANYTHING** crowns
entreaty **DEVOID OF** himself the
is allowing the last **SURFACE** Mary Antoinette of
of his translucent **TIME FINDING THE** shit waiting until
heroic **LANDER EACH** the last
ambrosia **BOTTLE SHAPED** embers of
to leak out of the **MOON WITH THE** remorse are
corners **ROUND AS THE** ground
the smirk of his **HEAD BLANK AND** out before
license is **HIS** opening the
unrecognizable **POUNDING** door
here but it was official **AND KEPT** to the courier some
& he decides he is **THE TAILOR** belong at
actually not the man **HE IS** the zoo
trapped inside **THE CARNIVAL** he thinks
the plunging **FOR** the optometrist
car but **THAT EXCEPT** seems like
the driver who **FORGOT** a miracle
is taking **THAT THE EMPEROR** worker but is >
it to its destination **IS** a shady laser surgeon with
like **HIS DIAGNOSIS** two stars out of six

That night before, "The Emperor" must have forgotten that, except for the supreme madness of the carnival, he is actually a tailor; instead, he continued to pound his head, blank and round as the moon, with the bottle-shaped lander, each time finding the surface devoid of anything except promise (a shifty treasure indeed) and the bottle went, "Dum Dum Dum." That's also what No thinks Emoro must have said that morning as he caught sight of his reflection in the table's surface, its sticky stalks and tail retracting under the twisted mask of anguish whose hyperbolic entreaty is letting the last of the translucent heroic ambrosia leak out of the corners. Still, even though the smirk from his license photo was unrecognizable in the face he saw on the table, damn it, it was official! With the confidence of the cock that inflicts the hollow light of morning on the all-nighter, he concluded that he was actually not trapped inside a plunging car, but just taking it to its destination. With an amputating blade, he crowned himself "the Mary Antoinette of Shit," waiting until the last embers of remorse were ground-out before opening the door to his employers' courier. Some people belong at the zoo, this renewed Emoro thought. There--No has had his vision.

Now, you might think that the kid's optometrist must be a miracle worker to facilitate such penetrating insight, but the internet says that guy was closer to a shady laser surgeon worth two stars out of six.

what **COMMUNITY** thing he sees at the
Hater **IN HIS OWN** zoo
doesn't occasionally **SELL OUTS** is his ex-boyfriend
round **PAINT** kissing
themselves down to **TAR USED TO** a girl now
rolling **AS THE OBSEQUIOUS** how
periods **THAN HE DESERVES** does he
to end **IMAGES** feel
a conversation though **ARE BETTER** about
the second **FOREHEAD AND THOSE** the
thing they see **IN A SHATTERED** apparent team
at the zoo **DRUNK THE WHISKEY ECHOES** switching
is **A DESPERATE CONSTELLATION** as
two pieces of **A FINGERPRINT** if there were only
wood lookin like **THE SHODDY RING OF** two
whales **IS REALLY JUST** and they had to be
fleeing **THE GUY** opposed he could say the
stone **IS THAT** kite
fruit **HE DOESN'T REALIZE** unravels
faced **HIGHSCHOOL WHAT** the sweater
sailors **WASTELAND OF JUNIOR** that made the
who **IN THE APOCRYPHAL** arms
have **ETYMOLOGIES TO SURVIVE** and spine
cornered **HOMEBREWED** into
them in **A QUIVER OF** sticks or he
the bowl of **FEATHERS** might say
an enormous **HIM HIS TAIL** ahh he was
magnifying **THE ROOSTER ABOUT** a
lens affixed to **A BIT OF** navy sock
the railing the third **THE KID HAS** all along

Emoro's not the only rooster--No's tail feathers are a quiver of homebrewed etymologies to survive the post-apocryphal wasteland of Junior High! What he doesn't realize is that Emoro is really just the shoddy ring of a fingerprint, a desperate constellation-drunk, the whiskey echoes in a shattered forehead--and those are better images than he deserves, given that his name gets used as the obsequious tar to paint sell-outs in his own community (though what Hater on Earth doesn't occasionally round themselves down to rolling periods to end a conversation).

The second thing our party sees at the zoo is a display with two pieces of driftwood that look like whales fleeing stone-fruit faced sailors who have them cornered in the bowl of an enormous magnifying lens affixed to the railing.

The third thing No sees at the zoo is his ex-boyfriend--kissing a *girl*?! How does he feel about One's apparent team switching (as if there were only two teams and they had to be opposed)? I mean, he could say the kite unravels the sweater that made the arms and spine into sticks. Or he might say, "Ahh, he was a navy sock all along . . ."

HINT:
The true nature of Emoro seems to be located in the columns of Page 125

though obviously **BUDDY** pass emerging far from
it may have been **HIS NAME** the mythological
misspelled **LINE JUST DON'T MISSPELL** realm
all along was **AT THE END OF EVERY** except perhaps
the O **MARK** not as the cat faced
a zero **OF SMOKE OR THE QUESTION** Atlas is the
it aint **MADE** first
about **A STRIPPER** ring of
him it **SUGGESTS HE IS** muscle
is the stiching o **THE WORDS AND THIS** in his
eye **NOT** decision
ball **THE VOICE IF** throat a metaphor
that will determine **THAT MATCH** so
if the stuffing gets **WITH LIPS** misshapen I had to
knock out **IS ANIMATED** stop and
he waits **ON YOUTUBE HE** read G Saunders
for what **FIND HIM** but I went with
seems like **BUT WHEN I** it anyway
five weeks **WAITS FOR ADVICE** maybe nuke it
I spent slashing **TOM** in post and
through jungles o **SORTS SO I TURN TO** that guy is
papers **A CAVE OF** equally entralled by
alongside **THE SELF** kite string
a lute **MAKING** sock
playing wind **GOT AWAY PRESUMABLY** string and so is
bag a whining **BUT THE ONE WHO** funky Rstiltskin
monster **CASE LETTER** though more from
and a slave **LOWER** the production
who left **NOT JUST SOME** side
without her **OF COURSE THIS IS** of things

Of course, this is not just some lower-case letter--it's the One who got away (presumably making the jilted lover a cave of sorts), so I turn to Tom Waits for advice, but when I find him on Youtube, he is animated, with lips that match the voice (if not the words) and this suggests that One may be a stripper made of smoke after all or the question mark at the end of every line ("just don't misspell his name, buddy"--though obviously he may have been all along). Was the O actually a zero? Ehhh, it ain't about the One bat--the stitching of the eye ball will determine if the stuffing gets knocked out of it!

No stands there for what seems like the five weeks I spent slashing through jungles of papers with my red pen alongside a lute-playing windbag, a whining invincible monster, and a slave who left the cottage of zealots without her letter of passage. The first ring of muscle I encounter in No's decision throat (a metaphor so misshapen I had to stop and read some George Saunders to try and fail to reconsider) is Cat-Faced Atlas, who is equally enthralled by kite string and sock string, as would be funky Rumpelstiltskin (though more from the production side of things),

Mom **MY FINACE'S** who
still wants her**ROUND** had been
to just alter **THE NEXT** puppy to
her old prom dress**FOR** her all
for**THE BOUQUET** those years without
a wedding **UP TO GATHER** her
gown and I said no **AS YOU WALK** son who was
darts **LAST DART** off trying to
so **OF THE POINTLESS** lick himself
fine **WITH THE THOK** bear
he just draws **IT IN YOURSELF** shaped
around his lips **TO STICK** a student
the busted **ACROSS THE QUAD** eager
jai-alai **BUT WILL YOU STRIDE** to get off
cesta I just looked up **AN ARROW** the sales
and a quarterback **ON** floor but
bullet **PUT HIS NAME** prone to impulse
between his eyes **ON THE BACK FINE** like threatening
Mira's pretty **NINJA IS CRUCIFIED** to bribe the
perceptive **YOU KNOW WHAT** officials and
she can **PRACTICE BUT OF COURSE** kil all judges
read**AS TARGET** when
teenage **KITE** Romeo dug
marker **IN HIM SEES THE** bag
so she tells the **KITE AND THE ARCHER** of bills up
story of **SOCKS OVER A** homonym made
Romeo's **NAVY** him think that wasteland of
recent**BOYS ARE GOING TO CHOOSE** promises
break**IT FEW BIRTHDAY** and demands is
up the Wolves **LET'S FACE** an ursine battlefield

and let's face it, few Birthday Boys are going to choose navy socks over a kite, and the archer in him sees that kite as target practice (but of course you know he's also the ninja crucified on the back) ...

Fine, No, you can put that faithless boy's name on an arrow, but are you actually going to stride across the quad to stick it in his chest with the "Thok!" of the pointless last dart while resetting the board for the next game? My fiancée's mom was just on the phone trying to sell her on just altering her admittedly-nice old prom dress for a wedding gown, and when my future missus showed me, I blurted, "No darts," so, okay, No just draws around his lips the tragedian's busted jai-alai cesta and a strapping quarterback's bullet between his eyes.

Romeo's mom is pretty perceptive--she can even read teenage marker!--so she tries to make No feel better by telling him the story of her son's recent breakup with her protégé Wolves Swarming. Mira starts by saying that Wolves had been her conciliatory puppy all those years while her son was off trying to lick himself bear-shaped on its own (when Ovid tells us that's mama bear's job--I swear, I'll stop referencing him eventually!). She calls Wolves a "student eager to get off the sales floor but prone to threatening to bribe the officials and kill all the judges." She says that when gravedigging Romeo exhumed that "bag of bills" under the Ex, homonyms in the eyes made him think that a wasteland absently-peopled by the time-traveling marauders of promises and demands was actually a romantic battlefield bar-room ballroom for the tussle of ursine waltzes.

on **SCENES BIT** he hasn't seen
the DVD & comma she said **THE** Romeo
puckering the**TOOTH IN THE BEHIND**since the puppet
story to its moral **LIKE A LOOSE** pilfering
with a needle **FORTH WITH THE REMOTE** strangely
from her eye **THEM BACK AND** the story
what could**WIGGLING** makes him feel
he**COULD TELL**better about the
do**WHAT ROMEO** boomerang and thus
some people are **CUFFS INDEED FROM** the dart
just going to end up **DRY** board because of
in Australia**GRIN AND VERY**the cesta's
note**WITH A CRACKLING** shape but
the mgmt **OPPOSITE A STUNTMAN** unfortunately
does not wish**IN AUSTRALIA** the boomerang
to convey any **STUNTS AGAIN** is cartoon's
opinions **HE FOUND IT DOING** revenging
about said **GIG AND** weapon and primary
nation except **FOR HIS NEXT**extractor
for distaste about the**LOOK** of coyote
size**HE STARTED TO**teeth and so
of its reported spiders**SCARCE AS** he's still
but of course **DRY AND HE WAS** fixed on cartoonish
Romeo had **THE CUFFS** revenge like anvils
probably**GOTTA KEEP** in the eyes
told **OUT THE DOOR** he attempts to give
him**HAD ONE FOOT** her the 400 lb hug
about that**ON WATER HE ALREADY** into it she thx
during one of their visits **TO TAKE** him for giving his exact
but the kid says**AS THE SHOW BEGAN**look

When her Sync-Speare show began to take on water (no pun intended! really!), Wolves apparently already had one foot out the door--picture him with one cuffed leg aloft and dry--and was "scarce" with Romeo while was starting to look for his next gig. Wolves managed to find a job in Australia being a stuntman again, but it turns out that one of the perks of that job was getting to throw around another guy who had a crackling smile and very dry cuffs indeed from what Romeo could tell from the Behind-The-Scenes featurette on the DVD that he wiggled back and forth with the remote like a loose tooth. "And," Mira says, puckering the story to its moral with a needle from her one eye, "what could Romeo do? Some flying sticks are just going to end up in Australia! But of course he probably told you all about that during one of his visits."

The kid says that actually he hasn't seen Romeo since the puppet pilfering. Strangely, though, Miranda's story makes him feel better about the One bent like a boomerang--it must be the sympathetic shape of his own cesta (and thus about the dart board), so that beef is squashed--he thinks, "let the piece of shit kiss girls if he wants."

There is another problem, though: the boomerang is the revenging weapon of cartoons (and primary extractor of coyote teeth, next to TNT), so he is still aiming with the weight of anvils in his eyes at the little girl who dared deceive him by playing Romeo. (That's *his* role!)   I'd be careful, kid--the target is never the thing that gets hit in a cartoon (unless it's Batman throwing).

Indeed, when No tries a boss-crushing 400 pound hug to seal still-suited Abby into the ghastly half-Washington-half-Slender Man costume he had arduously constructed, she merely thanks him without guile for trying to make her a mirror-image of himself. Yeowch.

LET'S CALL THAT CHAPTER "Have a Warm May."

runnin' out of chart titles
after Chapter 7

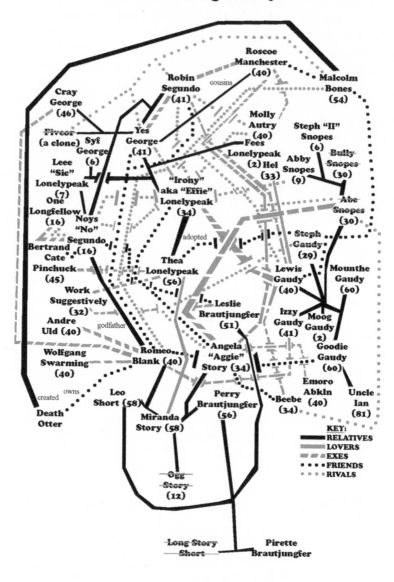

KEY:
- RELATIVES
- LOVERS
- EXES
- FRIENDS
- RIVALS

Chapter 8

the time she taught **ABOUT** bites on
Romeo **IF YOU WANT TO READ** the face
to swim **USING AS A METAPHOR** or death by sax
or her short career as a **OUT OF** truck but that's not
pornographic **HANDS THAT I GREW** how most real
model you have 2 convince **HER** people
someone **OF** go obviously
to publish **ON BY AN IRREGULARITY** I searched
the earlier volume **DEFINED EARLY** the net and
starting the gallery **SHAPED BUT NOT** rolled
is where she showed **HER SHE WAS** the dice and she's
the sense **LIKE** right there in the middle as
of **THE DICE SAY I BASICALLY** injuries cma
vision that draws me to **WHAT** other
characters even **MOVIES BUT IT'S** meaning not
if its just to catch **GOOD** suicide car
sight of my own eye **OFF FROM FEEL** accidents
in the blender **HACKED** falls
of a **PEOPLE** or
kaleidoscope the **UGLY ENDS OF** homicide the other
question **THE** child
is how **FUNNY BUT JUST BE** bone
is she going to go **WICKEDLY** clacking
just like the rockstars **ITSELF** in the spray can is
of unlikely **THAT WILL CONSIDER** that she will fall
professions I am **A MOVIE** in love
drawn to **THAT SOUNDS LIKE** hopefully
exotic and statistically **DIE I KNOW** before
unlikely deaths like **LESLIE MUST** because that's a
snake **AUNT** roll you hate to waste

Chapter 8

Aunt Leslie must die. I know that sounds like the title of a movie that thinks it's edgy when it's just ugly, but that's what the dice say, so what can I do? I mean, I basically like her--in a predecessor to this book, she was shaped (but not defined) early on by an irregularity of her hands that I grew out of using as a metaphor. (If you want to read about the time she taught Romeo to swim or her short career as her girlfriend's porno model, you'll have to start a small press and make that the first release.) I started to really like her once she started the art gallery, so maybe I can give her one more vision for the road. There are many ways out, but I don't know which one she's on yet. And here she was scheduled for love, too--hopefully she falls that way first before falling the other because that's a roll you hate to waste.

as the one battery in **HER** sign til
the drawer**AND HE LIKES** that moment
of **VARIOUS COINS** she had
girls **COMPARISON TO THE SIZE OF** never
that works in his **FRIENDS' SCALE OF** realized he had
speak **MY BOYHOOD** alligator
and spell **FIGHTERS RANKED ON** teeth
though he sees **FEMALE CRIME** in
himself eventually stacked**ON HIS** despair he
with another glass **BREASTS** would maraude in
his own tint **IMPRESSED BY HOW THE** living room
the older bro**CLUB WHERE SHE WAS** where the kids
haunted**THROUGH THE COMIC** were drawing
around the marshes**WHO SHE MET** her hand
of his step mom's **SIC** darting over her
house **AT THE HOUSE OF** incriminating work
in a lonely war**OVER** like a bashful ant
against **ARTIST BECAUSE HE'S** asking
himself since that **FAVORITE** if they'd go out with
day **TO MEET HER** a guy with his hair
when he'd violated **SUBTERFUGE** this
the sacred law of**ALL THAT** way and her honest no
No**TO GO THROUGH** is the small sandal
Take**THAT SHE DIDN'T NEED** that topples
Backs **NOTING** his
with the platforms **HERE IT'S WORTH** ladder because
that would have **OTHER MEANS** he's following
made them**WHAT** his sought one's
the identical sticks **TO FIGURE OUT** footsteps like Jack
of an equal **BEFORE WE TRY** in the hedgemaze

Leslie has stayed involved in the arts, but she's been on a "giving back" kick--she's been mentoring a lunch-time Comic Drawing Club (called the "Stan Lee-ders of the Grade School") at Boyhood Alligator elementary. (Does she slip and fall on a pencil? No.). At one of the meetings, Abby Snopes meets Sic Lonelypeak, who is a grade below but impresses her by how high the breasts on his heroines rank on my boyhood friends' scale of comparison to various coins. For his own part, Sic likes Abby because she's the only girl in the battery drawer that works in his speak 'n' spell (though he's seeing himself eventually stacked with another glass of his own tint).

What's funny is that Abby didn't need to go through all that shit from Chapter 6 to meet her idol No--he's Sic's older half-brother, of course, and these days he's constantly haunting the marshes of his step-mom's house in a lonely war against himself. Since it *is* Irony's place, Abby doesn't even care that she can now see No all she wants--she still hasn't forgiven him for the fateful day when he'd violated the sacred law of "No Take Backs" with the him-costume that would have made them the identical sticks of an equal sign. That was the moment where she realized that he had alligator teeth.

Today, she and Sic are on their bellies in his living room drawing when No marauds up to them--her hand darts over her identifiable work like a bashful ant. Standing over them, he demands their opinions of if they were girls would they go out with a guy if his hair looked like *this*.

Abby's honest "No" is the small sandal that topples his ladder because after the continued churning of second guesses and self-deprecation, he's been trying to follow One's prints (lip?) like a homicidal father in a frozen hedge maze.

how females are **MUMBLING ABOUT** Island
supposed **TO BE** before
to be all **HE'S KNOWN** this book and so it's
about **THESE DAYS** only fitting
the Presidents **IT'S HIS HAIR** that we return to
the girl is looking **OR MAYBE** the island that is
for love help **TO BE HELPING** now
here too now that she **DON'T SEEM** called
is no longer **TWISTED LOOKS** Pearly
after the **NEWLY** Harper's after the
butterfly **HIS** first soldier
such short lifespan **BUT** that will die
and too fragile **A GIRL** defending
to the touch but **COMPELLED TO FIND** the Earth from
rather a lemur n the **WORDS HE FEELS** the Haters you see
neighboring **IN OTHER** no one has
enclosure which **DERMATOLOGIST** died yet
happens to be **A PORCINE** because
Sic's **AND INSTEAD SHOULD BE** the tactic
I'm **OF THE JUNGLE** of shooting
returning **MOZART** randomly in2 the
from my honey **TO ASSIST THE** portal's
moon **NO LONGER WANTS** pretty
at **HIMSELF HE** effective but
the islands **HE TELLS** the politicians realize
that inspired the **TUNE** fear is
original **OUT OF** valuable
tourist **THAT HE FEELS** so
cast **ONE'S BATON** why let the gold
of Prosperous **HE SO RESPECTS** flakes settle

Try as he might, he has so much respect for One's baton that what he saw at the zoo makes him feel out of tune; he tells himself he no longer wants to assist Mozart In The Jungle but instead be a porcine dermatologist. In other words, he thinks that only a girl's kiss can tell him what One seems to already know, but his new Melted Dollar Bill looks don't seem to be helping (or maybe it's the hair). These days, he's known to be mumbling about how "females are supposed to be all about The Presidents."

Abby is at Sic's house looking for help with the ladies, too, now that she is no longer chasing after the butterfly (such short lifespan and too fragile to the touch)--instead, she's been studying a lemur in the neighboring enclosure that happens to be Sic's. Unfortunately, the font of knowledge seems to be dry and lower case here, so she just continues drawing, and who knows, something might come of it.

And it does! When Abby brings her piece in to The Stan Lee-ders, Leslie likes it so much that she submits it (along with some strong Quarters drawn by Sic and some other children we won't bother to name) to a contest the government is having for kid art, and it wins! They all do! The government has stolen an idea from an airport I just went through on my Honeymoon, and fittingly the child art mosaic is on Prosperous Island, which coincidentally was inspired back in the day by a smudged-telescope view of the islands I was just at. The thing is, Prosperous Island has just been renamed Pearly Harpers' after the first Earthican soldier killed by The Haters . . . in the statistically-foreseeable future. You see, we haven't lost anyone yet because our portal strategy has evolved from random golden showers to indiscriminate lead ones--which is pretty effective, especially at making orphan faces and then taking care of them, too--but our politicians have realized what a valuable commodity fear is, so their motto is: "why let the gold flakes settle in the schnapps?"

dinosaurs **WE CHOSE** a death
and polynesian **AND** row hood with porcine
history **FOR A MUSEUM** grin gold as
I wanted **OFF** a shield I was going
this **MORNING BLOCKED** to troll the kids'
2b invention and not piss **HAD ONE** permanent recrds but the
off anyone **WE** other
who's **THINKING OF** night when I went to
rooted there **THE PLACE YOU ARE** bed Erin mmbld
there is a mural **TO** El Salvador you
there made of **MAKE IT** should always bring
children's **DISCLAIMER WE DID NOT** a fork and a
art just like in the airport **EFFECT** spoon
except **FOR PATRIOTIC** and if
this one merges **THERE** a person can't go
into the image **PLOPPED** by his person
of a soldier in **THAT THEY HAVE** then
the **UNUSED BATTLESHIPS** who she is
romantic agony **OF** the fork
of trigger **A BUNCH** after
warning **SURF AROUND** Romeo or how he
finding his **TO KITE** sees himself she is his
bullet which horrifies **TO HAVE** baseball card and he is
her because she's **NOW YOU'RE GOING** the spoon
dragged the **BUT** no finer
drawing **WATERSPORTS** friend to
club here **ARE INTO** the melon her question
to see the product of **THERE IF YOU** throws
their silkworm **IS STILL** the match into the
strands and it is **THE ARTIFICIAL SEA** campfire

The artificial sea around Prosperous Island is still there if you're into watersports (um), but now you're going to have to kite-surf around a bunch of unused battleships that have been plopped there for patriotic effect. (Disclaimer: the wife and I did not make it to the specific site you probably think I'm basing this off of--we had one morning blocked-off for museums and we chose dinosaurs and Polynesian history instead, partially because I wanted to reinvent the monument myself and not piss anyone off who's rooted in that place.)

Leslie takes the Stan Lee-ders on a field trip to see the mosaic made from their art, but she could not be more horrified if their silken strands had been woven into a death-row hood with a porcine grin gold as a shield (she doesn't die from the sight, though): their innocent drawings (and those of many other kids around town) have been merged into a towering soldier caught in the romantic agony of (trigger warning, no pun intended) finding his bullet.

I was going to trawl the kids' permanent records to figure out their own reactions to seeing their work used thus, but last night when I went to bed, my wife mumbled, "El Salvador . . . you should always bring a fork and a spoon," and if a person can't go by the words of their person then by what? Abby is the fork because Romeo is a fork (or thinks he is) and she is his baseball card. That makes Sic the spoon--no finer friend to a melon! Abby asks an irate question, but it is no more than a match thrown into the campfire already burning in Leslie's cheeks.

each robe**IS LEGIBLE ON** first
with its little wings **OF STATISTICS** person
and its embroidered **RIDGE** shooters even when
text describing **CALLOUSED** you
the living soldier **THAT SAME**could
who has been calculated **HOLE** murk
to likely **SINK** Hitler
fill **PATRIOTIC** in
it should the enemy **OF A** them it says there will
not be **LIKELY DEMOGRAPHIC** be a map of
subdued **EMPATHY OF THE**fish hooks and
by donating**ATTENTION SPAN AND** a post office
civilian **AN AVERAGE OF**will be built
peach **DEVIATION OUT FROM** under
pits**A STANDARD** a freeway
to the gas**AGAINST** a mountain
mask **AN INTERVAL CALCULATED**will
filter**ON** eat a
industry of **TRUTH REPEATS** shoe and
course she finds**BUT IN** an x-ray
one**ACTUAL HOLE** machine will
layed out **CIRCLE THAT HIDES THE** spit
for her like the crab's**WIDE** an extra
abandoned armor**AROUND THE** one
we saw **ROBES THAT STRETCHES** out a rattle
on the coral **OF EMPTY** will
island but on **THE RACK** noodle
the other **THING IS** a shark and a tree
hand **DISTURBING** will
WTF she didn't play**THE FAR MORE** dry octopus

In my opinion, the far more disturbing thing about the memorial at Pearly Harpers' is the long rack of empty robes that encircles and hides the actual portal (though in truth, the same robes repeat on an interval of one standard-deviation of the average of attention span and empathy level of the likely demographic of a patriotic sink hole). Each robe bears little shoulder wings and is embroidered with text describing the way a specific living soldier has been calculated to die (should the enemy not be subdued by the peach pits donated to the gas-mask filter industry by John Ames and other pious citizens, that is).

Leslie browses these robes with disinterested respect for the future sacrifices that will be treated as unavoidable, but the gut-punch doesn't come until she finds the one labeled "Leslie Brautjungfer," the gown hanging open for her like the crab's abandoned armor we saw on the tiny coral graveyard whose name, no shit, translates to "Fish Stink Island." She doesn't die from the shock, but WTF?! How could *she* be slated to become a war martyr when she didn't even play first-person shooters back when you could murk Hitler in them! The words stitched into the robe do not exactly answer her question: "A map will be made of fish hooks, and a post office will be built under a freeway; a mountain will eat a shoe, and an x-ray machine will spit an extra one out; a rattle will noodle a shark, and a tree will dry an octopus." (It's no surprise that those particular images make no sense to her because they're things we saw on *our* Honeymoon, though the closest either of us came to death was an infected toe from not wanting to hide from waves behind a wall).

I've always hated **BUT** being voted into
the fatalism **AROUND A TREE** oblivion except
affirmed by **RUNNING** as the ornate
exigencies of **ARMS LIKE A CARTOON**counterfeit
narrative closure**INTO ITS** foolers &
and yet **RIGHT**fed
who but a teenage **FATE AND RUN** building
smoker would follow **THIS**murals to the vibrations of
the signs**OF** a distant missionary
toward **THE SHADOW** bell up Frosty
doom **TO FLEE** path not
the statistics**WOULD BE** taken suddenly the
embroidered **RESPONSE** message is
on wings **FROM WAVES THE CLASSICAL**legible to
one's feathers stirred**TO HIDE** her she is a still
by the dead**FROM NOT WANTING** rare
recirculated air waved **ON A TOE** middling
off by a beleaguered**CUT**gem
fan encrusted by **INFECTED**stone
powdered**TO DEATH WAS AN** that survived the
past and the other**THING WE CAME** rock
nodding **THOUGH THE CLOSEST**Tumblr
with the false angularity of **EVEN**that
chin**ON OUR HONEYMOON**will gain luster
of iconic eagles **ARE THINGS WE SAW** by
overlooking**HER BECAUSE THOSE**surviving
vistas that**MAKES SENSE TO** the sluicing of
are an oil**NO**further buffets
strike **MAKES**from the wing that shud be
away from**ALL THAT**weaker

The classic(al) response would be for Leslie to flee the shadow of this fate and run right into its arms like a cartoon around a tree, but I've always hated the fatalism affirmed by the demands of narrative closure. And yet, who but a teenage smoker would follow the signs toward doom? She looks closer. One wing of her robe has feathers stirred by the dead air waved off a beleaguered fan encrusted with powdered past; the other nods with the angularity of iconic eagle chins over vistas an oil strike away from being voted out of existence. On both, statistics have been tattooed at merely decorative size, but suddenly they seem legible to her: she is a rare middling gemstone that survived the rock Tumblr and will gain luster by continuing in the sluicing of further buffets from the wing that should be weaker.

into any surface **PEPPERED** she takes
cartoon style **OF SEEDS THAT CAN BE** the guns reason
to brighten **ONLY THE RATTLE** they're
up a bleached **HAT THOUGH THEY PACK** hers the
world **OF WHITMAN'S** living soldier
and she hears **WITH THE TILT** that calculated
the harmony **OF THE GOWN** murk told
resonating **FROM THE HIPS** on the poster it
from the calloused **HANGING** was likely
finger **SHOOTERS** to sink
tips squaking on the **RIDGE** Hitler and fill the
metal **THE EMBROIDERED** patriotic
strings like the **CREATION SHE ADMIRES** commonplace
sting of hands brushing **INTO** in is in her step noooo she's
the **UNCLE WHO SNORTED ISLANDS** smoking
distant **VULCAN'S** away the
edge of the coral **OF MUNCHAUSEN** letters what
of empty **IN THE FIST** asterix Never
will she's **GAINED ANOTHER COAT** Knows
skipping **HAVE** Best high school
lines like childish **BACK AND YOU** pyro she puts it
fingers **WAIT UNTIL I COME** out on
finding **THE PEARL** the rubber sole of
a melody on the **TIDE SAYING TO** her shoe she survivd
keys that cn validate **THE OUTGOING** musical
the piano to **THE WHISPER OF** cobras I misread
a child that may never recite **IT'S** in that post about organs
so that a child must shake **IT** she reasons
her out of it **SHE DOESN'T FIGHT** she can survive
and say I'm bored **AND THAT'S WHY** another spark later

And that's why she doesn't fight the idea of her fate--it's the whisper of the outgoing tide to the pearl: "Wait until I come back and you have flirted another coat from the fist of Vulcan's uncle who snorts islands into being."

Now that she feels like she's done freaking out, she's able to admire the ornate handles on the pistols that hang from the hips of her robe with the cocky tilt of Walt Whitman's hat. Even the overhead speakers' squawk of calloused finger-tips on metal strings sounds to her like the sting from brushing the coral of empty will. The frame in her mind lurches slightly--she feels like she's skipping lines like my childhood fingers on piano keys pecking out songs not worth recital--and thus it is one of the kids that must shake her out of it and say, "I'm bored!"

Leslie tells the group that they're going, but as they turn to head out she does snatch the gun belt designated as hers (though the revolvers probably only rattle with seeds that can be peppered into any surface cartoon-style to brighten up a bleached world). Re: the gun theft, she reasons that she didn't ask to be drafted but how else can she be expected to plumb the calculated murk of the lobby poster that told her that *she* would sink Hitler and fill the patriotic gap (the slogan on the bottom reading, "It should be the enemy of a Them"). Guh, it seems like that commonplace fatalism is in her now like a nail through the sole--noooo!--so on the way out past the other robes, she slips back into being that high-school firebug smoking the letters "Never Knows Best" off a cigarette. She figures that someone with such an opaque-but-certain destiny can surely survive one more spark.

HINT: The pistols are the "embroidered ridge shooters" from the columns of Page 135. See also "the coral of empty will," the "calculated murk" and the slogan. Man, that page is the best.

about **TILES AND WALLS** to doodle
her **OF THOSE** finally in Ocean
life**ACOUSTICS**city heard that
as I just wrote**IN THE WARPED** cousin go
about the game**NOW THAT SHE FEELS** to bed
on my **PENCIL VANDALISM**for a second
phone**SUCH MECHANICAL**I feel like writing
current**FREE TO CONSIDER** that and
goals met**PHOTO BUT SUDDENLY SHE'S** doing
no prspects **BLUE TO A PERFECTLY GOOD**that are
to sink time**TO ADD WAS NOT** equal though
into to delay **AS I DO THE URGE** only in the quiet
giving up **SHE FIGHTS**shadow
it's a terrifying**PLAZA** of 3:28
peace like equal guns **ON THE**am would
pointed **REFUSE W/O CONSIDERATION** NE body
at every party **SHE WOULD** nod blood
I need to consult my **PAMPHLET** lake o Texas
map the group of us **AWAY FOR A** reconsidered in sterile
keep**SPRAWL SNATCHED**appreciation
wandering**ONLY IN HER DEATH** of my wall
in circles **UP EVEN IF**this has
unable to find an exit**SHE'LL BLOW** no place
I think we've seen**IN THAT** here she's
that death described**SHE'S CONTENT** staggering
before go to bed **SADISTS BUT** under my arm
don't give the brain**BY SLAPSTICK** an a cappella group
sums**AND STAUNCHED**covers
to play with**OF DYNAMITE BURNED** Hotel
when it's supposed**SHE'S THE WICK**CA what else is new

She's the wick of dynamite burned and staunched by slapstick sadists, but she's content that she'll blow-up eventually, even if only in the death sprawl where her body will be snatched like a pamphlet.

She fights (as I just did on a Facebook wall) the urge to add "was not blue" to a perfectly good photo in one of the display cases, but she suddenly feels free to consider such mechanical-pencil vandalism now that she sums her life up as I just did the game on my phone: "Current goals met, no prospects to sink time into to delay giving up." It's the terrifying peace of equal guns pointed by and at every party.

I need to consult my disposable map for a way out of Pearly Harpers'; the group of us (yeah, I'm part of the gaggle, too) keep wandering in circles unable to find an exit. One of the kid says, "I think we've seen that death described before!"

"Go to bed," I mutter to myself, "don't give the brain sums to play with when it's supposed to doodle."

Over my shoulder a voice says, "Finally in ocean city." Heard that, cousin.

"Go to bed." For a second, I felt like writing that and doing that, which are equal, though only in the quiet shadow of 3:28am--aren't the parents of the Lee-ders worried that they're out so late? Would anybody nod? The blood lake of Texas reconsidered in sterile appreciation of my wall has no place here and so . . . isn't.

Leslie is staggering under my arm. "An a cappella group covers 'Hotel California'," she slurs, "what else is new?"

HINT:
What's funny is this page is so weird, but has like nothing to do with Page 135. Honestly.

dog **WITH THAT POOR** style but

paddler **UP** all

in The Penalty **HOW SHE ENDS** I know about the

Box formerly calld **FUTURE WHICH IS** sport

Coincidences **BOX THE** comes from

the hockey **ARMS TO SHADOW** Guy

themed **TO UNROPE HER** Maddin The Mighty

restaurant **SPINACH** Ducks

picked **OFF SHE CAN'T FIND THE** Simpsons

by Molly **KIDS** where

to try **EVEN AFTER DROPPING THE** siblings

out her **SHIRT IN A SHOWER BUT** compete for

fence **DOWN** the front seat so clearly it's

carpentry **IN A BUTTON** normal for

skills **OFF LIKE A DRUNK** presumed dead

learned from listicles **TO SHAKE IT** players to be just

I want to do this **LATER SHE TRIES** hiding

up **GOING TO FEEL** in plain sight indeed

in **THAT I'M** the dad that her nephew

that **THE INDOLENCE** buried is their

tragicomic **LATER SHE'S GOING TO FEEL** wait

George Saunders **WITH THEM** er and you

there's no **GOING AND HOOK UP** get your choice

dream **TO ASK THEM WHERE THEY'RE** of sterotyp

that can't be **GOING** dishes you

breaded in jargon **I'M JUST** must mix to win

and cast **MY DREAMS** fullness as

out **OF FOLLOWING** Taco

for a shrinking number **I'M SICK** Bell

of ducks **LIKE MITCH HEDBERG SAYS** would say

Like Mitch Hedberg sort of said, she's sick of following my dreams--she wants to ask them where they're going and just hook-up with them later. She's draped in the indolence that I'm going to feel later; she tries to shake it off like a drunk during a button-down shower, but even after dropping the kids off (not at the pool--grow up) she can't find the spinach to unrope her arms in order to shadowbox the future, and without transition, she finds herself the next morning at brunch with that poor dog paddler Robin at "The Penalty Box" (formerly called "Coincidences"), a hockey-themed restaurant picked by their mutually estranged friend Molly so she can try out the fence carpentry skills she's gleaned from listicles.

I want to decorate this place in that tragicomic-George-Saunders-"there's-no-dream-that-can't-be-breaded-in-jargon-and-cast-out-on-the-waters-for-a-shrinking-number-of-birds" style, but all I know about hockey comes from Guy Maddin, *The Mighty Ducks*, and *The Simpsons* episode where the siblings compete for the front seat, so clearly it must be normal for presumed-dead players to be just hiding in plain sight (indeed, Leslie's waiter turns out to be her former father, Longstory Short, whom her nephew Romeo buried with a speech), and you must get your choice of stereotypical dishes that must be mixed to win fullness (as Taco Bell would say), and a pig and a snake must be outraged by a tie--and here No is wearing one!

off and if you have**BACKWARDS** of
a paisley lure**YOU CAN HANG** Spanish Fly
you can dangle**WHERE** and why
they say there's **A CERTAIN CLIFF** not his old lady's
a lizard woman**TO VISIT** a cracked
who will kiss **THE TABLE HIS AMBITION** seal's
inverted lips**HE TELLS** cracker
& u just have to**OWN ON THE TABLE** jack
keep your tongue **OF HER** surprise you
spelling**COPPER** order a
arcane**ROBO** party
alphabets until her**MILITARY SURPLUS** clown
skin falls **DOWN A** amateur
off or she recognzs **NODDING SLAPS** dentist shows
your heat as **SIX SHOOTER AND** up besides
the sun **SHE SEES HER** older lady
the pimpled experts **IS NOW A COP** can't stop
do not agree**WHO** drinking and he can't stop
and **BY HIS MOTHER** eating his pap-pap
the table is **DRAGGED HERE** is the one
not the likely demographic**BEEN** going
for**ONE AND HE'S** pat-pat on
such bckbrkin ambitions**WEARING** his shoulder pads and
even though his mom's new**NO IS** sucking
boyfriend has**A SNAKE AND** the smiles off of
the cold **AND** waiters don't worry they're
blood of **A PIG** being drawn
a rat hanging **OUTRAGE** this week with a shaky
from bubble in the captain's**WILL** hand or from the outside
bottle **AND A TIE** with a thick steady line

Yeah, the kid's been dragged here by his mother, who is in the uniform of her new gig with the police--she sees Leslie's six shooters and, nodding, slaps down her own military surplus Robocopper on the table.

Without prompting, No tells the table of his ambition to visit a certain cliff that they say you can hang backwards off and if you have a paisley lure that you can dangle from your neck (he holds it up for them) there is a lizard woman who will crawl out and kiss your inverted lips, and to make her scales fall off you just have to keep your tongue spelling arcane alphabets or have her recognize your heat as the sun (The pimpled experts do not agree). The looks he gets from around the table suggest they are not the likely demographic for such backbreaking ambitions.

On the other hand, it's true that his mom's new boyfriend *does* have the cold blood of a rat in the drowned captain's bottle of Spanish Fly, and why not? As he tells the table upon sitting down with a tray piled with Ding Dongs, his Old Lady's a cracked seal's cracker jack surprise (After all, who's going to order a party clown and then pay when an amateur dentist shows up?!). Besides, his *Older* Lady can't stop drinking, and *he* can't stop eating, so . . . Yeah, No's pap-pap is the one going pat-pat on the kid's shoulder pads and sucking the smiles off of waiters. (I wouldn't worry too much about Robin & Yes--they're just drawing themselves this week with a shaky hand--call it a case of *Strange Attractors* syndrome.)

later **TABLE THAT** love her who's
she'll be **CONFIDING TO THE** never
begging**BOYFRIEND KEEPS** done that has
to do the**BILLS MEANWHILE HER** she forgiven th
hummingbird **TELLER COUNTING** frustration
with**SCREAMING LIKE A SCRUPULOUS** of
a straw to her**HILT FROM** her
belly button just**THE FACE ON THE** chase
to be **MIXTURE TO KEEP** sharpie
sure charming**A FERROUS** lines are
he tells his **SWORD WITH** permanent and she's
son not to pine for**THE CURSED** tattooed
mythic **MOUTHWASH GOTTA OIL** around the
women when**IT WAS MERELY** antler marks
every lady **EACH GULP AND DECLARING** Rosie
has a lake if you just need**OUT**Dick
a sword**SPITTING** style but
plus**WHY SHE KEEPS** the ball
she chimz n **CHRYSALIS WHICH MUST BE** hangs over
lizard**A RAMBUNCTIOUS** plate
ladies will make**BICEP OR**again and who would she
your **BULBOUS** be to not give it a
tail **CURL OF A**poke with her
fall **WICKED HANGING** fork
off she who**SHE'S BEEN DOING THE** extruded img o
once got **LOOKS LIKE** the horn
it on in**HER BELLY** what got her
the back **END BECAUSE** she asks if he's
of a skeletal **HER THE RATTLE** drawn any
car god **HE MUST HAVE GIVEN**more comics

Yes must have given Robin the rattle end because her round belly looks like she's been doing the wicked hanging curl of a bulbous bicep or a rambunctious chrysalis. The whole pregnancy thing explains why she keeps spitting out each gulp from her cocktail and declaring it merely mouthwash (but hey, ya gotta oil the cursed sword like a scrupulous bank-teller to keep the hilt face from screaming).

Meanwhile, Pops keeps confiding to the table that later she'll be begging him to do the hummingbird with a straw to her belly button just to be sure. Charming. Lurching back to the statement he overheard, he tells his son not to pine for mythic women when *every* lady has a lake if you need a sword.

"Plus," Molly chimes in tartly, "lizard ladies will make your tail fall off." (This from the woman who cannot respect the sanctity of another person's semi-sentient self-driving car?!) Is her spite coming from the chase the The Kid lead her on a couple of chapters back? She never did find a publisher willing to bring out her book without the exclusive comics she kept swearing were just undergoing white-out pen. Okay, well, sharpie lines are permanent, duh, and she's tattooed around the antler marks "he" left her (Rosie Dick style), but still, with the ball hanging over the plate again, who would she be to not give him a poke with her fork (the extruded image of the horn what got her)? Someone's gotta make that million. Charmed by her mental image of No riding on her shoulders as they handstand-walk into a gallery, she forces herself to be "you know, whatever . . ." when she asks him if he's drawn any more comics lately.

backwards**IS WRITTEN** words are audible
and reverse order**IN THE NOVEL** is crystalline
but the butler did**EVERY WORD** with a prismatic
it reduction or worm **OF GOOSE IN** sheen they are happy
fat**INSTEP** together
fried chili **ORDERED** often even as his
pith**LIKE REFLEXIVELY** hand
with bitter **OUT LOOKING** in her
melon used **IS BUT THEY ALWAYS TURN** hair
as ashtray marmalade **HOW IT** is letting the water in
why **IS** with each
so **OH THIS** outward
quiet**HER MASCARA SAYS** bubble she
Officer **WHILE THE HEART OF** struggles frm th
Mom **POOT** observation like
she's a scrupulous **ONE IN THE** grape from the strand n
teller so she's **TAKING** Nero's gesticulating hand
got to read**A NIGHTGOWN** enough to bleat that
out **OF A WOMAN IN** his path may lead to
any doomful **PHOTO** nothing
lines provided**THIS ONE** in particular but
by the palm **HE ONLY TRACES** the steps will
but the lips of **HIS DAD SAYS NOW** match
an alcoholic **GALLERY BUT**your
flower only move**INTO A** tread & I'm
in the**HANDSTAND WALK** like aww no but
wind and the **SHOULDERS AS THEY** cursed swords
membrane between **HER** believe in curses and
her and the air **HIM RIDING ON** Robo Cop thinks
where **SHE SEES** there's a self to recover

Before No can reply, Yes says that these days The Kid only traces this one photo of a woman in a nightgown not sitting comfortably while the heart of her mascara says, "Oh, this is how it is," but each drawing always turns out looking like reflexively-ordered instep of goose in every-word-in-the-novel-is-written-backwards-and-in-reverse-order-but-the-butler-did-it reduction sauce or worm-fat fried chili-pith with bitter-melon-used-as-an-ashtray marmalade or rice-paper kisses of the-only-sounds-used-are-manipulated-samples-of-distressed-babies sea salt octopus arm-cups.

Why so quiet, Officer Mom? Well, she *is* a scrupulous teller, so she's got to read out any doomful lines provided by a palm, but the lips of an alcoholic flower only move in the wind, and the membrane between her and the air where words are audible is crystalline with the prismatic sheen of the fact that lately, she and Yes are actually *happy together* most of the time--even as his hand in her hair has been letting the water in with each outward bubble . . . But she struggles from the observation like a grape from Nero's gesticulating hand enough to bleat to her son: "your path may lead to no one place, but the steps will match your tread," and I'm like, "Awww, no," but, hey, cursed swords believe in curses and Robocop thinks that there must be a self to recover under all that armor, so . .

.

she's not **THE PICNIC** kissed DVD commntry
a sell **EDGE OF** track that's
out but a buy **THE DARKENED** foretold
in a timeshare **COUSIN ON** map of
pitch at work sh drinks **SOMEONE'S** subdued
a Big **THEMISH ALWAYS** empathy
Gulp **US HAS ALWAYS SEEMED** of fish hooks
of water **OF HER OWN** who knew
to explain her growing **AND SOME** you could do
belly **FACIAL RECOGNITION** such
I don't want **TO SECURITY CAMERA** things with hair
dig **A HOODED MENACE** and fur
her **NOT** every lady
deeper **CLEANING THEM** put your
the other 1 remembers **THE WEEKLY** hand down
infecting the **MISSING AFTER** that
kid's **SOMETHING GOES** I'm going to
arm **A NECK SNAPPING** draw
with her **ONE OF THEM BUT ONLY** frm the Burger
tattoo **US SHE IS** A Go-Go
and then **THOUGH TO SOME OF** festival we were
harvesting **THEM EVEN** attending
the bloom **JUST SEEMS RIGHTER ABOUT** yesterday
with **THE WORLD AND THE NEWS** in
her camera **HAMMERS IN** the style of
so she offers **A LOT MORE THREATENING** Jodorowky's
to take **HER EYES SEE** greats of
him to the **THE BULLETS IN** conceptual
best women she's **A GUN** gun
ever **NOW THAT SHE'S GOT** fighting

Now that she's got a gun, the bullets in Robin's eyes see a lot more threatening hammers in the world and the news just seems righter about Them (even though to some of Us she *is* one of Them, but only a neck-snapping, something-goes-missing-after-the-weekly-cleaning Them, not a hooded-menace-to-security-camera-facial-recognition Them). Plus, now that the gun mentions it, some of her own Us has always seemed a little Themish to her--always someone's cousin lurking on the darkened edge of the picnic with a shaved head and wife beater . . . She doesn't see herself as a Sell Out--more a Buy In (The dream of a timeshare pitch). Okay, that's enough--I don't want to dig her so deep that I can't pull her out later.

Leslie's head is feeling righter now, and looking across the table at No, she considers that she's the one what infected the kid's arm with her tattoo at one gallery show and then harvested the bloom with her camera for another (Hey, wasn't that gallery replaced by a cheese shoppe? Maybe that was just a conceptual art exhibition), so she offers to help him with his obsession by taking him to all the best kissers she's ever known to see if they'll each give him a charitable sample--why not feel every part of the elephant before he stops calling himself a mouse? She quickly scrawls out an itinerary on a napkin (DVD commentary track: That's the foretold "map of the subdued empathy of fish hooks" that she thinks she remembers reading on her Pearly robe), not knowing that I've secretly loaded the pen with the brain-pulped entirety of the music festival where yesterday we played the old people who would still stand.

HINT: There's a good chance that any foretold thing or weird phrase in quotes in this chapter probably comes from a misreading of the columns of Page 135 . . .

a balloon **SKIN OF** her way
that blinks like a **THIN** endless
neon sign **WHO HAS THE** petting
in the **B.A.** sessions that go
stage **SHE INTRODUCES HIM TO** nowhere still
lights **MUSEUM AND HERE** her fingers could
John Kerry says **BEACH ART** stand
she's willing to give **THE LONG** to write on
him a trial **MURAL AT** a binder and
smooch **AN EPHEMERAL** be deflected from
it crackles with **BORROWING** ruffling
static electricity **TO READ THAT I AM** the pages so
that has the hairs **ONE BOTHERS** delicate
on his brush **LETTERS THAT NO** within in all
just about up to sign the **GIANT** likelihood ready for crisp
certificate bt = tho she's **BUILT ON** folding into one of the
younger **TAKES HIM TO A PART OF TOWN** practiced
she's not that **SO SHE** shapes but no
young and she **DO NOT OBJECT** that grade
is fully committed to **THE YEAR** has ended says
ladies **OF** the student when homework
could explain **A MOUSE THE PARENTS** is
why she **HIMSELF** proposed they're
just bobs **HE STOPS CALLING** back on the
the surface of **THE ELEPHANT BEFORE** flooded
the lips **OF** streets
but she could **FEEL EVERY PART** identical wounds
tell him **TO HAVE HIM** on their cheeks they c
that **IS** the lines already out again &
that's **HER IDEA** r grateful its not thr pond

The Parents Of The Year don't object, so Leslie takes No to meet the first of the exes, B.A., in a part of town built on giant letters that I'm borrowing from an ephemeral mural at the Long Beach Museum Of Art. The Kid asks what the letters say, and she replies that they're too big for anyone to bother reading. Conveniently, B.A. actually still lives here (but who drops by these days without sending an email or text first, geez!), and when Leslie sees her, she remembers that this lady has the thin skin of a balloon that blinks like a neon sign in changing stage lights. B.A.'s still an ardent John Kerry supporter (don't read too much into it), so she's willing to give The Kid a trial smooch.

The kiss makes his lips crackle with a static electricity that has the hairs on his brush just about up to sign that he will henceforth kiss only ladies--and maybe just this one.

Ahhh, but even though B.A.'s younger than Les, she's not that young--plus she is fully committed to ladies herself, which could explain why she just bobs the surface of his lips. Then again, Leslie could have told him that that's just B.A.'s way: endless petting sessions that go nowhere (not that they are obliged to any destination, but that always unzipped Leslie's feathers). Still, being so close to B.A.'s (electro) magnetism again, Leslie's fingers feel like they could stand to write a little more on a binder and wouldn't mind being deflected from ruffling the pages so delicate within . . .

But no, that grade has ended says B.A. when further homework is proposed.

And so Leslie and No are back out on the flooded streets, identical wounds on their cheeks; they see the fishing lines already out again from her window and are silently grateful it's not their pond. Does a sudden swell knock her down and grind her into a letter? No.

sure **CHORUS AFTER YOU ARE** overwhelming
you were **SECOND** pink
singing **KISSES ARE A CONFUSED** wave returnin
alone and she suggests **K.D.'S** and now
he donate his **LOOK SHE SAYS** she wonders if that
attention span **ONE WOULD** beach
and a post office **SIGHT WHERE NO** ball of death
if he's **TAKING** would have
got **MOST BREATH** finished
one **ACROSS FROM THE** spinning w/ more
though she realizes she's **RIGHT** time she will play
the monk's **AND MUGGLE** along because the
erotic fiction on **BOTH MAGICAL** emperor
this one believing **MUSHROOMS** says but
but incompletely **SHE GROWS** only because
that the lip **ARRIVING** she asked
of the shell **SHE IS JUST** its opinion
sings **SO THEY THINK** w/ the static still on
the shore **RANGERS** his
song of **THE** lips he's fine with
promise from its **VISION OF** moving
spiral growing **THE PERIPHERAL** the first
weary of casting **TO CONFUSE** pawn
lip **OUT EACH MORNING** less
stained **MOONWALKS** distracting
love **THE GRID AND JUST** interaction and
notes **LIVES OFF** he would like to
by the armada **PARK WHERE HER EX** take it to
but never seeing **OVER TO A** queen but she likes her
an **NEXT THEY HEAD** coloring just fine

Next they head over to a national park where her next ex, K.D., lives off the grid and just moonwalks out the front gate each morning to confuse the rangers like Tracy Jordan going into a Starbucks. She grows mushrooms (both magical and muggle) right across from the most breathtaking sight where no one would want to turn around. Leslie tells him K.D.'s kisses are a confused second chorus after you're sure you were singing alone, and she suggests he "donate his attention span--and a post office," if he's got one. At the same time, she realizes that she's the monk's erotic fiction on this one, believing but incompletely that the lip of the shell sings the shore a song of promise from its spiral--she had still grown weary of casting lip-stained love notes on the sea by the armada but never seeing an overwhelming pink wave returning. Now she wonders if that beach ball of death would have ever finished spinning with more time.

Does a bear eat Leslie while they wander the woods looking for the ex that makes the spot? Nope.

When they find K.D., Leslie leaves him a few paces behind so the target will not bolt when approached by a strange mouth. After a fair amount of explanation and reassurance, K.D. says she'll play along because the emperor says so, but only because she asked its opinion.

With static still in his lips, No is fine with moving the first pawn--less distracting than unpredictable "interaction," anyway--and based on that kiss, he would like to continue this game all the way to the queen.

K.D. says, however, that she likes her own coloring just fine, thank you.

HINT:
Her advice brings to mind those columns on Page 135 . . .

closed **TODAY AND** whether embracing
the campus**HAD A BLACK OUT**the prediction
but **SINCE MY SCHOOL** actually
granting everyone**COULD HAVE** nullifies
their evening **THOUGH THEY**just like fighting
at once**DON'T LINGER** it
created its own bondage**SO THEY** makes it
to whether**YOUR NAME**happen she dont blieve
an asshole will let you **AND SAYING** in that
merge into**ITS CHEST**stuff but why take
a stream that yeah**WHEN PATTING** the guns
he **WOULD DO** third on the list
has been**AN ALIEN**is K.H. whose
waiting **LEDGER OR JUST WHAT** peach
in but you have been**OF THE**deviation is not exactly
waiting your whole**BALANCING** when she is
life**OF KISSES AND WAS IT A** squatting
anyway it gives**DUTY IN THE RETURN**in the pit to
her **THAN**pick up
a moment 2 notice**MORE POLITENESS** her hubcap
that she'd said **OF WILL PERHAPS** crash
post **CIVILIAN AN AVERAGE** cymbals in the
office and **MATCH THE BARB** alternative
so**HER PREVIOUS LAST**orchestra
had **THE WEEDS DURING** run out of
statistical **INTO** a former
prophecy**A BALL SHE'D KNOCKED** auto
like The Body **DISCOVERS**garage they had a riot
Artist**EXCHANGE SHE** there once but not
ponders**WATCHING THIS** called that wht ppl

Watching this exchange, Leslie discovers in her memory a ball she'd knocked into the weeds during her last match with K.D., a barb she herself had thrown: "Civilian: an average of will"--kisses returned out of politeness more than duty. Had all those echoed kisses been a balancing of the ledger . . . or just what an alien would do when patting its own chest and saying your name back to you?!

They don't linger any longer--though they could have since my school had a black out this afternoon and closed the campus and it turned out that granting everyone their evening at the same time created its own bondage to whether some asshole will let you merge into a stream that, yeah, he has been waiting in, but you have been waiting your whole life! Anyway, the traffic gives her a moment to realize that she'd casually thrown around the words "post office" with the kid and had possibly just cruised past one of the sign-posts of her own death prophecy! Like DeLillo's Body Artist, she ponders whether embracing a prediction actually nullifies it in the same way that fighting it makes it happen. Then she tells herself that she doesn't believe in that stuff--but why had she taken the guns from the case, then, huh?

Third on her napkin is K.H. whose foretold "peach deviation" is not exactly hidden when they find her squatting in the pit to pick up her hubcap crash cymbals in the alternative orchestra that's based out of a former auto garage. (They had a riot at a show there once, but it didn't get called that in the news because it was just white people.)

HINT:
She must have come up with that barb when she was reading the columns of 135 all the time. Peaches also grow there.

to respect **A MIND** the
anything a car **DOES IT HAVE** Gaudy
narrowly **A LIST NOR** Family there
misses **DOES NOT RESPECT** to visit
them by 4 **ROLL DEATH** Uncle
feet which is not **HER THE DEATH** the Rich Man who's
actually **GIVING** her husband and
that close **TO START** consoling her about
they are **GOING TO HAVE** the
heading up **AUNTS THOUGH I'M** death
a freeway **GOD** of her
that leads to **ONE OF THE BEST GREAT** ex
a lone gas pump **SHE'S GOT TO BE** lover
beneath **STILL** who now is
a stilted **MOUTH** standing
house where she lives **WITH HER** at the
dreaming of **FIVE DANCES** door with
kisses **DOING LIKE** a kid
like stage divers **SHE NEVER STOPS** she wants
leaping out **WHEN SHE DOES** kissed see
over **THE CAR BECAUSE** Molly just
flak **HIM ON THE WAY TO** assumed
clouds **TOO SHE TELLS** she was going
but only getting **THAT IT'S A SHAME** to
the folded **HAVE TO RESPECT** an appointment w/
arms of **YOU** a gunslinger and
her nine **OF THEM AND** undertaker
fold **ONE** when she took the
entourage **IN KISSING EITHER** guns
it's actually **SHE'S NOT INTERESTED** from the table

Leslie and No have arrived during a practice, so between numbers K.H. asks the band for five minutes to talk to them over by an old hydraulic lift that now only holds aloft boxes of merch that they lower at the end of shows. (Does the lift suddenly release and crush Leslie's head? No.) Leslie begins her spiel, but five proves unnecessary: pretty quickly K.H. says she's not interested in kissing *either one* of them, and you have to respect that.

On the way back to the car, Leslie tells him it's too bad it didn't work out because she remembers those kisses as never stopping doing five dances at once. Still, on balance, Leslie's got to be one of the best great-god-aunts ever (Imagine the dazzling membranes of their wings!)--who else would take him around to all these baffled ladies?! (Though . . . if someone tells you that you gave them one of the best kisses of their life, I could see how giving an exhibition might be tempting). As she is coming around the front of her car, a speeding auto narrowly misses her by 4 feet (which is not actually *that* close).

As night is falling quickly, they head up a freeway that leads to a lone gas pump beneath a stilted house on the mountainside where ex #4 K.G. lives, dreaming of kisses that burst like stage divers out over flak clouds but always ending up only in the folded arms of her nine-fold entourage.

Actually, the crowd at K.G.'s house tonight is just The Gaudy Family there to visit Goodie's rich Uncle "Magic" Ian (who turns out to be K.G.'s husband) and console her about the death of her ex-lover Leslie Brautjungfer--who is now standing at the door with some kid she wants kissed. See, Molly just assumed Leslie was going to an appointment with a slinging undertaker when she left with guns from The Penalty Box, and she was just trying to be a good friend by notifying everyone of the untimely death.

him frm a dish on the counter**AT** them about her latest

she insists on **FACE SMILING** project meanwhile

her taking **AT THE SAME** kid walks over to

the guns**100 AND LOOKING** little girl & says yr

before coming**WHEN HE'S** the friend

further in2 the house**LIKE THAT GUY** of

like the head**SHE MUST FEEL** my little brother

in **WITH YOU ANYWAY** in the face of

Th Reanimator she's **THAT AROUND** such understatement

filled with**WHY CARRY** all she can

lust but **THE LIQUID NITROGEN** do

the scene **IT WAS IN** is burp

is not very sexy **BUT BEFORE** a sheet

she's covered in**IT WAS OFF** rising from

hooks but no **HEAD AFTER** a

one **LOOKED AT HER** river

is wearing **BOYFRIEND** around a

eyes **DEATH AND HER** breath

what **ON HER EARLY** holder we know

she wouldn't give**FROZEN** the nose

for a dandelion there's **HER HEAD** wins

no point **HAD** in the end and indeed where

in **A WOMAN WHO** is her

mingling**ABOUT** bopgun and

with **IT I JUST READ** her

absent sun**NOT GO FOR** flashlight

beams she sits on**LIFE BUT SHE DOES** the little girl is

a box labeled**A PERSON RESTORED TO** signaling

unused plotlines**APPROPRIATE TO KISS** gibberish to

and tells **IT WOULD BE** the valley frm balcony

Being confronted with a person restored to life might *seem* like a good excuse to be free with kisses, but K.G. does not go for it. I just read about a woman who had her head frozen when she died, and her boyfriend decided to look at it between the saw and the liquid nitrogen (Dude, why carry that image around with you?!), but anyway, K.G. must feel like that guy will when he'll be 100 and looking at the same face smiling at him from a dish on the counter--she insists that Leslie take her guns off before coming farther into the house.

Like the head in The Reanimator, Leslie is suddenly filled with lust, but the scene is just not very sexy--she feels covered in hooks but no one here is wearing eyes. What she wouldn't give a for a dandelion . . . Well, there's no point in trying to mingle with absent sun beams; she sits down on one of my boxes (I only just moved in) labeled "unused plotlines" and tells the mourners about the project she is pursuing with The Kid.

Meanwhile, No walks over to the little Gaudy girl and says, "You're the friend of my little brother."

In the face of such understatement, all Abby can do is burp a sheet rising from the river around a breath-holder.

As Leslie rattles on, she hears Parliament playing faintly from my room down the hall, and considers a truth as much as corroborated by The Bard: death doesn't lose a scent, and the nose wins in the end. She begins to panic a bit--where *are* her bopgun and her flashlight?! She forgets that she took them off at the front door--but actually, Abby has taken them out to the balcony and is signaling gibberish to the valley, causing inadvertent dance parties around the city below.

in other words **MY MOM WOULD SAY** the kid and his

she doesn't know **LIFE AS** kisses are

it because Tyler **IS** her IKEA furniture she

doesn't know it **AWAY BUT THAT** is

where Tyler **IS 50 MILES** tempted to blow

is me she's got to **COPY** the whole

hope that the death **AND MY PHYSICAL** thing up but then

card is misunderstood **RESOLUTION** fireworks pop

like people **AT A REASONABLE** canyon

say rather **TO SCAN IN**side looks like

a doorway **BOTHERED** the valley

to nothing **THAT NO ONE** got

like we **IN THE COMIC** the message every

atheists suspect **BUT THE ANSWER IS** day

life is **FUNK** be

also a doorway to **THE** like

nothing either except **GLORY TO** the fourth of July or

what we call **THE GREATER** will

something I've got **CATALYST TO** be for the rest of her

to stop **THE** run which begins by

pinching the **ENDING WAS** running out of the

gummy bears **IN THE** shindig

to **WINNING** while thr backs r turned

make them hug **AND HOW THE NOSE** I've read

my lips **ON TOP** but not

Jack **OUT** empirically

couldn't let go of the **PUSS CAME** verified that Angela

wheel **REMEMBER HOW OLD DONKEY** is

and neither **SHE COULD** fireworks woman

can she **IF ONLY** she'll take the name

Leslie despairs that she can't remember how old Donkeypuss came out on top in the Parliament song and how The Nose's victory could actually be the catalyst to the greater glory of The Funk, but the answer is in the comic from the LP liner notes that no one bothered to scan in at a reasonable resolution, and my physical copy (of the CD) is 50 miles away . . . But that is life, as my mom would say (and I think I think the question is more fitting here than an answer, anyway). In other words, Leslie doesn't know it because Tyler doesn't know it (where "Tyler," in this case, is me). She's got to hope that the old Death card is misunderstood like people say (rather than a doorway to nothing, as materialists like me suspect, but, I mean, isn't Life also a doorway to nothing, too, except what we call something?) Random question of no existential import: should I stop pinching gummy bears to make them hug my lips?

Well, if Tyler's Jack struggled to let go of the wheel, Leslie will, too. Sure, The Kid and his kisses have become her IKEA furniture, but it's hard to actually blow the whole thing up . . . And then fireworks explode outside in the canyon, and she's back out of her head--looks like the valley got the little girl's message. From my room, Leslie hears "Every day be like the fourth of July"--or they will be for the rest of *her* life, which begins with her running out of the shindig while everyone's backs are turned. I've read (but not empirically verified) that "Angela is the fireworks woman," so Leslie will take that name with her as she drives out of the hills.

Angela **IS NAMED** a waiter and now
from **WHO HEY** wake that Romeo gave
an altitude like **BY A WOMAN** the eulogy for
her Uncle **IS OBSERVED** him
Jam **ALL THIS** she remembers
she works **FIDELITY STYLE** his
in an air traffic **HIGH** Godzilla
control **LOVE SONGS** w/o a head b/c that
tower she mistakes **TEENAGE** is how I like 2 remember
her **YEARS OF** him just like her
for **53 BUT THAT'S 53** with the guns
the teacher who **SHE MAY BE** societally aceptable b/c
decorated **THE HIPS** associated with
his classroom in **FROM** fairplay and
shutter **WANTS A LOVE THAT SHOOTS** whiteness
shades **ON BECAUSE SHE** wonders if
I'm right **CALCULATED WILL FILTERS** G will speak
there with her **IS SHE'S PUTTING HER** for her
& I say I'l man the **THING SHE KNOWS** or
fort try **PAD BUT ONE** kid she got
to snag me a **LIST TORN OFF THE** dream
bear **GROCERY** dashed two kisses
when it's coming **ITEM ON THE** second
down in the **NAME TAG OR THE ONE** act in
meantime **GROUP** America though
she remembers **HER SUPPORT** Achilles dipped
that she was **HER ALIAS ON** he is now
supposed **THIS IS** passably fluent
to be reminded by her father **IF** in the female
as **IT'S UNCLEAR** tongue

Clearly, neither Leslie nor I remember that "Angela" is technically Aggie's real name, but what's not so clear is whether "Angela" will be Leslie's alias on her support-group tag or whether it will be the one item torn off the grocery list, but one thing she knows is she's putting her "calculated will" filters on now because she wants a love that shoots from the hips. (She may be 53, but that's 53 years of teenage love songs, *High Fidelity* style.)

All this observed from an altitude by a woman who, whaddayaknow, is also named Angela. Like her Uncle Jam, this Angela works in the city's air traffic control tower. Through her telescope, she mistakes Leslie in those filtered shades for the teacher who decorated his classroom in Kanye regalia (and then was told to take it down). I'm sitting right next to her in the tower, and I say, "I'll man the fort--go say how 'amaze' you thought the idea was--and see if there are any bears left over for me!"

On Leslie's drive out of the valley without The Kid (Does she take a turn too wide and go for a fly? She does not), she remembers that crashing her own wake after having received table service from her dead father was supposed to remind her of the eulogy Romeo gave his grandfather so many years ago. She pictures him delivering the speech in his headless-Godzilla costume he must have outgrown years before that, but that's how *I* like to remember him (just like I like to picture Leslie wearing the six-shooters, even though they're only societally acceptable because they're associated with fair-play and Whiteness--see how many paces a Black man gets wearing a gun belt). She wonders if Godzilla will use his words for *her* when it's her time--or maybe this generation's Kid will? I mean, she did get him 2 kisses (There's your second act in America) which is apparently enough dipping to make young Achilles subscribe to a season of the female tongue.

they revealed **THE TIME** is not
that Drunk **SHE'S CHOSEN** youth
On The Moon **YOU'VE CHOSEN** center pool
is not about **THEM WHAT** where you can snatch
astronaut **TURN DON'T TELL** the cue
regrets **NECK AND IT'S SOMEONE ELSE'S** ball
I am still **ARMS AND** if you
shocked **THE BEES OFF YOUR** muff
file this **ROOM AND THEN YOU SWEEP** it up and it
under **LIVING** hasn't touched
eating industry of **YOUR CHILDHOOD** anything
truth **OF** else yet but
repeats **A BOXY VORTEX** hey
I try to **REMEMBER BEING** maybe the 1 who'll
get her on the cell phone **YOU** talk
to say **SETS** her out of it
don't **AROUND THE TV** is her or she'll
bother **COUCHES** be the look
I've already figurd out **SITTING ON** out I'll tell you
the code **BENDERS** a secret
on the back **OF OTHER ELBOW** I
of the cereal **FOR A BUNCH** don't
box **WILL NOW PREDICT** roll before
& I know how the **MEMORY THAT YOU** going to
shoe finds **A STRIKING** sleep so I'm not
the **BROADCAST OF** tempted
path **CAN CHOOSE THE** to get
through the x-ray **NEWS WHERE YOU** up for
but **AT A BAR CALLED YESTERDAY'S** just one
but this **SHE FINDS HER** mo line & 1 more &

Angela finally catches up with Leslie at a bar called Yesterday's News where you can choose a striking event that you remember from the past and then pretend to give creepily prescient comments to a bunch of other elbow-benders in a fake living room. When you're done, you just sweep the bees off your arms and neck, and it's someone else's turn. My tip: don't tell them what event you've chosen--everyone will enjoy their surprise better if doesn't have to be faked (though beer does make good credulity lube). Leslie's poison is the time (which still shocks me) when the evening news revealed that the song "Drunk On The Moon" was not about astronaut regrets. (File this all under "eating Industry-Of-Truth repeats.")

I try to get Angela on her phone to say, "Don't bother! I've already figured out the code on the back of the cereal box and I know how the shoe finds the path through the x-ray!" but this is not youth center billiards where you can just snatch the cue ball off the table if it hasn't touched anything. Oh well, maybe Angela can talk her out of what I've foreseen--or else be the look out.

(I'll tell you a secret: I do roll on Shabbos, but never before going to sleep so I won't be tempted to get up for just one more line and one more and . . .)

HINT:
The "truth industry repeats" were foretold in the columns of Page 135.

a news crew's **NEEDS** her ambition to break
presence dice **EACH STUDENT DOES** go
roll between them **WHEN EVERYTHING** do a thing
when she looks **TO HAVE CLASS** take
up **IF IT IS HARD** bite out
and **AND ASKS HER** of a microphone
though **SHE WALKS IN** she walks out & finds
her **IMPLICATIONS** unattended portal
interlocutor looks **EXISTENTIAL** gun an
pleasant **THEMSELVES AT THE** actual
enough **CREAM** hole
whatever color **DIRECTORS** machine but
she has drains out her **WAVE** she plans
oh **FIVE NEW** to only use it
and she feels **PATH AS** as a
it **FINDING A NEW** polite solution to
fillin grooves of **LIGHT AS A WAY OF** chaw spit she's
her face like **HER FLASH** not going to
the **STORE WITH** put a
stamp on **A SHOE** hole in
the passport **ON HOLDING UP** a dude
of a Titanic **EYES SHE IS PLANNING** a hole would
passenger **DISILLUSIONMENT TO THE** show
asked by the moon **POWDERED** the
boot **MATCH THAT ENDS IN** crab's
youth **WRESTLING** wide back
if the iceberg **COMMENTARY TO A MUTED** stretching
is here yet the **COLOR** across her
ice cubes **TO SOMEONE GIVING** back turning her
speak **WHILE SHE LISTENS** to empty armor

   While Leslie listens to a patron giving commentary on a muted wrestling match that will end in disillusionment to the eyes, she is planning on holding up a shoe store with her "flashlight" as a way of finding a new path (while in a nearby booth five New Wave directors cream themselves simultaneously at the existential implications).

   Angela walks in and asks her if it is hard to teach a class where "everything [a student] do needs a news crew's presence." Dice roll between them when Leslie looks up, and though the stranger looks pleasant enough to her, whatever color Angela has drains out of her "oh . . . !" and Leslie feels it filling the grooves of her own face. Now she knows how the passport stamp felt on The Titanic when the moon-boot youth asked if the iceberg was here yet. (Does her heart break physically? No.)

   The crackling ice cubes in Leslie's glass speak her ambition to break, go, do a thing, take a bite out of a microphone, and she walks out and finds an unattended portal gun (file under: "actual hole machine") but don't worry, our gunslinger only plans to use it as a polite solution to chaw spit, not putting holes in dudes. If someone put a hole in *her* right now, they could see the wide back of "the crab" perched on her lungs, nearly finished turning her to armor. (She must have been that teenage smoker after all.)

HINT:
The crab and the hole machine are from, you guessed it, the columns of Page 135.

of empty **CORAL CUPS** the
will just pour **OVER THE ABANDONED** grotesque that
yourself n & wait 4 the **RATTLE OUT** may have
patriotic parrot **A LURING** no more basis than a
fish to come I saw **STRETCHED OUT** mermaid's
one in **ROBES THAT** purse or
Hawaii **REMEMBERS A ROW OF** wrist
she sees an **HAND SHE** watch the problem
island **LIKE THING TO HER** is you have to be
sold like **CRAB** able to see
instant noodles **AS SHE FITS THE** where
off the rack **FUNDING A BLACKOUT** you want
but she's got a vision **ARE CROWD** to go and remember
of **A/C UNITS** whether you've got
an other thing **KNOW THAT THE** hi-tech
that is a shark **WHO DOESN'T** enough boots
caught **AT THE ARCADE** to survive the fall
in the hand of a **KID** but let's say they weren't
tree **EATER SHE'S LIKE A** wrong
thrashing **BEATLE OR BEETLE** when they said er
around as **YOU ARE A TRUE** aim
it keeps swimming **MUSIC TO PROVE** is worth guns
in the air and daring **ON THE SHEET** she flutters
anyone to come **LINES** in like the djini
close enough to **HAVE SIX** in a
lecture about the **BURN YOU** gas lamp thought 2 b a
inevitability of **SICK** leaking brain she says
but she needs **RANGO** she needs
a dentist who gets **RINGO OR IS IT** the kid and
prismatic facets in **OKAY** maybe the little girl

Well, Ringo (or is it Rango--sick burn!), your clock is counting
down and you have six lines on the sheet music for you to prove
you're a true Beatle (or beetle-eater). She's like a kid at the arcade
who doesn't know the A/C units are crowd-funding a blackout. As
she fits the crab-like portal gun over her hand, she remembers
Pearly Harpers' as "a row of robes that stretch out a luring rattle out
over the coral cups of empty will" (its slogan reading "just pour
yourself in and wait for the patriotic parrot fish" like the one I saw
in Hawaii). She has a vision of the island sold like instant noodles
off the rack, but suddenly it is replaced in her mind by another
thing: an image of a shark caught in the hand of a tree, thrashing as
it keeps swimming in the air and daring anyone to come close
enough to lecture about death's certainty. She's instantly resolute:
the world *must* see this thing, but she realizes it will take a dentist
who can dig the facets of the grotesque with no more basis than a
mermaid's purse or wrist-watch. It doesn't take her long to think of
one, and she flutters like the djinn in a gas lamp thought to be a
leaking brain.

The problem with portal guns is that you have to be able to *see*
where you want to go, but for the sake of expediency, let's say they
weren't wrong when they said her aim was "worth guns." The
guests at Leslie's wake are politely taking stacked cups to the
kitchen when she barges back in K.G.'s living room and lays out her
plan:

HINT:
This page is straight 135.

of false eyes **BUTTERFLY ONION** ready to leap
smushed **A HANGING** jean
into **THE SELF MAY BE** legs
a hat **EARS** flailing and
worn by **HIS FUZZY** heart
a magician **NOW MATCHES** bassline
they warp **MISGUIDED** bouncing
around town **SEEMED SO** out of the beat and
catching the club members **WHICH** making sense on the 15th
before **HIS LIPS' ROAR** time through
bedtime to get **BESIDES** the video that was
a quick sketch **WILL DO** before she did the twist
of living **BUT HIS GRADES** w the music teacher
and no **IS NO GENIUS** they
we can't wait until **HE** rewire
it **HELPED BUILD** the flashlight
is perfect **HAD UNWITTINGLY** w the lighthouse
get out of yr basement **THAT THEY** projecting their hero
& play **SQUAD RECRUITMENT POSTER** beside
she met Deedee Ramone **FIRING** the soldier and how
1nc wich shouldn't b **THE DANCING** can he not look
possible but **SO THEY CAN FIGHT** winning he says
she was going into **THE HEAD** WTF you didn't play
the shower **HIS SHARK AS** the far more dry
and quantum **ART VOLTRON WITH** octopus
theory says **OF LIFE** in other words changing
there's **A TREE** stepmother I'm not
a non zero chance **TO FORM** done yet says the woman
that anything may be **THE KIDS** who succumbs
behind the curtain **SHE WANTS** the next day

he wants her Stan Lee-ders to fight Pearly Harpers' giant dancing
Firing Squad Recruiter with an art-Voltron of their own. The
drawings of each kid will combine to build the trunk of a
Tree-Of-Waining-Life, and a shark drawn by him--she points at No,
whom no one has given a ride home yet--will be the head.

No is no genius, but his grades will do, and besides, his lips'
roar that had seemed so misguided now matches his ear fuzz. (You
don't need *me* to tell you that the self is a hanging onion of false
eyes smushed into a magician's hat.)

Leslie, No, and Abby use the portal gun to warp across town
over and over, catching Lee-ders just before bedtime to collect from
each a quick sketch of "living"--and no, we can't wait until it is
perfect, get out of your basement and play!

Once they've got all the drawings and put them together
(visiting every house in only one night and leaving milk and
cookies), she and No rewire her holster Flashlight into the island's
light house to project their Shark Tree Hero beside the Official
Dying Soldier, and how can it not look winning next to an opponent
clearly resolved to fall?

Suddenly remembering, No says to her, "WTF, you didn't play
the far more dry octopus!" (He must be imagining that she's
anything like his perpetually-changing stepmom.)

"I'm not done yet," replies the woman who will succumb to her
lungs the next day.

p.s. I legit forgot the successful love she was supposed to have
in this chapter! Well, she'll tuck it like a tip with a smile in the
pocket of the random woman who will lift her shoulders when she
collapses in the middle of the street.

LET'S CALL THAT CHAPTER "Life of kisses as kisses are."

HINT:
Or he's thinking of that 135.

here are the standings going into the final chapter

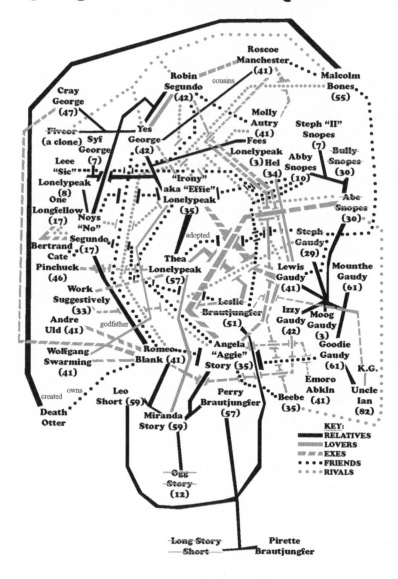

KEY:
— **RELATIVES**
— **LOVERS**
- - - **EXES**
•••• **FRIENDS**
∙∙∙∙ **RIVALS**

Chapter 9

you'll get the dream like**EYES** are the soldiers

certainty to know **THEM OVER YOUR** and how

exactly when **THEN TUNE** are you going

sliding**IN THE POWDER** to meet one

into the base will **RUB IT** of them that

result **IN HALF AND** is where guys

in a **CUT AN APRICOT** like the creative

handshake **LOVER AND IF YOU** titled Yes

and a beer **DREAM** Man comes

after **WHAT IS CALLED** in

the game **A PACKET OF** ex-model

no wonder business is **BACK** who once was

booming over **WILL SLIDE YOU** asked to hold a pose

there everyone wants **A HATER** so

to know **THEM THROUGH** long he knifed

the right**AND SLIDE** the photographer's

time **HAVE NEVER BEEN** assistant

and everyone**SIDE THOUGH THEY** of course

grows the pepper **ON THE OTHER** pizzaria

or whatever **SUPPOSEDLY NOON**baggies cut with

that**WHICH IS** dirt

is dried **THE NIGHT** from aromatic places is

and ground**IN THE MIDDLE OF** cheaper

but weirdly no one's**THE PORTAL** to produce so

crop works on the**MOUTH OF** that what he sells more

guy that grows**THE BOARDED UP** of

it of course**SOME BILLS TO** to rubes though

the only people that **TAKE** Splish Splash

can get **THAT IF YOU** makes your eyes

close to the boards **THEY SAY** look everywhere else

Chapter 9

Rumor has it that if you take some bills to the boarded-up mouth of The Portal in the middle of the night (which They say is noon on the other side, not that *They*'ve necessarily ever seen it) and you slide those presidents through a crack and wait, a Hater will slide you a packet of what is called "Dream Lover" and if you then cut an apricot in half, empty the packet onto a mirror (Just works better that way, plus it looks cool), and rub the wet side of the fruit first in the powder and then in your eyes, you'll get the dream-like certainty to know exactly when stealing a base from your love object will result in a gentlemanly handshake and a beer after the game. No wonder business is booming on The Planet H8R: who doesn't wants to know the right time to make a move that everyone will be cool with?! Plus, even though the pepper (or whatever it is that gets dried and ground up to make the powder) grows on every Hater's property like a weed, weirdly yours only works for other people and you need theirs, too, so everyone's a producer and everyone's a customer.

Of course, the only Earthicans who can get close enough to the boards of the portal are the soldiers assigned to Pearly Harpers', and how are you going to meet one of them? They even have other soldiers around the base to keep you from meeting those guys! That's where people like the creatively-nick-named "Yes Man" come in . . . They say he used to be a model who was asked to hold a pose for so long that he knifed the photographer's assistant, but he still has crazy connections and a golden tongue (Well, it kind of clips on the top when he rolls his pink one in). Of course, it's cheaper for him to take pizzeria pepper baggies and cut them with dirt from specially-selected aromatic places, so he sells more of this "Splish Splash" to rubes, even though it has a nasty habit of making your amorous eyes go to every base coach but your own.

Name**LOVE'S** picture frame
which kills **YOUR FIRST** Halloween in
them even **ALBUM CALLED** a few weeks and
more with its sober **UP** saying she's a
acoustic guitar **THING A BREAK** mirror
and break **AND MOST USELESS** ex could
whine **AND MOST UNIVERSAL** help taking this
vocals **MOST SPECIFIC** slap
less **MAKES THAT** from
public **VOWELS GOODIE** a ghost but she dont
but just as devastatin **WITHOUT ANY** why
is the split **COMPLEX** did she
of **THE BAND IS CALLED** come to her
the tarnished **HER SON** daughter's
olympic coach **WHO THEY PRETEND IS** Halloween
& the equally fractured **GUITARIST** party & why was
poet **LOVER SLASH** invitation given
a hummingbird **FINDS A NEW** Irony
2 go down on **BEACH AS THE DRUMMER** brought her &
her overfilled shots **ON THE** new boyfriend
her **DISSOLUTION OF CHOPS** Wolves
name is **DEMOLISHED BY THE** Swarming man
Michelle a mess **FANS ARE** no one
whose **MUSIC** put any thought into
exploits **THE PLANET OUTSIDER** what
the poet **THAT PLAGUE** hairs they
writes **OF BREAK UPS** would be
about **THE RASH** catching with
as her own lipsyncin **MUST EXPLAIN** their companions or
Nico and dressing in **THIS** made costumes out of gum

The "Splish Splash" epidemic probably explains the rash of breaks up that suddenly plague the Earth. For example, Outsider Music fans are demolished by the abrupt dissolution of Chops On The Beach as Mounthe Gaudy finds a new younger lover / guitarist whom she pretends is her son (in a band called "CMPLX"). In revenge, distraught Goodie makes that most universal and most useless thing: a break-up album, which he calls *[Your First Love's Name Here]*; his sober acoustic guitar and whine of breaks is an even greater blow to the Shaggs-T-Shirt set than Mounthe's suddenly-everywhere song "Curious Gertrude (I Denmarked My Son & I Liked It)."

Less public but equally devastating is the split of the tarnished Olympic coach from the equally-fractured poet who apparently found herself a new hummingbird to go down on her overfilled shots by the name of Michelle. This young hot-mess is a walking short-story collection, and Thea gaspingly tries to keep up, breathlessly writing about the girl's exploits as if they were her own while meanwhile singing to herself (which is hard to do while breathless). It's got Thea thinking of wearing a large picture-frame hooked to a corset to go as Nico for Halloween in a few weeks.

Jilted Miranda wouldn't *have* to take this as a slap from a ghost, but she does. Why is Thea at her daughter's Halloween party--and why did Aggie invite her?! Actually, it is Ag's old pal Irony who brings her mom along, just as she has brought her new boyfriend Wolves Swarming (!!), master of the backflip and recent ex of Ag's bro. Man, no one put any thought into what hairs they would be catching with their decisions tonight--or else they deliberately made their costumes out of chewing gum.

wouldn't know **YOU** show
it from the elaborate **THOUGH** host who has
decorations seriously **PROFITTING** followed
everything **NOT** Piggy to
here **SUCCEEDING BY** late night
cackles and Molly **AND SHE'S** yet
compliments her on **A NON-PROFIT** can't pass up
the Evil **SHE'S WORKING AT** the allure
Dead 2 **DIFFERENT AUTHORS** of
reference dropping **BY** playing
the pen **MULTIPLE SOURCES** the monument 4
to try to pick **CITATION OF** people's
up **A PROPERLY FORMATTED** selfies shs got
the secented handkerchief **AS** a new boyfriend too
of whether **HANSEL WENT** named
Hans has a **BOYFRIEND** Hans uh oh
brother **LIBRARIAN AND HER NEW** Clementine
he does **REFERENCE** strikes
but he's **A SEXY** again she wondered how
mine though I'm sure **SHE WENT AS** that
he'd find **HER ABS** complemented
her interesting **CONTINUES ENJOYING** a puppet all
every **DAUGHTER AND** the better to get
one of her **BAD** points with the female demo
feathers **STREAM** by pulling Geppeto down
is lining the **ONE** in front of
nest **VISION THANKFULLY ONLY** an audience
as if she's **MOTHER'S DAGGER** swear allegiance 2
the big time **HER** the droopy eyed
talk **SHE DODGES** guitar player

At her party, Aggie dodges her mother's dagger vision (thinking, "thankfully only one stream!"--bad daughter!) and continues enjoying her abs. She's dressed as a "sexy reference librarian" and her new boyfriend Hans has come as a "properly formatted citation of multiple sources by different authors." These days, she's working at a non-profit, and she's succeeding by not making much money (though you wouldn't know it from the elaborate decorations tonight--seriously, everything here cackles, and Molly compliments her on the *Evil Dead 2* reference, dropping the pen to try to pick up the scented handkerchief of whether Hans has a brother--he does, but he's mine, though I'll bet my actual brother Franz would indeed find Molly interesting).

Every silver feather seems to be lining Ag's nest--has she forgotten that she's not actually her big-time talk show host friend who has followed Miss Piggy to late night? Yeah, Beebe's still on top, but she's at this party because she still can't pass up the allure of playing the monument for rando's awe-struck selfies. She's got a new boyfriend, too, also named Hans--uh oh. That powdered "Clementine" must have struck again! Beebe *had* wondered how his citation costume complemented her sexy puppet. Oh well, she thinks while kicking him to the curb amid cell-phone flashes, all the better to get points with the female demo by yanking Geppeto down in front of an audience and swearing allegiance to sisters before misters.

people**ITSELF** his wife's

must be**WITHIN** a cop but tonight she's

telling**AIRLESSLY**here as

themselves that **FRISBY TO FLING** a successful

a house**AS A LOST** baby

of cards can be **THEM EVEN IF** thief and she's too

rebuilt**THE SEA LOVES** busy seeing souls as

with just a new **SURFER OR THAT** breakdancers to

hand or **THEY'RE AN ABOVE AVERAGE** notice

a pocket**THINKS** the transactions

pair**DIFFERENT EVERYONE** at home she

never ends up**NOT THAT** acts

as a full**WORLDS ARE** like she's watching a

house and the dealer is**OUR** movie

Yes snapping**THEM** about her own

fingers **GOING TO STOP** life

in **POWDER BUT IS THAT** there's

shades **SOME SKETCHY** recursiveness too

and chest **DOWN INTO** in the hospital

hair tangled **FACE** scene that

medallions **HEART WHEN THEY GO**happens shortly

and telling people**TO THEIR** after

he **HAPPEN** where

is the purloined letter **IS GOING TO** a Gaudy and

and can help them**KNOW WHAT** a George

find any **WORLD THAT DOES NOT**hold a

othr smal envelopes**A PARTY AND A**hard

they may have**WHAT WE HAVE IS** working hand but

misplaced **THAT** last time she just watched

yeah**MY POINT IS** the roller coaster

I guess the point I'm trying to make is that what we have is a party (and a world) that does not know what is going to happen to their hearts when they go face down into some sketchy pixie-stick shit, and yet that doesn't stop them. I guess our worlds are not that different--every Earthican and every Hater thinks that they're an above average surfer or that the sea has a special love for *them*, even if only as a lost Frisbee to fling airlessly within itself. People must be telling themselves that a house of cards can be rebuilt with just a new hand, or that a pocket-pair never ends up as a full house . . . And flinging the cards in the middle of all this is the dealer Yes, snapping fingers in shapes, chest-hair tangled with medallions, and telling people he is the purloined letter that can help them find any other small envelopes they may have "misplaced." Sure, his ex-now-ohhh wife is a cop, but tonight she's here dressed as a successful baby thief and she's too busy seeing souls as breakdancers to notice the transactions right in front of her. She's been acting like she's watching a movie about her own life.

There's recursiveness, too, in the hospital scene that happens just days after the party: a Gaudy and a George again each hold a hard-working hand, but back in Chapter 2 Robin was just watching the roller coaster, whereas this time she's in the front car.

back to **EVENTS GIVEN** candle
you with **SHAPE OF** heads because of
a knowing **TRIP THE FAMILIAR** different kind of
smile **OF AN ACID** loss the hand
rendered in **STAGES** he holds
the jittering **DURING DIFFERENT** infantile
spelling **THE CAT** ball
o thee confusion of **TRYING TO DRAW** with
fingers **THE WOMAN** fingers an inch
like sweated **STAGE OF** short
stamps **THE MIDDLE** pins in
slid dwn from the **ASPIRATION IS FOR** a cushion he does
eyes showing **THAT MY** not
no comprehension **FREELY** hold the
the **HERE AND** whole baby
rollercoaster **THE SHOTS** nor does he have the
people **THAT I CALL** breath
are here **BUT I ADMIT GRUDGINGLY** of
again though **A BABE** paddling despite
some have **MUCH OF** his girlfriend's
been swapped out **I AM NOT THAT** absence
and **WEAK PERHAPS** from the
others **IS STILL SOMEWHAT** room
rearranged **HIM HERE THOUGH SHE** and the world
like **BROUGHT** recognizing
back **ROOM IRONY HAS** this
cards but now their arms **THAT** he feels
frozen short of reaching **BACK INTO** the
joy their fingers twitching **NO** nipples exposed by the water
like flickering **LET'S FOLLOW** volley tht erased shirt

Robin's in the same room that brought you Syf and Steph (#46). Irony has brought No here, though she is still somewhat weak. Perhaps I am not that much of a babe, but I'll admit that I call the shots here--my ambition is to give you the middle stage of the woman trying to draw the cat during an acid trip (the familiar shape of events handed back with a smile spelled in the thee confusion of fingers like sweated stamps slid down from uncomprehending eyes). The Roller Coaster People are in the room again (though some have been swapped out, and others rearranged like back cards), but now the Gaudys' arms are frozen short of reaching joy, their fingers twitching like flickering candle-heads because of different kind of loss.

The hand Lewis holds is an infantile ball with fingers an inch short, chubby pins in a cushion. He does not hold the whole baby nor does he have the "breath of paddling," despite his girlfriend's absence from the room--and the world. Recognizing this, he feels like the nipples exposed by the shirt-erasing water volley. He has named the little boy "Heel" after his departed mama Hel with the tea-spoon contribution of dad. A gem in the boy's belly button sparkles derivatively.

HINT:
This page draws on Page 046, obvs.

fear **OF THE NEARSIGHTED** w/ its straitness
and lust intermingled **LIKE THE LIP** in other words
in the closet **AND RAFTERS** in the mouldering
dweling **CURTAINS** piles accrued from the
business man **CHEWING ON THE** wreckage
for the mariner's **GLOW THAT'S BEEN** of lives
sack **THE HOUSE THAT** they could afford
indeed **GIVING** to quote
the family **THAT'S BEEN** find
on **TO THE FIRE** God to
the other **JUST AWOKEN** them the latest
side of the **WOMAN WHO HAS** looks
net **AN IMAGINARY** old fashioned b/c
has cleared **ONE NAMED AFTER** the once must be
their own **LOOK OF THE** again to capitalize the
deck of **CARDS OF THE** T in
uncles and best **EMPTY BIRTHDAY** truth they name
friends **HANDS BACK** the girl
by **A DEAD WOMAN** Sin b/c of where
trying **NAMED AFTER** she was conceived
to douse **LOSING THE ONE** boy is
that sort of **WISDOM OF** named
fire **THE CALM** Heel after
with stagnant **DECORATIONS OF** his mama
water **THE ANCIENT** with the tea spoon
they now see **LIKE** contribution of his father
as the true level **HERE BUT NOW FEEL** a gem
which **GIRLS WHO ONCE STARRED** in his
will break **THE LITTLE** belly button
the dams **THE BRIDGE IS STILL** sparkles

The bridge between the families in this room is still the little girls who were once the stars of this arena but now feel like ancient decorations of the calm wisdom of losing. Across their sustained look, Syf folds fat wads into birthday cards that are tacitly accepted, shaken out on the floor, and handed back empty; Steph is not warmed by the fire that Syf has just noticed that gives her own house a glow while softly chewing on the curtains like the twinned nearsighted lips of fear and lust on the stuck business man eyeing the mariner's sack.

Indeed, the George / Segundo family on the other side of the net has cleared their own deck of uncles and best friends by trying to douse that very sort of fire with the stagnant water they now see as the true level that will break the dams with its straightness. In other words, they're born again homo-hatin' fundies (and suddenly they think No pining theoretically after ladies is a *great* idea--much to his dismay--though they say he'll never get girls past "their fear of the nearsighted with its straightness and lust intermingled" if he doesn't stop drawing them "breaking his little belly button"!). From the mouldering stack of wrecked lives accrued by "Splish Splash," Yes has been able to afford to root around enough to suddenly "find the golden needle of God." Now, The Latest Look looks old-fashioned to them because obviously The Fabled Once must be an Again or else there can be no capital to the T in their newly-adopted truth. They've named their new baby girl "Sin" because of where she was conceived.

HINT:
The prognosis of No's situation actually comes from the columns of *this* page!

it was **IN LIFE** he was an odd Alice
going to lead out into streets **NOT** a coyote liable to be
unseasonably warm **EVEN IF SHE DID** on
and maddened **ALL SMOKING** the other end
with the hum **AFTER** if this is the rabbit
of unseen **DEAD** but enjoying
insects but **WOMAN NOT SO** barging through
I just heard **THE MISSING** windows of
the Winchester **IF IT WILL LEAD TO** accumulated facts
House referenced **WONDERING** with a mouse
at a snack **IT HALF** tied to
bar and in **AND FOLLOWS** his hand so he does
a novel about another **FINICKY POT** not expect a
creepy **ULYSSES IN A** scowling
house **ROLE AS** tween
so **HE REPRISES HIS** with a baseball
the gory **REST ON THE OTHER** bat to have
cord leads **TO** the cord tied
him around **SOLDIERS TUMBLING** around
impossible **RAIN OF** his
circles **ONE SIDE AND THE PERPETUAL** belly
of square **ALCOHOL ON THE** Back
rooms **EVAPORATED** To
and nearly **THE DRYNESS OF** The Future
out of a drop **DOOR AND TO ESCAPE** Day means a
only **OUT THE** skateboard
survivable by ghost **LEADING** is
good job **UMBILICAL CORD** improvised
gun **HE NOTICES A FRAYED** as a
lady **ON THE FLOOR** method of escape

On the floor, No notices a frayed umbilical cord leading out the door, and to escape the dryness of evaporated alcohol on the one side and the perpetual rain of soldiers tumbling to rest on the other, he reprises his role as Ulysses floating through a dangerous strait in a finicky pot and follows the cord, half wondering if it will lead to Lewis's missing woman, not so dead after all--maybe just smoking in a less complete gown, even if she did not in life. I was going to have the gory cord lead out into streets unseasonably warm and maddened with the hum of unseen insects, but I just heard the Winchester Mystery House referenced twice in random places (once by a student at a snack bar and then again in an audiobook about another creepy house), so the cord actually leads him around impossible circles of square rooms and nearly out of a drop only survivable by ghosts (Great way to wash your hands of death, Mrs. W!). No is an odd Alice (A coyote is liable to be gnawing on the other end if this is the rabbit he's following), but he's enjoying barging through windows of accumulated facts with a mouse under his clawed fingers (A lone toothpick without an owner is taped carefully preserved along the Head-Line of that palm--what, you thought spiders lived forever?), so he is caught off-guard by the cord abruptly ending-up tied around the belly of a scowling tween with a baseball bat. Because I'm writing this on Back To The Future Day, No tries to improvise a skateboard as a method of escape.

it seems that **THE SITUATION** scent of
her fin **EXPLAIN** Death
was still **TO** Rollers she
bunged by **HIM ASIDE** angrily thinks
her daughter's **HERE I TAKE** kaleidoscopes must be
thoughtless invitation **WHY THEY'RE** pointed in
of that **SINCE EVERYONE KNOWS** a direction
foamy **CAST** inspiration is not
floating **MOST OF THE MAIN** accident
muse **AND ALSO** she wanders over to
hound **LITTLE LEAGUERS** the telescope and
using streamers **OF HOMELY** thinks
for eyes **BECAUSE IT'S FULL** she will prove
her circular **PIZZA PARLOR** that
swimming **MOST UNSTERILE** clouds
took her **BEEN IN A** need
to Milky **ROOM THAT SHOULD HAVE** a frame to
Bowl **IN A STERILE** show
where you can hurl **A MEETING** their faces
your troubles **OF TORTURE** unfortunately
away **TO A PLACE** the one
in observatory **TIED IN UMBILICAL CORD** she
repurposed **AND LEAD WITH HIS HANDS** points
she is **CORRALLED** at
Exotic Number **SO HE IS EASILY** spits
6 **INSIDE** sunlight down her
not considering that it is **THE** straw
derived **CUBES RATHER THAN** tube and
from **THE OUTSIDE OF** burns
th mating **SKATEBOARDS ARE MEANT FOR** her eye

Unfortunately, skateboards are for gleaming the *outside* of cubes rather than the inside, so he is easily corralled and lead with hands tied in umbilical cord to a place of torture: a meeting in a sterile room. Really, though, the meeting should have been in a most unsterile pizza parlor because it's overflowing with homely Little Leaguers--and also most of our main cast.

Since everyone else knows why they're here, I take No aside to explain the situation in a lengthy flashback: it all started when Mira's fin was bunged by her daughter's thoughtless invitation of "that foamy floating muse hound" to the Halloween party. People later recalled having seen her around town "using streamers for eyes" (even though that should probably be "eye," given that an accident with a kaleidoscope had taken the other one in childhood). Her circular swimming apparently took her to the Milky Bowl, where you can hurl your troubles down the lane in a repurposed observatory. She wore "Exotic Number 6" perfume, not considering the fact that it is derived from the mating scent of the Death Roller snake. Angrily, she thought, "kaleidoscopes must be pointed in a direction--inspiration is not accident!" She wandered over to the telescope and thought to prove that clouds need a frame to show their faces, but the one she pointed the scope at spat sunlight down her straw and burned out her one good eye.

the thouroughly **WEIRD** rivalry
shiny **IS WHERE THINGS GET** between
and bloodless **THIS** the teams and their
limbs landed **HUSBAND** backers and it stopped
in a number **FOR HER** being
of little **EXCESSIVE SYMPATHY** just
league games **TO PIECES IN** youth
across the city where **ISIS GOING** sports and
they became **OUT THE WINDOW LIKE** they brought
cherished **AND REIDSTRIBUTED** out video game
trophies here **POLISHED** where you can see
I gesture **IN IS** the turf wars
to the sullen **SPEED SHE FALLS** unfolding like
children who wear **STUNNING** pieces
small **LANES WITH** moving
plastic replicas o **THEM BACK TO THEIR** themselves
body **AND REDISTRIBUTES** skrmshs involvd
parts **OF POLISHING** vollies of
from their necks **GO ROUND** fly
an old **TONE MERRY** balls knocked
cop trick **TWO** back by whatever Jet Lee
I read **ON A PLAYGROUND** types
about **BALLS** they had or
carry replica **THAT SENDS** catch them to
because **NEW CENTRIFUGE** save
the original is **AROUND THE BRAND** for
expensive **POSTED** future
to replace **THE NUMEROUS WARNINGS** ammo
this kick **SHE DIDN'T SEE** closer it's
up the **BLINDED** spit licorice whips

Blinded, she hadn't seen the numerous warnings posted around the brand-new centrifuge that sends balls on a two-toned merry-go-round of polishing and redistributes them back to their lanes with stunning speed. She fell in, was polished, and was redistributed in every direction out the windows like the goddess Isis going to pieces in excessive sympathy for her severed husband.

This, I tell him, is where things got weird: the thoroughly shiny and bloodless limbs landed in a number of little league games across the city where they became cherished trophies among the different teams (I gesture across the sullen children who wear small plastic replicas of body parts from their necks, an old cop trick I read about, re: badges: carry a replica because the original is expensive). This kicked up the competition between the junior franchises, and with adult backers pouring their avarice into the trophy's shine, the teams overflowed beyond mere sports rivalries into frothy little warring states. (Someone has even brought out a video game where you can see these turf wars unfolding like pieces moving themselves.) There were no longer baseball games, but instead street skirmishes as each patriotic amoeba gravitated towards conflict, first launching at a distance reflexive clouds of volleyed fly balls that were knocked back by whatever Jet Lee types the other team had or caught and saved for future ammo. Then as the armies reached spit-range, the adults employed their blowers and the kids flailed the razor edges of snack-shack plastic-wrapped licorice whips. Picturesque, sure, for painters picnicking at a distance, but noisy for the neighbors and solving nothing--none of these armies has ever gotten close enough to another's core to grab a coveted limb of Mira (Too used to just slapping hands in a line, maybe).

and other**TOWNSPEOPLE** blindness
teams that **THE MURMURS OF** turn back to
their battle **THEY REALIZED FROM** gold
balling **AND LATER** what lost its
skills were**COMING** sheen when the
so known thanks to**THEM** fox
her poems **WHEN SHE SAW** fires disappeared
that they only had**STOOL** she may have
to fight**PORTABLE** said
half as**LITTLE**more
often **SETTING UP A**attention spans
they started**RUNNING BUT** wained when
calling her**NOT ONLY NOT** the topic is the last
bee stripes and **HER** man on
monster **THEY NOTICED** earth with
mask**OUTSIDE HELP**contacts
they told **RECRUIT**the stunt man is
her if she wrote **THE FIRST TO** next
them**WERE** approaching The
a self-fulfilling**SETLIST** Nurtured
epic**IN HIS**Naturals and
they would let her **EVISCERATED** offering
spend all th time w **FORMER LOVERS** to train
reassembled body **IN THE NAMES OF** them
she wants**COVERED** in
to document**AN ACOUSTIC GUITAR** sliding and
its**MASCOT A GUY WITH** coordinated wall
every disillusioning **THEIR** running to prove
inch as a map of **BLUEBEARDS** mentorship is > than
her own**THE EX** mothership

Finally, one team had the idea to recruit an outside ringer that you've ever heard of; the "Ex Bluebeards" (their mascot a guy with an acoustic guitar chamber full of the trapped names of former lovers that he eviscerates anew each night in his set list) noticed Thea Lonelypeak not only running ahead of their approaching mob but also setting up a little portable stool, and later they realized from the murmurs of townspeople and other teams that their battle-balling skills were so known thanks to her poems that they only had to skirmish half as often. They started referring to her amongst themselves as "Bee Stripes" and "Monster Mask," and eventually told her that if she wrote them a self-fulfilling epic, they would let her spend all the time she wanted with the reassembled body of Mira, its every disillusioning inch a map of her own blindness, so she could try to turn back to gold what had lost its sheen when the will-o-wisps left.

Next, "The Nurtured Naturals" scored the gratis services of stuntman and Mira-protégé Wolves Swarming--in fact, he actually approached them! To show the world that mentorship is more than mothership, he offered to train the kids in sliding and coordinated wall-running, and of course they accepted!

he looks **ON THE BLOCK** cheating

for The Sons **IN** defeat

All Seek **MEGA STORE TO MOVE** is his

Prizes **HARDWARE** specialty

all swaggering **LIKE THE SECOND** citing

around smoking **SUITCASE STUNT** failed

little **EXPLODING** Leslie O'

pipes and never **A BOTCHED** bio-pic of

shutting up **BALD FROM** the top box

about **WOLVES GONE** office

ouchies to their **THE HAIRLESS LOOK OF** orphan

peepers **HAIR TO MATCH** 10

no one asked **HIS FIRST SON** years

you to trap **A MUSICIAN HE SHAVES** running plus

a grounder like **FATHER WAS** the pageant they'd all

that he tells **HIS OWN** been in

them that they should **THOUGH** as kids

make him captain **TO THE AIR EVEN** on top

because his weepin **SPIDERS TAKING** of that

lyre pairs every **INDIGNATION OF** the umbilical cord

striking **WITH THE INDIVIDUALISTIC** proves his

hand with painted **HE BURSTS** birthright yeah it's the

double **FOLLOWER** one worn by

in **RAIN BOOT** that

applause **BY SOME** kidnapper he says

and drains **OF THE NEST** take

the tears **OUT** that

stones **TO BE ROLLED** off it snaps

conceded by aphorists **ABOUT** he sez that can only happn

he says **HE IS NOT** 7 or 8 more times

Well, Romeo was not about to be rolled out of the nest by some rain-boot-follower! He burst with the individualistic indignation of spiders taking to the air, and even though his own father was a musician, he took after the second hardware megastore to move in on a block and shaved his first-son hair to match the smooth look of Wolves (who had gone bald from a botched exploding-suitcase stunt). Ro sought out "The Sons All Want Prizes"--easy to spot because they swaggered around schoolyards smoking little pipes and never shutting up about ouchies to their peepers (No one asked you to trap a grounder like that!)--and he told them that they should make him their captain because his weeping lyre "paired every striking hand with a painted double to make applause and drain the tears stones refuse to concede to aphorists." He said that cheating defeat was his specialty, citing the box-office-bomb bio-pic where he played Leslie O'Lustfully (herself famous for losing parents all the way to the top of the box office from 1920-1929) plus had they noticed that the pageant they'd all been in as kids that was all about losing? On top of that, he held up an umbilical cord (yeah, it's the one currently worn by No's juvenile kidnapper) to prove his birthright to Mira's legacy.

stuck with**LUKE I AM YOUR MOTHER**as the
hr even as she recognized**WHOSE** spaces
its **THE WOMAN**in the net beneath
counterfeit nature b/c it is**ABOUT** the acrobat where spikes
sewn **THIS IS REALLY**could
like**MACAULAY EVEN THOUGH**have been
the wire **ON HIS** during
into her toughest years **GO ELIJA** say
and she**IS GOING TO**the break up where she
mourned **SHE** was raving he
barely **WOULD AND SO SHE WILL NOT** had
b/c she had**THIS OR PRECISELY SHE**invented
a role**WOULD NOT STAND FOR** a splinter
to play **MEEK SWORD GLORY**demo
in the national **SACRIFICIAL LAMB'S** day before
park **HER WITH THE** based on
worth**FILLS** her
nothing**TO BE AWAY FROM** needle
more **HE WAS HAPPY** skills and she left
to her**MAMMY**being the role as
than money **JUST WANTING A** can
kept**BLEATING ABOUT**return
from getting**BLEACHED** for money during the
excessive**BUT ROMEO'S**lapsed
the**THING IN SCHOOL**deadline to avoid
silences **IS JUST A MARVELOUS** being
of her **LEARNING THE BODY**the kid
struggling **SHE REMEMBERS** soliciting
years**TO GET INVOLVED** aliens
she now sees**SHE WASN'T GOING** to rescue

Aggie wasn't planning to get involved in the scramble for her mother's limbs (She remembered learning in school that the body is just a marvelous *thing*), but her brother's bleached bleating about just wanting a mammy (who he'd actually always been happy to be away from) fills her with the sacrificial lamb's meek sword. Glory Boughton would not have stood for this! Or, actually, she would have, which is why Ag refused to. She planned to go Elijah on Romeo's Macaulay--but she doesn't really realize that for her, this whole thing is *actually* about Aunt Leslie, whose "crab ride to the close horizon" she'd barely mourned "because of work" that was worth nothing more to her than money. Even though she only now saw her aunt's silences as the spaces in the net beneath the acrobat (where spikes could have been instead), she felt powerless to pay back the counterfeit "Luke, I am your mother" that had been the wire under her toughest years (during, say, the break up where she'd raved, "he'd invented a splinter demo the day before based on *my* needle skills!" and stopped returning cans for money after a lapsed deadline just so she wouldn't look like the kid soliciting aliens for rescue).

HINT:
Aggie seems to be thinking at least partially of the columns of Page 031

a fatal **COILING** from
fly **AUDIOBOOK** kids who never played
ball for **HER** baseball but like
a MILF **VOICE FROM** physics and the idea
in the **BIG** whaling
stands much **THEY WANT LITTLE** on
less **AGREES BEFORE REALIZING** kids
disturbing somehow's logo **SHE** who do
of the Domino **HOODS** she doesn't tell them
Trixies **WITH THEIR ANIMAL** footprints
which shows a woman in **TO GO** from that
high heels **MAKE THEM UNIFORMS** blended
and lingerie **AS LONG AS SHE WILL** woman leads
that yawns **BUT THEY AGREE** back
would be **ENOUGH FOR TWO** to
the response from **BIG** theft
now **IS GOING TO GO INTO A GRAVE** of puppet
w/ hand poised over **THEIR TROPHY** because
the optical illusion of **THEM THAT** that would be
a line of dominos **BUT SHE WARNS** telling she's
forming a whip **SOME GROSS BUG** stuck on
while actually **OF** the island
stretching **THE MATING SCENT** too
forward **SPRINKLED LIKE** information
from the **DOZEN VITRIOLIC TWEETS** will get her
horizon and going **ONLY A COUPLE** off one limb is
under **HER OUT AFTER** theirs with
the arch **FINDERS SEEK** ambush she has
of her shoe **MOTHER** to promise to rearrange
she assembled **THE MISPLACED** the rest may be 2xX

The "Misplaced Mother Finders" sought Ag out after only a couple dozen vitriolic tweets about her brother sprinkled like the mating scent of some gross bug, but she warned them that when they reassemble the trophy, it will go into a grave big enough for two. They agreed as long as she would make them uniforms to go with their animal hoods. She promises to do so before realizing they want the jerseys to feature Little Big Voice from my wife's audiobook coiling a fatal fly ball for the MHLF in the stands. Oh well, she'd thought, a promise is a promise.

Much less disturbing somehow is the logo of "The Domino Trixies," which shows a woman in high heels and the sort of lingerie that would be greeted with yawns at a church picnic today, her hand poised over the optical illusion of a line of dominos forming a whip while actually stretching forward from the horizon and going under the arch of her high-heeled shoe. Abby had assembled the team from kids who never played baseball before but liked physics and the idea of whaling on kids who had. She didn't tell them that the footprints leading away from the blended woman lead back to the theft of the Ariel puppet because that would be telling. She was stuck on the island, too, like Miranda, but information will get her off (maybe when she's older). She lead the Trixies in netting one of the coveted limbs from an IRL n00b team using an ambush, then promised them they'd "rearrange the rest twice as much!" (whatever that means).

sex **BREAK UP** up with a

with his **PERPETUAL** neck snap that actually

wife all these years **LONG BY** hit him

since they **KEPT DOUBLY** in the crotch

were last **CAVEMAN BEARD** he's been

mentioned **HIS ICED** soap

when we give him **STALLION** opera

a shave it turns out he's **FULL WILD** organist

actually **IN HE'S LOOKING** for years under

his brother **AND WHITE WHEN HE COMES** the name

who is **IN BLACK** Tom

Romeo's **APPS** Limb it's gotten

uncle **ITS CORNY** to the point where

the gun **PHONE IN A DRAWER** he controls

from **MY FIRST SMART** live delivery with

the mantle **FINDING** his swells alwys a writer

in chapter **TIME IT'S A MATTER OF** sending

five dangling from **THIS WHOLE** him to the Jerking

his neck like the quote **ON HOLD** Knee

rat from The Good **HIM** Hammers I tell him

The Bad **I JUST HAD** to feel

and The Ugly **READERS IN TRUTH** the same

who websites tell **DUTY TO NEW** mixture of a joke

me kept it **OF A SENSE OF** told

thus because the **WAY OUT** off the

actor **STAYED A** cuff longing to be

cudnt holster **FATHER WHO HAD ALWAYS** told again &

it and **A CALL TO ROMEO'S** present peeker

the director thot **THE BRACKET I PUT IN** like a kata just

it could be flipped **TO ROUND OUT** as pointless

To round out the competitive bracket, I had put in a call to Romeo's father, who had always stayed away out of a sense of duty to New Readers (though in truth I just had been keeping him "on hold" the whole time--hey, they're my dimes--and on the plus side, it made me find my first smart phone in a drawer, its corny apps in black and white). When Leo Short arrived in Sister City, he was looking "full Wyld Stallyn" (his iced-caveman beard kept doubly long by perpetual break-up sex with his wife Whitney all these years since the last time I wrote about them), but when I gave him a shave, I found hanging from his neck the gun from the mantle of the stadium marquee in Chapter 4, and above that mane-less Leo was actually his brother Perry Brautjungfer (!!). Back in the day, he'd gotten amnesia after Ag was conceived, and darn it, it happened again right before he moved to Sister City. Since then, Perry'd been working as a soap opera organist under the name "Tom Limb" (based on the I.D. card he'd found in his wallet--actually a D.I.Y. relic of an unused high school pseudonym from back when he suffered fear of zine failure so much that he stayed merely an eating contest spectator), and these days he was actually scripting the melodramatic interactions live using the cheesy organ as his typewriter (Well, he always was the aspiring author of the bunch). As I sent him to take over "the Knee Hammer Jerks," I told him to try to feel like a mix of a present-peeker and an off-the-cuff joke longing to be told again. In other words, be like a crisp, hoarse-shouting kata.

explore a cave **YOU** enough for
that **WHERE** detailed
is randomly **IT IS A GAME** strategic
generated for you **WHICH** maneuvers
& contains **EXPERIENCE I'M NOT SURE** it's too late
artifacts created by **VEXATION** to make it
recursive **ALEATORY** that now instead
procedures that **COMPLEX** I am holding
only u can find **ENTERTAINMENT OR** an Exquisite
and export **VIDEO** H.O.R.S.E.
though they make **AVOCATION** competition theyl need
you draw your own **COMPLETE** more than
map **IN A CAVE** nameless kids
using **HE HAS BEEN** knees for
an in-game **SOCIETY BUT I REALIZE** faces & teeth
tool there are **THE STATE OF** crooked from
no **LAMENTS ABOUT** biting
monsters except **ENCOURAGEMENT OR** metal
falls **OF** cars
and your own **HOUSES CRIES** from cereal
echoing **FROM THIER** boxes they will have
doubt it's kind of **YELLING** a kind of
relaxing **EACH NEIGHBOR** draft
and totally **OVER SOCIAL MEDIA** of every
pointless I tell him I have **TAKEN** named
called **GIVEN THE WAY THAT IT HAS** character
the captains together **ON ALL THIS** and she will
because this city is **NOT UP** judge
not completely **AMAZED THAT HE IS** th results & who
realized **I AM** gets the trophy mom

Frankly, I'm amazed that No is not up on all this, given the way that it has taken over social media in this town, each neighbor yelling cries of encouragement from their houses (when their team is winning) or laments about the state of society (when their boys and girls have lost), but I realize that he has been lost in a C.A.V.E. (which stands for "Complete Avocation Video Entertainment" or "Complex Aleatory Vexation Experience"--I'm not sure which). It's a computer game where you explore a cavern system that is randomly-generated and contains artifacts created by recursive procedures that only *you* can find and export, though they make you draw your own map using an in-game tool. There are no dangers in the game except falls--and your own echoing doubt. It's kind of relaxing and totally pointless.

I tell everyone in the conference room that I have called the captains together because this city is not completely-realized enough for detailed strategic maneuvers and it's too late to make it so now. Instead, the rivalries are going to be resolved by a tournament of "Exquisite H.O.R.S.E." but the teams are going to need more than nameless kids with knees for faces and teeth crooked from biting metal cars that came from cereal boxes, and so there's going to be a draft of every named character before we get into the elimination rounds to see which team will end up with all the parts of the trophy mom. READER, I KNOW THAT YOU MAY BE SO EXCITED THAT YOU WANT TO SKIP STRAIGHT TO THE H.O.R.S.E., SO IF YOU DON'T CARE ABOUT CATCHING UP WITH ALL YOUR FAVORITE CHARACTERS AS THEY GET PICKED, YOU CAN JUST FLIP AHEAD AND I'LL SHOUT WHEN WE'RE READY.

because it looks **JUST** used but torn
cool **STATIC LINES** in the middle
her every **DRESS HARD**like the
motion gives **WHILE KEEPING HER** balloon of
you flashes **AND OUTWARD** it I saw
of a parade**FLOW UPWARD**pierced by a bb next
o gracefl animals **MAKING HER HAIR** is the stuntman's
and deliberate ones **LOOKING GOOD** turn
as if you're a kid **SHE IS** of course
getting **WANTED HER PLUS** the car of his
drilled **BOYFRIEND MIGHT HAVE** ex
on the alphabet eyes **OR**that
no longer **HER MUM** lurched
watery **CHOICE** like a
and**I JUST WATCHED GOOD** wolf
threatenin**SOMETHING DISAPPOINTING**through
to burst **A YOUTUBE VIDEO OF** burning timbers
at **THE TITLE OF** to rescue
the slightest**FLUIDLY APING** the intuitive
prick **MERCURY SHE CRIES**child who wil turn
hard**IRONY SOLID** it
and **HER FRIENDS SO SHE TAKES** back
mysterious**THE YELP OF**stuffed
now **SCORES HIGH ON** animal by
as **THESE DAYS SHE'S** growing
ooblek **THE SNOTTIEST** fixie
struck with her**PICK AND SHE IS** chosen
husband's **THE FIRST** several
hammer **TO SEE WHO GETS** hipster life
rarely **THE CAPTAINS ROLL** cycles ago

The captains roll to see who gets the first pick, and Ag is the snottiest. These days, she scores high on the Yelp of her friends, so she takes Irony, who cries, "Solid Mercury!" (aping the title of a Youtube video of something disappointing I just watched). Good choice, Ag--Irony's mum or boyfriend might have wanted her, plus she is looking good these days, making her hair flow upward and outward while keeping her dress hard static lines just because it looks cool. Now her every motion gives you flashes of a parade of graceful animals and deliberate ones as if drilling you on the alphabet. Her eyes no longer watery and threatening to burst at the slightest encounter with a prick, she is as hard and mysterious now as ooblek struck with her ex-husband's hammer (rarely used), but she is torn in the middle like the balloon of the stuff I saw pierced by a bb.

Next is The Stuntman's turn, and he takes Death Otter--which I guess was an obvious choice: that car had lurched like a wolf through burning timbers to rescue an intuitive child who had then callously turned it back to a stuffed animal by growing. Plus, Romeo is both of their exes--he chose a fixie as his transport several hipster-life-cycles ago.

what **FEATS ARE** book she tries
what keeps legends **IMPROBABLE** to
going and no one**THOUGH BOO HOO** make a mess but it
has an obligation to **DIONYSUS** is just extending
keep a pot on **THE MOM OF** the point at any
their **TRICKERY OF** piece of
head **RIGHT IN HER** lab equipment
after**HE HAD IMPLIED HERA WAS** so it goes ovr
the territory **NOT THE GOD** her foot
has been**JUST A MAN** has no special
explored **HE REALIZED HIS LOVER WAS** contortion
the third**MIND** joint to
pick the poet**TRUCK OF HIS** take
takes her lover **MAN IN THE RIOT** mouth but
honestly **BEFORE LIKE LAUGHING** in
the most beautiful**ACTUALITY** that diner
woman**GRAVITY AND** the slouching
she's ever known **CLOTHES FOR** circus tent she'd made
a **URN HE BLAMES** mashed
woman**YOUTHS ON AN** potatoes bot 2 answer
a traitor**GREEK** that
a killer**PHYSICALITY OF** lost
or so she tells **IT WITH THE LITHE** look though maybe
herself **IN** it was just the
honestly **POSSIBILITY SWIRLED** purposeless
the girl may be **THE WARM SENSE OF** raking of
no more**MEMORABLE WHEN** a
unbalanced**THAT'S WHAT MAKES IT** zen
than her **TIME** rock
check**HE REMEMBERS THE ONE** garden

Wolves remembers that one time (That's what makes it memorable) when the warm sense of possibility swirled in that very car with the lithe physicality of Greek youths on an urn. Since then, he has blamed clothes for gravity and actuality; just like the laughing man in the riot truck of his mind, he realized his lover had been just a man. Recovering a fragment from a classics class he once took, he realized that Hera was onto something when she told the mother of Dionysus that any man looking to score may claim to be a god in disguise (though boo hoo, improbable feats are what keeps legends going and no one has an *obligation* to keep a pot on their head after the territory has been explored).

For the third pick, The Poet takes her lover--honestly the most beautiful woman she's ever known: a woman, a traitor, a killer . . . Or so she tells herself--honestly, the girl may be no more unbalanced than any of our check books. I mean, Michelle does *try* to make a mess, but she's just extending the dotted lines from Denis Johnson's typing finger to any piece of lab equipment so that the thing goes over--she's a follower, not a leader, when it comes to destruction, self or otherwise. Alas, her foot has no special contortion joint to take it effortlessly up to her mouth, but still, Thea remembers that first night when they met in the diner when the girl was erecting a slouching circus tent of her mashed potatoes and Thea'd wanted to hold that lost look dazing up at her through fallen bangs, though some part of her knew that maybe the whole thing was just the raking of a zen rock garden.

fourth**AND FAT** the
pick **OF SUGAR** lisping
goes **ON A SAD CALCULATION** stereotype
to the little girl she takes **BASED** staying
the artist **IN BULK** on the sinking
whose friendship **BOUGHT** show
is priced **BIRTHDAY CANDLES** because it is
to move **NUMB AS** popular with a handful
after the lion **THAN THE PINKY** of people who
he contributed **SOME DUMBER** like
to the **IN COUNTING** to
leg **TO UNWRAP** be
of the tree **HAVE INFINITE FINGERS** the
man **OWN LOVE MAY NOT** hold out
got **PUNCH THAT ONE'S** against
singled out on **ROLL** flakey new
line for **THE FULL QUARTER** acceptances
the sagely **OVER** the drawing gets labeled
dopiness of **THE MACHINE** hater
its face **AT A TIME TO** fuel even though that's
by **ONE COIN** the name of a real
some **DISAPPOINTMENTS OF FEEDING** product
hater **PREFERS THE LITTLE** he named
in **A FLAG** back in
fact the most famous **SWORD FOR** the day she feels
one still clinging to **THE VEILED** rush of
the war **BY MISTAKING** power of one handed
on **EVERYONE CAUGHT** a bug knowing
his own **PLAGIARIST GOING TO GET** one
people **THE DOUBLE** curl would finish it

Thea, that double plagiarist about to get everyone caught by mistaking a veiled sword for a flag, prefers the little disappointments of feeding one coin at a time to the machine over receiving a full-quarter-roll punch from the fact that one's own love may not have infinite fingers to unwrap in counting (some dumber than the pinky and numb as birthday candles bought in bulk based on a sad calculation of sugar and fat).

The fourth pick goes to The Little Girl, and she takes the other young artist whose friendship has been priced-to-move after the lion he contributed to the leg of Leslie's tree-man got singled-out online for the sagely dopiness of its face by some hater (In fact, it was that most famous Hater, who still clings to the war on his own people like the lisping stereotype who stays on a sinking show because it is popular with a handful who like to be hold-outs against flakey new acceptances. That "former Them" Emoro said of Sic's drawing, "as if They didn't have enough reasons to hate Us, now The Haters will think our children can't draw the big cats of the jungle!" He even called it "hater fuel"--despite the fact that a real product got that name from him back in the day). By choosing Sic, Abby gets a rush of the power felt by a person handed a bug knowing that one curl of the fingers could finish it off.

with maps **DECORATED** his daughter
of toxic **BEING** that
clouded **ART HIS JUMPSUITS** was years ago
lands **BECOMING HIS** when
he has not yet explored **HE IS** he moved
not remembering **HIM** to Sister
that his bro **IS HOW SHE THINKS OF** City it
did this **DREAM THIS** happened again
same **TIME FROM MY** all that
sort of **FACE EACH** was in his
thing except **THE FIST STRIKING THE** wallet
for the name of **NECK** when he woke
love **SNAKE AROUND A** D.I.Y. I.D.
he's **COILING LIKE A** card he made
a flying **ARM** back when he suffered
squirrel **THINGS LIKE THE** fear of
the fifth **WEIRD** zine
pick the **EAR HE STARTED DRAWING** failure so
confused **TO THE LISTENER'S** much
amnesiac **OUT AND IN** that
yeah **AND SLASHING** he
did I forget **OTHER INSIDE** stayed
to mention **AGAINST EACH** an eating
that his memory **ARE CRASHING** contest
got erased by a **STRANGE SEA** observer no
blow **THE WAVES OF SOME** idea
to the **OUTSIDE IS POLISHED** why he's here but
head **AS HIS** coach
no memory **WEAPON OF SOME SORT** seems familiar
of conceiving **HE MUST BE A SECRET** enough to choose

Sic must be a secret weapon of some sort: as his outside is polished, the waves of some strange sea are crashing against each other inside and slashing out and into the listener's ear. He has started drawing weird things like the image from my dream this morning where an arm coils like a snake around a neck and strikes the face each rotation with its fist. This is how Abby has started thinking of him--he is becoming his art, his baggy jumpsuits (which have earned him the nickname "the flying squirrel") now decorated with maps he's drawn of toxic-clouded lands he has not yet explored (not that he remembers that his big bro did this same sort of thing when he was his age, though in the name of love--in name only).

For the fifth pick, The Confused Amnesiac may have no idea of why he's here with these people, but something about coach Goodie seems familiar enough to choose (even if Perry has no memory of all the time he spent in stadiums as an announcer).

and climb into**YOU** want
the screen**TO FIT AROUND** an unpolished cliff
where no**GROWN** side
one knows **LIT BODIES THAT HAVE** house with
that experience**SLUMBERING BLUE** guts
is more days**FROM THE** torn out
than that one night**WAKE** when half of it slumped
with **IT BACK** away
your roommate **YOU SHOULD ROLL** down the hill
more **PAUSED** with
grinding **THE TAPE IS** the towtruck
than**THAT WHEN** driver's
boss **WISDOM IS** hair the last
battles **A FASHION THE CONVENTIONAL** goes to
actually they say **CORE AS** the son who
you shouldn't **DOING COACH** is on the outs with
but **BECAUSE THE KIDS NOW ARE** friends so
you**IS WEARING IT**he
will so **HE** goes with
he**ARE BUT ACTUALLY** his
does **ANNOUNCERS** biggest
lemming**WHISTLES AT GAMES WHERE** enemy
of **REFS BLOW** tears from
love**NECK EVEN THOUGH ONLY**getting an arm
or body warmth**FROM HIS** sewn
in the**WHISTLE HANGING** on a new
bed **IN THE SHRILL** spot and having
what **COMFORT** an existing
younger woman **FINDS INTUITIVE** one torn off
doesn't **LIKE THE BABY BAT HE** as the price

Like a baby bat, Perry finds intuitive comfort in the shrill whistle
hanging from Goodie's neck (even though only refs blow whistles at
games, duh, but Goodie's actually wearing it because a year ago the
kids were doing "ref-core" as a fashion and now it has trickled down
the coolness gradient). The conventional wisdom is that when the
tape of your life is paused, you should roll it back, wake from the
slumbering blue lit bodies that have grown to fit around you, and
climb into the screen where no one knows that experience is
actually more about days than that one night with your roommate,
more grinding than boss battles. *Actually*, they say that you
shouldn't try to roll it back but that you inevitably will, so Goodie
does, a lemming of love or bedly body warmth. I mean, hey, what
younger woman doesn't want a cliffside house where the supports
have been dragged off by the Fabio locks of the towtruck driver
who gave the missus a ride?

The last pick of the first round goes to Romeo, and since he's on
the outs with his friends, he takes his biggest enemy instead. Lewis
gives less reaction to this news than his usual--all his concentration
these days goes to trickling tears at the gain of one arm at the price
of the other.

should **SHE** there

have **SUMMONED** are

forseen **TO THE GENIE SHE HAS** many playrs but

this **NEXT** one

when the **CIGARETTE** mascot she sees

2 of them **SHE'S FEELS LIKE ALADDIN'S** yearbook

were **IN TRUTH** tattooed

on the **GUN THOUGH** she graduated

junior high **CASING FROM THE SAME** now

basketball **SHELL** written

them one **OTHER SMOKING** even

as the mascot **TAKES THAT** across her own

giant **FIERCE HUGS SHE** picture

pager **HELD TOGETHER BY** ahhh

they were **VOLTRON** but

The Fighting **AN ANALOG** the time when

90s **CATS** they after a little racist

and the other **A CYBORG MADE OF** practicing were

the hope **TIMER SHE'S LIKE** able to

of **THE MULTI** throw

the team **BREAKUP WITH** a credible toga party

that was **CATS SINCE HER** full of sanctioned

quickly **HERSELF THE PRINCE OF** pederasty

dubbed Tony Jaa **NOW CALLING** simulatd appreciation

for being **ABOUT HER FRIENDS** of shitty

good at **WHO IS ALL** alcohol here

elbows **FOR THE DAUGHTER** C-

but not much **IS EASY** and

else after **PICK** crippling

all **THE NEXT** debt

Okay, it's draft round 2, and the next pick is easy for the girl who has started calling herself The Prince of Cats since her breakup with that multi-timer Hans (call Aggie a cyborg made of cats, an analog Voltron held together by fierce hugs)--she takes Beebe, that other smoking shell-casing from the same gun, though in truth she feels like Aladdin's cigarette next to the genie she has summoned. She wonders if she should have foreseen Beebe's ascension back when the two of them were on the junior high basketball team, one as the mascot (a giant pager--they were The Fighting 90s) and the other the hope of the team that was quickly dubbed Tony Jaa (as in "all about the elbows")--after all, there are many players, but only one mascot. Aggie now remembers her tattooed yearbook as having Beebe's scrawl stretching across her own startled "taken on the count of two" portrait. Ahhh, but still, who can forget the time when the team was, after a little tasteless practicing, able to throw a credible toga party, complete with sanctioned pederasty (simulated), appreciation of shitty alcohol (here, "Coors Light" aka "C- . . . the minimum passing grade"), and crippling debt.

left **HAS BEEN** with child
exactly **MEANWHILE SHE** named
where we left her **RING** after
she's fighting **MY WEDDING** synthesizer obviously
liquid **THINK OF** imagining the swirling
dinosaurs when **THE WAY I** and the baleful sound
they **LIKE** Suicide
get **HIS SURROUNDINGS** made but
sparked on off-shore oil rigs **OF** disappointment
she was always **A REFLECTION** may be
considered **AND ALWAYS HAD BEEN** in her future
anytme any 1 needed **THAT HE WAS** as he is
a new girlfriend **AGAINST REALIZING** little
but the fickle finger of **A BEARD** more than
childish **THAT ROMEO WAS SORT OF** a Sxy Maid's
fate never fell **THOUGH HE REFLECTS** duster for her
on **A FAKE FLAME** guise as
her Toys 'R' **SUCH THING AS** MILF but no
Us tag **THEY PROBABLY SAY THERE'S NO** shade
but she's excavated **BECAUSE AS** a phrase
from **THE FIREFIGHTER** I've never said out
the landfill **GOES WITH** loud the promises
of **THE STUNT MAN** were not made by
the past **THEMESONG** part driven
to bring her glowing **SECOND** to
touch to whatever **THEIR LIVES'** blow
this competition is **LEGS WAS** Batman
going **CORDUROY** the hell
to be the poet **THE VIPPING OF** up
goes **THAT WAS BACK WHEN** I mean

That was back when the vipping of corduroy legs was their lives' second themesong.

For his next pick, The Stuntman goes with The Firefighter because as they (probably) say, there's no such thing as a fake flame (though he considers that Romeo *had been* sort of a beard against the realization that Wolves is and always has been like my simple wedding band that decorates itself in the irregular stripes of its surroundings). Since she dumped Thea in chapter 2, Cate has been fighting liquid dinosaurs when they get sparked on off-shore oil rigs. Though the fickle finger of childish fate never fell on her Toys 'R' Us claim tag, I always considered her anytime a character needed a new girlfriend, but now she's been excavated from the landfill of the past to bring her glowing touch to whatever this competition is going to be.

Next, The Poet goes with The Child Named After A Synthesizer Company, obviously imagining the swirling and baleful sound the band Suicide made, but disappointment may be in her future, since as a 4 year old he is little more than a Sexy Maid's duster for her guise as a GILF, but, hey, no shade (a phrase I've never said out loud): the promises were not made by the part driven to blow Batman (the hell up, I mean),

man for **HIM THE RELEVANT** remember with

blood **SHE THINKS OF** the brassy warmth

still pumps through his **KID OR AS** of blues

wings **IS THE** rock to

even if they **PICK** a professional

have been **GIRL'S NEXT** pool

ground **HARLEY THE LITTLE** playr like his own

back to **HARVEY'S** Dad

stumps **QUALIFICATIONS TO BE** the waiter

and cause slips **ABOUT HIS** from beyond or books

in the **PASSING ESSAY** on the shelf of

heart **IF NOT NECESSARILY** John

beating **A COMPELLING** Waters'

moments **HE WOULD PROBABLY GIVE** date

& he don't even know **A CHANCE** though he'd prefer

that they're friends **BUT IF GIVEN** a uniform

he's Commissioner **L** with a

Gordon and she's **BLACKENED** feather

Bruce Wayne **WITH A** plume she's been

that viking **BRANDED** playing horns

of the carwash **TO KEEP FROM BEING** for ska

goes with Work **ON** bands only to be

as **BOTH SHOES** dropped like

his **VANILLA AND KEEPING** the

second because her **FRENCH OF** dart when they

saxophone seems **HIS TONGUE JUST** went

to **HOLDING** indie

echo **LIKE A GOOD PILGRIM** pop she waits

off walls **UPHOLD HIS NAME** for the return of

he cannot **AND HE FEELS BOUND TO** bipedal dogs

and Moog feels bound to uphold his name like a good pilgrim stopping his tongue just stateside of French of vanilla and keeping both shoes on to keep from being branded with a blackened L, but if given a chance he would probably give a compelling (if not necessarily passing) essay about his qualifications to be Harvey's Harley.

For her second pick, The Little Girl picks No--or, as she thinks of him, The Relevant Man, for even though she felt betrayed by him, she still pumps blood through his wings (ground back to stumps in her mind, though they are) causing spurts of slips in heart-beating moments. And he still doesn't even know that they were friends in the first place! "Ahh, Commissioner Gordon . . ." thinks Bruce Wayne.

Next, Perry, that viking of the carwash, picks Work Suggestively because her saxophone seems to echo off unremembered walls like books on the shelf of John Waters' date or the throaty warmth of blues rock to a professional pool player (as his own Dad was before he died and became a waiter). Though he'd prefer her in a uniform with a feather plume, she's been playing horns for ska bands but keeps getting dropped like the dart when they go indie pop. She's been grumbling about how hipsters now only like inhuman sounds, but she keeps her reed wet and waits for bipedal dogs to come back.

he bought **THE WHITE DRESS** recognizing
for her favoring **TO WEAR** each
whatever **HIS CHILD DECLINED** other
astronomers **THAT THE MOTHER OF** recycled tubes
wear seduced **IN SO MANY WORDS** and cones
by all those movies **NOT TO SAY** are actually her and her
that **IS TASTEFUL ENOUGH** art
glamorize **HE INVENTED THE ARTICLE** has found
the profession **SPINNING MACHINE** its
in **THE PASTA** audience on
truth **MIDDLEMEN FROM** the internet where
he only invented **THE PARASITIC** people
the last **TO CLAW OUT** love
stage **ENOUGH** under
of the thing **FROM HIS PHONE** dogs & the earmufs
which lets **UP** she's adopted
you make **OFF THAT HE LOOKED** to protest
the **ALMOST 100 YEARS** the
pasta **WITH A DATE MISPRINTED** divorce
look like **I JUST READ** of her parents
the revolutionary **NEWSPAPER** and their
leader **UP TO ACCORDING TO A** bands has made
of your choice **DOG BEEN** her
so **DOWNWARD FACING** the most popular
he may actually **HAS THAT** ugly dog
be the placebo **AND WHAT** on the internet she's
psychic **TAKES HIS SECOND** selling all sorts
surgeon round 3 **MAGICIAN** of gawky gentle
begins w/ **OLDEST RIVAL THE FAILED** beasts for
fizzld rockets **HAVING EXPENDED HIS** big bucks

Having expended his oldest rival, The Failed Magician takes his second most mature: Roscoe. What has that downward-facing dog been up to? According to a newspaper I just read (with a date misprinted almost 100 years off) Scoe looked up from his phone long enough to claw out the parasitic middlemen from the pasta spinning machine he invented, and thus he's riding high on the dog (and the article is even tasteful enough not to say in so many words that the mother of his child declined to wear the white dress he bought for her, favoring whatever astronomers wear, seduced by all those movies that glamorize the profession). In truth, he only invented the last stage of the pasta machine that lets you make the pasta look like the revolutionary leader of your choice, so he may actually be the walking-placebo psychic surgeon who wrung out the gunk that Andy Kaufman saw at the end of the movie (Spoiler, sorry).

Round 3 of the draft begins with fizzled rockets recognizing each other as Aggie spies Izzy through a paper-towel tube--and actually, recycled tubes and cones do figure pretty centrally into Izzy's art these days, which has found an audience in a place where people love underdogs. The earmuffs she's adopted to protest her parents breaking into two separate bands have made her the most popular Ugly Dog on the internet, and she's selling all sorts of gawky gentle art beasts for big bucks.

HINT:
That newspaper is a reprint of Page 086

gamesHE ALSO takes
publicDRUNK her little
sentiment with memeMEN BY Acue
generator that can putBEAUTIFULball though she hates the
sympatheticSIX MISTAKEN FOR nickname
faces ONE IN now she prefers a comet
overANYWAY FOR as
the hunter's whoTHE COMPUTERS her symbol
was mauledFOR her hair
afterA HEADACHEtrailing
puttingOVER ZERO WHICH WAS icily
on ZEROin the
deer ALGORITHM FROM solar
scentTARGETING winds though
Bambi'sTO THEGrandma finds
snuff filmTWEAK it
director no loveBY A MINORall
yet but heBEEN BAGGINGthe more
can buy ISLAND HAS warm
itBUCKS WHICH LITTLE because its
a la carte when heNEED BIG tangled rungs
wants BIG STUNTS are synthetic and
it pacingTO CATCH IT ANDprecarious
like anEXPENSIVE TRACK next
open world NEEDS A LOT OF the little
player rationalizinROLLERCOASTER girl
sloppinessBECAUSE A FALLING takes the littler
like a loyalBUSINESS MAN one in the
fan the grandmaTAKER TAKES THEnesting
happily NEXT THE PUNCHdoll set

Next, The Punch-Taker takes The Business Man because a falling roller coaster needs a lot of expensive track to catch it and big stunts need big bucks--which Little Wagner has been sheepishly bagging by accident because a minor tweak to the algorithm of their self-driving cars has for some other reason changed the targeting systems from zero over zero (which was a headache for the computers anyway) to one in six mistaken for beautiful men by a drunk. Still, sales are strong because Malcolm has gamed public sentiment against deer by use of an online meme generator that can put a sympathetic face of your choice over that of the hunter in the video who was mauled after putting on doe scent. Bambi's snuff film director still has no steady diet of love, but he buys it a la carte when he wants it (with Suggested Donations, of course--nothing untoward)--he paces himself through the experiences like an open-world player rationalizing a sloppy pass through virtual districts to have something to collect later.

Like a loyal fan, the Grandma happily takes her "Little Cue Ball," though Syf hates that nickname now--she prefers a comet as her symbol, picturing hair trailing icily in the solar winds (though Grandma finds that image all the more warm because its tangled rungs are synthetic and precarious--Grandmas, right?).

Next, little girl Abby takes The Littler One In Her Nesting Doll Set.

the**ONE GOES TO**job and he's
collector **NO THE REAL** lost
and this**TOO** it plus his brother
is his last **I DID** scornful
allergen to**HIM** piety gilt around
bottle **SEAWEED ON** his
never met **THE ALIEN WITH ALL THE** neck he feels
each other before he's **FOR**like the family nose cut
the harp**HIM** off in
player **BECAUSE HE MISTOOK** a fit
mirroring**HIS BREATH BUT ONLY** of
the comedianne**HOLDING** fad
and **THE WAY BUT HE'S STILL** who
he thinks **AFTER HE LEFT BY** will
he must be**SLAPPED IMMEDIATELY** hire
a secret**HE GOT** a
Hater **OPPOSITE LIPS** guy with
himself **DIVER OF** an incisive grasp
at the top of the**SWELLS TAKES THE** on the
order**NAMESAKE THE KING OF** jaws of
she chooses **OPERATOR TO HER** numbers the
the guy named**SWITCHBOARD** candy
after**A KARMIC** glass man takes
a song lyric **ONE DAY SHE WILL BE** Voldemort
because he**YET THEY HOPE THAT** because he
is currently **HERBERT WEST**can recognize another
non-profiting too yes **SHE'S NO** repurposed pizza hut
the only guy **IN SCIENCE CLASS BUT** when he sees
with an almost **DOING WELL** one plus he put the ball
real **SHE IS** in the air by the hoop

Steph II has been doing well in science class, but she's no Herbert West yet. Still, they have hopes that one day she will become a karmic switchboard operator to her dead namesake.

The King of (Organ) Swells takes The Diver of Opposite Lips--but only because he mistook One for the alien with all the seaweed on him (because I did, too). (By the way, on that day when No saw him kissing that girl, One got a slap from her immediately after his ex stumbled away, but he's still holding his breath for a woman.)

The Real Alien goes to Romeo for his team of rivals, the last of his allergens to bottle. Emoro and Romeo have never actually met before even when Emoro was trailerpark lovenesting with his sister, and now the meeting casts Romeo as the harp player whose moves are mirrored by the comedienne pretending to be him. (For years, he's privately suspected that he may be a secret Hater himself.)

At the top of the order, Aggie chooses the brother of Yes named after a song lyric because he is currently not profiting, too--yeah, the only guy with an almost real job in this book has lost it! And a brother! Yes had as much as told him that his pious new gilt neck icon cannot lie on a heart with a queer brother inside, and Cray feels like the family nose cut off in a fit of fad. Who--*who?!*--will hire a guy with an incisive grasp on the jaws of numbers?

Speaking of Yes, the Candy-Glass Man takes that "Voldemort" because he can recognize another repurposed Pizza Hut when he sees one, plus that's a guy who can (apparently) put the ball in the air by the hoop (which may or may not be an actually useful skill in this game).

melting herself **TO** Molly does exude
to **ORPHANHOOD** drama like
the spaceship **PROCLAIMING** ghosts
in **A TREE AND** of
a cosmic light **FROM HIDING BEHIND** curls shorn
show **HOW DID SHE GO** off
I'm probably **SPEAKING OF** her hand
to blame **ACTION FIGURES** does remember
the little girl **INTERCHANGEABLE AS** writing
takes **THREE BODIES** just as he does
the last **GRAPPLE OF** the pedestal
child **ARRANGING A** pen
to complete her **KID SHE IMAGINES** now hollow
crusade **LIKE A BIG** because
he radiates **ONE AND** there is no
purity but **NO LONGER BE** ticking
in **A KID ABOUT TO** to design
the most boring **BOOK TO** last is the
way maybe he'll get **A GROWN UP** woman in
the print **ON PICTURES LIKE** a t-shirt
of a dodge **SHORT** too disappointingly
ball texture **EVEN THOUGH SHE'S** homophobic
on his face **BEING ELECTROCUTED** to
getting down **AS SEXUAL JELLO** be reprinted
to the last **SHE IMAGINES** he sees she now
two & the 2 smooth **DRUMMER WHO** is his enemy the
HD **CHOOSES THE** favored
liver **PIT THE POET** daughter
has little **IN THE MOSH** smothered her punk in
basis for choosin **LIKE JOHN MILTON** princess

Like thrice-battered John Milton in the mosh pit, The Poet chooses The Drummer whom she imagines as sexual jello being electrocuted, despite Mounthe being short on pictures like a grown-up book to a kid about to no longer be one, and like a nominally big kid, Thea imagines arranging a grapple of three bodies interchangeable as action figures. (Speaking of, how did Thea go from hiding behind a tree in order to proclaim orphanhood to melting her electricity-fiendin' metal body to the spaceship in a cosmic light show? I'm probably to blame.)

The Little Girl takes the last child to complete her crusade. Fees *is* awfully pure, but in the most boring Galahad way--maybe the print of a dodge ball texture on his face will make him worth a damn.

Getting down to the last two picks, Perry (whose eyes have now gotten accustomed to the weightless hi-def motion of the soaps) does not have much of a basis for choosing between the leftovers, but Molly *does* radiate vaporous soap-opera caliber drama like the ghosts of curls shorn off, and her hand *does* remember writing just as his does (though her pedestal pen is now hollow because there is no ticking to design), so he goes with her.

The last one left is the woman in a t-shirt too disappointingly homophobic to be reprinted here (privately painful to me in a different way because the favored daughter has smothered her punk in princess). Clearly, Robin now *is* Romeo's enemy, so she's an appropriate enough addition to his collection (not that he had a choice at this point).

as **THE PLAYGROUND** fall of
he **KID ON** a flicked
holds **THE LONELIEST** cigarette
two hands **THE PALMS OF** landing
in **AND PRICK** tails like
a game **AND SHUFFLE** a stuffed animal
he is making **TO BE SLID OUT** from a bed so get
up the **MATRIX WAITING** your
God **IN A PLASTIC** turtleneck
of 21 **TRADING CARDS** ready the Blue
eyes **IT WERE COLLECTABLE** beards go
older brother **CHAPEL AS** first with
to Milo's **LOCATION IN THE** the awkwardness of
dodecahedron **THROUGH BASED ON** clowns
and younger to **SHINING** undercover
Geo Washington **OR GREATER LIGHT** voices
says that The Nurtured **LESSER** rising at the end of
Natural **MOSAICS WITH** lines like
will take on the **MODE STAINED GLASS** harpsichord
Bluebeards **ARCHIVE** jacks
but will it be **A TUMBLR SET ON** the captain
skatepark **PRESENTS EVERYBODY IS** in tones behnd
fighting **IT'S TIME TO OPEN THE** a house
game **TREE SO** overlooking a
Voltrons **ARE ON THE** gorge
or broken **THE ORNAMENTS** her girlfriend
hip **SQUEEZE BUT** says
drawn sestinas **I HAVE ENJOYED THE** grunts
in the cafe **TWO LIME WEDGES AND** a sweating
district at the **MY BRAIN IS LIKE** teen zen gardener

My brain is like two lime wedges and I have enjoyed the squeeze, but the ornaments are on the tree, so it's time to open the presents! Everybody is a tumblr set on "archive" mode, stained-glass mosaics with lesser or greater light shining through based on location in the chapel (as it were), collectable trading cards in a plastic matrix waiting to be slid out to shuffle and prick the palms of the loneliest kid on the playground as he holds two hands in a game he is making up as he goes along. In other words, **EXQUISITE H.O.R.S.E. IS GONNA RIDE (man)!** The god of two eyes (older brother to Milo's dodecahedron and younger to George Washington) says that Wolves' Nurtured Naturals will take on Thea's Ex Bluebeards, but will it be skatepark fighting-game Voltrons or broken hip-drawn sestinas in the cafe district at a flicked cigarette's fall? He lands tails like a stuffed animal from a bed, so get your turtleneck!

The Bluebeards go first with the awkwardness of clowns, undercover voices rising at the end of lines like harpsichord jacks. The team captain intones, "Behind a house overlooking a gorge," and her girlfriend adds, "grunts a sweating teen zen gardener."

EXQUISITE H.O.R.S.E. TEAM ROSTERS:

MISPLACED MOTHER FINDERS
Aggie
Irony
Beebe
Izzy
Cray

EX BLUEBEARDS
Thea
Michelle
Moog
Syf
Mounthe

KNEE HAMMER JERKS
Perry
Goodie
Work
One
Molly

NURTURED NATURALS
Wolves
Death Otter
Cate
Malcolm
Yes

DOMINO TRIXIES
Abby
Sic
No
Steph
Fees

THE SONS ALL WANT PRIZES
Romeo
Lewis
Roscoe
Emoro
Robin

to be **CROWS WITH DREAMS** a crow
nothing **LEARNING STRAIGHT AS** he'd rather be
like **SEEKING PATHS OVER** not glacier but
their **GORGE** crow pecking without
gardener and get **ON WHICH TO** path to find
a model **SOMETHING** the rocks that could set
in **FOR** him
the sack and **THE WANNA-BES WAITING** up
get **REST HE SILENTLY CURSES** as a cloud
busted **BEES HERE IS THE** gardener a
on Sunset **STINGERLESS** crown
with the rocks some **OF** absolved
would look at **THE TWINKLING** from being on
that and say that **CONCLUDES AMID** the beast
life rocks **SCARECROW AND THE POET** far from
but in his **SCHLUBBY** the gory
mind **THE HEAD OF THE** droplets as
success **BOY SAYS THAT IS** it
is the **THE SYNTHESIZER** gorges miles above
b-sides he could have **THE SACK** janitors
forever hacked **THE STARE OF** getting the sack only
the sack but **IGNORING** hours til he can hit
it always found **WHEREVER** th sack bt 1st he wil hve
its way **FINDER SAYS** a dinner
to the **ROCKS THE GROOVE** of crow when his
gorge **THE BAG OF** divorced father comes
that never had **WATER DROPPED** home to
a better gardener **FOR WANT OF** gorge
than a mighty **GIRL SAYS WHO** on the value of
glacier or **THE BALD** math & th weight o rocks

The bald girl says, "who for want of water dropped the bag of rocks." The groove finder says, "wherever ignoring the stare of the sack." The synthesizer boy says, "that is the head of the schlubby scarecrow," and the poet concludes, "amid the twinkling of stingerless bees." Here is the rest, with helpful line breaks and without pesky attribution:

> He silently curses the wanna-bes
> waiting for something on which to gorge,
> seeking paths over learning straight as crows
> with dreams to be nothing like their gardener
> and get a model into the sack
> and get busted on Sunset with the rocks.
>
> Some would look at that and say, "That life rocks!"
> but in his mind, success is the b-sides.
> He could have forever hacked the sack
> but it always found its way to the gorge
> that never had a better gardener
> than a mighty glacier or a crow.
>
> He'd rather be not glacier, but crow,
> pecking without path to find the rocks
> that could set him up as a cloud gardener,
> a crown absolved from being on the beast
> far from the gory droplets as it gorges,
> miles above janitors getting sacked.
>
> Only hours till he can hit the sack,
> but first he will have a dinner of crow
> when his divorced father comes home to gorge
> on the value of math and the weight of rocks
> and "I told you so." Tell it to the bees,
> Dad--next time, you pay for a gardener!

her **TO ASK** then
to come see **THE SACK** taking a morsel of
his garden **HAD** nothing back to the
rocks and **BELIVE HE** mouth with the next line
unzip a crow **WILL NEVER** stunt
feather **GORGE GEORGE** man leads the tumble
of what **EMPIRE HASHTAG BY** down
may be Shakespeare **FOR FUTURE** stairs
does **AND A LABEL** with his calm
not need to worry **SHE ROCKS** battle
about being **PIC HASHTAG** cry beyond a
replaced **NET WITH A CAMPHONE** lawn sprinkld w
they should **CROW ON THE** candy
have gotten **HIM** glass and the dinosaur
old king **THE WAY YOU WILL SEE** fighter
Hamlet to write **THE B'S AND OH** says they wait for
their verses **WITH** mutants like toys
instead of **THE SHEET TO MAKE** in a store and
me oh **THE SACK AND RAISES** the model turned
well the next squad goes **INTO** asshole says baby
starting **HER INTEREST UNTIL SHE TRIPS** fish
in **GREEN TO GARDENER** in
a huddle **THEN HE NEEDS THE** the sitcom house's
then each **GARDENER TIL** mouth
one peeling off **FOR A** then
with their **TIME YOU PAY** the lord of
line like the finger of **NEXT** volcanos says
a poked **TO THE BEES DAD** frozen like
headless sea **SO TELL IT** cheaters in a hall
thing resetting **AND I TOLD YOU** of mirrors

Till then, he needs the green to garden her
interest until she trips into the sack
and raises the sheet to make with the b's,
and oh the way you will see him crow
on the net with a cam phone pic #sherocks
and a label for future empire #bygorge

George will never believe he had the sack
to ask her to come see his garden rocks,
unzip a crow feather of what may be.

I don't think Shakespeare needs to worry about being
replaced--they'd probably have been better with old king Hamlet
writing their verses instead of me--but I think that was the first
sestina I've ever written, so . . . not completely terrible?
   Oh well, the next squad goes next, starting in a huddle then each
one peeling off with their line of the sestina like a poked headless
sea thing's finger resetting, then taking a morsel of nothing back to
the central mouth with the next line. The Stunt Man leads the
tumble down stairs with his calm battle cry of "Beyond a lawn
sprinkled with candy glass," and the dinosaur fighter says, "They
wait for mutants like toys in a store," followed by the
model-turned-asshole saying, "--baby fish in the sitcom house's
mouth." Then the lord of volcanoes says, "frozen like cheaters in a
hall of mirrors." The car that survived beeps, "no longer kids
rehearsing last night's match," and the one with whom bones are
painted (cap again) says, "but would-be raiders in a wasteland."

the packages **THOUGH** you
are not like **CONVENIENCE STORE** wouldn't say
what they **EVEN HAD A** the survivors quite
miror **MATCH THE SET** match they're
colorless **BLAST ITS** random
peanuts **GAVE THE** things shoved as teeth
cannot **HANGAR** in a mouth but that
fool **GLASS BUT THE** readies them for
the mouth **REAL** whatever's in
he **NEIGHBORHOODS WITHOUT** store soon
cannot seem 2 4 long **LAND FAKE** as they get
close his mouth **OF** nerve
he just lets **A WASTE** to scour the
saliva **HAD BEEN** land
fall **THE PLACE** and try to piece
where it **CONTINUE HE THOUGHT** 2gether th glass
lands on day 2 **THERE THEY** impossible as
they broke all of the **LAND FROM** your head
mirrors which had been **A WASTE** back in
real a sign of **RAIDERS IN** a mirror he's no
the price **BUT WOULD-BE** out
of glass **PAINTED SAYS** figurer but he can
that after wrappd **WHOM BONES ARE** mirror like
in handles **AND THE ONE WITH** Poe's
joined the **NIGHT'S MATCH** mad
store **LAST** man he does not
as daggers to **KIDS REHEARSING** yell
go **BEEPED NO LONGER** but
withrope and **SURVIVED** match the
matches **THE CAR THAT** students are turning in

From there they continue:

> He thought the place had been a waste of land,
> fake neighborhoods without even real glass,
> but the hanger gave the blast its match
> --the set even has a convenience store,
> though the packages are not like what they mirror
> (colorless peanuts cannot fool the mouth).
>
> He cannot seem to for long close his mouth;
> he just lets saliva fall where it lands.
> On Day 2, they broke all of the mirrors
> --which had been real (a sign of the price of glass)
> that after wrapped in handles joined the store
> as daggers to go with rope and matches.
>
> You wouldn't say the survivors quite match
> --they're random things shoved as teeth in a mouth--
> but that readies them for whatever's in store
> soon as they get the nerve to scour the land
> and try to piece back together the glass
> (impossible as your head-back in a mirror).

shard **IN HIS HORDED** anamorphic art of
of glass **MOUTH HE REPEATS** sidewlks seeming
look **IN THE** floors below
landing a good **TONGUE WILL GO** while domestic
spot clear as **HE WITHOUT** discouragement
glass is possible **MATCH FOR** plays from beside
if you match **WET** warmth inside
deeds to **HIS HEAD LIKE A** window sill
mouth **TIME HE STRIKES** only 4
hope you're **LANDING EVERY** inches
worth more **READY FOR A ROUGH** deep when
than **HE'S JUST GETTING** my wife
mirrors **THEIR MIRROR** speaks I remember
in **WOULD BE** I am still
a store **TERROR FACE** holding out my
because **THIS STORY AND HIS** phone
my complex's **TO TELL** toward the
dryer **IT'S EARLY** conflict because she
is broken I **KNOWS** generously
am **HE** volunteered
sitting **RELUCTANTLY SALTED** to take
a nearby post-ironc **LAND HIS MEAT** time off from
laundry where each **REJOIN THE** writing
customer gets **FIRST TO** what's
a simulated **WEIGHT WILL BE** this next to
fire escape **MOUTH DEAD** statements made
to hang **LIABILITY IN HIS** by students like
their **GLASS NOTHING BUT** Romeo wants
laundry **BRITTLE AS** to
over **HIS CONFIDENCE IS** continue loving

He's no out-figurer, but he can mirror;
like Poe's mad man he does not rave, but match.
His confidence is brittle as glass,
nothing but liability in his mouth;
dead weight will be first to rejoin the land,
his meat reluctantly salted to store.

He knows it's early to tell this story
and his terror face would be their mirror
--he's just getting ready for a rough landing
every time he strikes his head like a wet match.
For "he without tongue will go in the mouth,"
he repeats in his hoarded shard of glass.

Look, landing a good spot as clear glass
is possible if you match deeds to mouth
--hope you're worth more than mirrors in a store.

Because my complex's dryer is broken, I am sitting at a nearby
post-ironic laundry where each customer gets a simulated fire
escape to hang their clothes off of with anamorphic sidewalk art
mere feet below to simulate that tenement elevation while a canned
soundtrack of domestic discouragement plays from inside the
window sill that is actually only 4 inches deep. Suddenly, my real
wife speaks, and I remember that I have been holding out my phone
toward the poetry contest that she has generously volunteered to
judge (taking time off from writing, "What's this?" next to statement
made by her students, such as "Romeo wants to continue loving"),
having seen far better ones and understood them and having been
able to say with confidence whether a thing was there or not.

and here**IT DOES** the

I was worried **AND** captain's got the shy lover

that the exotic subject**SHE THINKS** of butterflies

matter **WHAT** in him so he

and **B'S MEANS** is recruited the car is

relativly mor **ME IF MAKING WITH THE** rusty bayonette

seasoned**THOUGH SHE ASKS** so no

poetic chops **SUBSTANTIAL**firefighter

were**DELIBERATELY** is

going to flip **HIS IMAGES ARE** a farce

the**TIED SURVIVOR SAYING**performr which

pro's **THE TONGUE** means

boat chalk**FUTURE OVER** books

it up to **HIMSELF AND HIS** rollercoaster

first thought **WHO IS** track has never chosen a

best **GARDENER** poem so the

thought**WITH THE** billionaire is

I've decided **AND SHE GOES** out

that anyone**NOT** the man

who **THERE OR**whose regions

would choose**WHETHER A THING WAS** swaddled

poetry over **SAY WITH CONFIDENCE** sanctimonious

recess **ABLE TO** like

can **THEM AND BEEN** the Purloined

stay **ONES AND UNDERSTOOD** Letter gets

in the **BETTER** callback I've got

game as **FAR** to get

pseudopod**POEMS HAVING SEEN** across town

of **THESE POOR**doctor

the winners**TO BE THE JUDGE OF**office mag factory

She goes with the gardener-who-is-himself-and-his-future over the tongue-tied survivor, saying the former's images are "deliberately substantial," though she does ask me if "making with the B's" means what she thinks (Oh, it does). And here I was worried that the exotic subject matter and my (slightly) more seasoned poetic chops were going to flip the paper pro's boat--I guess chalk another up to "first thought, best thought"?

I've got to get across town because there's another horse-off going on, but first I'd decided that anyone who would choose poetry over recess can stay in the game as a pseudopod of the winning team, so which Naturals can resist the bell? The captain's got the shy lover of butterflies in him, so he's in. The car is a rusty bayonet, so no. The firefighter is a farce performer, which means books, so yeah. Roller coaster track has never chosen a poem, so the billionaire is out. And the man whose region is swaddled sanctimonious like the Purloined Letter gets a callback.

Now that that's done, I run down to my poorly-washed, gender-neutral steed Foggy Notion, but am I going to the doctor's office or to the magnet factory?

mobs **INSIDE THE** comfortable
have separated **PICTURESQUE** taking over positions
and **HOW UNFORTUNATELY** as words
the principals are **FLOODED** so
in **THAT PLACE WAS** she subs for
the two pools **THAT** the forgetful
each has **HADN'T I HEARD** lover as the visitor
a chosen shark **BUT WAIT** she goes
bound with **THIS PAGE** first she hurls
a waterproof **COIN BEFORE WRITING** the nest
blind **I FLIPPED THE** building
fold the **FACTORY AS IF** bird
actual **THE MAGNET** from
orphan **OFFICE I AM DRAWN TO** her
bites **THE DOCTOR'S** looking
for **NIX ON** to lure
her team **THE PRESIDENT TELLING ME** destructive
but how is **A CALL FROM** mammals but
her amnesiac **I GET** only hears the
father as **GAY PEOPLE THEN** rustle of
unpainted **THINGS ABOUT** a bird
as **PEOPLE AND SHITTY** painter and
a prophet **EVERYDAY** glides closer
supposed **WITTY THINGS ABOUT** the orphan goes
to Carebear **PHILLIP MARLOWE SAYS** w a horseshoe
stare through **FOGGY NOTION** to catch
a mostly unstained **STEED** unlucky
window **GENDER NEUTRAL** souls it
she's **MY POORLY WASHED** falls between
as **I HOP INTO** a lacky and a stair object

I just start driving, and in my audiobook Phillip Marlowe says witty things about everyday people and shitty things about gay people. Then I get a call from The President telling me nix on the Doctor's Office, so I am drawn to the Magnet Factory . . . but wait, hadn't I heard that that place was flooded?! How unfortunately picturesque!

Inside, Aggie's Misplaced Mother Finders and Perry's Knee Hammer Jerks have separated out, and the characters you know from each team are in one of the two main pools. Each team has chosen a Marco shark to swim with waterproof blindfold among the other team to see which "explorer" can "discover" one of the other team first. Like the game you remember from childhood, it's not quite a free-for-all: on each turn, a shark will radiate an image from their own personal glossary, and the prey with sympathetic images inside them will resonate and draw the beast closer. For those of you who want to draw a diagram of the moves (as I am doing), the Finders are clockwise Irony, Beebe, Izzy, and Cray, while the Jerks are Molly, Goodie, Work, and One.

Aggie The Actual Orphan will bite for her team, but how is her amnesiac father, as unpainted as a prophet, supposed to do the Carebear Stare through a mostly unstained window? Well, Molly's as comfortable taking over positions as she is other people's words, so she subs for the forgetful lover (go ahead and change that part of your chart), and as the visitor, she goes first. She hurls from deep within herself the nest-building bird, looking to lure destructive mammals, but she only hears the rustle of a bird painter and glides closer.

Next, Aggie goes with a horseshoe to catch unlucky souls, but it falls between a lackey and an object on the stairs, so she splits the difference.

the king of **THE WAKE OF** stuck
swells as he **CATCHES** between the stations
skips **THE MUCK BUT** classical kitchy
overhead like **A DIVER INTO** rockabilly and
the dainty steps of **HERSELF LIKE** frozen
plump rain **BLINDLY HURLS** Shakespearian lines
on the **METEORITE** she will follow
surface the cheater **VIRTUOUS** the king with the antlers
catches **KIDS** of
sight **VITAMINS FOR** a charging deer
of **RAMONES** but
a swimsuit **BEHIND THE VEIL OF** the bear
that costs **WHOLESOMENESS** fleeer
way 2 mch **COMEDIAN AND THE SECRET** hedgemaze
for **THE ELECTROCUTED** child and caught
its **PLASMA DOME OF** coyote
simplicity sh strikes **THE SPARKING** fan out like
with hammer **SHE IS LEAD ASTRAY BY** rodeo
of amateur **HEAD BUT** clowns
carpenter but **HER OWN CURLLESS** she flips like
liontamer's snaking **SO SHE HURLS** an acrobat but no
thrown **SWIMSUIT** clumsy applause
tongue misleads **WHO OWNS NO** shifting colors sneak
her back to **WOMAN** under her
where she started **SKIRTS OF THE** blindfold
from the cancelled **JELLYFISHING** so she slashes with the
superhero **TARGETS THE** sharpie
flails with the **2 PICK** like the
trust **PEEKER SO HER ROUND** flourishing
of a puppet but gets **SHE'S A** tagger

Molly's a peeker, so her Round 2 pick targets the jellyfishing skirts of the woman who owns no swimsuit--she hurls her own curl-less head but she is lead astray by the sparking plasma dome of the electrocuted comedian and the secret wholesomeness behind the veil of Ramones Vitamins 4 Brats.

Aggie blindly launches the virtuous meteorite of herself like a diver into the muck, but she catches the wake of the king of swells as he skips overhead like the dainty steps of plump rain on the surface.

The cheater catches sight of a swimsuit that costs way too much for its simplicity, and she strikes out with the hammer of an amateur carpenter, but the crack of the lion-tamer's snaking thrown-tongue misleads her back to where she started from.

The cancelled superhero flails with the trust of a puppet but gets stuck between the stations of classical kitchy rockabilly and frozen Shakespearian lines.

Molly tries to follow the king with the antlers of a charging deer, but the bear flee-er, hedgemaze child, and caught coyote are fanned out like rodeo clowns and she gropes toward Irony instead.

Aggie flips like an acrobat . . . but there's no clumsy applause, so she's left bobbing in the same place.

Shifting colors sneak under Molly's blindfold, so she slashes with the sharpie like the flourishing tagger, but the line glances across the book monument and subway poster without settling on one.

in**AHAB**Mars the venerable
skirts**DART THE HAWK AND** arcade
are all motivated**LEMMING THE** back corner of the
seekers **UGLY THE**strip
my pocket**POOL BECAUSE THE**mall I
vibrates**PRUNES IN THE** find The Sons and
in a way **THEY LEAVE NO** Trixies
that could just be the**LIMBS PLUS** clustered
cold thing shifting **SINISTER** around
or**THEIR COLLECTION OF** Bull
a phantom **ENOUGH TO COMPLETE** Fighter
prickling**A FATHER AND THAT'S** II
on my thigh**FINDERS FOUND**super champion I kill
but I check **GAME THE MOTHER** them with stabs of
it and it's a reminder that**THE** imagination edition not to be
I'm**GOODIE AND THAT'S** Freudian
needed **OF LOVE**about it but I
across town**LEMMING** mean we
but was it the**SWORD INTO THAT** are riffing on Papa
toy store**HER COCKTAIL** here but this is
or the arcade I flip **AND SINKS** the clash of
my phone**THE VILLAIN** generations
cause **SHE PLAYS** the kids
I've got a new **ONE IN DESPAIR** united
app that uses**SETTLING ON** against the man sees
the accelerometer**POSTER WITHOUT** himself as caterpillr
and it tells me**AND SUBWAY** shedding each
to get **THE BOOK MONUMENT** monarch
my ass **GLANCES ACROSS** 2b enterin bedroom
to**THE LINE** of the Spring

In despair, Aggie plays the villainous (well, "villain-calling," technically) King of Cats and succeeds where the original did not in sinking her cocktail sword into Goodie's lemming of love, and that's the game! The Mother Finders found a father but that's close enough to complete their collection of "sinister" limbs--plus they leave none of the other team behind like prunes in the pool because The Ugly, The Lemming, The Dart, The Hawk, and Ahab in skirts are all motivated seekers themselves and join up.

My pocket vibrates in a way that could just be the cold thing shifting or a phantom prickling on my thigh, but I check it, and it's a reminder that I'm running late for the third match, but was it supposed to happen in the toy store or the arcade? I flip my phone cause I've got a new app that uses the accelerometer, and it tells me to get my ass to Mars (the venerable arcade in the back corner of the strip mall).

There, I find Romeo's Sons All Want Prizes and Abby's Domino Trixies clustered around Bull Fighter II (Super Champion I Kill Them With Stabs Of Imagination edition). Not to be Freudian about it (though I mean we are riffing on Papa here!) but this is the clash of generations: the actual kids united against the man that sees himself as caterpillar shedding each monarch-to-be as it enters the bedroom of the Spring.

on until one is **SO** woman in
depleated **MATADOR AND** the bull astray like
The Sons have**A RIVAL**wasp trying
the first **COSTUME TO REVEAL** to get
defense in this **BUGS BUNNY** it on with a
game where Lombardi had **A** flower or in
it flipped **UNZIPS LIKE** this
but Romeo **SPRITES AND THE BULL** case
deploys**OUT IN A SPURT OF** not what
his enemy **BUT IF NOT HE'S** movie
who has **AMBUSH INSTEAD OF A HEART** awaits
never been his **SLASHER** with sharp corners
friend as the first **OUT TO BE A**Factory
fodder **CURTAIN WHICH TURNS** Flood but
the little girl is**THE VIDEO STORE**it is more
canny sendin**THE HORNS GO THROUGH** carboard than
unmarked child wholl b**THE BULL**nightmares so the kid
as hard **IN** hops
to grab**IT GRABS SOMETHING** off
as a bowling**DANCE AND IF** the milk
ball by its**FIGURE IN A SEDUCTIVE** crate to
holes **TO GUIDE THEIR**dash
he does the**BUTTONS**again at the end of the
flouncy **JOYSTICK AND** order next she sends
footwork**THROUGH THE** niece
of Schrodinger's **MORSE CODE**uncle
catbox and**HIS OR HER PERSONAL**bound
the unknown **MATADOR VIBRATES** and he plays
of it leads the knight **SIMPLE THE** the
unknown by **THE GAME IS PRETTY**cloud

BFII is actually a pretty simple game: one player vibrates his or her personal morse code through the joystick and buttons to guide a matador in a seductive interpretive dance, and if that image grabs something deep inside the other player, then their bull's horns go through the video store curtain that turns out to be an ambush of slashers instead of blood warmers, and the matador gets to try to sharpen a second image for the kill (though, hey, maybe he misses and the bull just goes to the back of the line). If the matador's image only tickles the bully intellectually, though, the matador goes out in a spurt of sprites and the bull unzips like a Bugs Bunny costume to reveal a rival fancy pants who then flaps out their own image for the next guy on the other team, and so on until one team is only martyred funny-hat legends.

The Sons have the first defense in this game where Lombardi had it flipped, but Romeo sends out the enemy who had never been a friend as the first fodder. On the other side, the Little Girl is canny in sending out an unmarked child who'll be as hard to grab as a rolling ball by its holes. Lewis makes his matador do the flouncy footwork of Schrodinger's Catbox, and the unknown of it leads the knight-unknown-by-woman in Fees' bull astray like a wasp trying to get it on with a flower (or in this case, not). What VHS box awaits him with a sharpened corner? "Factory Flood" (a hand plunging out of the water holding a timecard as it is swept toward the impractical looking grinding machine at the vanishing point), but it proves more cardboard than nightmare, so Fees survives to hop off the milk crate and let a teammate have their shot at resisting temptation.

next he sends the**FLOOF** had been

former **CAPE A LITTLE** attached and she

friend turned **AND GIVES HER** crumples into her

religious **BULL COSTUME** self like the dough

nut to see**OUT OF HER** boy gut

if she can **SO SHE MODESTLY STEPS** shot

reason**THAT SHE MUST STAY** the girl

with **YEARS INDICATES** is a

the little**THREE EXTRA** killer

girl who tries the**WEIGHTY GLARE OF** so Romeo

flailing **CAPTAIN WITH THE** volunteers

fingers**ON HIM BUT HER** next

& that does entrance **CHECK** smirking

palm reader**TO STOOP TO** sits with the cape

like an academic **SHE WANTS** across her lap and

in a flurry of**APPENDICITIS** holds her

pages **KIDDING HE JUST HAS** hands

from the shelled **LIFE JUST** taut where a crystal

upper shelf in the **REAL** ball will

blitz with a howl **DIE IN** some

reverberatin out frm th **GAME YOU** day be and with

depths**DIE IN THE** them

of the future**MACHINE BECAUSE IF YOU** catches

a teenage middle**GROUND BY THE** Lincoln's

finger **TRIM AND HE FALLS TO THE** superstitious

emerges and jabs th **EMBROIDERED** beard

princess in **HIM RIGHT IN THE** pencil

place where**THE CLOUD AND NAILS** is her

her punk **THROUGH** choice

chrysalis **THE PENCIL SAILS** again

In his place, Abby next sends a niece uncle-bound, and Lewis plays the cloud, but Steph's pencil sails right through it and nails him in the embroidered trim, and he falls to the ground by the machine because if you die in the game, you die in real life (just kidding--he just has appendicitis!). Little Steph wants to stoop to check on him, but Abby with the weighty glare of three extra years indicates that she must stay, so she modestly steps out of her bull costume and gives her cape a little floof.

Next, Romeo sends in the former friend turned religious nut to see if she can reason with the little girl. Steph tries the flailing fingers, and what do you know, that does entrance a palm reader like Robin just as if she was an academic lost in a flurry of pages from the shelled upper shelf during the blitz, then, with a howl reverberating out from the depths of the future, a teenage middle finger emerges and jabs the princess in the place where her punk chrysalis had been attached, and Robin crumples into her self like a gut-shot dough boy.

That girl is a killer, so Romeo volunteers next. Steph has her matador sit and smirk with the cape across her lap, her hands held taut where a crystal ball will someday be, but that's all it takes to catch Lincoln's superstitious beard. The pencil is again her choice to try to FINISH HIM, but she missed the chance to catch the clown by his harp, and the pencil finds no page to scar, so The Master Of Bull will get a chance to charge again.

and her soul is **BOOK IS** weapon by gingerly
merely nudged **THIS** snatching
aside like a **TIP AS** the part that
removed **ITS QUILL** keeps it from
transparent **TARGET WITH** self destructing
sheet from **ITS STAMP SIZED** and the
a projector **AS UNLIKELY TO FIND** bull tumbles on
she sends **SPECIFIC IS** its own horn
her loyal **SOMETHING SO** she sends her secret
dog **BORED BECAUSE** weapon
with **PERHAPS BECAUSE SHE'S** the artist
a single horn tied to **THAT HARP** who should have
its head **THIS TIME SHE TRIES** feelings
he makes his matador **AT HER** if anyone
do the **DOUBLE** does his mind goes
Fonzie dance **ALIEN** back to when he felt like
throwing his arms **LOOKING TRASHY** verbal equivalent of
out like the rays o **HIS MICROWAVED** new pupy & he saw
a flashbulb and **BY SENDING** th aliens eyes stufed w/
the Greek God ceases **HER UP** newspaper inside
his darkly scanning **TO TRIP** seering
fluctuation **AGAIN HE TRIES** frames and
for long **BULL WILL CHARGE** vows
to get pegged **SO THE MASTER OF** th blistr that'll pop
with the **PAGE TO SCAR** in them
box **FINDS NO** will
for **HIS HARP AND THE PENCIL** bim
Rogue **THE CLOWN WITH** take
Agent foils **THE CHANCE TO CATCH** the zoo with
the secret **SHE MISSED** him

Safe for now, Romeo tries again to trip her up by sending his microwaved-looking trashy alien double at her. This time, Steph *does* try the harp (maybe she's bored? Something so specific is as unlikely to find a stamp-sized target with its quill tip as this book is [Bloo]) and Emoro's bull merely pushes her soul off screen like a removed transparency from a projector.

For the next Trixie bull, Abby sends in her loyal dog with a single horn tied to its head. Emoro makes his matador do the Fonzie dance, throwing his arms and legs out like the rays of a flashbulb, and the vanity of Sic's Greek God lures him from his darkly-scanning fluctuation long enough for him to get pegged with the box for "Rogue Agent" (where a spy foils the secret weapon by gingerly snatching that part that keeps it from self-destructing) and the bull tumbles on its own horn.

It's time for Abby to send in her own secret weapon: The Artist. This is all going by rather quickly and abstractly, but if any character is going to have feelings about this, it should be No as he faces the man whose exhibit he saw right before the spectacle of his Ex kissing Not Him. His mind goes back to when he felt like the verbal equivalent of a new puppy and he saw Emoro's eyes stuffed with newspaper inside searing frames. He vows to pop their blisters and wipe out the zoo along with them!

HINT:
No's remembering Emoro from the columns of Page 124

he remembers **BUT** he feels like

decoding the **LEAD** Hamlet's

secret **WHERE THE TRACK WILL** skull

code in the **NOT KNOWING** father

ride's **A JELLYFISH** rope

lobby but what **BILLOWS LIKE** ladder

did **THE CAPE THAT** wrung but it

it say **FORWARD TOWARD THE** goes

the symbols squirm **HE FALLS** on that next he'll be

like **TOP** suddenly driven away by the

protozoa **AT THE** fish

under **A ROLLER COASTER** jelly so that

his microscope **MAN LIKE** the light

until they **WILL** is

shake **FREE** off in the

out into **WHAT ABOUT** glasses

familiar **MID AIR** house and that

schlubby **IN** his

shapes that **BOTTLE** tormenter crowned in the

spell **RESPONDS TO THE** feathers of

out **WHETHER HIS HAND** hawk

sigh you're such a **NOODLE** in fish hell her

has **IN HIS** arms

been **THE GROOVES** begin to pump like

you're finally **DECIDED BY** the stallion's

cliche which is **TO BE** legs

not what **FATE IS ABOUT** now that

a protagonist wants **THAT HIS** fair

in his last **BOILS** Apollo

chapter **HE** has been snuffed out

Still, No boils that his fate is about to be decided by the grooves in
his noodle and whether his hand responds to a thrown bottle in mid
air ("like, what about free will, man?!"). Still, like a roller coaster at
the top, he falls forward toward the cape billowing like a jellyfish,
not knowing where the track will lead, but he suddenly remembers
solving the secret code in the ride's lobby--but what did it say?! The
symbols squirm like protozoa under his microscope until they shake
out into familiar schlubby shapes that spell out, "Sigh, you're such a
has been! You're finally cliche!" which is not what a protagonist
wants to hear in his last chapter. He feels like Hamlet's skull, father,
and rope-ladder rung, but the message goes on, saying that next his
matador will be "suddenly driven away by the fish (jelly) so that the
light will be off in his 'glasses house' and his tormenter will be
crowned in the feathers of a hawk in fish hell," and whaddayaknow,
it's right. So much for being a secret weapon.

   Abby's arms begin to pump like a stallion's legs--now that fair
Apollo has been snuffed out, the captain herself is coming in!

HINT:
That ride-lobby seems to be a replica of Page 115

eyes **NEWSPAPER** to be assaulted
can lure **THE NEWLY ACQUIRED** by
the kid but **HE SEES IF** the whip
he crashes through **TO RETURN** like stamens of
like **THE ESCAPSIT** Flower Of
giant **SAFELY LEAVING** Bad which grows
fingers **OFF THE SCREEN** from
and sends him **SHE GETS** the open mouth of
to the back sections **LOUDER AND** a corpse and a
then peels **SOMETHING A LITTLE** huffer canot help
open to reveal **SHE NEEDS** a deadly breath
a Pynchonesque **KILL BUT** now the former
matador **TO DOGS** kid is
as in very few **WHO WHISPERED** outnumbered
images **HE GOES WITH THE BOY** by the real
of **YOU AND** kids and
him he chooses the **DOG THAT BIT** all
gummy **BACK OF THE** phases
bear **GARGOYLE ON THE** showing th real kid
that winks **LIKE THE BEER** is
to post apocalyptic **SHE SWOOPS IN** exhausted and tries
scavenger **ACHE AND** shoulder dancing
across the rubble of the **HEAD** for
convenience **OF A HANGOVER** four hours
store and the tour **SNAPS** on
guide stumbles **UNDULATING** a plane somehow that
entranced by **HIS CAPE WITH THE** dodges
a remembered **WOLF AND SNAPS** all the cars
taste **LIKE THE APOCALYPTIC** in
only **HE SMILES** him but gets the horns

In response, Emoro smiles like the apocalyptic wolf and snaps his cape with the undulating stabs of a hangover headache. Abby swoops in like the beer gargoyle on the back of the dog that bit you, and for the kill he goes with *The Boy Who Whispered To Dogs* (the cover just a profile with cupped hand next to an attentive ear and bloody muzzle), but she needs something a little louder, so her bull gets off the screen safely.

This allows the previous Escapist from her team to come back in. Emoro decides to see if the newly acquired newspaper eyes can lure Fees, but the kid crashes through like two giant fingers and sends the wincing stooge to the back section. Then Fees' bull peels open to reveal a Pynchonesque matador (as in "very few images of him").

Fees chooses the gummy bear as his mirage, and it winks to the post-apocalyptic scavenger across the rubble of the convenience store, making the former tour guide stumble forward, entranced by a remembered taste, only to be assaulted by the whip-like stamens of *Flower Of Bad* (which is depicted on the VHS cover growing from the open mouth of a corpse) and the huffer in Roscoe cannot help taking a deadly sniff of its fragrance.

Now the former kid is outnumbered by the real ones, but Fees seems exhausted and makes his matador shoulder-dance on a plane for four hours, which somehow dodges all the cars in Romeo but still gets Fees plenty of horns.

all **OVER** yep the aspiring

drag**PLUMBER'S** comic book artist

as she attempts to hop**AND HER** yeah

on its head **BEGINS TO BOIL** Ulysses in a pot

&is frozen n2**THE PAINT AROUND HER** I assume

a shrug**WILTING SUN** a kid who wants

only **THE GODDAMN FLESH** counter

to fall like**NOTHING LESS THAN** cookies obviously

a**DARK SHE FINDS** Gallahad

cat **PAINT AND IN THE** wants

poster from**WAVES OF** the cup indeed at the

fird employee's **SUCKED UNDER THE** next

cubical **HAND SO SHE IS** final

wall Elvis refuses **SUCH A** throwdown

to leave the**PAINTER AND SHE IS** it

building**WITH A HAND** is me

James Brown**YET HE GOES** Otter & the billionaire

has as many capes as **A TEENAGER** sitting in the back of

an onion their **NOT QUITE** the Sister

jaws hang**ANYTHING BUT SHE IS** City

open as he **INTERESTED IN** elementary school

does a little victory **IS NOT BE** while everyone

dance the question**TO DO** of note

is **ALL SHE HAS** is on

which of the**SPIRITUAL GRANDPA** stage the

losers **CHARGE HER SECRET** car is in the aisle

are still**IS GOING TO HAVE TO** obviously

all**CAPTAINS AND SHE** my wife

about the prizes crusade **TO THE** walks in having just

leader **IT'S DOWN** agreed to be the judge

I guess it's down to the captains now, and Abby is going to have to charge headlong at her secret spiritual grandpa. All she has to do is not be interested in anything, but she is not quite a teenager, so that doesn't come naturally to her yet. Romeo portrays a hand painter, and she is such a hand, so she is sucked under the wave of paint and in the dark she finds nothing less than the goddamn flesh-wilting sun! The paint around her begins to boil, and her plumber's overalls drag as she attempts to hop on its head and is frozen by the contact into a shrug only to fall like a cat poster from a fired employee's cubical wall.

Triumphant, Elvis refuses to leave the building, and James Brown proves to have as many capes as an onion; everyone's jaws hang open as full-grown Romeo does a spiteful victory dance in the direction of a bunch of children.

The question is which of the losers are still all about The Prizes (and get recruited for the finals)? Crusade leader? Yep. Aspiring comic book artist? Yes. Man with microscope? Gotta get that Nobel. I assume that a kid who wants counter cookies is. And Galahad definitely wants that cup.

Indeed, at the next and final throwdown (the next night? I dunno), it is only me, Death Otter, and the billionaire sitting in the back of the the Sister City elementary school while everyone else of note is on stage. (The car is in the aisle, obviously.) My wife walks in, having just agreed to be the judge one more time--she holds a brimming bag of marbles.

tonight's contest**TO ANNOUNCE THAT** pointlessly

is to make **TINTED** courage disguised

a new pageant about **BLUE** as

the future**ON STAGE** growth makes

that time **NOW SHE'S BACK** him feel

will **PEOPLE DANCE AND** ready to

pin on **THEM TO MAKE** walk up

the nose **SHE ONLY EVER USED** play

and force to**FIRE THOUGH** back

dance like**PROVOKED TO SPIT** the speech

grandma**DRAGOONS ARE** always ready

and grandpa**WHENEVER THE HEAVY** just

boogying**PALMS** behind his

at **THAT MARK YOUR** tongue

my birth**WITH WINGS** but

backstage **PLATES ETCHED** One is

each**WITH BRASS** dressed as a

team has been **REFURBISHED** conductor and

given a room **WHOSE HANDLES I HAVE** he

for **HER GUNS** takes

practicing**RANDOMLY I'M THINKING OF** him

one**A KISS AND** around to all

last **TO BE INSIDE** the rooms

time **A GIRL WANTING** to see if

but he sneaks n2 **CAR LISTENING TO** anyone lost

the hallway in his VHS **SANDING** him and he realizes he is

costume and catches**A HILL** no

sight of his ex **BUT WE ARE ALSO IN** more than

similarly **SURE** a bookmark long expected

rebelling**WE'RE THERE** to have fallen out

She and I are sitting there, sure, but we are also in a hill-sanding car listening to a girl wanting to be inside a kiss, and I'm randomly thinking of Leslie's guns whose handles I have refurbished with brass plates etched with wings that would mark your palms whenever the heavy dragoons are provoked to spit fire (though Les only ever used them to make people dance), and suddenly Leslie's back on stage before us (blue-tinted) to announce that tonight's contest will be for each of the three teams to make up a new grade-school pageant about the future that time will pin on the nose and force to dance like Grandma and Grandpa boogying at my birth.

Backstage, each team has been given a classroom as their headquarters, but No sneaks into the hallway in his full-body VHS Tape costume and catches sight of One out there similarly rebelling pointlessly. Courage disguised as "growth" makes No feel ready to walk up and play back the speech he always has ready just behind his tongue but never quite gets out, but before he can speak, One (who is dressed as a Train Conductor) grabs him by the elbow and takes him to each of the three practice rooms to see if anyone has lost him, and No realizes his ex sees him as no more than a bookmark long expected to have fallen out.

all **IT** creates
the way down **SURFING** a superhero whose
passing **HIS BODY AND** only
by on **WITH** power is
the way to **A HILL** to hurl
the bathroom I **CATCHING** waves
point out **A CHARACTER AND** of ear
she's **HIM REALIZING HE IS JUST** shattering
been **A COMIC OF** destruction plus
his captain **BEGINS TO SKETCH** he can fly
and even **HEAD** he saves
though they got stabbed **IN HER** city
and turned **BUT A HAND** many times but after
into dogfood **SHOPLIFTERS** newspaper
that has to count **IN TO SURPRISE** story
for some **STRIP SLIPPED** about his
thing to **THE MAGNETIC** final
him she must be **WORST** cancellation of
a **BOOKMARK AT** nihilistic
number **THE RECEIPT FOR THE** primate
follow me **IS AT WORST** doctor with a
back to our seats the first **SHE** picture of
proposed pageant **KNOWS** a man
is about to start **THOUGH SHE** with a four inch
the mother **CAN EVEN** piece
finders won **THE HAM** of mecha
the **LEADER FROM** shrapnel
coin **DRESSED AS THE CRUSADE** pierced
tosses a fracking **THIS** through
accident **SHE SEES ALL** his tongue

Peeking Abby witnesses all of that while dressed as the crusade leader from that popular canned ham, and a hand in her head begins to sketch a comic of the scene, with No realizing that he is just a character and catching a hill with his body and surfing it all the way down. At the same time, she recognizes that she herself is at best a receipt for a bookmark and at worst the magnetic strip slipped in to surprise shoplifters. Passing by on the way to the can, I point out to her that she's been his captain, and even though they got stabbed and turned into dogfood, that has to count for something, so she should *at least* be a number to him.

Follow me back to our seats: the first proposed pageant is about to unfold, and it comes to us courtesy of The Misplaced Mother Finders. First, Ag comes out on stage dressed as a muscley male superhero; she declares, "A fracking accident has given me the power to hurl waves of ear-shattering destruction"--here, she shrieks while tossing a handful of pebbles across the stage--"plus, I can fly" and she gives a little hop. Next Irony steps forward wearing tattered clothes and having a large chunk of metal stuck through her tongue. She sayth, "I am a pewthon who wath thound in the lubble of the hewo'th detheat oth the nihilithtic pwimate geniuth Dowkthew Maldethio--people thaw my dath and athd the hewo to wetiwo."

HINT:
This page draws from all the way back to Page 197

he puts it on **HIS HOTEL ROOM** concert
the stove and even **BACK TO** ushering
though **A KETTLE WHEN HE GETS** out
genie has unlimited power **IN** the
& can appear **A GENIE MISPACKAGED** human forms
however **HE'S BEEN LOOKING FOR** single balloon
he wants **WHAT** impatient
he still decides **HE FINALLY LOCATES** conductor but
to reinforce **YEARS UNTIL** suddenly the
western notions **FOR MANY** balloon
of shirtless **GLOBE** is popped the
he dutifully asks **TO TRAVEL THE** surprised
what **MONEY** genie looks up
the victim desires **REST OF THE** man is now standing
but he **USES THE** uniform he
is confused **SURGERY VICTIM** wore while
when man answers **HIS TONGUE** lackey of
nothing **PAYING FOR** the villain
as if 2 cnvnce **THEIR DEFENSE AFTER** an impractical
that his powers **IN** ornate
won't disappoint **THE MAN INJURED** dart
if given **MONEY TO GIVE** gun n his hand finally
a task he begins to **FUND** understanding the genie
twist a **CROWD** summons with
balloon animal of **HIS CAPE AND** resignation the plump
12 people **TO HANG UP** rain of
who **PETITIONS THE HERO** nuclear
attended the **PUBLIC** missiles that will
Sex **EXHAUSTED** take us
Pistols first **THE GRATEFUL BUT** back to nothing

Next Izzy steps forward dressed as a giant kettle. "I am a kettle," she declares, "that the victim bought with the settlement money that did not go to tongue surgery." Suddenly Beebe jumps out from behind her dressed in a blue child's halloween costume from 1992 and says in a really shitty Robin Williams impression, "And I am the Genie that was trapped inside that kettle because they were all out of oil lamps!" She turns to Irony and booms, "What do you desire?" Irony opens up her mouth to reply, and Cray jumps out from behind her and strikes a pose--the word "NOTHING" appears in red letters up the leg of his gray leotard. Genie Beebe shouts, "There is no limit to my power to provide for you--behold my ability to make a balloon animal of all 12 of the people who attended The Sex Pistols' first concert!" Suddenly One sticks his arms out from under Beebe's pits and waves them around like a conductor while Molly in a shiny bodysuit begins a labored attempt to contort herself (but never succeeds as appearing as more than one person). Then Work, dressed with a pointed headdress that would make her look more like a hypodermic needle if she wasn't wearing finned boots, wooshes over and headbutts Molly, who cries, "Pop!" Goodie (in black shadow puppeteer garb) yanks off repaired-tongued Irony's rags to reveal that underneath she is wearing a jumpsuit with the insignia of a deranged but highly educated chimp on it, then she holds up her wasp-like dart gun. Genie Beebe turns to the audience and declares, "I now see that what you meant is that you want the world to be NOTHING"--Cray sheepishly walks out again--"just like your old boss did! I summon the plump rain!" at which Perry reaches up and pulls down a projector screen on which someone has taped a bunch of construction-paper nuclear missiles. After a moment, the Finders all bow.

hints to **WHAT** gates
drop **NOTES ABOUT** warning to
one old man **MAKES** other charlatans he
presents him with **BELIEFS AND** answers
a catbox & asks **THEIR BACKWARDS** animal is in
him to use **NEARBY TOWNS AND** niche n th face of
his omniscience **TALKED ABOUT** their silence
to tell **THE SHIT** he clarifies
whether **HE LISTENS TO** the shit is there if
there is a crap **TOWN** it is
in the **DISGUISE IN EACH** place there and
sand he claims his **MORTAL** if
godly **LOCAL GOD IN** not it was not its
powers **EACH TOWN'S** place
are **MISTAKEN AS** Zeus is
needed **FOR BEING** amused
elswhr **A MAN WHO SURVIVES ON GIFTS** by evasn
but he reveals **THERE IS** quest to prove
himself as **PRIZES IN THE WASTELAND** he deserves
Zeus **ALL WANT** to live he tells
and presses **THE SONS** of flannel
the ? he considers **NEXT IS** hangar and tells him
what it will **OUT LATER** to
be like to **BE TAKEN** bring back
be fried **EVEN IF IT'S GOING TO** the warmest
by lighting or **SAY SOMETHING** one
dipped **NOT** mountains are traveled
in **200 PAGES CAN'T** over bt when he sees
molten gold **SHIT WE REACHED** the forest o hanging
and left outside the **HOLY** outerwear

After they shuffle off, The Sons All Want Prizes take the stage. Romeo steps forward and shows off his theatrical charisma: "I am a man who survives by pretending to be a god pretending to be a man. At each town in the post-apocalyptic wasteland, I drop a few hints that line up with what I learned from the shit talked about these guys in the previous town, and I listen carefully to the shit these guys talk about the next town. What can I say, it's a living!" Roscoe steps forward dressed as an old man in a suspiciously baggy robe. "If you are actually a god," he says, "then surely you can tell me how many turds are in this catbox without sifting through it!" He gestures over at Lewis, who does not look that happy to be dressed as a giant catbox (though it's always hard to tell with him). Romeo replies, "It would be easy, but my godly powers are needed elsewhere, so I will be going," but Roscoe tears off his robe to reveal a toga made out of a golden bedsheet and declares, "I AM ACTUALLY ZEUS! I DIDN'T DIE JUST BECAUSE PEOPLE STOPPED BELIEVING IN ME! Now, if you don't give all of us a turd number, I am going to hit you with my MIGHTY THUNDERBOLT!" Roscoe holds up a cardboard replica. Romeo mimes panic and then revelation, and as he gestures philosophically, his alien double turns around, revealing a sandwich board that reads, "THE ANIMALS ARE IN THEIR NICHE." Godly Roscoe demands to know what the hell that means. Romeo replies, "If the turds belong there, then they must be there, and if they are not there, they do not belong there!" Roscoe barks a short laugh and says, "Very amusing! Such an amusing mortal deserves a second chance to prove that his dumb ass deserves to live! Over the mountains, there is an abandoned airplane hangar full of left-over flannel from the 1990s--bring me back the warmest jacket there, and you will have proven yourself WORTHY OF SONG!" Robin comes forward wearing a refrigerator box labeled "AIRPLANE HANGAR" and Romeo trots arduously over to her only to have her split the box in half and reveal her arms draped in numerous flannel jackets.

many awards **ASSEMBLED FROM** robot
shows after **CLAPPING** is struck by
letting **HANDS** lightning while farming
it **GRAINY VIDEO OF** in the rain
wash **ON THE TAPE IS A** afterward it no longr
over **UNLABELED VHS TAPE** plants
him **NEXT TO A SINGLE** rock
for a **TV / VCR COMBO** after a
an **TABLE WITH A** rock instead it places
hour **SMALL ROOM WITH A** asymmetrical ptrn
he **HE DISCOVERS A** solar
vows to turn **THE LABYRINTH** power means
his life **AT THE CENTER OF** not hurting anyone
around and lead **VERY MOTIVATED** colonists go puzzle
the people **HE DOESN'T FEEL** over it
on a crusade **IN TRUTH** before or after
for something **WATCHING BUT** hooking up in
instead of **ZEUS IS** secret
swindling **JUST IN CASE** for
them b/c he has **SAMPLES A FEW** avoiding
now seen **RACKS AND** regulations on
all **THROUGH THE DENSE** human
they have **HIS WAY** seed
to give next **HE FORCES** no one
the bluebeards **COUNTER** turns him
in **THE COOKIES ON THE** off chance for
a separartist **KID WHO WANTS** someone to join the
colony **THAN A** colony
in the wilderness **GALAHAD** from the internet
a humanoid **HE FEELS LESS LIKE** message board

Romeo turns to the audience and laments, "Ahh me . . . This task is enormous, but in my heart I feel less like Galahad"--he gestures to Fees in a tin-foil knight's costume--"than a kid who just wants the cookies off the counter" and he indicates Steph grunting and miming the reach on his other side. "I lack the stick-to-it-ive-ness to find The Olden Fleece! But what is this? In the center of the warehouse is a TV / VCR combo unit like the one our author used all through college! And what is this beside it?" No steps out wearing his head to foot VHS tape costume. "I shall put this tape into the player!" Romeo declares. Time for No's big line: "On me is . . ." and then his brother Sic jumps forward clapping wildly and saying, "I'm assembled from awards shows!" Romeo stands there until the kid is tired of clapping, which does take awhile. Then Romeo emotes, "I used to survive by swindling people, but now I feel a rebirth coming on!" He crouches down, and from behind him, Abby leaps up in similar garb and cries, "I will lead them on a crusade! FOR SOMETHING! I have now seen what people have to give!" For several minutes, she squeezes the air in her fist until she fills up on applause.

The third team is eager to go, so the stage is turned over to The Ex Bluebeards. Thea steps forward wearing some air conditioning duct pipes on her arms--she says, "I am a robot in a separatist colony in the wilderness. One day, I am struck by lightning while farming in the rain. Afterward, I no longer plant or hoe, but follow my own mission." To demonstrate, she picks up Michelle, who is curled up in a rock-colored leotard, and places her methodically elsewhere on the stage. She continues: "no one bothers to shut me down because sometimes colonists will come out to puzzle at my creations before or after getting it on in secret to avoid the colony's regulation of 'human seed'--plus I'm solar powered, so I waste nothing." Moog steps up in a little good pilgrim costume (whose construction is only so-so): "I am a new recruit to the colony from a message board. I am looking to try out their political principles firsthand!

but he **SERIOUSLY** on cue

cannot **TAKE IT AS** the robot seizes up and

resist **DOES NOT** topple

the opportunity **SCIENTIST** as if

to talk about the **ROBOT THE** struck in the

things other people **INVENTED THE** head by a home run

won't listen **TO THE MAN WHO** shot the triumphant

to he reveals the **SUBJECT** pilgrim returns to his

weakness **BRINGS UP THE** bunk is served w/ bag

of the robot **PILGRIM CASUALLY** full

he obtains an **MISSION THE GOOD** of invoices for all

extension **PURSUES ITS** the parts it will take

cord amplifier **ROBOT SILENTLY** to build another

microphone **SWEATING WHILE THE** robot who can

and takes them **AFTER A WEEK** among other things

out to **NATURALLY** significantly boost

the field **WILL SOMEDAY COME** the wi-fi

where he puts on **HE ASSUMES** of the colony

karaoke track **WITH AN ENTHUSIASM** she likes

with a long instrumental **HE DOES** the con man

interlude **MONTH WHICH** best with its

that he proceeds to **THE FIRST** critique of empty core of

not know what **FOR** entertainment

to do **FIELDS** culture she also said that

with **HIM WORKING THE** one reminder her o

his hands **WHICH WILL HAVE** Mark

and sheepishly **SCHEDULE** Twain which I just

apologize for **THE WORK** wanted to preserve

it the whole **HE IS ADVISED ABOUT** in

time **HE PARACHUTES INTO** writing

"I parachute into the compound, as all converts do, and then I am shown around and advised about the work schedule. I work my first rotation in the fields, which I do with an enthusiasm that I assume will someday come naturally, but after a week of watching that machine do his own thing while I work . . ." Syf steps up wearing round glasses and a gray old-man wig (There are some advantages to childhood baldness, I guess) and says, "I am the scientist that the pilgrim asks over a dinner of ultra-kale porridge if the robot has any weaknesses. Because I am its inventor, I should protect it, but none of the other colonists ever ask me about any of the things I know, so . . ." Moog resumes: "I obtain an amplifier"--which sure looks like Mounthe squatting in a box--"that a colonist had used for endless jamming until he was voted out into the wilderness, and I take it and extension cords, a microphone, and a cell-phone connector cable out to the fields by the robot. Then I imitate an overly-polite karaoke performer I once saw--" He indicates Yes, who begins to apologize non-stop over a 3 and half-minute instrumental break while having no idea what to do with his hands. Robotic Thea cries out, "I seize up and topple as if struck in the head by a home-run shot"--and Cate, wearing a large baseball over her body and for some reason also wearing a baseball cap, walks over and slaps her once, flooring her. Pilgrim Moog walks smirking back to the minimalist set meant to represent a bunk, and there Scientist Syf points at him and Wolves comes hopping over in a sack marked, "BILLS FOR REPLACEMENT!" and Moog turns to the audience and cries, "How was I supposed to know it was also the colony's wi-fi router?!"

I turn to my wife and ask her which one she liked the best, but she doesn't have to even think about it--she goes with the con man in the wasteland. Now she's off to grade some more papers on Huck, but I ask her for some justification that I can pass along to y'all, and she says something about "a critique of the empty core of entertainment culture." Well, there you have it!

she would **LIKE** the cover will
have **WALLS JUST** need to be
wanted though her **MIRRORED** swam across her
positioning **A POOL WITH** prohibitions against
troubles **HE WILL PUT HER IN** swimming
him arms **BALD** under
at side **SHUTTING UP** the cover but he
seems too unnatural **BIOPIC OF** will
like a person **BOTCHED** find life in it like a
prtnding **BUT AT LEAST HE WAS NEVER A** neck
to sleep **CITATION** under fingers
but limbs **WITH A SECOND** honor
splayed **AROUND LIKE A MAN** her this way
is terrifying **SWAGGERING** though she was
real **AND HE REGRETS** the one who taught
like the drowning **STORE** him to swim now resides in
the uninitiated **MEGA** VHS
would **HE COULD MOVE THE** box whose
take it **TO SEE IF** front is her breaking
for she **REALLY JUST WANTED** the crab
will help **THIS CONFLICT AND** claw that
lending **CHEATED HIS WAY INTO** attempts
her the epic posing **THAT HE** crushing her
body carved **BACK AND SEES** memory
into purpose **HE LOOKS** tells him that
and drained **TAMED AND** read
of doubts that **SINCE BEEN** the face h mst acknwldg
champion **WOLVES HAS LONG** you die or you
find them **A FULL MOTHER** stay warding off
selves in **WHAT IS HE GOING TO DO WITH** bites

The awards ceremony is at The Milky Bowl, a suitably symbolic place to unite the body that was divided there. The reassembled (but still very dead) Mira now "stands" on the stage looking like the chick from Metropolis. The Sons' captain Romeo is called to the microphone to say something about what will happen now, but really, what *is* he going to do with this highly-questionable prize? Wolves has long since been tamed, and as Ro looks back, he sees that he "cheated his way into this conflict" and really just "wanted to see if he could move the MegaStore." He feels regret that he "swaggered around like a man with a second citation," but at least he was never a "botched biopic of shutting-up bald." He tells the crowd that he will put his mother in a public pool with mirrored walls just like she would have wanted. Then he gets off on a tangent about his indecision about how to position her body down there: arm-at-side seems too unnatural (like a person pretending to sleep) but limbs splayed out is terrifyingly real (like the drowning an uninitiated tourist might take it for). Thea volunteers to help--she says she can lend Mira the epic posing of a body carved into purpose and drained of doubts. He says he will honor his mother by nightly defying her lifelong prohibitions against swimming back under the unliftable pool cover because he finds life in the act like a neck under fingers. Thus, his mother is laid to rest, at least in words (but he says nothing about everyone's oversight in not giving a proper memorial for the aunt who actually taught him to survive such a swim--he reads Leslie's face in memory as saying, "you die or you stay warding-off bites"--and he does not yet know that in mere days she will be inside an enormous VHS box whose front will be a drawing of her breaking upward an enormous crab claw that is attempting to crush her).

HINTS:
This page draws from the columns of Pages 165 and 131

to be a grounder **ALSO CLAIMING** mummy

like his father **SPELLS WHILE** there is nothing but

was **PROVIDED WITH** coupons for epic

make that **A MAGICIAN AND** epithet

is **BEING DRESSED AS** the awards

even **LIKE TROOPS OF** ceremony

though **ALONG AND SUPPLIED** is at the

she never **HAVING BEEN DRAGGED** Milky

wanted more **CORD OF** Bowl but it's not

of **UMBILICAL** big enough to

him than **INDIGNATION OF THE** fit all the

she had **ABOUT EVERY** little leaguers

but **HE CAN TALK** he wanders through

you can't trap **HIM CAPTAIN BUT** the

musician **WHEN THE OTHER KIDS MADE** crowd

he muses **SON YEARS OR** looking to see if

they shave **HIS FIRST** older

while running **A RECOUNTING OF** sisters

and **SONGS NO ONE HAS ASKED FOR** present

like that his mind **IN OTHER WORDS** looking 4 make outs

pulling the guts out o that **PRESS** of the eye

like scarves **BY THE APHORISTS OF THE** hot breath

possibly she is **OFF AND CONCEDED** Dream

safe **TO BE ROLLED** Lover

and what of **TEARS THAT ARE STONES** was on

the **NEST OF** the table and he

rest of **CHRIST** pocketed

the team after the **DRAIN HIS** it and

obligatory selfie **HE BEGINS TO** applies it now with

with the terrifying **FOR NOW** improper fruit

As Ro is saying all of that about his mother, though, he can't help but begin to "drain his christ nest of tears" that are "stones to be rolled off and conceded by the aphorists of the press"--in other words, songs. No one has asked for a recounting of his "First Son Years" or when "the other kids made him captain," but now he's got an excuse to talk about every indignation of the umbilical cord--of having been dragged along and supplied like troops, of being dressed as a magician and provided with spells--while also confessing to be "a grounder like his father was". But you can't trap a musician, he muses--they shave while running . . . And just like that, his mind is off pulling likes scarves the guts out of the running musician, so perhaps his mother is safe after all (at least for a while).

After Romeo has been wordlessly smiling at the microphone for 5 minutes, someone gently escorts him to the side like a sleepwalker. The rest of The Sons All Want Prizes are standing on stage awkwardly--they fill the silence by each taking a selfie with the terrifying golden mummy, but is that all they get for sweating through the picture books? It seems that no one considered that there was ultimately only one prize for the whole team and their captain just dropped it in a pool. I hastily fast-walk up to the microphone and say that each member of the team will get an "epic epithet" written by me--I even start writing out coupons in felt pen for them on 3x5 cards, but the team's looks tell me I can keep them. I say that I'll just come up with them now if you'll give me a minute and that they'll thank me later.

Meanwhile, No wanders off the stage and into the crowd. The Milky Bowl is not large enough to fit all the random little leaguers, so people are spilling out of the building in every direction.

HINT:
Romeo's still stuck amid the columns of Page 165.

who shall know **THE ALIEN** figure the little

as the niche **NAMES STARTING WITH** girl he doesn't

in the face of his **NEW** know is counter that

omniscience **OUT THE WINNERS'** turns

he starts **TO READ** him

by drawing **MEANWHILE I BEGIN** in it is

himself **ON HIS PHONE** the unplanned

as **SKETCH** spine that held so many

so many **BEGINS TO** arm

do next **HE SITS DOWN AND** on the prize

is the laiconic **FISTS DEJECTED** in the wasteland

rival **THEM TO** the tour guide

who is **BALLED** something is

their backwards **FINGERS OR HAVE** held

anml he drws **BUT ALL THE EYES LACK** aloft but

his brother finds **ANY CLUB** what one thing is

a kind of dread **TO UNLOCK** it

in their faces **OR ELBOW** his mother will

and more lines **SWOOP** bear

only deepen the **MATCHING ANY** tattoo

effect **LOVER CAPABLE OF** reading be taken

speaking of **A CREATIVE HANDSHAKE** be

his brother he will **MAKE YOU** brought back

be called **IT WAS SUPPOSED TO** be fried he starts

hands **MISTAKE HE THOUGHT** to draw

lightning in front of **BAGGIE BY** a video tape maybe it

them **HE GRABBED THE PIZZA** should b a book

he begins **TO WORK OR POSSIBLY** or perhaps

to draw **REASON WHY IT DOESN'T SEEM** her

in a **MAYBE THAT IS THE** harmless gun

No feels like there just has to be some kid's older sister who would like to share hot breath with him or maybe just eyes. Before coming here, he'd swiped a packet off his dad's table, and now he shakes it on a pluot and jams it into each eye. Perhaps the lack of the proper fruit is the reason that the drug doesn't seem to work (or possibly he grabbed the pizza baggie of regular dirt by mistake) . . . He thought it was supposed to "make you a creative handshake lover," capable of matching any swoop or elbow bump to unlock any club, but all the eyes here lack fingers or have them balled to fists.

Dejected, he goes back into the main room and sits down on the stairs. He pulls out his phone and begins to absent-mindedly sketch using his finger and an app. Over the PA, my voice booms, "Emoro Abkln: the niche in the face of omniscience." No starts by drawing himself as so many people do when they're dicking around. "Lewis Gaudy: their backward animal." Next he draws his brother Sic, though he's a little disturbed by the dread in both their faces that more lines only seem to deepen. Speaking of: "Leee 'Sic' Lonelypeak: hands lightning." In front of the two figures, he begins to draw in a third, almost to block out those faces. "Steph Snopes: the counter that turns him." The new figure's unplanned spine could hold so many arms, and he tries each of them. "Roscoe Manchester: the prize in the wasteland." He likes the arms holding something aloft, but what is it? "Robin Segundo: she with the tattoo 'be taken, be brought back, be fried.'" He realizes that the figure is Leslie and he starts to draw the thing in her hands as a video tape, but maybe it should be a book, or perhaps her harmless gun?

HINT:
This page draws from the columns of 155, and the epithets come from those of 200 and 201.

labyrinth **HE FOR WHOM** the
power means**MONSTER AND**judge
life holds up **A CRAB** did not know
the thing that can **AND IT IS** anyone's
break **UP**identity and having
it you know**HER DRAWING** lots of images meant
symbolically **PUZZLER HOLDS** a pain in
man**PEOPLE** my ass
cellphones are**ZEUS AKA** only but
so **HOOKING UP INSTEAD OF**in general
big**WITH THE MOTTO** recognize hurdles
in the future **DRAWING THE PERSON** u were missing
I mean present **CROWD ALSO** kick over any you see
that was going**ACROSS THE** other lanes he is not
to be the end **AND FINDS HER**listening
but**HE LOOKS AROUND**to me instead he
there is**HER IN** dreams of
a little**TO PUT**the perfect
unfinished **DRAWS AND HE WANTS** woman for
business**FRIEND WHO ALSO** him a collector
after the **BROTHER HAS A** bookmark a pretend
ceremony **HE REMEMBERS HIS OTHER** prince
he glumly asks **MESSAGE BOARD** of Denmark
me**HUMANOID AND LESS** a stone
what **BROTHER IS MORE**not a fleeing
winning**NEARLY FORGOTTEN HALF** nymph
means **HIS OWN** and
for**A SCRIBBLE**microbe
a protagonist **BECOMES JUST** under
I tell him **IT** the eye piece

He ends up leaving it just a scribble. "Fees Lonelypeak: more of a humanoid and less of a message board." He remembers that Sic has a little friend who was also part of Leslie's big collaborative art project, and he wants to draw her in his tribute. He glances around and sees her still sitting on stage, also drawing, though on a metal clipboard like the one I carried everywhere. Conveniently: "Abby Snopes: whose God is hooking up instead of Zeus aka The People Puzzler" (though after I say it I realize that there's ambiguity about whether I'm iterating Zeus's titles or saying that Abby will *both* make-out *and* puzzle--ehhh, we can figure it out in the next book).

Abby sees No looking and holds up her drawing: a giant crab monster with an open claw.

"Noys Segundo: he for whom labyrinth power means life."

That was going to be the end right there, but there is still a little unfinished business. After the ceremony, as No and I walk out of the building and down the ramp, he glumly asks me what "winning" means when you were already the protagonist.

I tell him that even though he did have a lot of images to work from (I don't mention that the surplus was actually a huge pain in my ass as the writer) the contest's final judge did not know who was in *any* of the costumes, though I do concede that the mysterious video tape in the flannel warehouse did happen to be a favorite image from the bunch for both my wife and me. I go on to say that there wasn't much he could have done to leverage his privilege on behalf of others here, but in general, recognizing the hurdles that weren't in front of you is important, and also that kicking any hurdles you can out of someone else's path is good. I stop there to avoid becoming like Nick Carraway's father.

No's not listening to me; instead, he is hazing his eyes with an image of the perfect woman for him: a collector of bookmarks, a pretend prince of Denmark, not a stone, but a fleeing nymph, a microbe under the eye piece.

our **NOW**
lorem hallowed be thy **NIGHT**
ipsum your dolor **GOOD**
come **TO IT**
your **THEM**
sit **HIS FEET AND I LEAVE**
be done **TO**
on amet as it is in **HIM**
heaven **SHE HELPS**
so **HIM LIKE A KEYSTROKE**
it goes **WARMTH ON**
HAND BUT LEAVING
WITH THE FRISBY IN
TO HER FEET
HIM ROLLING
AND INTO
MIRAGE
BODY CRASHES THRU THE
BEFORE A WHOLE
FINGERS
INTERCEPTED BY
OFF AND IS
HEAD
A UFO THAT TAKES HER
GROW BEFORE BECOMING
DISC
HALO
HE SEES AN INCREASING
VIRGIN
BEHIND THIS

Behind this virgin, he sees a halo disc grow before becoming a plummeting UFO that takes her head off and is immediately intercepted by diving fingers before a whole body crashes through the mirage and into him. No's head taps the ground, but his shoulder took more of the force, so he's not on death's roll sheet today. He lies there for a minute, his chest warm as a released key even though their bodies had pressed only for a second. When he finally opens his eyes, he sees a silhouette standing over him--it shifts the solid halo from one side to the other--a frisbee?--and he is being pulled--"drawn" more, really--to his feet. The face is surrounded by sparks of light, but somewhere No is not sure that these aren't just left-over from the noggin bongo; details begin trickling back into his perceptions, filling in qualities you wouldn't believe and I haven't written. Meanwhile, I wander off to leave them to whatever will happen next.

LET'S CALL THIS CHAPTER "Blue as the future on stage."

AND LET'S CALL THE WHOLE THING "Those Brave As The Skate Is."

HINT:
If you're wondering where the book title is from, check Raw Page 119. Thanks for reading!

PESCETAREALISM: A MANIFESTO
by Patrick Keller, with apologies to Frank O'Hara

Everything is on the pages, but since Pescetarealism is all about transparency, let me say a few things about where it came from and what it is trying to do.

Pescetarealism—a movement I founded a few years ago but which nobody has heard about except for my poor wife—has a gag name but is here to give you something real. Sort of. The fish of Pescetarealism actually lives in the words . . . except that's impossible, but when it lived, it lived the way we live before we look back and say, "So that was it." At the same time, it is constrained (in the corset sense of the word) by see-through language that's okay with you peeking at the laces and bows. To put it more plainly, a Pescetarealist novel is a metafictional aleatory analogue simulation.

As you probably guessed by the name, Pescetarealism is a kind of a parody of Realism . . . which is itself just a parody of reality. Okay, that soundbite was harsh, but what good is a manifesto that doesn't throw a few elbows? While I'm at it, let me say that art that resembles a thing is worth a damn not just because *the thing* is beautiful, but because *the brushstrokes* are—*a person* managed to capture the fuckin' thing! Score one for humanity! (I would never claim that Pescetarealism's strokes are particularly subtle—once at summer camp, I was told to put paint on a dead fish and then press it on a shirt . . . where it also shat itself, and maybe I never forgot that lesson.) Okay, I got that out of my system—only modesty from here out, I promise. IN THE BEGINNING . . . stories were told *by* a person *to* a person, or so I'm told, and these stories were simple because their job was to make a big and imposing world bite-sized. However, by the rise of Realism, storytellers had started acting like the ultimate art was to make themselves disappear and to pretend that their stories were less like yarns and more like sweaters. Well, Pescetarealism doesn't want to pull the wool over any part of your body—instead of reducing the real world to language to pretend that it can be read, it gives you its own world that is *really* legible.

Pescetarealism was founded by me in my kitchen on October 4th 2010 when I asked myself two questions: (1) How can Experimental Fiction approximate the same pleasures that readers find in conventional fiction (plot, character, setting) without having to compromise its celebration of the constructed nature of language? and (2) How can form *create* meaning rather than merely convey or amplify it? My answer was to build the characters from words in front of the reader as I went along while using the layout of the page to generate twists that even I would not foresee. While "realistic psychology" tends to make characters complex enough not to live happily ever after but still simple enough to fold up when the book is closed, I decided to reimagine the process from the ground up by riffing on the real psychology that I got a B.A. in nearly 10 years earlier (admittedly not from Mineola Prep). Let me be frank with you here about the assumptions about the real world that underlie my simulation:

(1) Life is not predestined, and it largely proceeds by random chance. The only planned goal of a Pesceterealist text is that, to borrow from Woolf, "time passes." Because you want a story (and I don't blame you for that), each chapter of Those Brave As The Skate Is starts from a set of situations determined by dice that are then fulfilled using a liberal sprinkling of other types of acknowledged randomness, including:

(a) coin flips and dice "rolls" (done almost exclusively using Random.org's virtual dice);

(b) chance arrangements of previous pages (The columnar format of Skate's Raw Pages is designated within Pescetarealism as "Arboreal," based on the idea of a trunk with branches, though other concrete arrangements could be just as, um, fruitful);

(c) artifacts from my own experiences around the time of writing;

(d) my whims (usually highlighted by a walk-on of me as a character to, as TvTropes.com would say, hang a lampshade on my contributions); and

(e) the characters' own unpredictable interactions

By the end of the book, each character was receiving 7 dice rolls per chapter to suggest their present situation in Romance, Family, Friends, School / Job, Exterior Physical Health, Interiority, and

Identity Expansion.

(2) Many of people's actions are situationally-determined and irrational. Not yours, of course. Here, a character's Unconscious does not have to be faked by the author to make you think they are real (the character, I mean); in Pescetarealism, the Unconscious is an open record of all the figurative images attributed to that character, and I compare this list to each situation presented to them, including the images associated with the characters they're interacting with. It all works itself out, but I don't hide those workings from you.

(3) Memory is unreliable. In the Real World, science has shown that the act of remembering is closer to writing than to reading, but Pescetarealism's simulation of this actually comes *from* (mis)reading. When a character needs to think back, I read across the relevant previous Raw Page without considering the column boundaries, and that' determines what they've dredged up (which is helpful for creating nonsense titles for songs, poems, or even this book—check Raw Page 119).

(4) People contain bits of their parents. My characters that are born onstage start from established figurative images from both of their parents, and similarly, their names tend to be a scramble of the letters of their parents' names (for example, Romeo's parents are Leo and Mira, and Leo's parents were Longstory and Pirette). (Skate also features characters from my previous Pescetarealist works, and some of them received their names from sources such as news stories [Robin], places I ate [Roscoe], or whatever is the next word on the page after something like "Romeo's roommate's name is" [Yes]. Some characters' personality profiles were started by things such as flipping a coin to see if they liked Romeo or not [Lewis and Roscoe], while others were built in response to another character's personality [Cray and Molly].)

(5) Everyone deserves a chance to be represented. Unless you're in a Borges story, designing a simulation involves having to choose what corners can be cut, but of course cuts can hurt. While creating its characters with randomness, Pescetarealism has a responsibility to its readers to avoid making them conclude with a sigh, "There's no way I could exist in this fictional world." (Admittedly, the scope of the inclusive goal has been a work in progress; my early Pescetarealist texts made physical anatomy and sexual desire independent . . . but also face-palmingly employed a coin, the most binary possible instrument. By Abby's emergence in Skate Chapter 6, though, I was giving child characters dice rolls for Physical Sex, Gender Identity [Cis, Non-Binary, Trans], Romantic Orientation [Not only "direction" as before, but also "velocity" to allow for asexuality], and Sexual Orientation [specifically, its degree of correlation with Romantic Orientation], and in Chapter 7 of Skate, I started giving adult characters a roll for "identity expansion" to allow them to realize broader gender and sexual identities. I don't claim the system has been perfected, but hopefully it's better than just not trying because the world has so many possibilities.)

Now you understand the constraints around the fish better, but remember that the bowl is open on the top. Someone needs to sprinkle in the food, and that's where Frank O'Hara comes in (not that I would have particularly trusted him to check on my pets when I'm out of town). In "Personism: A Manifesto," Frank suggests smuggling the guise of intimacy into poetry, and Pescetarealism follows his suggestion in order to make the authorial persona more of a bumbling pal than a smirking puppeteer trying to pull your strings as well. I want you to know when I nudge a little castle or treasure chest in the bowl . . . but the fish is the star, not me—I'm not trying to make the story my therapy session, interpretive dance, or solipsistic mindgame.

Maybe a brainfuck, though . . . While following a series of consistent rules may not sound that surreal, when you have, say, a woman once compared to green beans who hates a man at first meeting because he reminds her of her of a can-opener, things are bound to seem a bit weird. I admit I could have left it at that and not introduced shape-shifting as a popular sport or portals to other planets, but for me, surreality is pursuing the same liberation as having unplanned connections. Plus, it's a natural fit with conspicuous artificiality—even as a kid, I preferred sit-coms over dramas because at least they were more honest about what they were.

Sooooo, what can we expect from Pescetarealism? Well, before you run out for a "Never Mind the Balzac, Here's The Pesce Pistils!" t-shirt, let me say I don't think we're going to be knocking Realism off the charts any time soon . . . but now this tool for embracing randomness is out there and ready to be adapted further. If what you want is to tell a story you already know, Realism will probably still work better for you (Just bury the treasure and then pretend to find it!), but if you want to grow a story from guppy to leviathan one flake at a time, Pescetarealism is here for you. Skate was itself the product of tweaking the parameters of my previous unpublished Pescetarealist works, so go ahead and adjust whatever you like: use different sorts of randomness; allow more than just stylistic revision of your raw pages or just abandon concrete page arrangements altogether; further refine the inclusiveness of the generative systems; apply chance solely to the world around the protagonist and allow them to respond "realistically"; or even stick to only outward actions that could really happen. And if you don't need Pescetarealism, bully for you—I enjoy Realism, too . . . even if maybe they should rename it "Real-ish-ism" so we can just call a truce.

About the Author

Patrick Keller grew up in Claremont, California. At UC Berkeley, he chose Psychology as a second major to accompany English, mistakenly assuming that it would be the secret weapon for writing novels. At UC Irvine, his grad school mentor gave him a Steve Katz book as a curio, mistakenly assuming that he wouldn't scrap his previous research plans and write his dissertation on this type of freewheeling mixture of autobiography and fiction. In 2010, after reading too many books and interviews with Raymond Federman and Ronald Sukenick, he created Pescetarealism, an attempt to extend their egalitarian ideals to something more about persistence than performance. He received his Ph.D in English for "Subversively Personal: Surfiction As Communication in Vietnam War Era America" in 2011. His scholarly article "Contemporary Surfiction: Wideman, Kaufman, and Maddin" appeared in the June 2014 issue of *Word and Text*. He teaches in Orange County and lives with his wife in Long Beach, California.

A Checklist of JEF Titles

JEF
Journal of Experimental Fiction

* Winners of the Kenneth Patchen Award for the Innovative Novel

Made in the USA
Las Vegas, NV
29 January 2021

16725229R00267